I0654397

DARKNESS

COMES

REAPING

A NOVEL OF THE ASCENDING DARKNESS
#2

DARKNESS COMES REAPING

Published by Damn Fool Press
www.damnfoolpress.com

ISBN 978-0-9936983-4-7 epub
ISBN 978-0-9936983-5-4 mobi
ISBN 978-0-9936983-6-1 pdf
ISBN 978-0-9936983-7-8 trade paperback

First Edition : June 2015

This is for Lynn and the cats.

CHAPTER ONE
The Fist of Tolerance

It was the sound that got his attention when awareness returned to him. A soft meaty thudding that sounded vaguely familiar. Then came the feeling of a sharp twisting movement. It puzzled him at first, then he realized that the former always seemed to precede the latter. Following the movement came a sensation of pressure, building quickly to a dull pain that spread from the point the pressure occurred. He fit the pieces together and realized that all of the events were related, somehow, and the process of figuring it out gave him a vague sense of accomplishment. After some indeterminate time the process was repeated. Then again. And again. It gradually occurred to him that not only were all of the events related, but that they were happening to *him*. Something was hitting him. He tried to think, but the sounds and motion of the repeated blows made it impossible to hold together a chain of thoughts. And he was tired. So terribly tired.

The various sensations stopped, finally, and he felt grateful for the quiet and a chance for his thoughts to coalesce into something vaguely coherent. He became aware that something new was happening; something trying to get his attention. Voices. That was what they were - voices that were saying something. He tried to focus his shattered attention on what they were saying. Maybe it was something important. Everything felt so thick to him, thick and disconnected.

"Mister Franklin," he heard the voice say, over and over again.

This confused him. He didn't know anyone named 'Mister'.

The voice continued speaking in a slow, melodic manner.

He finally came to the realization that the voice was talking to *him*. With this realization came a limited return of awareness. He had a body, with a head and torso and arms and legs. He had forgotten about them, somehow. And he was lying horizontally on a hard surface, unable to move his arms or legs. The trickle of awareness increased, and memories started coming back to him. Memories of imprisonment and beatings. He was being beaten. Again. But he couldn't remember why. Everything hurt, and he was so tired.

"Mister Franklin," the voice intoned, "the Fist of Tolerance takes no pleasure in these activities. We only seek to guide you to The Path, but we require your assistance. Please, we beg of you, help us to guide you."

Yancey carefully shook his head as if to clear it, and opened his eyes as much as the swollen flesh surrounding them would allow. The bright light cut like a knife, and he quickly shut his eyes again and tried to move his head away. Strong hands firmly held his head, and a cool cloth was placed over his eyes. Yancey made a soft sigh that rustled through dry chapped lips.

"We have dimmed the lights for you, Mister Franklin," intoned the voice, "and we will try to make you comfortable, for a time. You must realize that coming to The Path is inevitable, for it is the will of God that we do so. Each and every one of us. This scourging of the flesh is necessary only because you resist the inevitable. All that is required is for you to confess. Confess and tell us everything that is in your heart. Tell us how you found this place. Tell us where your friends are. Tell us about the Shattered Palace. Confess. Confess and receive God's blessing and forgiveness. Confess and be comforted in body and soul."

Memories started to come back, like a broken mirror reassembling itself. Yancey remembered that he was in the hands of the Sword of Infinity Ascending. He remembered being captured. He remembered the interrogations. Most importantly, he remembered that his friends were now safely away from the Sword. Nothing could force him to betray or endanger them. Nothing. He tried to form words, but his lips refused to cooperate. He felt a moist cloth against his mouth, easing the dryness. The cloth was removed and he tried again to speak. This time his lips worked, or at least well enough to form words.

"Fuck you."

Not many words, and not everything that he wanted to say to his captors, but it would suffice.

He felt the cloth around his eyes being removed, and then felt the heat of the blinding lights returning.

"You have only yourself to blame for this, Mister Franklin," said a deep, sad voice, "the Fist of Tolerance exists only to guide sinners back to The Path ordained by God. You are a lost soul, and we will help guide you back to The Path. Remember that as we scourge the flesh."

The beating began again. As before, his inquisitors were puzzled by the laughter that bubbled out of their captor's mouth before he lapsed into semi-consciousness. Yancey knew something they didn't, and the realization always made him laugh. He knew that the beatings couldn't break him. As a child he had grown up with similar sorts of beatings, and from long practice knew how to retreat into himself to escape the pain.

Some things never change, he thought, just before the kaleidoscope of memories claimed him once again.

CHAPTER TWO
New Beginnings

Yancey and Simon drove through the darkness without speaking. The horrors of what they had seen, and what they had done, at the battle of the Shattered Palace weighed heavily upon them. After driving for several hours Simon's attention was grabbed by a passing sign.

"Take the next road up ahead, on the right," he said sharply.

Yancey's attention snapped back to the here-and-now. He made no query of his friend, but did a quick glance, moving his head briefly to the right. Then he gazed intently ahead as he slowed the car. Up ahead was what looked like the beginnings of a small forest, with a dimmer darkness entering into it.

"That one up ahead?" he asked Simon, slowing the car to a crawl.

"Turn," was the curt reply.

Yancey slowly and carefully made the turn as a road revealed itself. As they travelled slowly along, he noticed that the trees on either side shielded them from sight. The road itself was gravel and had seen better days, but it wasn't too bad for northern Ontario. He had seen worse. They had travelled along worse, and not that long ago.

That thought caused him to inhale and exhale sharply, the sharpness of the breath amplified by the bumps.

"I remembered seeing this road number indicated on the map as we travelled up," said Simon softly, "I damn near memorized that damn map trying to find our way to the Shattered Palace site. If I recall correctly, there is a clearing about a dozen klicks ahead. Might be a campground or abandoned sawmill or something. No towns or houses indicated on the map. Worth checking out. We really really need to stop for a while, Yancey. We really do."

"Yah," agreed Yancey, "and we seem to be going uphill. That'll be a help in hiding, too. I've been taking a few random zigs and zags since we left the battle, to make our route less obvious. There are all sorts of abandoned whatnots around here. You've got a good memory, Simon."

A half hour of careful driving brought them within sight of a relatively cleared area, with what looked to be a couple of smallish buildings not too far off. Yancey stopped the car, and after the two friends conferred briefly they decided to park next to some brush that looked big enough to hide the car from the road. After a brief look around while sitting in the car, he moved the car forward slightly to force its way deeper into the brush until it was reasonably well hidden by the branches.

"May as well do the best we can to hide from aerial view," Yancey noted with a grunt "and, no, I'm not gonna worry about scratches to the car. OK, so we just sit tight until morning, I guess, and then we can look around. I don't want to go exploring in the dark, or take the chance of someone seeing the light from our flashlights waving around."

He then forced his door open, using it to batter aside the

branches and forming a bit of a pocket in the brush. He motioned to Simon to do the same, and then he got out, quickly closing the door to extinguish the interior light. While he stood and stretched to ease his cramped muscles, he heard his friend get out and do the same. Yancey tried very hard to focus on the cool sweetness of the air, and not think about what they had just been through only a few hours ago. Then he looked down at his torso, and saw the dark stains that had once been the blood and brains of a soldier of the Sword of Infinity Ascending. A wave of nausea forced him to clamp his jaws very tightly, and several involuntary shudders racked his body. He heard the sounds of Simon retching, and knew that he was not alone in his shock. Forcing himself to move, he opened the rear door of the car and removed a couple of containers of water. He put one on the hood and silently passed it over to Simon, who nodded miserably and took it.

"Take off your clothes," commanded Yancey, "and wash yourself off. We have enough spare clothing that we can burn these damn things later, but for now just toss them into this plastic garbage bag. Keep sipping at the water to keep something in your stomach. For right now we'll sleep in the Flush, and work out something better in the morning."

Simon simply nodded. They cleaned themselves, changed into fresh clothing, and got back into the car. Each huddled under several blankets not expecting to get any sleep, but their emotional exhaustion caused both of them to sink into something resembling it. The rising sun shining into their eyes caused them to awake with a start, throwing their blankets off with a convulsive shudder.

"OK," said Yancey blinking his eyes at the bright sun, "time to take a look around at our new home. Why don't we look around for a bit, then eat later?"

Simon nodded and grunted his agreement. His appetite hadn't yet returned, and he felt curiously deflated, yet anxious. Maybe walking around would snap him back to something approaching normal, he thought to himself.

The pair pushed through branches to emerge into the clearing. Looking back they could now see that the Busted Flush was reasonably well hidden inside a copse of brush, which in turn was surrounded by trees of medium height.

"Not a bad spot, considering we couldn't see much in the dark," muttered Yancey. "It'll do, Simon, it'll do."

He pointed to the low buildings a few dozen metres away, and they trudged towards them. The air was cool, with just a hint of a breeze, and their spirits rose a bit as the sun warmed their faces. Arriving at the buildings and doing a quick outside walk-around, they saw that the site consisted of what looked like a maintenance shed, an office building, and a couple of other smaller buildings of indeterminate function. The shed's large doors were open, so they decided to take a quick look inside it first. At first glance there didn't seem to be too much of anything around, but it looked as if it could offer a place to store or service the larger sorts of industrial trucks and equipment one found in the bush. The roof and walls looked to be in reasonable shape, with few holes. After a cursory inspection, they decided to check out the other buildings.

The other large building was indeed a former office, and consisted of a pair of office trailers pushed together and sharing a common roof. Both the roof and the inside were in pretty rough shape. One of the trailers seemed to be the main office, and there were a couple of dilapidated filing cabinets and cheap desks. The other held a somewhat nicer desk, a few chairs strewn about, and a couple of thoroughly rotted cots. Without bothering to speak, they each started poking around to see if there was a clue as to what the site had been used for. After a couple minutes Simon chimed, "I've found something."

Yancey raised his head and turned towards his friend, who was waving some papers.

"Looks like this was a secondary maintenance site for a logging outfit. The most recent dates on these papers are from sixteen years ago. 'Course, these are just leftovers from when they packed up and left," Simon mused.

He took a look around, shook his head, and continued, "But that jibes with the condition of this place. Cheap office trailers were all that these sorts of places got, little more than the bare minimum to store and handle the paperwork. I've seen these sorts of places before. Dime-a-dozen little outfits that would do logging and sell to the bigger loggers or maybe a mill. Some of them specialized in fixing up equipment for others, rather than doing the logging themselves. Or maybe set up by one of the big outfits, doing it as cheaply as possible. In any case, it was abandoned a long time ago. It hasn't been maintained or fixed up in all that time, I'd guess, so not even used by hunters."

Yancey chimed in, "Makes sense. No towns anywhere near here, so why would any hunters come? Lots of good hunting closer to home. Would also explain why the maintenance shed was built decently - that's what the place was for. Hey, those small sheds might be storage sheds for something, if we're lucky. Outhouses if we're not. We should go take a look at those."

Simon nodded his agreement, and off the two of them went. A quick investigation showed that Yancey was correct on both counts. Although built identically, one shed turned out to be a multi-hole outhouse, and the other held a variety of tools and supplies. Almost like a small commissary or industrial pantry. They ignored the bulging cans of food with a shudder, but the hand tools and building materials were still in good shape. There were even a few first aid kits, which appeared to have been stocked properly for a remote industrial site. Behind an inner door they found a concrete pad on the floor, a number of electrical wires dangling from the ceiling, and a small-diameter metal pipe going up into the roof. They decided that this was where the electrical generator had been located. After poking around for a bit they agreed to return to the maintenance shed for a more thorough look-around. Yancey was leading the way, but at the door he stopped and blocked Simon from continuing.

"Wait a sec," was all he said, as he carefully scanned the area and the sky. The thin, high clouds of the early morning had turned into lower, darker clouds that covered much of the sky. Yancey grunted approval and led the way out.

At Simon's pointedly enquiring glare, Yancey laughed and explained, "You're not paranoid if they're really out to get you. Yah, we're on top of a slight hill out of sight from the road, but that's no reason not to be careful. And satellites are pretty good at picking up IR signatures in remote areas, don't forget, but the clouds eliminate that potential threat, at least for now. I suppose that there could be aircraft or drones looking around, but I can't see that sort of active search as being too likely."

"Fair enough," admitted Simon, "hadn't thought of that. But how long are we going to keep this up? We can't stay here - there's no electricity for one thing. And just hiding won't solve anything. We can't find Gretchen by just sitting here."

They entered the maintenance building, and Yancey pulled the big doors shut. This made things dim enough that they could more easily see any holes in the roof and walls. The glass in the windows was intact, except for one small window at the rear that had a number of cracks.

Yancey pointed at the few holes in the roof and walls. "There's enough material and tools around to fix those pretty quickly. It's cold, bad weather seems to be coming in, and we're going to need decent shelter for the next few days. With an hour or two of fixing, we can make this place weather-proof enough for our purposes. It's large enough that we can have a small fire inside for warmth, and if we board up the windows then no one will see the light. We have enough food for a week - more if we're careful. As for electricity, don't forget the UPSs that we packed at the start of the trip. Our laptops don't consume much, and we can use the Busted Flush to recharge them, or even the UPSs if it comes to that. We've got work to do, Simon, and this place is safe enough for the few days we'll be using it for."

Simon just gaped at his friend. Normally he could keep up with Yancey's thinking, but his brain still felt fuzzy. "Wha ..." was all he could get out.

Yancey smiled gently and said in a firm voice, "The shit has well and truly hit the fan, my lad. We've got information that no one else has got, and we've seen things and done things that we need to process. In emotional terms as well as data analysis terms. Too much has happened in a very short time. We need to figure out what to do, where to go, and who to trust. We need a safe place to crash, and this is it. But first we need to make this place more weatherproof. Then we can dig into our data some more for clues about just what the hell is going on. Let's get some tools and supplies from that storage shed and patch the holes before the bad weather hits. We only have a few hours of daylight left, and a lot to do. Then we can stop and crash for a bit. I promise."

With that he took Simon by the arm and gently pulled him towards the door. Simon moved a few steps, then looked stubborn and shook off Yancey's hand with a glare. He looked wildly around for a moment, then closed his eyes, took a long deep breath and slowly let it out. Yancey watched calmly as his friend adjusted to the realities of the situation. They had known each other since childhood, had been through several types of hell together, and he knew that the stresses of this situation were going to tax them to their limits, if not beyond. Simon opened his eyes, grunted, and said, "Let's get 'er done."

Working quickly, but carefully, they got hammers and nails from the storage shed. Yancey grabbed some of the many stray pieces of lumber and clambered up onto the roof. With Simon inside telling him where the holes were, they made quick work of the repairs. The two of them then went around the structure patching the worst of the holes in the walls. By this time the light was fading and snow was beginning to fall. As Simon began moving their tools into the shed, Yancey moved the Busted Flush from its hiding place and drove it into the shed, then they closed the doors. The door fit the frame pretty well, so they didn't need to add any caulking, at least for the time being. They turned their attention to the windows. These weren't very large, but there were quite a few of them, presumably to take advantage of natural light. Most had inside shutters, so with those closed they quickly boarded up the remaining windows. The wind had picked up and the snow was beginning to fall heavily as they boarded up the last of the windows. Snapping on a flashlight, they moved tiredly back to the car. Neither had eaten all day, and the exertion had overcome their emotional distress to the point where they were feeling almost normal, and hungry. Exchanging the briefest of glances, Yancey began digging through the car for food while Simon put together and lit a small fire on the concrete floor. The fire, although small, provided comfort as well as warmth and light.

"I've found a bit of Mama's cooking left, so we'd better finish that off. Should still be OK," Yancey remarked, and Simon quickly agreed. While it was being warmed up by the fire Yancey filled up a pot with some of their rapidly-diminishing supply of water. Without saying a word Simon took one of the empty water containers, went outside briefly to fill it with snow, and came back inside.

"One of the few advantages of winter is having a large supply of clean water," he said with a slight smile. "All we have to do wait for a bit until it melts."

They waited in silence until the food warmed up enough to eat. The silence continued while they ate. It was only after they had finished eating and settled back to slurp on their tea that either of them was ready to talk.

"So what's the plan?" asked Simon looking at Yancey.

"Well, I guess we need to brainstorm something ..." began Yancey.

"No. You're the big-picture planner, Yancey," interrupted Simon, "that's what you do. 'Sides, you seem to be able to see that we've got some hope. I can't. I just can't see it. Over the past few days Gretchen has gone missing after giving us some data from a murdered reporter, we uncovered an international conspiracy to corrupt and control Canada's political system, and we uncovered and stepped into the middle of an attempt to steal nuclear and biological weapons that were being stored at a secret military base. Oh, and we have no idea of who in authority we can trust. Did I leave anything out?"

Yancey stared into the fire, choosing his words carefully. His friend was no quitter, that was a certainty, but he didn't have the experience to put this sort of thing into perspective. "Simon, you've been knocked on your ass before, and managed to get back up. Nothing this hard or nasty, but you've always bounced back. The only reason I can see a little further than you is that I've been hit harder and more often. Thing One is to get a few hours of decent rest and some food. We won't do or plan anything until tomorrow for the simple reason that we are fried. But it is OK to feel bad about what happened. It is very much OK."

He raised his head and looked at his friend, "We need to be strong and tough enough to get through this and continue to fight. But we can't allow ourselves to become so hardened that we stop caring, that we stop thinking about others. I'm sorry we had to kill that Sword soldier, but he gave us no other option. I've never killed anyone before, but I've had to fight, and I've seen death. The only thing that gives it all meaning is to accept that it happens, without allowing the anger and hate and fear to consume you. Otherwise we lose ourselves and become like the Sword."

Simon sat silently staring into the fire for a while, lost in his thoughts. Yancey opened his mouth to say something - anything - to keep his friend from getting lost in his dark thoughts. Simon spoke first, "How do we stop becoming them? And why should we? They're willing to kill without hesitation. Kill innocents, strangers, as if they don't matter. Maybe we need to become as hard and strong as them, to be able to do whatever it takes."

"*No!*"

Yancey's loud, sharp reply startled Simon into looking up with surprise.

"No," repeated Yancey somewhat more calmly, "they are *not* stronger or harder. To them, everything is black or white, right or wrong. They are in the right, therefore anything that stands against them is wrong. Nothing must stand against their absolute rightness, therefore anything and everything is allowable in their struggle. That sort of attitude is always fuelled by hate. The only thing that is forbidden is failure, and that is what they fear most. That is *not* strength, Simon - that is insanity, or the next best thing. They are fanatics, nothing more. Whatever their initial reasons, whatever noble aims their cause once had, all that has been burned away and all that remains is hate and fear that overrides any pretence of critical thought. That makes them dangerous, Simon, not strong. Their narrowness of thought makes them fragile, not hard or tough. It's important that you understand that - it's something that I've had to learn the hard way."

Simon was taken aback by the intensity of his friend's words. Yancey had always been somewhat dispassionate, being able to detach himself from emotional turmoil. And yet Simon knew very well that his friend cared deeply about others, about trying to improve the world. Simon dropped his gaze back to the fire, trying to force his tumultuous thoughts into some sort of order. Yancey understood his friend well enough that he knew that this was the time to keep his silence.

"I shot him, Yance," Simon began, "I put the gun to his head and pulled the trigger. The stupid fuck was trying to kill us but I put the gun to his head and pulled the trigger and then all that crap came flying out and sprayed over us and ..." Simon's voice stopped as his throat choked up with emotion. He drew a ragged breath and paused to wipe his eyes, which were still fixed on the fire. Yancey kept a carefully neutral expression on his face. This was a battle that his friend had to fight through alone.

Several long minutes later, Simon raised his head. His

eyes were clear and bright now, and the darkness that lay behind them was, if not gone, at least diminished.

"OK, so we take a few more hours to get our heads straight and our shit together," Simon said simply, "but even with the best of intentions and purest of hearts, how do we even begin to fight back?"

Yancey kept his face under control, but inside he was celebrating the healing of his friend. In truth, he had never doubted that Simon would work through it. The harshness of their childhood had given them both the strength to endure and bounce back from pretty much anything.

"We've got a shit-tonne of data that we've only skimmed the surface of. We know a lot of the players and how they are connected. What we haven't bothered to do is to analyze it for operational intelligence. How the Sword and whoever is behind them is organized. We learned enough to stop the attack on the Shattered Palace, but there's more there that we didn't have time to look at in any detail. There were at least hints of people and places connected with the Sword. The armed forces now know about them, and that means the government knows. Not everyone in the system has been corrupted, so there's going to be pressure on them from that front. Then there's us - we're the wild card in all this. We know enough to be very dangerous to them, and they don't know that we are still alive, much less where we are. Hell, it's doubtful that they even know *who* we are, if it comes to that. We'll stay here to analyze the data for a few days, then head down to somewhere with Internet connectivity. We'll do our damnedest to find Gretchen. Someone gave her that data, and we'll pick up them as well. A team like that is one *hell* of a good start at fighting back, I would think. As for right now, we should get some sleep. Neither of us is in any shape to keep watch, so we may as well both sleep."

Simon liked the plan, spare though it was, and his face plainly showed it. With tight predatory smiles on their faces, the two friends prepared their new home for a good night's rest. Tomorrow was going to be a busy day.

CHAPTER THREE
Home Is The Soldier

Thomas Thansworth the Third, former General in the United States Armed Forces, walked woodenly into the study of his family home, glass in hand. He had been drinking heavily for some time. He had lost his rank, his command, and evaded a general court martial only because of his family's influence. Thansworth had spent a lifetime in his beloved military career, and now he was cast adrift. Rarely introspective for much of his life, he now found that to be his default state these days. His family had accepted him back among them and gave him a place in the family home, but definitely as one might accept an impossible-to-get-rid-of burden. So he started drinking again, for lack of anything better to do. Over the years he had developed a prodigious tolerance for alcohol, and had learnt that it was very useful to keep that particular talent to himself.

It was a bright and beautiful day and the others in the household had left to pursue their careers and lives of cheerful infinite promise. Rather than wander outside, Thansworth stayed inside the house to savour a rare interval of solitude and peace.

His feet had found their way to this room, which he

remembered from younger days and happier times. Thansworth closed his eyes with remembrances and a faint smile came to lips long unused to such exercise. The study had been used by his father as an office, before his sudden death, and then by the uncle after that time. He opened his eyes and gazed at walls filled with books, with a few paintings scattered about to break the pattern. Nothing of any great value, really, but pleasant to look at and enjoyed by both his parents.

The room held a pair of large wooden desks, of the type meant for actual work rather than showpieces, which sat facing each other. One had a computer terminal on it, but the other was obviously meant for older means of work. Thansworth sat heavily in the chair at the desk that his father had favoured, the one without the computer terminal. He placed his drink carefully on the surface, careful not to scuff or mar it. After his father's death, his uncle had taken over the desk. Thansworth still felt the sense of betrayal that his much younger self had experienced when this was done, but his adult self dismissed the feeling as foolish and unworthy. His uncle had always been there to help him, from the time of his mother's death to that of his father a few years later. Afterwards, it has been his uncle who had steered the course of his life, introducing him to the various pleasures due to one of his station, obtaining the posting to West Point, and even offering a bit of family influence after that. His uncle had initially opposed Thansworth's military inclinations, and rather strongly at that. But after he succeeded in the entrance exams on his own merit and did so very well at the academy, his uncle's attitude had softened and grown into support.

Thansworth gently poked around the desk, and ran his fingers lightly over the top. He had loved to watch his father at work here. So much so, that even after being sent from the room he would sometimes sneak back and peer carefully around the door, and just watch. Thansworth had loved his father very much, but memories of his mother were vague.

Sometimes his father would fiddle with some of the decorations on the side of the desk, the only real outward sight of distraction that Thansworth could recall. He softly smiled at the memory and ran his own fingers along the same decorations. As he lightly toyed with them, he felt a section of them move slightly. Horrified at the thought of breaking something, he examined the area with great care. They weren't broken, it would seem, but slipping as if designed for that purpose. A puzzle! Thansworth had delighted in such things as a child, and it was only the pressures of West Point that drove that interest into the background, to be forgotten until now. With care and patience he teased at the various decorations, and found that if he moved this area just so and another area in such a way, the original piece moved aside to reveal a button. Without thinking, Thansworth pushed it and a larger section along the side of the desk dropped down to reveal a book-sized storage area. Peering inside he saw a pair of books. With slightly trembling hands he carefully removed them and placed them reverently on the top of the desk. He sat there staring at them, afraid to open them. Almost afraid to even look at them. He felt like an errant child gazing at forbidden secrets, but he washed that feeling away with a large gulp of his drink. Replacing the feeling was one of eagerness and, perhaps, a hint of hope. This might have been his father's! Thansworth had so little around that was his father's, as his uncle had determinedly purged much of that, stating brusquely that it was best not to dwell on the past.

With trembling hands he opened the larger of the two volumes and began to read its handwritten contents. To his immense surprise, it had belonged to his grandfather. That stern and frightening man had died two years after his father, but had little time or patience for a small, frightened boy. Thansworth decided to do a quick skim-read, then go back and read it all in detail later. There seemed to be so much information and it was written in a small, careful style that took some care to decipher. As he read, his confusion grew. There were references to an important plan and the important part that his family had played and had yet to play in it. A plan seemingly blessed by God, but promising great material rewards for those strong and pure enough. Thansworth skipped over many pages of what seemed to be dry philosophical arguments, and then came across a chapter referring to his father. Reading speedily and hungrily, he became horrified to discover that Grandfather had become convinced that his son, Thansworth's father, had committed a great sin. "Turned from the Ordained Path by sinning against The City", as his Grandfather had put it. Despite scouring the chapter, all that Thansworth could see was that his father had married a woman that Grandfather had not approved of.

He stopped reading, breathing heavily, with his mind spinning. He remembered few details of his mother, but the memory of the love between his parents was one of his oldest and dearest ones. That and the obvious grief of his father in the years before his own death. Grief for a lost wife had never stopped him from ensuring that his young son always felt loved and never alone. Thansworth was forced to close his eyes at the strength of the memories that came surging back through him, as if fresh. Those had been the last times that he had felt as if he were truly loved and not alone in the world. The world which to that point had felt so large and full of promise - then became smaller and harsher and lonelier.

With a sudden intake of breath, Thansworth forced his eyes to open and his mind to focus. Wiping away the traces of tears, he began flipping through the pages. Not reading the details, but more to get a sense of the overall pattern of the writing. About three quarters of the way through the book the handwriting changed. A closer examination of the transition period showed that it was his uncle who had taken up the narrative. A cursory reading of the first couple of pages revealed pledges to continue along something called "The Path", as well as obedience to "The Plan", without any obvious indication of what those were. He resumed flipping until the end of the book, and read the last couple of pages with more care. The format of his uncle's writing seemed more of an outline form, rather than the narrative form favoured by Grandfather. Thansworth saw columns with names and lines between the columns. He puzzled over those, and was struck by how some of them seemed to refer to vaguely-remembered relatives and their spouses. Some held names of what looked like companies or organizations of some sort, and for these the lines seemed to refer to other notes. Putting down the first book, he took a quick look at the second. A cursory look-through seemed to indicate that it was a continuation of the first book, but the notes got even briefer, with more references to what looked like on-line resources. The words "sword" and "city" seemed to be cropping up more frequently, too, but capitalized as if referring to a company or organization. Some of the other references were familiar, though, with names of people and organizations that he recognized. This had the feel of something that a CEO or organizer of something would keep at hand, but it was for nothing that he had ever heard of or even heard rumours of. Whatever it was, it involved his family in some way, and had for several generations. This needed to be studied in a much more detail. His mind started to organize itself into patterns of analysis, just like in his student days. Plans on how to properly analyze this trove of information began forming in his mind, and his hands reached for a pad of paper.

The distant chiming of the main clock brought his head up with a jerk. He had forgotten all about the time, and was shocked to discover that several hours had passed. That meant that the others would be returning home soon, and until he knew more about this information it would be best that no one else know that he had found it. He placed the books back into their original location, taking care to place them exactly as he had found them. A careful manoeuvring of the various decorations returned everything to its original position. He quickly policed the desk to its original state as he heard doors thumping outside the room, indicating the arrival of his family.

Thansworth quickly moved to the room's liquor cabinet and filled his glass with the first bottle his hand could find. Grabbing a book at random, he sat down in a nearby easy chair, sprawling with his legs over the edges. As the door opened, he raised the glass to his lips and began sipping. "Hello, uncle," he belched, carelessly moving the glass down from his lips.

"Thomas," his uncle replied in clipped tones, "have you been spending the day drinking? Again? And must you do that here, of all places?"

"Sorry, sir," slurred the nephew in question, "I just got here, actually. Haven't been in this room in years, and just felt the urge to soak up the atmosphere."

"Well go get soaked somewhere else," his uncle said peevishly, "I have work to do and I don't want you around to ruin the evening. Supper will be served shortly, so why don't you go upstairs and get cleaned up? Try to look respectable for supper."

"Yessir," slurred Thansworth, "I'll go do that right now."

Thomas Thansworth the Third, disgraced scion of a rich and influential family, tottered off to his room to the disgusted head-shaking of his uncle. His hidden secret self was excited at the prospect of a mystery to solve, but his body stumbled like the drunk that everyone believed him to be. That was alright. This was a game he had played before, and now he had a game with an exciting mystery to solve. Things were looking up.

CHAPTER FOUR
The First Ascendant Speaks

"I am the First Ascendant, speaker for Infinity Ascending. Hear my words."

The words came from the communications console in a calm and measured manner.

"I am the First Apostle of the Sword, and I attend the words of my master," was the equally measured response of the room's sole occupant. He was dressed in plain dark clothing, suitable to a soldier in the field. Around his waist was a utilitarian belt, of the same colour as the rest of his clothes. The only sign of decoration was a knotted cord on his shoulder, the colours of which were simply different shades of black.

The remote voice continued, "The Council of Ascendants has become concerned about the increased level of activities. This increased militancy seems to be dangerously close to straying from The Path, and the recent adventures in Canada have the potential to bring unwanted attention upon us all. Worse, the other powers are becoming more active in response. Our most recent projections show an increase in world instability, which would more than counter our recent successes in enforcing control and stability. Our purpose along The Path is to function as guides and protectors to increase stability and order, not to act as agents of chaos and instability."

The First Apostle stood calmly without speaking for a handful of heartbeats. When he spoke, his voice was calm, measured, and unrepentant.

"I am aware of your projections, and am also aware of their flaws. The Council of Ascendants has for too long focused on arcane and academic concerns. It is the Sword who has had to interact with the world all these years, creating the necessary social structures and measures of control. We have the practical experience that the Council lacks, and our experience tells us that the time is right to begin a more active phase. Any instabilities will be transitory and controllable. The other players have been minimized, and the actions of the remaining ones constrained. We are now the dominant player."

After this the only sound was the soft background hiss from the communications console speaker. The First Apostle stood with calmly assurance, aware that the other was observing him carefully. Finally, the First Ascendant spoke, "Explain to me, please, why the increase of activities in Canada?"

"We have always been active there," was the quick reply. "It offers a wide range of natural resources. As a former colonial nation the habit and social structures of obedience have been long established. It has a well-educated population that is concentrated in only a few areas. Its deep ties to both Europe and the United States allow our associates easy access to the nation's wealth and social control mechanisms. Our current operations there have taught their ruling elites that resistance to our guidance is impossible, further solidifying our control. It is weak and rich enough to serve as an enticing battlefield that cannot do harm to anyone that matters. It is home to a large number of different races, which only recently have started to debase themselves by intermarriage. And finally, it is large enough that if necessary it can be sectioned off to appease the other players and bring them into our sphere of control. Your projections are correct in that events are coming to a head. It is important to properly prepare for what is to come. Only the Sword has the necessary experience and expertise to do this."

This was met with a period of silence from the communications console. The silence was finally broken by the First Ascendant, "The Council of Infinity Ascending was chosen by God to be the guides of our movement, to be the ones to show all others The Path. Do you now reject The Path we have set before you?"

The response by the First Apostle was still calm, but he spoke with increased strength and confidence, "We have always accepted, and will continue to accept, your guidance in all spiritual matters. But The Path is ours to define and choose, for we are the ones who see and deal with the world as it is. We are the ones who know what is to be done to bring order out of the chaos created by The Darkness. The Darkness grows ever stronger, and we must strengthen ourselves and act swiftly to prevent its spread. The Sword will continue on its Path and call upon the Council for guidance as required."

The First Apostle reached toward the console, "We both have much work to do. I thank you for your words of wisdom, First Ascendant. May the grace of God be upon you," and with that he terminated the session and strode out of the room. There was much work to be done - among them a number of the Canadian-based projects that were coming to fruition, and it was time to harvest their successes.

The one called First Ascendant leaned back into his

chair, his eyes thoughtful. An inflection point, perhaps even a crisis point, had come - and perhaps more than one. The Sword itself was the cause of at least one of those. The First Apostle was also a source of trouble to be reflected upon. His use of the term "players" might indicate that he now thought of the process as a game, rather than a Divine Mission. Also troubling was his use of the term "race" - that was an obsolete concept that was better suited to the world of a century ago.

A small sigh escaped from him, as he bowed his head and offered up a short prayer for calm and serene thought. The increased militancy of the Sword had originated after the horrifying events of World War 2 and the Cold War that followed. The darkness of that time had unleashed such chaos upon the world that it was decided that Infinity Ascending must take a more active and expanded role in imposing order lest The Path be lost to The Darkness. There had been some fears that the Sword would take so much upon itself that it could grow out of their control, but its successes had stilled all but a few contrary voices.

Their order had increasingly relied on the Sword to do most of the practical hands-on work. Most, but not all. In an attempt to mitigate the foreseen inflection points, he had been able to do a few small things to try and mute the Sword's actions. He smiled wryly to himself and tried to take some comfort in the thought that the flapping of a butterfly's wings could influence great events - if properly applied. The question was, what form should his wing-flapping now take?

One thing was certain - he would have to proceed very carefully.

CHAPTER FIVE
Harvest of Souls

Yancey and Simon awoke the next morning greatly refreshed in body and mind. Although the stresses and horrors that they had experienced were still on their minds, they were no longer crushed by them. After a cursory breakfast and quick stint of personal hygiene, they were ready to start the day.

Looking around, the two friends proceeded to put together a suitable work area. There were several rough benches that they moved to the centre to be closer to the fire, the car, and light from the windows. Short lengths of planks and some stumps were rapidly converted to quite serviceable chairs. Several pieces of plywood ("They don't make this stuff like they used to," observed Simon) became general-purpose whiteboards. Pulling their laptops, UPSs, and printouts from the Busted Flush, they completed the setup.

"OK," said Yancey, "let's concentrate on the areas that might help us understand the structure of the Sword, how they work, and especially on any facilities that they might have."

Simon readily agreed, and they came up with a division of files for each to look at. A couple of hours later they took a break for some tea, and to compare notes.

"I may have found a few things," said Simon. "There's some references to what seem like various divisions or groups or something, and what might be the names of facilities that they seem to be using. A lot of them have Biblical sounding names, or names that have that sort of pretentious sound."

"Yah," agreed Yancey, grabbing some paper and handing it to Simon. "Write off a summary on this and tack to the board. I'll do the same with my stuff. The tea should be done by the time we are."

As he predicted, everything came together at the same time. After pouring themselves a cup of tea, they sat back for a moment to savour it.

"Damn, Yance, that is good tea. You always manage to get your food and caffeine right, no matter what."

Yancey slurped his agreement, and passed a biscuit over to Simon, who accepted it gratefully. After taking a small bite and chewing, he sighed and took a bigger bite. Several bites and slurps later, each had finished his biscuit and turned back to the task at hand. Taking their notes to the closest of the benches, they each spread out their notes, one above the other's. They spent a few minutes looking at the others' notes, eyes flicking back and forth among the pages.

"OK," said Simon, "it looks like I've picked out a few of the same names you have. In terms of organizational stuff, I've got a few names. One interesting one is the 'Fist of Tolerance'. Now that is a strange and scary concept."

Yancey glanced down at his notes, and stabbed a finger at one page, "Yep, got that. It appears to deal with the handling of prisoners, I think, although they refer to them as 'lost souls awaiting salvation'. As you say, that is a scary way of putting it. Maybe something to do with incarceration? But no, something more. Maybe interrogation?"

"Sounds feasible," admitted Simon, "but it seems to be an order within the Sword. Not a very large order, and the only ranks referred to are acolytes and Deacons. The job of the deacons seems to be to 'save souls'. Sounds like something out of the Spanish Inquisition."

They both shuddered at that.

"Does it seem associated with any facilities?" asked Yancey.

"Hmm, well, there are references to what seem like place names. Stuff like 'River of Mercy', and 'Tears of Joy'. Spanish Inquisition stuff, indeed."

While Simon was talking, Yancey was furiously tapping away at his laptop, "Gimme a sec. Those names ring a bell, somehow."

It took more than a second. More than a few minutes, in fact, but Yancey sat bolt upright, did a fist-pump, and hissed out a rather predatory, "Gotcha."

Simon sat with a more-or-less patient look on his face, waiting for his friend to calm himself and start sharing what he'd found.

"I may have a location for them!" Yancey preened. "Buried in the operational details for the attack on the Shattered Palace was some reference to the Fist and Tears of Joy. It didn't seem important at the time, so I ignored it. But I just looked at it again and it seems like any captives were to be handed over to the Fist at this Tears of Joy place. There's coordinates here, but they're map references. Some sort of internal reference system that the Sword uses. If we can find out how to convert it to latitude and longitude, we'll have a location! I would assume that it'd be relatively close by. Can't think of any good reason they'd want to transport prisoners very far."

"Hmmm," muttered Simon. "What sort of reference system? Gimme what's there. I've got some references to maps in my stuff."

Yancey quickly passed on the information, and shortly thereafter it was Simon's turn to proclaim the end of a successful hunt with a fist-pump. A quick check of their maps showed that the location appeared to be west of their current location, near Dryden.

"Is that right?" said Simon numbly. "That doesn't look too far off the beaten track."

Yancey zoomed in on the maps stored on the laptops and said, "A small town near Dryden, actually. Makes sense when you think about it. It'll be real close to their transportation network, close to an airport, close to a larger town but located in a small place that can be controlled. Seems to be some sort of private sanitarium or spa or something of that sort."

They looked at each other blankly.

"Crap," said Yancey finally breaking the silence. "That's something right out of a spy novel. But it does make a lot of sense, both in terms of location, accessibility, and local cover story."

"Yah," agreed Simon, then added "Say, did you see anything about something called 'Harvest of Souls'? Not sure if it's a place or what, but it seemed to be something that was supposed to be done or seen or something after the attack on the Shattered Palace."

Yancey bent down at his computer and began muttering softly to himself. Shortly thereafter, Simon sat typing at his own laptop. Their small fire died down and then went out completely, casting the shelter into darkness that was broken only by the light emanating from the laptops.

Suddenly, Yancey sprang back from his computer as if attacked, his eyes wide with horror. Simon glanced up sharply from his labours and stared at his friend. He started to ask what was wrong, but the look on Yancey's face stopped Simon, and sent cold chills down his spine.

It took several long seconds for Yancey to find his voice. "Harvest of Souls is an ongoing operation of some sort. The soldiers from the Shattered Palace op, and others drawn from other in-province sites, were to be assigned to that operation to provide security, at whatever level was required. This was something big and important to them. Important enough to guard with soldiers equipped with heavy weapons."

Yancey looked up at Simon, the look in his eyes changing from horror to ice.

"It's about children, Simon. Harvest of Souls is an operation that involves children."

"Yance ..." began Simon in an uncertain voice.

"Shitfuckshitfuckshitshitshit," chanted Yancey in an increasingly emphatic voice. Then he caught himself, inhaled deeply and exhaled in a rush before continuing. "OK, we gotta calm down and check this out, Simon. We need to confirm this, and possibly the money angle will give us a clue. There's always a money angle when it comes to ops involving kids. Always."

Yancey looked up at his friend. The raw desperation slowly fading from his eyes, to be slowly replaced by his normal professional detachment. Momentarily at a loss, Simon looked at his friend, and drew strength from his resolve. Yancey was back on track, and it was time for the two of them to get to work. In clipped tones they discussed the division of labour, and general plans of analysis. They were experienced professionals when it came to teasing useful information out of a morass of raw data, and they prepared to get to work. First of all they attended to the human basics, re-building the fire and boiling up some water for tea. While snacking on a protein bar and a cookie to help fuel their next efforts, they made sure that they had a supply of pencils and paper for note-taking, and mugs of tea to sustain themselves. Then they got down to the task at hand.

A couple of hours later, a muffled but heartfelt curse from Simon broke the silence. He stood up, and his stretching elicited both groans and the sound of joints protesting after being too long in one position. A glance at his friend was enough to inform him that Yancey was still lost in the depths of data analysis. Fair enough, he smiled, so he decided to take brief break to tend the fire and make a quick bio-break. When he returned, he saw some faint indications that Yancey was beginning to return to the world. After a couple minutes of furious note-making, Yancey raised his head and yawned, shook his head while uttering incoherent sounds, then stood and shook his entire body before performing a prodigious series of stretches.

"We got any tea?" he enquired.

"I just put the water on to boil," smiled Simon. "Take your bio-break, then we can start comparing notes."

As it was spoken, so it was done, and in a couple of minutes the two friends were at the desk staring at their notes, deciding how to start.

"Maybe if I start," said Simon, "and you chime in as appropriate?"

Yancey nodded his agreement and Simon began.

"OK, working backwards from 'Harvest of Souls' got me some references to projects that seemed to tie into it, and then companies that tie into those. Actually, it seemed as if some of those were feeder operations, supplying something or other to the final goal. Harvest of Souls, I mean. Interestingly, all of those feeder companies are part of a single cadre. And since that's the cadre associated with the election fraud side of things, that's got to be controlled by the Sword."

Simon paused, and Yancey nodded at him to continue.

"Another interesting point is that those feeder companies all have their operations in northern Ontario, and are doing a variety of things. But all of those things are transportation-related. Some are hauling general freight, some move heavy equipment, and some move foodstuffs. None of them are big companies, but each of them has their particular niche all to themselves, and they don't overlap spheres of activity with each other on either the operational or geographical side. Or so it looks like, so far. Anyways, between them they have exclusive access to a very wide area. Even areas that aren't terribly cost-effective to operate in. It's all a bit sketchy, I'm afraid, but there's enough there to start looking hinkey."

Yancey nodded his agreement, "Hmph. OK, so they have their own transportation network set up, but the question seems to be *what* they are transporting in addition to their nominal business. Then there has to be a human side of the distribution, for both the legal and illegal merchandise. Operating that sort of setup costs money to establish and run, and it sounds as if the legitimate products wouldn't pay the costs of running the network. So whatever the illegal side of things is, it has to generate enough to pay their basic costs plus balance their risks. Especially since this has been going on for some time. Hasn't it?"

Simon nodded and added, "These companies are all based on the acquisition of smaller companies over time. Those smaller companies are the ones that were around forever, then ran into hard times, or were family businesses that couldn't handle the succession issue, that sort of thing. It's hard to get too much more out of the data that we've got, though."

"OK, then," Yancey mused, staring off into the distance, "we've got an organized distribution network created by merging together existent small companies, but optimized to minimize overlap. As to what is being transported, I rather suspect that it would be pretty diverse. There's the obvious stuff like booze and drugs, although that would probably get them noticed by the regular organized crime types. Or maybe not, if all they supplied was a distribution service to keep those groups supplied without trying to take over territories or profits. Prostitutes, maybe? Though I'm not sure how profitable that might be, these days."

Yancey's eyes lit up "Hey, how were they going to transport all that stuff from the Shattered Palace? There was a lot of stuff to be taken out, and large in terms of both volume and weight. And not to mention getting the Sword troops with all their equipment in place, in the first place. That's a helluva lot of long-term planning for a single op, big as it was. No, there's more to this transportation network than that. Maybe a bunch of smaller ops, with the occasional big one?"

"No," answered Simon, "That doesn't sound right. It has to be something reasonably profitable and ongoing. Maybe part of their operational mode is to transship across Ontario, say across the country? Or to act as a means of distribution for goods coming in from out of the province?"

Yancey said thoughtfully, "Hmm, acting as a tie-in for a more national distribution grid? That would up the ante. OK, say they move stuff from out of the province to within the province. For what purpose?"

"Well," answered Simon, "Ontario is still the major

province for damn near everything. Manufacturing for one, even though that's been cut back a lot. Finance, for sure. Hey, physically transporting money for laundering might be the sort of thing they could be doing. Lots of people and companies still use cash for all sorts of legal reasons, especially up north where banks and e-commerce networks can be few and far between. Lots of little towns with lots of little and not-so-little resource companies. Spreading the dirty cash around the North would be a good way to launder it."

"The advantage of that," added Yancey grimly, "is that it would help establish their hold on any company or politician that they got into contact with. Infinity Ascending is all about control, remember. This brings me to my own research. But first, let's grab some of that tea."

They took a brief pause to pour and slurp some tea. It was getting a bit strong by this time, but they didn't mind at this point.

Yancey started talking about what he had found by looking at things from the IA and Sword side of the data. "OK, we know that the attack on the Shattered Palace was to obtain nuclear and biological weapons. I think we can be pretty sure that this distribution network was how they planned to get the weapons out of the area. They obviously planned to use the troops on another op, and probably fairly quickly - that's the Harvest of Souls. All fine and good, but where did those troops and equipment come from, and what were they doing? I think that we can assume that the attack on Toronto with the tank was probably one of their ops. OK, so we've got a cadre of highly trained troops, trained to the level of Special Forces, complete with all the equipment those forces would require. Where would they be stationed? Where would they train?"

"Having established their transportation system, moving troops and equipment around would be pretty easy. As for where, well there's not as many places as one might think. Northern Alberta is out, because of the Cold Lake air force training area. Northern Saskatchewan and Manitoba have mines and hydroelectric facilities under a lot of supervision. The Maritimes are just too small. That leaves Ontario and Quebec, and Quebec is xenophobic enough to make non-natives stand out like a sore thumb. Which leaves northern Ontario, with its plethora of little towns and abandoned remains of mining and logging camps. A few big towns and a few big cities, the country's economic hub, Toronto, and the nation's capital, Ottawa. Major crime hubs in both Hamilton and Toronto would give easy access to anything illegal. Then there are the Great Lakes to easily move stuff illegally to and from the United States. Yeah, if someone wanted to grab control of Canada, then Ontario would be the place to infest and infect."

Yancey paused for a moment to slurp at his cooling tea before continuing. "We know that there are powerful groups using Canada as a battleground, and their war is heating up. At least one of those groups, IA and the Sword, are on a self-proclaimed holy mission to save us all, to restore the natural order of things, with them on top and the rest of us grateful for their wise leadership. We don't know exactly who those other players are, but we can take some good guesses. Some of them are bound to be nations with state-owned multinationals like China, or state-encouraged ones like the US. Canada was founded by European countries, and their influence has never left us. Then there are the ultra-rich robber barons that are expanding to near-warlord status on an international level, in both the US and Europe. Think about it. Canada is one of the few places where all of their interests intersect on all sorts of levels. We have lots of natural resources, sure, but we've got a well-established civil infrastructure, a strong financial system, and our banks have worldwide reach. Not to mention being physically situated kind of in the middle of all of them, or within spitting distance. No, Canada was chosen for a reason, and it won't be for our good - that's the only thing we can count on."

Simon looked unhappily thoughtful. "Remember the term 'banana republic'? Less than a century ago, American private companies pretty much owned a lot of small countries that did nothing but produce what was good for those companies - like bananas. Private individuals, even whole governments, lived or died at the whim of those corporations. And don't forget how a few British and American companies pretty much carved up South America for themselves at about the same time to control the exploitation of their natural resources. I always thought that those sorts of things were ancient history. Guess it's our turn now."

Yancey cleared his throat, "Actually, I think it is worse than those times."

That got Simon's full attention, and his gaze bored intently into his friend's eyes.

"Simon, this time we've got Infinity Ascending, and they appear to be controlling a lot of those previously private companies. A single group that is on a holy mission from God to save us all from ourselves. They seem to truly believe that. Worse, much like the Spanish Inquisition, they believe that saving our souls by bringing us to this 'path' of theirs is more important than saving our bodies. It is a strongly religious group that has maintained their zeal for over a century, spreading its influence from the top of society downward. They have infiltrated and influenced all sorts of organizations over the years. Hell, they've probably created some of them as false fronts. All for one all-consuming goal - control. Control for a holy purpose with no doubts entertained or allowed. There's a dangerous allure to that sort of certainty, Simon. Think about how dangerous fanatical suicide bombers can be, for example. But IA isn't just about religion, as much as they profess it to be, but also a mindset from over a century ago. It's all there in the databases, Simon, if only in sketchy form. These crazies are evangelizing an expansionist vision from the late 1800's. Europeans were supposed to go forth and impose civilization on a chaotic world. White man's burden. Separation of the classes and of the races. All ruled by an elite - the self-appointed natural ruling class. Looked real good on paper. Even worked, on the surface, for a while. But those inbred intellectual halfwits caused World War 1, and learned so little from that that they set up the conditions that guaranteed World War 2 a little bit later. And those conflicts set up the Cold War, which in turn set up the various Ethnic Cleansing Wars and suchlike that are still ongoing."

Yancey paused to take a shaky breath before continuing. "The important thing to remember is that these crazies will do anything at all if they think it will advance their cause. Do anything to anyone. But they have their weaknesses, too. They don't have absolute control. In fact it is pretty tenuous right now because they have to work from the top down, for the most part. That means setting things in motion takes time to set up. This implies limits on their communications, and *that* limits their ability to control things once an op starts. Sort of like a clockwork mechanism. Looks really impressive, but throw some sand into it and it goes out of whack. Get enough out of whack and it grinds to a halt, or even self-destructs. They've got a distribution network, but the illegal stuff has to be carefully coordinated. Coordination means communications, and all that sort of stuff is carefully monitored by a lot of different people in a lot of different agencies. IA and the Sword can't control all of that, so that means they have to be careful. Maybe communicate only at certain times when they can ensure that the few people they control in those agencies are on duty."

Simon was beginning to look thoughtful, especially when he saw the evil gleam in his friend's eye.

"And, Simon me lad, they've only got so many of those elite troops at hand here - and a good chunk of those got wiped out at the Shattered Palace. That means their local organization is going to be scurrying around trying to keep the clockwork plan on track. At that's at best. At worst they're running around like chickens with their heads cut off, although I wouldn't count on that. In any event, they are going to be disorganized and off-schedule. We don't know enough about this 'Harvest of Souls' op to stop it, but I'm guessing that it'll be postponed until they can put together another security force. Which will probably be drawn, at least in part, from any of their front organizations that have Sword soldiers. Like that 'Tears of Joy' place, where they hold 'guests'. Check out that transportation system you've dug up, and check to see if it has a depot in that area. I'm guessing it does. And if that's their holding cells for Ontario, that's where Gretchen will be. If their planning is being as thrown for a loop as I think it is, then now is the time to pay that facility a visit. It's time to bring Gretchen home."

CHAPTER SIX
Changes At The City Desk

Several reporters gathered around the coffee machine, swapping stories and complaints. The biggest of these was the sudden and mysterious departure of Charlene Blaverston, editor in chief. She had been at the paper literally longer than many of the reporters had been alive, and was something of a legend. She had taken time off before, sometimes at short notice, but to simply fly off without warning was unheard of. There were mutterings that it might be connected to the death of Herman Flagsworth, a long-time colleague of Charlene's. Maybe his death made her realize that she wasn't getting any younger, and that she needed to grab some good times while she still could. Others muttered that the two of them seemed to be working on something prior to his death, and maybe she was following up on the story. Others pointed out that Charlene's sense of duty and order would never have allowed her to simply vanish without ensuring that her beloved newspaper was organized for her absence. The only thing that everyone agreed upon was that it was damned peculiar.

Peculiar or no, the fact was that she was gone. In her absence a new acting-editor had been brought in - one of the new MBA-trained favoured sons from 'upstairs'. This was not treated as a good thing by any of them, and the unhappiness went beyond the traditional grousing about management. There had always been grumbles about Charlene's hard-headed approach, but those were complaints about the impossibly high standards of journalistic quality and integrity that she demanded from everyone for every story, great or small. Under the new editor, standards seemed to be somewhat arbitrary. Assignments were more and more being doled out based on personal favouritism. The most shocking thing was the spiking of stories, even of some good investigative ones that Charlene had championed, to suit the whims of advertisers or influence peddlers. There was even talk, in voices lowered to mere whispers, of 'requests' to slant stories a certain way.

Things had changed in the short time since Charlene had left, they agreed, and no one thought that the changes were for the better.

CHAPTER SEVEN
Defence Department Press Conference

The press conference room had but a handful of reporters, and no video crews at all. The furniture on the stage consisted of a lectern and behind that a small table with two chairs .

The press conference had been lightly advertised, and the press release gave only vague information about what was to be discussed. The 'rumours' in Ottawa - actually carefully leaked information that all the media depended on -implied that it was to discuss some minor training accident.

Into the press conference room strode two uniformed soldiers and one civilian. The soldiers stopped behind the table and sat down. The civilian stood behind the lectern. The civilian was a young man, and wore a dark coloured suit, with a maple leaf pin on one lapel, and on the other a pin with the insignia of the Prime Minister's Office. The latter was a new development of the Government's 'deep think' teams. The official reasoning was that it helped the media know who was speaking for the Government. Everyone understood that it was to show who was in charge.

"Thank you for coming today," said the PMO

representative. "It is my sad duty today to inform you of a fatal accident that occurred during a recent military field training exercise. The exercise was a small part of one of the larger annual US-Canada joint exercises. The purpose of this smaller group was to take part in live-fire training. Apparently something went wrong during the helicopter insertion portion of the exercise, and two helicopters went down, killing everyone aboard. Early reports indicate that some sort of explosion occurred on one helicopter that caused the other helicopter to explode as well, but those reports remain to be confirmed. The resulting crashes occurred next to the troops on the ground, causing some injuries, several of them serious. Thanks to the quick thinking and decisive leadership of the on-scene American commander, General Thomas Thansworth the Third, the injured were treated promptly, resulting in the minimization of casualties."

The young man paused, as if to emphasize the seriousness of his report. The military representatives sat stone-faced, as if at attention.

"Among the casualties was the Canadian senior officer, Colonel Frederick Brown. Unfortunately, the preliminary investigation would seem to indicate the Col. Brown had insisted on holding this particular exercise against the advice of the American advisers, but pressed ahead despite the lack of training and readiness of his troops. I would like to extend the thanks of this Government to the United States military for their prompt response to this incident. Survivors of this incident have been transferred to a military base for treatment and debriefing. Because of the preliminary nature of our information, I will not be taking questions at this time. Thank you."

The young man turned and walked away from the lectern to the exit. The military representatives stood, spun on their heels, and followed him. Their expressions never changed from stone-faced silence.

One bored reporter turned to a colleague and complained what a waste of time this had been. Another, from the AJF News Agency, tartly commented that if a country couldn't properly train its soldiers, then maybe it should get rid of them and hire professionals to take over.

CHAPTER EIGHT
Into The Tears Of Joy

"Okey dokey, Smokey, let's bust some data and get this rescue plan run up the flagpole and see who salutes."

Yancey looked askance at his friend, shaking his head sadly.

"No, I'm serious," insisted Simon. "We gotta go SEAL team on this op, and ... uhm ...uhm, well, anyways, we gotta start some serious planning."

"One step ahead of you, old chum," Yancey laughed, "I really wish that we dared to get on the Internet, but at least these road maps and topo maps are pretty current. We can see where this Tears of Joy place is physically located ... uhm ... here."

Yancey struggled to smooth out the topo map on the rough surface of the bench, and added a few stray pieces of wood as weights to keep it flat. Then he tapped at his laptop to bring up the road maps.

"OK, the road map shows us where the facility is located, and the topo map gives us an idea of the terrain. There's a semi-major road going north of Dryden here, and the facility is located along there," Yancey waggled his finger indicting the area of the map he was talking about.

"If we look at the topo map, it looks like flat to gentle hills all around. Can't tell exactly from these maps, but the facility is probably located on the top of one of those low hills. Would make sense, strategically, I would think, since it lets them get a look at anyone coming their way. You'll notice that there are several small roads passing quite nearby -probably old logging roads, or something like that. Something to look at when we reconnoitre."

Simon peered at the maps, moving his head back and forth as he carefully examined them. Then he sighed, folded his arms, and leaned back against another of the benches. Again, he looked from one map to the other, and began to puff up his cheeks and rhythmically puff out air. Unfolding his hands, he steepled his fingers and banged his index fingers against his puffing mouth. He stopped puffing, lowered his hands, opened his mouth to speak, closed it again, then opened it and finally spoke up. "Nope. Not seeing it. How, exactly, are we not totally screwed here?"

Yancey smiled and said quietly, "Have faith, my friend. I've done some, shall we say, surreptitious checking-out of places before. Under normal circumstances you'd probably be correct to assume that anything other than a light reconnaissance would be impossible. But keep in mind that these are not normal times for the Sword. Their elite soldier reserves have got to be seriously depleted, and we know that they're going to try and replace those with their second- and third-level forces, which are going to be drawn from their various facilities. Gotta be, if they want to do that Harvest of Souls operation. Whatever it is, it is going to require troops, or at least trained security personnel, to accomplish. Yes, our information on all this is a bit thin, but it's all logically consistent and ties together coherently. So, that leaves all of the various facilities short-handed, as they accumulate troops for the op. This Tears place looks to be small to begin with, so removing any of their personnel is going to leave them shorthanded. And keep in mind that they won't be expecting anything, and they've had it soft and easy for a long time."

Simon interjected, "Won't what happened at the Shattered Palace put them all on high alert?"

"Not in any way that'll affect us, I wouldn't think," was the quick answer. "They've got to be still trying to piece together what exactly happened. All they know for sure is that the op went spectacularly bad. So, yeah, they'll be a bit on edge, but they can't be on high alert and maintain all their various active operations at the same time. With nothing else happening, any state of alert is going to wear off in a few days, and it has been that long, so it should be OK. But, yeah, we'll take care to look for any problems when we reconnoitre."

"Sounds reasonable," Simon admitted, "but there are so many unknowns. It's just real scary thinking about breaking into a place like that. I mean, if it is a holding facility for enemies of the Sword it'll be like a jail, won't it?"

Yancey pondered that for a moment before he replied.

"Only to a certain degree," he decided. "It still has to maintain its cover, so I really doubt that there will be jail-like cells. More likely to be rooms with good locks, and locked windows. Just as good as a medium-security jail, for all practical purposes."

A troubled look came over Simon's face, and he asked, "I know that our objective is to rescue Gretchen, but what if we find others being held? What do we do with them?"

"Ah, shit. Hadn't thought of that," answered Yancey. He paused briefly before continuing, "Well, I guess it all depends on how many there are. A couple or so extra is no problem, I guess. Just cram them into the back seat. More than that, though, would be a logistical problem. Hmmm, well, I guess that's got to be something that we worry about when it happens. We've only got the one car."

Yancey was silent for a few moments as he thought furiously.

"OK, I can't see that they're going to have a large number of people. I mean, how much call are they going to have to store prisoners? Probably just have a few at any one time, at most. This is the Sword, after all. If anyone is a truly serious problem, the Sword will just bury them."

Simon look startled by this piece of reasoning, and his eyes opened wide.

"No, no, I'm sure Gretchen is OK," Yancey hastened to add. "I mean she just doesn't know all the much that can harm them."

"Yance," said Simon slowly, "that does *not* reassure me. They took her to find out what she knows. A low-level catch is all she may be to them, but I doubt they would let her go if they thought she was harmless. They might, if they've taken care to make sure that she hasn't seen or heard anything about them. Or if they thought that causing her to disappear would cause more problems than letting her go. I dunno. That's an awful thin hope, no matter how you look at it."

Both of them fell into an unhappy silence at that.

Finally, Yancey broke the silence. "Well, if they've got her, then that's probably where she is. So we have to check it out. It's about a 4 hour or so trip there, maybe less if the roads are good or we can figure out a decent backroads route using some of the lesser roads. Why don't you check out the maps looking for the best route, and I'll pack up our stuff. We'll grab a quick meal and then head out and get there while there is still some light left, maybe. Do a quick check, then observe it when it's dark. If we watch how they light things up, that'll help us figure out which rooms are in use. There's no use just sitting around here and speculating without hard information."

Simon couldn't argue with that, so he turned his attention to the maps and studied them intently. While Simon studied maps, Yancey gathered up their loose belongings and stored them in the Busted Flush. That done, he sorted through their meagre supply of food, and put together a light meal. Simon finally heaved a sigh and got up from his maps and went to get his food. The small amount on the plate caused him to look up inquiringly. Yancey shrugged. Getting more food was going to be their next top priority, they decided.

They finished their meal, cleaned up and stored what little remained of their gear, then opened the large doors of the equipment shed that had been their home and refuge. The sky was cloudy but bright, a good day for driving. So they got into the Busted Flush and started down the road towards the Tears of Joy facility.

Simon's map reading skills proved to be up to the task, and through a combination of back roads and main roads they got to Dryden with almost of hour of daylight left. The gas tank was only one quarter full, so they decided that they'd best fill up. Pooling their money revealed only enough for a full tank of gas. Sighing at the prospect of no food for the time being, they pulled into a large gas station and began filling up. When they were done, they went inside to pay and to use the washroom before continuing. At the register they were told that the data lines were down, and the station was low on cash, so would it be alright if they paid using a credit card? The owner explained hurriedly that he had one of the old manual swipe machines used before the data lines were available, and kept it because it came in useful every once in a while. The two friends looked at each other, and Simon asked if they could put some more stuff onto the bill, like food? The owner happily agreed, and pointed them to an attached room that served as a small store. They eagerly filled up with enough to keep three people going for a week or more, then went back to the cash register. The manager totalled everything up, made up the bill, and Simon handed over his credit card. They even got a couple of cardboard boxes to carry their booty out to the waiting car. Getting in, Simon told Yancey where they needed to go, and off they went.

"That was a piece of unexpected luck," chortled Simon happily.

"Yep," replied Yancey, "but now we for sure have to be out of here in a couple of days. That's all it will take for those manually-created credit card transactions to be sent down to the main office and entered into their systems. If we're on any sort of watch list, this transaction's gonna pop up. We're on the clock now."

"Killjoy," snorted his friend. "We've got gas, food, and a target. What more do you want?"

That got an answering snort out of Yancey before he asked, "Have you finalized an initial approach to the facility?"

"Yep. Figure that we could simply drive by as a first pass reconnaissance. The road continues on to other towns, so it will be normal enough for traffic to be on it. I'll use my phone to take pictures, and maybe use yours to take a video record. With those, and our eagle-keen eyes, that should give us enough to decide how to proceed when it gets darker."

Yancey nodded his agreement, and handed Simon his phone. They had taken out their SIM cards days earlier, and ensured that they had turned off all the radio functions. Not too long afterwards they began their approach to the facility. Simon had arranged himself across Yancey, angling everything so as to hide the phones as much as possible. To anyone looking at them from a distance, they would look like two lovers out on lovely drive. Although the situation would have normally caused them to giggle and crack idiotic jokes, the seriousness of the situation had thoroughly dampened their sense of humour.

The facility was beginning to come into sight. They drove by at the speed limit, not daring to go any slower. Simon held Yancey's phone in his left hand recording a video, and attempted to track the area as they drove by. In his right hand he held his own phone, with the camera set to a slight zoom, and snapped anything that looked interesting, including the surrounding area. All too quickly they drove out of sight of the building, and Simon gratefully leaned back into his own seat. Before doing anything else, he carefully closed down the camera app on both phones, and let out a long exhaled breath, then said, "OK, keep going for another five klicks, then there should be a small side road to the right. Take that and we should be able to find a place to stop."

Before too long they had reached their destination road, and Yancey turned onto it. They drove along for a few minutes, then were able to pull over when the shoulder widened off into a small meadow. Yancey made sure that the Busted Flush was pulled forward enough to be hidden by the low brush, and not able to be seen from the main road. Then he turned to Simon and suggested that they each make a sketch of what they had seen prior to looking at the cameras. Simon thought this was a good idea, and for several minutes each was busy at his own sketch.

Yancey was the first to finish, and he lowered his pad of paper to stare at it thoughtfully. Seeing this, Simon quickly put the final touches to his. They each held up their sketches to better compare them, but the fading light made it hard to distinguish details. Simon suggested turning on the dome light or using flashlights, but Yancey insisted on blocking the windows before showing any bright lights. Simon could certainly see the logic in that, so they spent a few minutes making the windows light-tight using tarps, blankets, and duct tape. It wasn't long before they had the car light-tight enough to risk turning on flashlights.

Comparing drawings, they noted a lot of similarities though each had focused on different aspects. The facility looked to be a single building, rectangular in shape, about twice as long as wide, set about fifty or so metres from the main road. There was a single access road into the facility off the main road, with a hefty-looking gate controlling access. There was a modest sign in the front, reading "Tranquil Roads Executive Spiritual Retreat". There was a fence, at least a couple of metres high, surrounding the site on the three sides that they could see, so it was a safe bet to say that the fence went all the way around. The fence was mostly hidden by a hedge, but it didn't look as though the hedge was hefty enough to offer any climbing opportunities. There were a lot of trees of varying sizes, but all of them were safely within the perimeter defined by the fence. The access road to the facility appeared to be of the standard for such facilities, with a small parking area in front, then looping around to the back. In terms of topography, the building was on top of a low, flat hill, maybe ten or fifteen metres above the level of the main road and surrounding area.

"Well, it looks like we pretty much agree that it is pretty secure without looking like a fortress," Yancey mused. "Let's take a look at the photos and video to see what they picked up that we missed."

Simon decided to show the video first, so they peered at the phone's screen. They both agreed that it had turned out amazingly well, all things considered. As it reached its conclusion, both inhaled sharply at the same time, and Simon quickly rewound it a few seconds back.

"Is that a hole in the fence?" Simon said hopefully.

He rewound the video again and they watched it carefully.

"Yes, I truly think it is," Yancey said. "Let's take a look at the photos you took."

Once again, Simon proved to be an excellent photographer. There were enough good photos to see the potential hole in the fence, as well as windows and external doors on the facility itself. The more they looked at the damaged section in the fence, the more excited they got. That looked like their way in.

"Hmm, that damaged section looks suspiciously the size of a large car or truck," Yancey mused. "Looks like it didn't happen too long ago, too. Probably some local losing control on the gravel or snow and skidding into it. Gee, do you think that alcohol might have been a factor?"

Simon grunted his assent, then added, "Can't see that ever happening in a small town out in the middle of nowhere. No, sir."

Yancey was carefully studying the photos, then marking up his drawing. He rescaled his sketch of the building to be more accurate, then added the locations of the windows and doors. Things were looking, if not up, then not quite as down as he had feared. Enlarging the photos to their maximum usable extent, he studied the doors carefully, and noted what looked like access control boxes. He was confident that he could take care of those. Then he returned to studying the damaged section of the fence. Simon was watching carefully, knowing enough not to interrupt. Finally, Yancey leaned back and sighed irritably. As Simon raised his eyebrows in query, Yancey pointed at the photo of the fence, "Can't tell if the fence itself is still intact, or not. The hedge is taken out, that's for sure, and that helps a lot 'cuz it's thick enough to be a barrier all on its own. It all depends on if the idiot who hit it, hit it a glancing blow or hard enough to go all the way in. And if he did go all the way in, how well the fence was fixed, or if it got fixed at all. It's gonna be wired for alarms, but maybe that got taken out as well."

He paused and let out a hearty, "Oh, shit," to the great surprise of Simon, who was somewhat taken aback by this outburst.

"Wi-Fi," muttered Yancey. "We forgot to check to see if they have a Wi-Fi hub."

"No way," insisted Simon, "this is the Sword we're talking about. No way they'd do something as low-level stupid as having an unsecured or low security Wi-Fi hub."

"My friend, if there's anything that I've learnt is to never underestimate the carelessness of the supremely confident adversary," Yancey laughed. "You would not believe the dumb things supposedly brilliant organizations do. Helps keep me employed and able to buy nice toys, it does. I've got a Wi-Fi sniffer in amongst the gear and a small antenna for extended range sniffing. We'll use it when we go back to check out the level of activity there."

Simon perked up at the idea of their odds improving, "When did you want to go back?"

Yancey thought for a moment before replying, "We'll sneak back now, get on the main road, drive a bit further north to see if we can get up on one of those other hills, then do some Wi-Fi snooping as we check to see how many interior lights are on, and where. That'll give us a good idea of activity. Maybe watch for a bit to see if there are any changes. Maybe grab a bite to eat as we wait. One must keep up one's strength."

Simon acceded to his friend's wisdom, then they doused the flashlights and removed the curtains from the windows. It was getting fairly dark as they made their way back to the main road, then headed north for a kilometre before turning off onto a small road that looked like it went up one of the many small hills. There was no marker of any sort, so it looked as if it were simply one of the many such minor roads that seem to dot the northern landscape. It was a short road up a low hill, and lead to a relatively flat top. There were the remains of a long-dead campfire, so perhaps it was a local picnic area or make-out spot. In any case, it offered a good view of the Tears of Joy facility. They got out of the Busted Flush, and Yancey opened the trunk to get out a large plastic tub that held his 'detective stuff' as he called it. First he handed binoculars and an extensible pole to Simon and told him to start examining the building, extending and using the pole as support to steady the powerful binoculars. With Simon carefully scanning the building, Yancey pulled out a small box and a tube. The box was actually a compact scanner, and the tube a directional antenna, and he set it to work as he held the tube in his hand and aimed at the facility. After about a minute he stopped the scanner, then took it back to the car and plugged it into a laptop that had its display carefully dimmed. He wasn't expecting much, so a happy smile spread across his face as he saw not only cell phone activity, but Wi-Fi activity as well. A quick analysis of the data showed that the Wi-Fi was secured, but only with WEP, the weakest and most easily broken security ever created, in his opinion. Humming happily to himself, he went back to the trunk, grabbed a tripod, and spent a couple minutes securing the antenna to it and getting set for a proper data breach.

Simon had paused in his examination as he heard Yancey scrabbling around setting up the tripod, and grinned as he watched his friend set up.

Once he was done, Yancey looked up and smiled a predatory smile, "Wi-Fi. WEP encryption. How's you doing?"

Simon laughed, "I bow to the superior wisdom of the master. Most of the building is dark, actually. I can't see the rear of it, but I can see lights on the ground that have to be coming from windows at the back. What we assumed to be front office section has lights, and that is about all I can see from here. I'll keep watching while you work." He went back to his work, smiling, as he heard the gentle clacking of the keys on the keyboard.

All it took to enter the facility's network was a few seconds and one of Yancey's standard programs. His humming stopped as he focused on the task at hand. Being on the network was not the same as having access to any computers that might be on it, or evading the system's security measures. However, the more he looked, the more astonished he became, and the more worried. It was almost too easy, in some ways. As was his wont in such cases, he paused to think about things for a bit before continuing.

"Problems?" asked Simon. "I don't hear you clattering away anymore."

"Hmm? Oh, no. Quite the contrary. It's the lack of

problems that has me pausing to ponder. The Wi-Fi was set to the manufacturer's default password. The regular unit probably died, and someone grabbed a spare out of the box and hooked it up quickly, then either forgot or didn't know to reset the password. Happens all the time, actually. There's a firewall, but it's nothing special and I bypassed that, being careful to spoof the network monitor with a standard program. So I'm in and can see several computers, including at least one that looks like a server, judging by the name. Aside from the Wi-Fi, this hasn't been easy but certainly not top level security. We're only going to get one chance at this, Simon. I'm pretty sure, actually quite sure, that I can get in without getting caught. But not one hundred percent. Do I take the chance?"

Simon sighed heavily as he lowered the binoculars and his head. Pausing for a few moments, he shook his head, raised it, and looked at Yancey, "Yance, we aren't even positive that she's here. But if she is we have to get her out sooner than later. The Sword is off balance right now, but won't stay that way for long. OK, what if you take a peek at the non-server stuff first? That should have a lot lower chance of detection, right? Why not take a look at those? Then we'll decide what to do from there. By the way, what if someone notices your computer on the network?"

Yancey knew that this was not an easy decision for his friend to make, and he fully agreed with the reasoning. "Heh. I set the name on my own computer to 'Security'. It's pretty rare for someone to mess with anything labelled 'Security'. Watch the facility as I do this, will you? Let me know if any other lights come on."

And with that, Yancey began logging into one of the computers that probably wasn't a server. Probably. He hoped. Then he was in, and it became quickly obvious that this was someone's personal computer - probably a laptop or a tablet. A quick glance showed nothing of obvious interest, so he kept that window minimized as he looked at another computer. This, too, turned out to be a personal unit, which didn't look like very interesting, so he minimized that window and looked at the last computer he was targeting. This one was a little more interesting - it looked like a smart phone plugged into one of the other two computers. Hesitating only for a moment, he decided to download the data from it for later examination. This looked like it might take a minute or so, so he started that going and maximized the window to the phone's host computer. A quick look showed that the only mail client was the standard default one, so he started to download the email database. He repeated the process for the other computer, then went back to check on the progress of the phone download. A quick look showed that the download was finished, so he logged off of that. The other downloads were done so he logged off those computers as well. Pulling up another program, he started taking a quick look at the emails from each system, but first checking with Simon to see if there were signs of new activity at the facility. Simon answered in the negative, so Yancey focused on the emails.

"Jackpot," he breathed. "Simon, you can stop watching for a minute. You'll want to hear this."

Simon gratefully lowered the binoculars and turned to his friend.

"There are a series of emails here apparently from one of the workers here to a friend in another facility. The recent ones talk about having no guests, then the arrival of two women as 'special deliveries'. One is younger, described as 'kinda cute', and an older one, described as an 'old battleaxe'. Stored 'out back under lock and key'."

Yancey looked up at Simon, "OK, that could be Gretchen, but who's the other one?"

Simon thought furiously for a moment before replying, "Not entirely sure. Although she does know an older lady that works at a newspaper or something. That might be her, I suppose."

Yancey bent down to read from the screen, "Well, it seems that the email's author is right royally pissed at the low staffing levels, right now. All the 'high and mighty' types have buggered off to some other facility after 'the shit hit the fan about something'."

Both of them couldn't help but grin at that.

"And the worst seems to be that the two that are left are stuck here at the mercy of someone called 'the Deacon'. Hmm, then he talks about how bored he is, and how hard done by he is, yadda yadda, and here we go. Seems that they caught a break today, and this Deacon person took the day off to go somewheres and will be back tomorrow morning, so he and someone named Donny are taking it easy tonight."

The two friends stared at each other, hardly daring to believe their good timing.

"Simon, there's somebody being guarded. There's only two guards or whatever they are, and they sound like they're a bit on the slack side. But their boss is coming back tomorrow. The boss sounds like a right bastard, but all that probably means is that he makes them do things correctly, and that's bad for us. I'll keep monitoring to see if they're both on duty, or if they're taking shifts, or what. Once we know that, we'll know when to attack. But we have to hit them tonight, if we're going to do this at all."

"Yance, have you ever done anything like this? Rescue someone, I mean?"

"Not for a while," Yancey answered with a small laugh,

"and nothing this hairy, to be honest. Just a couple of times to track down underage runaways living in squats with friends. Just show up with a known relative, distract the others while the runaway gets grabbed and tossed into a car, and run like hell. Sorta like this, but those didn't involve the Sword."

"Still," he mused, "not all that different. Whether it's one or both on duty, we still have to create a distraction to draw them away. Then we go in, grab the ladies, and get the hell out of Dodge, fast. Hmm, how 'bout we ponder the distraction question while I see if I can find anything about their schedules from their computers."

Simon could only nod, but his big grin showed his feelings. He knew that this might not be Gretchen, but it certainly looked like it could be. Yancey was right, though, it was now or never time.

Several anxious minutes later, Yancey tapped at his computer for the last time, and leaned back with a heavy sigh.

"OK, I'm logged out. No sense taking any more chances until we do the deed. You still up for it?"

Yancey carefully didn't look at his friend. This was dangerous work, and no fooling, so he didn't want to apply any pressure. Simon was bright and brave, but this was totally outside his experience and expertise. Yancey was going to have to work hard to ensure his friend's safety, as well as the success of this mission.

Simon carefully considered the question. He knew that this was dangerous and totally out of left field for him. The women being held captive might not be their friends. The Sword operatives, slackers though they appeared to be, were still bloody dangerous. And they had guns. He was developing a real loathing for guns, he realized. But none of that mattered. This had to be done, if he were to live with himself. So he looked at Yancey and simply said, "Let's do this."

They gave each other a small smile. Yancey had known what Simon's answer was going to be, and Simon knew that he knew. They had been through several different types of hell together growing up. What was one more between friends?

Yancey described what he had discovered about the scheduling. Because of under-staffing, the guards were supposed to be doing two hours on, two off. With luck, there would only be one of them on active duty, and the other off sleeping. No big deal if they were both up, so long as the distraction affected both of them. The only open questions were the exact time, and the nature of the distraction.

"Well," said Simon, "the only thing that I can come up with that would force both of them out would be a fire of some sort. Fire always gets people's attention."

They both had to grin at shared remembrances of a youthful indiscretion or two.

Yancey thought furiously for a moment. "Well, it has to be big, and it should be at the opposite end of the building to where we enter. How about at the south end of the building? That's away from the front and side entrances, and away from cells at the back that seem to be occupied. Hey, do we still have those small cans of propane and paint thinner we found at the shelter?"

Simon was pretty sure that they did, so he rummaged about in the back seat and brought forth the requested items. "Yep, and both mostly full."

Yancey smiled happily, "My friend, I think we can do this. The paint thinner will make a dandy Molotov cocktail, and the propane will make an improvised fuel-air bomb, if we're lucky. If we're not lucky then it'll just add fuel to the fire. We just need to somehow toss them as a package against the side of the building."

They debated how to throw or catapult the homemade bomb package, but couldn't come up with any workable solution.

"Crap," spat Yancey with feeling. "Setting it off at the fence is just too far away to be of much use as a real distraction. We can't throw it. That means one of us is going to have to place it and set it off."

Simon looked at him with something approaching horror. Yancey didn't look too happy either as he grabbed the binoculars to look at the site again.

"Simon, I have a cunning plan."

Those simple words sent a chill up Simon's spine. He was not going to like this, no not at all.

"Oh stop looking at me like that. This will work. Really," Yancey said irritably, as he explained his brilliant plan. Well, Yancey thought it was brilliant. Simon was less than impressed, but couldn't think of anything better.

The plan itself was simple, and only relied a very little bit on luck. From their current vantage point north of the facility, Simon would drive the Busted Flush south past the Tears facility. Slowing near the damaged part of the fence, Yancey would get out, and Simon would keep going about a kilometre down the road then stop and wait. Yancey would go through the damaged fence, hopefully without setting off any alarms, and then make his way around the perimeter to the south side of the building. The perimeter was actually quite dark, as there were no lights anywhere except at the front gate and along the driveway. There he would set up their firebomb, light the fuse, scurry to the north end of the building, and wait for the explosion. When the firebomb went off he would wait a few seconds, then break in, find the ladies, extract them, and get back outside. Simon, meanwhile, once he saw the fire go off, would head back to the damaged fence, smash through and head for the door at the north end, pick everyone up, and then drive like hell.

"See?" said Yancey proudly. "Easy peasy."

"Uh huh," was Simon's dubious reply. "How do you break through the outside doors and the cell doors?"

"I thought you'd never ask," was the grinning reply. "As part of my handy dandy detective kit, the flash for my camera has an extra power outlet and I just happen to have a prong attachment that plugs into that. Did you realize that modern electronics really don't like having a burst of high voltage being fed into it? Does a dandy job convincing electronic locks to open."

"What if the cell doors have mechanical locks?"

A heavy sigh answered him, "I can pick them if I have to. Or grab the keys from the guard station. Or something."

Simon just glared.

"Or," Yancey said softly, "if I can't open it, then the operation is a bust and we just run away and figure something else out. There'll be cops and firemen here after the fire, so maybe things could sort themselves out that way."

Simon sighed heavily. He knew that the odds were stacked against them and that suicide wouldn't help get Gretchen out.

"Yeah. I don't like it, but ... yeah."

Yancey continued, "In any case, our escape route is towards Sioux Lookout. There are lots of back roads around here, and once we get to Sioux Lookout there are main roads, too. With even the tiniest bit of luck, the guards won't see the direction we take when we leave. But even if they do, there are too many routes to be covered in time to catch us. Hmm, it occurs to me that we might be able to catch two birds with one throw. What we might consider doing is hacking into that server I saw on the network while all this is going on. I could set up a script to log into the Wi-Fi and then into the server, then download whatever it found. Thoughts?"

Simon though intently for a moment before replying, "Damn good idea. It won't matter then if the intrusion sets off their security alarms. But I'll be too busy to deal with that so it'll have to be purely automatic, and there's only going to be a few minutes of download time. Can you set the script so that you download whatever file is below a certain size?"

Yancey's eyes got a faraway look as he thought. "Hmm ... yah ... good idea. Well, I can automate the accessing of the server, and then ... hmm ... yep, it can be done. Say set it to grab directory listings and anything smaller than, oh, 20 megabytes or something. Have to take a best guess as to where the good data is stored, but everything else is out-of-the-box standard, so that has a good chance of working. Yes, indeed, it is worth the ten minutes or so that it'll take to set up, even if all we go after are emails. Whatever we get will be a bonus in case we need to access it later."

He paused a moment to take a deep breath before continuing, "The only really big potential snag is the damaged fence. I *must* be able to get through it without tripping an alarm. The Flush *must* be able to break through without damaging itself. The ground itself should be OK for driving on to get to the driveway. It's not very far. But if the fence is intact, the whole thing is off. When I jump out, I'll do a quick look at the fence. If it's intact, I'll wave a flashlight at you. If that happens, wait a few minutes then come back to pick me up, and we'll head off to Sioux Lookout to work out another plan."

Another long pause, then he said in a calm and even voice, "Simon, one more thing. And this is really important. Once I go in, you can't wait at the doorway too long. Seconds, is all. I'll get the ladies out, don't worry about that. Once they're in the car, you drive. You don't look back, you just drive. I'll do my damnedest to come out with them, but whatever happens, you just get away."

The two lifelong friends exchanged hard looks.

"Yancey, I ..." began Simon.

"No."

Simon had never before heard that sort of steel in Yancey's voice.

"Simon, this is Crunch Time. One of us has to make it out of here with the information. One of us has to go in, and that's me. Gretchen can help you analyze the data as well as I can. If that's her friend in there with her, then those newspaper contacts will be essential. Simon, it's time."

After a slight pause, they gave a terse nod to each other and then began prepping for the rescue.

A short time later, the Busted Flush was carrying the rescue party towards the Tears of Joy. Both of them knew their tasks, and had their equipment at hand. Approaching the damaged section of the fence, Simon slowed down, and Yancey easily jumped out without mishap. Simon leaned over and pulled the passenger door shut. The *thunk* of the closing door sounded so final, somehow.

Yancey approached the fence and examined it carefully with a dimmed flashlight. The fence itself was indeed broken through, with only orange plastic temporary fencing in its place. He carefully pulled down the temporary fencing, then jogged around the darkened perimeter to the south end of the compound. Along the way he had examined the rear of the building, and saw a single door at the south end. He had looked carefully at the cameras, and found a blind spot in the coverage that allowed him to approach the south end of the building without being seen. He placed the improvised firebomb on the ground next to the building and began setting it up. A length of cloth soaked in paint thinner served as the fuse. He wrapped the improvised fuse around the bottle containing the rest of the paint thinner and the propane, then forced the propane tip down and taped it open. The hiss of the gas indicated that all was ready to go, so he stepped back, then carefully lit the fuse. Once he saw that it was burning, he knew that he only had seconds, so he ran along the side of the building back towards the north entrance. Just as he got there, he heard a satisfyingly loud 'bang', and a flash of light that continued to flicker.

Smiling, he dug out the flash unit that had been turned into a very effective taser, pressed it against the electronic lock, and pressed the trigger. He was rewarded with a loud *fizzing* sound, and a click indicated that the door solenoid had retracted. He opened the door and stepped inside carefully, but quickly. There was a short corridor towards the rear, so he ran down there and carefully peered around the corner. He was rewarded with the sight of two figures running down the corridor away from him, a door closing behind them. He ran towards the door, noting the locked doors along the corridor, and the light that came from the bottom of two of them. He got to the corridor door, noted that the door opened towards him, so he jammed a wedge underneath the door to hinder its opening. For good measure he took a small bottle of cyanoacrylate glue and squirted it quickly into the crevice between the door and the frame. Spinning around he ran towards the first of the occupied rooms, smiled happily when he saw the electronic lock, and then zapped it open. Opening the door carefully, he looked inside and was rewarded with the sight of Gretchen standing and staring at him open-mouthed. She was about to speak when Yancey interrupted her, "Hi, Gretchen. Simon and I are rescuing you. We gotta go, *now*."

To emphasize the last, he grabbed her wrist and pulled her towards the doorway, releasing her once he was confident that she was moving. Moving quickly to the next room, he got his zapper ready, then quietly asked Gretchen, "This one, too?"

Gretchen nodded emphatically, while urgently looking back and forth to either side along the corridor.

Yancey zapped open the door, and saw an older lady inside. He said simply "Hi. Rescue. Move. *Now.*"

The woman stood there gaping until Gretchen stood in the doorway and said quietly but intently, "Charlene, love, let's go. *Move.*"

Yancey stood to one side of the doorway to let the ladies out, then he pushed them urgently down the corridor and towards the exit.

"Go, go. Simon's got the car outside. Open the door and get into the car," he said urgently to the two women.

"This is going to work," he thought to himself with some amazement, "it really is going to work."

Just as they got to the outside door, a figure stepped into the corridor yawning and stretching. "Hey, you idiots, what's all the noise ..." then he saw Yancey and the ladies, and with a shout came running at them.

"He's not supposed to be here," thought Yancey frantically. "The data said TWO, not THREE guards."

Despite the shock, Yancey got the door open and shoved the ladies out.

"GO!" he yelled, then shut the door and turned to face the guard. He had to buy the others enough time to get safely away. Seconds counted, now. There was a dull pounding coming from their rear. Yancey realized that the other two guards must be trying to get back to the front. Yancey pulled his improvised taser out and held it before him, which caused the guard to pause and halt his charge. Yancey waved the zapper at him, and the two faced each other. The sound of pounding feet from behind him began to get closer. This was not going to end well, he thought, then he felt a tremendous sharp pain at the base of his neck and everything went black.

When he regained consciousness, Yancey realized that he was very cold. Blinking rapidly to clear his head, he realized that he was on some metallic horizontal surface, and there were restraints on his head and all of his limbs. He was naked except for his underwear. There was an array of lights above him such as those one might see in a surgery, currently turned off.

A deep, warm voice spoke up "Ah, I see that you are awake, young man. I don't believe we've met. I'm the Deacon of this facility. Won't you please tell me your name?"

Yancey clenched his jaws and tried, but failed, to shake his head. "Nugh ugh," was all he croaked out.

"Well, never mind," the voice calmly said. "We'll find out soon enough. For the sake of your soul, young man, I hope that you will confess all your sins to me. That is my only concern, you know. That your soul be purified of sin, and that you are set upon God's true Path. Let us begin."

CHAPTER NINE
Dagger To The Heart

The party was a great success, or so everyone kept telling him. But Thomas Thansworth the Third, former General in the United States Armed Forces, was having problems believing it. He had always enjoyed parties, to some extent. Growing up, his uncle made sure that 'special lady friends' were present to provide entertainment, and 'medicines' to lighten the mood. Simpler, happier times to be sure.

And yet, drifting among the people at this party, supposedly his peers, he felt quite distanced from them. Oh, yes, everyone smiled and politely enquired as to his health after that horrible training accident in Canada. Then they turned their heads and continued talking about their own lives and concerns. Such empty and vacuous lives, it would seem, filled with nothings and rumours of nothings. Through it all he had the uneasy feeling that their conversations were of more consequence when he wasn't part of them. But he continued to smile and drink and drift amongst them, exchanging meaningless chatter, amazed at the dazzling outfits that they all seemed to be wearing. It all looked quite wonderful. And yet … it really was all quite dull. Excruciating dull, with a sense of vague wrongness that niggled at him during the night.

He finally escaped them by pretending that his excessive drinking required him to get some air, and he stumbled off to a little-used alcove off to the side of the main areas of the house. Everyone shook their head as he passed, clucking their tongues about what a shame and a burden he had become to his family, and that his drinking really was starting to become a problem. Thansworth especially enjoyed the latter, given that after a long lifetime of excess, alcohol didn't really affect him much anymore. The appearance of a problem did, however, provide a convenient cover for him. It made him seem small and harmless, and that allowed him to be ignored and generally unseen. This was proving to be quite useful while pursuing the mysteries revealed by those secret books he'd discovered in his father's old desk. Such fascinating, if puzzling, reading those had been. The opportunities to read them had been few and far between, so his study of them was still incomplete. They did, however, point to other records that were more easily accessible, and he was currently beginning his study of those. But before he went any further he really had to come up with a way to make copies of those books and the subsequent records, and to make notes. Ah, but how to keep those copies and notes away from prying eyes, that was another real problem. It really was quite delightful to have problems to occupy his mind with.

Despite his current condition in life, Thomas Thansworth the Third, was no fool. He was possessed of a keen mind and above average intelligence, with a fondness for analyzing puzzles and riddles as a youth. He had achieved admission to West Point almost entirely on his own merits. Almost - since coming from a 'good family' had always counted there (and even more so these days). Once in the academy he began to shine on his own merits. He had a remarkable talent for military matters, and even managed to make a few friends. Once he graduated, the patronage system had no problems getting him promoted since his innate talent helped to silence critics. And at every step of the way his uncle was there to help celebrate his successes with special parties, and introducing him to the right people who could help his career. Somehow along the way of developing his career with the right people he had lost touch with the friends he had made. Encouraged by his uncle, everything became subservient to advancing his career, making the proper contacts. His only social release had been the special parties thrown by his uncle. But through it all he kept his love of, and respect for, the military. Over time, however, that had become tempered with his sense of entitlement. He was intellectually brilliant, a general, and from a good family with the right connections. Then finally there came that one excess too far, that one thing that couldn't be covered up, and then exile to that hole in the ground. The Poisoned Chalice, as he called it. It was only now, and only in the private corners of his own mind, that he could admit that perhaps he had failed his command. Failed in his military duties. Failed his sworn oath as an officer of the United States Armed Forces. That thought both shamed and chilled him to the depths of his soul.

It also made him realize what the vague wrongness was that he had been sensing all evening. All the bright glitter and colours that jarred his eyes hadn't been what he yearned for. What he wanted more than anything was to see a room full of military people in their uniforms. Not the dress uniforms, but the uniforms worn on duty. It was the concepts of duty and honour that those uniforms represented that he missed - and would never be his again. Because he had betrayed those ideals. Because he had allowed his weaknesses to control him, to cloud his judgement, and finally to break him.

In a desperate attempt to wipe those thoughts from his mind he gulped down his glass of raw whiskey as quickly as he could. Even with his prodigious capacity, that much alcohol consumed so quickly made his eyes water and his head spin. Throwing the glass towards the lawn, he put his head in his hands and sank to the floor, sitting with his back to a stone pillar. Then, sitting with his knees bent upwards, he lowered his arms to his knees and used them as a pillow for his head. He allowed his breathing to soften and slow, using the techniques he had developed over the years to force calmness upon himself.

Lost as Thansworth was in his own thoughts, he dimly sensed footsteps and voices coming towards his location. Soon, he heard a voice almost above his shoulder speaking as if to someone else, "Yes, he's here. Passed out or sleeping, although with the amount he's been drinking he should be dead. God, you can smell the liquor on his breath from here!"

Another voice that sounded very much like his uncle muttered, "Just leave him be, then. It's for the best, really. Some of the women see him as a tragic figure, and seeing him like this makes him appear too pathetic to be bothered with. He has served his purpose, and that is all that matters. We'll keep him around, for appearances, so long as he stays in this condition."

The first voice enquired, "If you keep him around, mightn't someone in our social circle decide he should be married off, despite his … uhm … current status? There are some who would marry anything to obtain a child that would enhance the standing of their lineage."

The voice of his uncle snorted, "There'll be no siring of

offspring from this one. I made sure of that years ago, when he was in his teens. No, nothing surgical ... one of the chemical sterilization agents from China. Had it done after one of his sessions with a prostitute. The idiot thought the subsequent bruising and swelling came from his magnificent performance."

Both men laughed at this droll humour.

The first voice persisted, "But what of the harlot? Could she ever say anything about this?"

"Not likely," snorted his uncle. "I passed her along to the Sword. Ended up as a training exercise for the Fist of Tolerance, I understand. No matter, she was getting past her prime. Better that she be used for something useful."

"And what about him?" the first voice enquired. "Will he end up be used for something useful?"

"Oh, he's done his part, never fear. We'll keep him around for a bit. You never know when he might be useful for something, damaged though he is."

Both men laughed again, this time sneeringly, and agreed it was time to get back to the party. The real entertainment would come later, of course.

Thomas Thansworth the Third sat quietly, with full knowledge that he had barely escaped with his life. His heart sang, filled with the knowledge that the great puzzle had just got more interesting. The game was most definitely afoot.

CHAPTER TEN
Into The Breach

"Dammit, Simon, we have to go back! Right away!" yelled Gretchen, and not for the first time.

As before, Simon stood with his back to the two women, gazing at something far away that only he could see. Finally he spoke, the first time he had addressed the issue at hand. "No. Yancey knew what he was doing when he locked that door on you. He did the only thing he could do to keep the two of you safe."

Charlene spoke for the first time, and said in a mild voice, "I know what he did, Simon. I was there."

Her eyes teared up, and her voice choked slightly, "You're right that we can't just go charging in there, but Gretchen is right, too. We need to get Yancey out, somehow. Can't we just go to the police for this? Look, I know that the election-rigging scandal is a big thing with lots of nasty types involved, but why can't we involve the police?"

Simon's face darkened. Not with anger, but with the burden of having seen too much. Gretchen had seen many of Simon's moods over the years, shared good times and bad, but this look was new to her. And it made her frightened for him.

He sighed heavily and looked wearily at the two ladies. "I keep forgetting that you don't know about all this. Charlene, the election-rigging was just the tip of the iceberg. Yancey and I did a preliminary analysis of the data and uncovered a much larger conspiracy, and an imminent attack on a secret military base northwest of Thunder Bay. We didn't know who to trust or contact, so we decided to find it and warn them ourselves. We got there just a few minutes ahead of the bad guys, just before they attacked the base."

Simon paused and took a couple of deep calming breaths before continuing, wondering how much it was safe to tell them.

"The attack killed most of the defending Canadian soldiers, but they managed to kill all the attackers. It was pretty bad."

Again he paused, and his face went grey.

"Gretchen ... we ... uhm ... there was an enemy soldier ... uhm ... and ... and we fought him. We ... there was a struggle. The three of us. And ... uhm ... Yancey and I got away."

Both Charlene and Gretchen could see the pain etched on Simon's face, the rapid blinking of his eyes, the struggle to catch his breath. Gretchen walked up and held his left hand tightly, trying to give her friend strength through sheer force of will.

Charlene's face softened as she quickly grasped something of what the two young men must have gone through. She now realized that things had gotten very much uglier than she could ever have imagined. Her years of experience as an investigative reporter and experience with dangerous stories made her realize that they needed to pool their information before they did anything else. This wasn't just about a story; this was a matter of their survival. And the rescue of Yancey Franklin. She wasn't going to give up on him, not for anything.

"Simon, dear, it's alright. Come, sit down over here. Gretchen, love, get some water, would you? You're absolutely right, Simon. We need to rest for now. We need to make proper plans. Now, you just sit there for a few minutes, and ..."

Gretchen had returned with a cup of water, which she held out to Simon. Simon surprised the two ladies by grabbing the water, taking a big gulp, then splashing the remainder onto his face. His hands scrubbed furiously, as if he could wash away what he had seen. Wiping his face with his sleeve, he looked at the women, first one then the other. Gretchen saw that her friend of many years had been changed by his recent experiences. Harder ... no, not harder so much as worn but tougher.

When Simon finally spoke, his voice was even and clear. "How much do you want to know about this?" he asked simply. "The more you know, the more danger you're in."

Charlene and Gretchen looked at each other, startled by the question. Charlene quickly, but carefully, replied, "Simon, whatever you tell us, everyone is going to assume you've told us everything, anyway. So you might as well do that."

Simon had to give a slight, lopsided smile at that simple statement of truth. So he began with what they had discovered in the databases Charlene and Gretchen had passed on to them. That Herman Flagsworth had died for. He told them of Infinity Ascending and their Sword, the ones behind the attack on Toronto. He told them about the previously hidden groups that fought each other using Canada as their battleground.

Then he told them about the Shattered Palace, its store

of nuclear and biological weapons, and how the Canadian soldiers protected those weapons with their lives. The ladies tried to interrupt, but Simon waved aside their questions. It was important that they get an overview of everything. The details could wait. He told them of how he and Yancey had fled the battle, found refuge, and then dug into the databases more deeply.

He told them how they uncovered the Tears of Joy facility, about the northern transportation network controlled by the Sword. He paused briefly, then told them about the Harvest of Souls. Over their gasps of horror he told them of Yancey's analysis of the Sword's operations, and how they now had a little more time to figure out where and how to stop the Harvest operation. And with that he simply ran out of the will to continue.

Yancey, his oldest and dearest friend, was now in the hands of a merciless enemy. He sat there for a time, the ladies respecting his silence, as they furiously tried to absorb what they'd just been told. They were both well aware that what they'd heard was just a thumbnail sketch of the horrors the two young men had uncovered and endured.

Simon finally raised his head, and said in a quiet voice, "I don't know what to do, now. Yancey's the planner, the one with experience in this sort of action stuff. Gretchen, Charlene, I don't know how to go about saving the two of you and saving Yancey at the same time. He is my best friend, but I can't risk you two. Not after what he sacrificed to save you. He and I talked about it, and we knew that something like this might happen. We need to stop this Harvest operation, and we need to stop the Sword, and we need get this whole evil mess out into the open. Somehow. I … I just don't know how, any more."

He lowered his head and wrapped his hands around it,

scrubbing away at his hair. Then he stopped and raised his head again and said in the same quiet voice, "I'm sorry. You're safe, and I'll keep you safe as best I can. That's all I know how to do right now."

Charlene surprised everyone by laughing. Not much of a laugh, perhaps, but something more than a chuckle. The other two looked at her with total surprise. "Simon, Gretchen, I'm an old newspaper woman. I've lived through Moscow during both the Soviet and Putin days, and dealt with mobsters and crooked cops. Simon, hon, you and Yancey have a done a better job with this than anyone I have ever known in my life. I'm absolutely astounded and amazed, and you've only told us the tip of the iceberg, I know. Look, you've been through hell the past few days, and absolutely need a breather. No, don't argue with an old editor who's lived through meat grinder stories before. Gretchen and I have been scared out of our wits, but at least nothing physical was done to us. But even we need some down time to decompress. Right now we couldn't even rescue a kitten from a humane shelter. Sorry, but that's the truth. Does that pile of supplies in the car include food? Good. Now, here's what we're going to do, boys and girls. First we get some hot food into us. You've got more of the big picture than us, so while we're eating, Gretchen and I will fill you in on what we've learned about their setup. That may jog some ideas in you. If not, you fill us in on a few more details. That may jog some ideas in us two. Kids, we ain't done yet. Bet on it."

Simon and Gretchen could only gape at her. Then they turned to look at each other, then back at Charlene. Neither had ever seen Charlene in 'battle mode' as her reporters liked to call it. They were about to learn why she was one of the most beloved and respected editors in the country, whose very name filled her targets with dread.

As she had spoken, so it was done. Simon got the supplies out of the Busted Flush, and they set up for a long night's work. The two younger ones had deep technical skills on their side, but Charlene had a long lifetime of experience on hers - not to mention the leadership skills to pull a team together under stressful conditions.

"Herman would have loved these kids," she thought to herself. "Those Sword assholes are gonna find out that you do *not* mess with the press."

CHAPTER ELEVEN
Prayers For Salvation

The Deacon of the Fist of Tolerance was not satisfied with the progress his subject was making. Not only was the subject no closer to finding The Path, his resistance to the teachings was extraordinary. *Quite* extraordinary, in the extensive experience of the Deacon, but not unknown.

He stood before the alter in the small chapel contemplating alternative strategies, his hands folded before him, making no unnecessary movements whatsoever. He knew that it was all but impossible to resist the salvation that he offered. All it took was time, and the acceptance that sometimes salvation came only moments before death. The complication in this case was that the subject had information that the Sword required, which made it imperative that salvation occurred while there was enough time to impart that information. A pretty problem, indeed. A true test of his abilities, and one that he relished.

Although this was a small facility, even a minor one, the Deacon was satisfied with it. There were other, larger facilities that did the same sort of work, but the Deacon preferred to work saving one soul at a time. Normally only the most difficult of subjects were sent here, although sometimes lesser souls were sent to assist in the training of new acolytes in the order, or to instill obedience. Although he usually preferred to focus on the task at hand, he always did his best when instructing. It was important, he felt, that the hard-won lessons that his Order had learnt be passed on properly to the next generation.

One of his assistants entered the chapel and stood before the Deacon, with head bowed and holding a folded piece of paper before him. The Deacon took the paper and nodded in acknowledgement. The assistant came to attention, spun on his heels, and left. The Deacon read the communication, paused for a moment, then allowed a small sigh to escape. It would seem that his subject had gained the attention of the Sword in the past, and the Council had decided that the information held by him was more important than saving his soul. The Deacon bowed his head and offered up a small prayer for the young man. In such cases, extraction of the information usually occurred before salvation was achieved.

His prayer completed, the Deacon turned and walked without haste out of the chapel. He had done what he could, and now was the time to complete his task. His subject had spent quite enough time in respite, contemplating his sins and his options. It was time for Mr. Franklin to choose his fate.

CHAPTER TWELVE
Rescued By The Maidens Fair

Yancey regained consciousness amidst the smell of burning flesh. The pain shrieking through his torso reminded him that it was his own flesh that was burning. Bright lights shining hotly upon him added their part to the orchestrated torment. Suddenly, the lights and their heat went off, and his flesh stopped burning, although the pain from the existing burns still throbbed.

"Mister Franklin," intoned the hated voice, "I regret that this extreme scourging is necessary. It pains me more than you realize to do this to you, to bring you to this point without saving your soul. Unfortunately, you have information that my superiors have deemed essential. Please, use this brief respite to reconsider. Please, I beg of you, for the sake of your soul. Offer up your confession and tell us all that we ask of you. In the name of God, help me to help you."

The voice sounded sincere, even earnest. But Yancey knew from long experience that those sorts of voices lied, and could not be trusted. This voice wanted him to betray his friends, to give them up to the Sword, and that was something that he would never do.

A gentle trilling sound penetrated his awareness. It was

something different in the routine. He heard footsteps move away from him towards the trilling, muttering something. The trilling stopped, and the voice got louder and more irritated than Yancey had ever heard it. Something about never interrupting God's work, and incompetence. The voice was silent for a moment and then snarled an agreement. Footsteps approached him, and the voice said in a slightly less calm voice, "Mister Franklin, it would seem that God has granted you a longer respite than I had planned. I could restart the scourging, but I want you to take this opportunity to offer a prayer of thanks to the Almighty who grants you this boon. I urge you most fervently to reconsider your resistance. When I return, the scourging will be more intense than what you have experienced before now. You will tell us everything we want to know, but of a certainty your body and mind will be beyond salvaging. Your soul will not be able to be cleansed and receive grace. I will return shortly for your final answer."

With that, the voice grew silent and footsteps indicated that someone was walking away from Yancey, followed shortly by the sound of a door softly opening and closing.

Yancey drank in the silence and cessation of the assault as if it were the sweetest elixir. He took a few moments to take several deep, calming breaths, and then began to test his restraints. Pain answered his every movement, but he overrode those messages from his body, realizing that this might be his last chance to escape. His vision was still unclear, overloaded by the bright lights and stress. He was on a table or some sort of flat surface, lying horizontally. The restraints on his head, arms, and legs refused to budge to any useful extent. He refused to succumb to the panic that was bubbling up within him, but his weakened condition was making that increasingly difficult. Despite the bravado he tried to project to his captors, Yancey was well aware that these sorts of interrogation techniques were all too often successful, especially when the inquisitors were not concerned with the final effects on their subject. Despite his heartfelt desire to take any information about his friends to the grave, if need be, he was all too aware of the possibility that he might fail. All he could honestly hope for was to buy enough time for his friends to get beyond the reach of the Sword.

His attempts to free himself were becoming somewhat frenzied, despite his efforts to remain calm and preserve his remaining strength. For the first time in his life, Yancey was forced to confront certain death - and worse, failure that could bring harm to those he held most dear. He was beginning to desperately try to think of ways that a bound man might commit suicide. Could he bite off his tongue, perhaps? Then he heard the door open again, and a soft voice whispering his name. A woman's voice.

"Yancey. Yancey, it's me, Gretchen," he heard.

Yancey tried to protest, but all he could do was moan. His failure was now complete.

"Shut up, dammit," he heard. "We're here to rescue you. Simon and Charlene and me. Now hold still, you idiot, and I'll undo these straps."

He felt, rather than heard, his restraints being undone one by one. He also heard a sharp intake of breath when Gretchen got a good look at his damaged body. Finally, all the restrains were gone, and he began to gasp with the relief of it. He felt almost as light as a feather after being held down so cruelly for so long. So very long that it seemed like forever.

"Hold still," Gretchen ordered quietly but firmly, "the others will be here at any moment, and I need to put dressings on these wounds."

Despite the gentleness of her touch, Yancey flinched with pain as Gretchen hastily put bandages over his torn and charred flesh.

"Good thing they keep this place well stocked with medical supplies," she said with forced levity, "almost as if they expected injuries or something."

Her voice caught a bit at the last, somewhat ruining her attempt to keep things light.

The door opened softly, and Gretchen spun around.

"It's us," a familiar male voice hissed. "You ready to go?"

"Just about, Simon. Gimme a sec to finish this dressing. We need to grab as much of this medical stuff as we can - dressings, antiseptics, and such. Yancey's in bad shape."

Yancey felt a firm hand on his forehead, then heard Simon whisper, "Hey, guy. Glad we found you," and his eyes filled with tears as he felt his head spinning.

He was so overcome with emotion that when another female voice began whispering, he couldn't make out the words. He took a deep breath to calm himself enough to focus on what was happening.

"Gretchen, just do enough with the dressings to get Yancey ready to move. Forget clothes, the underwear he's wearing will do. Simon, stop grabbing medical supplies and go take a look at that computer terminal over there, and see if you can access those data files we talked about. I'll take care of the medical supplies," said an older woman's voice in calm, measured tones, "I saw some boxes of MREs stacked not too far from here, so we'll grab those on the way out, too. Now *hurry*, people, I want to move out in ten seconds, fifteen tops."

Feeling Gretchen's hands remove themselves from his body, Yancey steeled himself and began to sit up. He quickly realized that this was going to be difficult, so he rolled slightly to his left side to shift his centre of gravity and roll off the table. Strong, gentle hands grabbed him and began to help with his movements.

"Just get to a sitting position first," said Gretchen. "Sit upright for a few seconds and then we'll try standing."

Yancey bit down a scream as he was moved to a sitting position, his legs dangling over the edge, naked toes barely touching the cool floor. Blinking rapidly, then rubbing at his eyes to clear the accumulated gunk, helped his eyesight to clear well enough to focus on his surroundings, even if everything was still a bit blurred. Gretchen urged him to take it easy, but he managed to grunt out, "No time for that. Simon, grab all the data you can get. We need it bad," and the effort to do that much left him feeling a bit dizzy. His mind was still a bit fuzzy, but he had managed to decode the gist of what was happening. He felt rather pleased with himself for that.

"Thanks a lot, hoser, I would never have thought of that," came Simon's softly-spoken rebuke. "Now stop farting around and get your ass in gear. Time for a road trip, me lad."

As he spoke, Simon's fingers furiously tapped away at the keyboard. He removed one data stick from its slot in the computer and inserted another one. "Gonna need almost a minute to copy everything," he said as he looked up, his fingers finally finished with their dancing. "There's a lot of stuff here. Might be important."

Charlene began to object, when Yancey interrupted her, "He can keep downloading up to the last possible moment. It's gonna take almost that long for us to get moving."

His voice was slightly mumbled and rasping from pain, but it was obvious that the mind behind it was reasonably lucid.

"Gretchen, help me to stand. I'm kinda weak, but you could probably sling at least one of those shoulder bags onto me."

Charlene had been stuffing medical supplies into a pair of large shoulder bags. In addition to bandages and dressings, she had discovered a cache of medications, including antibiotics and pain killers of various types. She paused to give a Yancey a penetrating look, then shrugged and looped one of the straps over Yancey's head onto one shoulder, then a second strap over the other. Gretchen was concerned, but realized that time was short and their options few. While Yancey carefully adjusted to the weight of the load, Gretchen moved to the door and took a careful peek outside.

"Coast is still clear," she whispered over her shoulder.

"OK," said Charlene, "that's it. Time to go, Simon. *Now.*"

Simon clattered a few keys, grabbed the data key, stood up, then made for the door. Along the way he grabbed Yancey by the elbow and helped his friend towards the door.

"I'll make it," said Yancey grimly. "Just go and I'll keep up even if it kills me. Anything's better than this place."

The group moved quietly out of the room and down a hallway. Charlene forced them to pause and make a short detour to grab a few cases of the MREs that she had noticed on the way in. Then it was a quiet and brisk march down the corridor towards a heavy door. Yancey wondered at the lack of alarms, but was coherent enough to realize that silence was more important than satisfying his curiosity.

They got to the door, opened it, and were outside. It was night, and the air was cool and fresh. Yancey wanted to stop and drink it all in, but satisfied himself with taking some deep breaths. The group continued walking for a few dozen metres, turned a corner, and Yancey saw his beloved Busted Flush sitting in the shadows. As they approached the car, Yancey grew uneasy, as it seemed somehow different. It suddenly dawned on him that the colour was different. It was painted in the colours of an OPP cruiser, including the markings. He tried to stop and warn the others, but urgent hands caught him and urged him forward.

"Sorry 'bout the new colour look and markings," was all the explanation that Simon gave before stuffing Yancey into the back seat and tossing a couple of blankets at him. Things were moving too quickly for Yancey to process, but he realized that now was not the time to ask about The Plan.

Simon got into the driver's seat, with Gretchen riding shotgun and Charlene in the back with Yancey. Simon started up the Flush, and carefully moved down the lane towards the main road. Yancey recognized this lane from his own rescue attempt, and opened his mouth to ask about the gate when he spotted said gate standing open before them. The Flush slowed a bit, went through the gate, and Simon made a sharp left turn onto the main road, accelerating up to the posted speed limit as quickly as he dared. The escape appeared to be a success, at least for the nonce.

Still stunned by the rapidity of recent events, Yancey's head was swivelling left and right in an attempt to figure out what was going on. He caught sight of Charlene, calmly smiling at him as she made sure that the blankets covered him warmly. Gretchen had leaned back into her seat with eyes closed, and was working at controlling her breathing. Simon was focused on driving the car, and appeared to be calmly confident of what he was doing.

Yancey was never one to sit back and let others take charge, but he decided that just this once it might be just as well if he did. Still, his mind was working well enough to turn to Charlene and ask, "How the hell did we just manage to do that? They should have been as stirred up as a hornets' nest 'cuz I got you two out. And why is my car dressed up like an OPP cruiser?"

Charlene gave a low, throaty chuckle. "They *are* still stirred up like a hornets' nest. We just ... redirected their attention."

"It was Charlene's idea," Simon piped up. "It was like you and I figured for our rescue attempt of these two. Any troubles or alarms would be passed off as false alarms to the local cops. Charlene had us trigger a few more false alarms, let the local OPP detachment's superiors know about the false alarms, and that made *them* order the local detachment to do an on-site inspection. The Busted Flush may be an obsolete model of police cruiser, but people will still think of it a real cruiser if the paint scheme is right. So we got some of that thin plastic covering stuff of the right colours to cover the car and make the markings, and it looks perfect. Well, if the light is low, anyways."

Yancey turned to Charlene, his eyes wide with admiration. "You're *good,*" he breathed.

Charlene nodded in acceptance of his praise. "Well, you two boys were the ones who figured out the original staffing arrangement here. And arranged for the defeat of the Sword at the Shattered Palace, which in turn drew away most of the security people from here. I just took advantage of their confusion."

"Keep in mind," she continued, "no matter how crooked or bought the local police might be, they have maintain at least the forms of regular police functionality. And I just happen to know that the OPP got so sick of false security alarms a while back that they mandated on-site inspections of any false-call situations. So the local police have to at least show up despite any protests, and what is one more police cruiser if one shows up on the security cameras? Although I will take credit for making sure that the local police were upset enough to demand that the building employees and management be front and centre when they arrive. Which left the back way open and unguarded. I almost felt bad about that. Almost."

She didn't look as if she felt bad about that at all. In fact, she looked quite pleased with herself. Her young companions might have superior computer skills that she couldn't match, but her experience had taught her how the police system worked. She knew which buttons to push and when. Sometimes, just sometimes, old age and treachery trumped youth and skill. That said, she enjoyed basking in the respect earned from such as these young ones.

Yancey gave her one of his big, sloppy, lopsided smiles, "OK, oh mighty leader, Maker of Plans. To what refuge are we off to now? Enquiring minds want to know."

Charlene snorted at this, and Gretchen actually laughed.

"Another idea of Charlene's," Simon interjected before anyone else could say anything. "A cabin. In the woods. What could possibly go wrong?"

That movie trope reference got everyone giggling. It took a couple of minutes before all the guffaws were done. It wasn't much of a joke, but they were in dire need of a laugh to take the edge off the stresses of the past few days.

"Actually," Charlene said, wiping her eyes, "it belonged to a friend of Herman's. Herman Flagsworth, the reporter who obtained that set of databases that Gretchen passed on to you."

Even now, talking about Herman still brought a lump to

Charlene's throat. She caught herself, cleared her throat quickly, and then continued.

"Well, anyway, sometimes he needed a quiet place away from everything to write. A friend of his owned a cabin not too far from Kapuskasing, and Herman loved to go there. Went at least once or twice a year, for many years. His friend passed away a couple of years ago, and his surviving family had no interest in it. They knew that Herman loved the place, so they let him use it so long as he kept the place in repair. An informal arrangement, with nothing in writing, which is perfect for our purposes. No paper trail leading to Herman, or to us. I only went there once, years ago, but I think I can get us there. The area is used to seeing transients and tourists, so we shouldn't attract any attention when we pick up supplies."

Simon piped up "We should be able to get there in half a day, if we don't stop. And I don't think we should. Both Gretchen and Charlene are OK to drive the Flush, so between the three of us we have enough drivers to keep going without a problem. We figured to head straight for the cabin and lay low for a couple of days before venturing out for supplies. Those MREs that Charlene made us grab will help out with that, a lot. We're running low on cash, and I don't think that we want to use any of our credit or debit cards just yet."

Yancey nodded his head as he listened to the unfolding plans. Now that the adrenaline rush from the escape had worn off, his wounds were beginning to scream at him and it was becoming increasingly difficult to focus his thoughts. Charlene had been noting the drawn look on Yancey's face, and suggested pulling over soon to rearrange the supplies that they had gathered. Yancey gave her a grim smile of thanks, both for her thoughtfulness and her attempt to spare his feelings.

A few minutes later Simon pulled over to a picnic area that was shielded from the road. They all got out of the car, and Simon began putting their purloined supplies into the trunk, and the precious data keys in with the laptops. Charlene and Gretchen tended to Yancey, who apologized for being a burden. First they tried to put some shoes on his feet, but had to settle for two pairs of thick socks because of the extensive swelling. Charlene dug out a container of the stronger pain killer pills, and gave a couple of them to Yancey, with a few sips of water to help wash them down. They carefully helped him hobble over to one of the picnic benches, where he sat down heavily. Charlene went to help Simon peel off the coverings that had disguised the Busted Flush.

While the others worked on the car, Gretchen began worriedly examining the wounds on Yancey's body. There were numerous bruises on all parts of his body, some of which were starting to turn ugly colours, which meant that the others would soon follow suit. These bothered her on an emotional level, but her health-related concerns centred on the oozing burns on Yancey's torso, arms, hands, and legs. Those needed immediate attention, and she was worried about what would happen if they got infected. As she studied the wounds, Yancey was studying her.

"They used some sort of electric prod to make those," he told her as he waited for the pain killers to kick in, "but I strongly suspect that it was sterile. The whole thing was handled like a medical procedure, almost clinical."

Gretchen accepted the information with a detached nod. Given that, the only problem would be where the burnt skin had cracked and exposed the underlying flesh. She decided to put a simple dressing over the areas that looked merely burnt, and then apply antibiotic cream to any cracked burns before dressing them.

"Are there any other injuries I should be aware of?" she asked quietly.

Yancey paused before answering; his face still pinched with pain as the drugs slowly took effect.

"Just the usual beatings with a padded rubber hose, mostly to my feet and legs and hands. Some to my ribs, just to keep things interesting. The scrapes and minor cuts were probably caused by me while trying to get free. They slammed the base of my neck to knock me out when they captured me."

Simon and Charlene had finished removing the car's disguising coverings, and had quietly moved closer to Gretchen and Yancey.

"At first, they weren't trying to extract information out of me. That came a bit later. At first it was a gradual escalation of pain, trying to get me to confess. That's what he called it - the one who interrogated me. He wanted me to confess to save my soul. To accept God's will. To accept 'the path', whatever the hell that is. Scourging of the flesh, he called it. No permanent damage, he claimed, but it hurt like hell."

Thanks to the drugs, Yancey's pain was beginning to recede, and he was able to feel the fatigue from his ordeal rapidly setting in.

"Then after a while, maybe a day later, something changed. He came in and told me that his superiors told him to get the information by any means, regardless of the cost to my soul. This actually seemed to concern the son-of-a-bitch, but not enough to stop him. I thought what he had done before hurt a lot, but I was wrong. This time he was trying to rip it out of me; not just convince me to give it up willingly. It got real bad. I thought I was done for. Then you guys saved me."

Yancey's head was drooping by this time, and the last was mumbled but still understandable.

Gretchen's hands had paused in their task, and quivered slightly as they hovered above him. All of them were looking at Yancey with horrified expressions on their faces. Then Yancey began to slowly topple to one side as sleep claimed him. They quickly kept him upright while Gretchen completed her ministrations. Once that was done, they carefully moved him back into the car, wrapped blankets around him to keep him warm and keep the seat belt from rubbing his wounds too much, and then fastened the seat belt around him. Ensuring that no litter remained to mark their presence, they all got into the car and continued their journey.

No one spoke as they drove through the darkness.

CHAPTER THIRTEEN
The Prime Minister's Press Conference

"And that, ladies and gentlemen, is a general overview of my government's new Natural Resource Action Plan for Canada. Although it is important that we continue to show appreciation for the support of our traditional allies in Europe and the United States, we need to ensure that our new partners from China and India are made to feel welcome. Their past and future investments in the West and East coasts respectively will continue to ensure the prosperity of those regions. I will now take a few questions."

Yes, you there, ma'am," said the PM pointing at a young lady.

"Zandra Faheed of AJF News. Sir, can you shed some light on recent reports of dissatisfaction at the Shining Leopard liquid natural gas facility in British Columbia?"

The PM beamed expansively. "But of course. As you will remember, the Shining Leopard is one of the facilities constructed on defunct and long-unused coastal communities, some of which had belonged to the First Nations. Because the site was declared abandoned, any applicable treaty conditions were automatically voided, and the land reverted to the Crown. Under the guidance of my government, and in an effort to stimulate economic growth, the area was made available for development under the new Homesteader Act. The Chinese government put together the best overall plan for the site, and were given economic homestead rights. They have expended a great deal of capital investment to build up their current facility - to the economic benefit of the area, the province of British Columbia, and the great nation of Canada."

"Thank you sir, but I was referring to reports of complaints with the security forces that were deployed on those sites rather than the use of provincial police forces."

"Ah, yes, Ms. Faheed, of course. Well, it makes perfect sense that the Chinese government would want to ensure the security of their considerable investment. Taking into account the cultural sensitivities of the local workers, something my government supports fully, we worked closely with the Chinese government to ensure the security of that, and other, sites. Of course, given the different cultures involved, misunderstandings are bound to happen. But the professionalism and good will of the Chinese security forces has ensured that any issues are handled quickly and fairly. My government has looked into each and every complaint, and I can assure you that these reports are quite overblown. Next question, please."

Another hand went up, and was recognized by the Prime Minister, and the appropriate answer given. The whole process was done quite efficiently and without the asking of any questions that might embarrass either the Government or any of its commercial partners.

While this was going on there was a lively, if whispered, discussion going on amongst the media folk at the rear of the room. Specifically, those from whom no questions would ever get asked.

"Well, this is certainly a better behaved lot of questioners than the last press conference the PM had," sneered one scribe.

"Are you trying to imply that the questions were scripted? I'm shocked, sir. Shocked to my core," his compatriot opined, with eyes open in mock horror.

"Laugh all you want, you lot, but this all stinks like pile of rotting fish," interjected another. "That facility, like the others, was built entirely with imported labour. They got around the hiring quotas by claiming that no Canadian tradespeople were competent to work to their standards, or understood the supposedly special building technology being used. It was all so special that any inspections were carried out by their own specially-imported people. And those so-called security forces? Talk is that they're regular army troops. Certainly equipped like an army, at any rate."

"You might want to ask yourselves how that area got to be abandoned in the first place," whispered yet another. "Years ago, the local First Nations people of the area got involved in some scheme that was supposed to create work for dozens of people. Get them economically independent and in control of their lives, that sort of thing. Somehow it just didn't turn out that way. As soon as the paperwork was signed, financing kept getting put off. Equipment was ordered and never arrived, or somehow never managed to work properly. Lots of people lost their life savings, the whole area just faded to a mere handful of die-hards. Then some chemical spills happened, and no one really knows how it happened or where the chemicals came from. Local yahoos got the blame, but no-one knows for sure. But the spills wiped out fishing for kilometres around, and made the beaches unsuitable for people. Not toxic, mind you, just not safe according to the environmental standards. And this isn't the only place where that sort of thing happened, and it didn't happen only to areas owned by the First Nations. Then a few years after that the Abandoned Site Act and Homesteader Act got passed, and all those abandoned sites were suddenly bought up for next to nothing. Damn peculiar. Especially given the lengthy time spans. But, still ..." the speaker's whispered words came to an end of their own accord.

They all nodded sagely in agreement of all the peculiarities. None of them planned to mount any serious investigation into it, of course. For one thing, such musings would never get printed. For another, it had become unsafe to voice opinions that strongly contradicted Government policy.

CHAPTER FOURTEEN
Healing Waters

After nearly a day of tense, silent driving, the Busted Flush and its passengers arrived in the late afternoon at the cabin that Charlene had told them about. Worry about pursuit and the inevitable empty feeling that comes at the completion of any large effort kept them all in no mood for anything but essential talking. Yancey had slept the entire time, but his sleep was frequently interrupted by what were obviously bad memories or even worse dreams.

As promised, the cabin was off the beaten track, but not too far from several small towns, including Kapuskasing itself. That promised to make getting supplies less risky than if they had to depend on a single place. Simon was driving, and he pulled up behind the cabin so the car could not be seen, then turned off the engine. The silence was palpable, which was not surprising after such a long drive, much of it on gravel roads. The three of them quietly exited the car, leaving Yancey to the sleep that he so badly needed.

"Is the door locked, Charlene?" enquired Gretchen.

"Yep," replied Charlene with a smile, "but I think that breaking in is the least of our worries right now."

Gretchen laughed softly, "I can probably pick the lock if we can make some suitable tools."

Simon laughed at Charlene's expression, "She's not just a pretty face, you know. At the office, she was the go-to person to open doors when someone forgot their keys. Hey, half a tic - Yancey has a box of his detective stuff. Maybe there's something in there we can use."

Popping the trunk as quietly as he could, he pulled out the box in question and put it on the ground. As he opened it up, they all peered inside it with interest. Simon pulled out the scanner that had been so useful, various sets of cabling, a small leather case, and some unidentified boxes.

"Gimme that slim leather case," Gretchen commanded quietly, tilting her chin at the object in question.

Simon handed it to her, and she opened it up. Inside was a collection of lock picking tools. Gretchen's eyes widened. This was a very nice set, indeed, with picks and rakes suitable for opening anything from a filing cabinet to a good quality padlock. The lock on the door shouldn't pose a problem, she thought as she walked up to the cabin with a grin. The lock was a good one, of recent manufacture, but all it took was a minute's work to open the door. Once inside, they all took a quick look around to familiarize themselves with the layout. The main room had a small fireplace for heat and a small wood-fuelled stove for cooking. There were two much smaller rooms that were obviously used for sleeping, although there were no beds in them. Off to one side was a small, but serviceable, bathroom. The layout of the cabin was small and cozy, but would suit them just fine.

As usual, Charlene took charge of organizing them. Simon was sent to collect some wood for a fire, while the ladies examined the cabin in greater detail. Gretchen asked if Charlene remembered anything, but it turned out that she had only been there briefly for a couple of hours when she had picked up Herman.

There were a couple of small lights in the ceiling, and a bit of searching revealed a pair of switches on the wall. With no expectation of success, Gretchen flicked a switch and to her surprise the two lights came on. The lights made the room suddenly more inviting. The ladies decided that the lights must be solar powered, and to investigate further in the morning. Simon came in with an armful of wood, and proceeded to set up the fireplace for a small starter fire. He informed them that there was a good-sized woodpile not far from the cabin. The low shelter blended in with the brush quite well, which is how they had missed it when they first pulled in. With the small fire started they watched carefully for signs of smoke, but the chimney was drawing well, so Simon gradually increased the size of the fire. Once that was burning properly, he spotted a wood carrier off in the corner of the cabin, which would make fetching wood a lot easier.

Charlene decided that with light and a fire in the cabin, it was probably a good time to bring in Yancey, and then the supplies. They all trooped out to the car and found Yancey in what appeared to be a troubled sleep, moaning softly and rocking his head back and forth slightly. They watched him silently for a few moments, afraid to disturb him, yet needing to get him inside. With a sigh, Gretchen leaned forward and softly began calling Yancey's name. His head stop its rocking, and his moans were replaced by heavy breathing, almost panting. Gretchen called him name more loudly, and told him that it was time to wake up. Yancey's breathing became more normal, then he coughed quietly a couple of times and opened his eyes, blinking them as if trying to make sense of what he was seeing.

"Yancey, we're safe now. We're at the cabin. We need to move you out of the car," Gretchen said quietly and slowly.

"Huh? Whah? Uhm, yeah. OK," Yancey managed to mumble, and he tried moving, but was blocked by the seat belt. A look of panic flashed across his face.

"It's just the seat belt, Yancey," Gretchen assured him. "Just sit back and I'll unfasten it."

He leaned back, breathing a bit heavily, as Gretchen unfastened the seatbelt and moved it out of the way. She helped him to carefully swing his legs out, and pull him upright from out of the car. With support provided by Simon on one side and Gretchen on the other, they managed to get Yancey to the cabin, being careful to keep the blankets around him for warmth. Once inside, they sat him in front of the fireplace, then turned to start bringing in the supplies.

"Gretchen, why don't you sit with him while we do this," said Charlene quietly. "The two of us can manage. He shouldn't be alone."

With a nod, Gretchen went back to sit by Yancey, who was staring at the fire. The momentary panic they had seen at the car had vanished, to be replaced with a vacant gazing.

Charlene and Simon made several trips back and forth, bringing in their meagre supplies. With the transfer of supplies complete, they settled in to prepare for the evening.

"Lock up the Flush, Simon."

Their heads swivelled around looking for the source of the low voice. They suddenly realized that it had come from Yancey, who then repeated his demand, and then

104

continued his vacant staring at the fire. The two ladies swivelled their heads to look at Simon, who mumbled an agreement and went out, to come back in a short time later. He squatted next to Yancey and said with a smile, "Good call, Yance. I had left the keys in the car."

Yancey made no indication that he had heard, so Simon got up to help with getting the supplies squared away. They had little enough to set up 'home' with. What had once seemed sufficient for a road trip for two now seemed quite inadequate. Charlene refused to be distressed by that. There were enough sleeping bags and blankets for three people, which was fine since they needed one person up at all times anyways. There was a pantry, of sorts, which held a few things of dubious utility - but it would suffice to store their non-perishable supplies. There was a carton of eggs and a small container of milk that the guys had indulged in when they had last got gas. These, Charlene decided, could stay in the cooler in one of the 'bedrooms' furthest away from the fireplace. The various pieces of equipment they decided to put in the same bedroom as Yancey would be in.

While Simon and Charlene saw to the housekeeping, Gretchen decided that the cabin was warm enough that Yancey's wounds could be examined again. Gently tugging on the blankets, she tried to take them off him. He resisted at first but then gradually loosened his hold, although he continued to sit staring at the fire. The cabin's lights and the light of the fire gave Gretchen a better view of Yancey's wounds, and the sight of them created an ache deep inside her. Taking care to let nothing of that show in any way, she examined all the wounds she had bandaged. Everything looked as good as could be expected. However, there were some wounds on his back that she had either missed the first time around or had been opened up by the long trip. She cleaned and bandaged those that required it, then pulled the blankets back over Yancey. During all this, he had not flinched or spoken or given any indication that he was aware of her ministrations.

"Yancey," she said softly, "it's time to go to bed, now."

"No," he replied softly. "Here."

Simon and Charlene had been standing quietly off to one side.

"Yance," said Simon, "did you want me to bring your sleeping bag in here?"

Yancey made a slight nod of agreement. So Simon went and got the bedding and arranged it off to one side from the fireplace, explaining that otherwise it would get too hot. Yancey made no sound or movement, so they took that for acceptance. Once the bedding was set up, they gently moved him over to it, gave him a couple more pain killers with a few sips of water, then helped him out of the blanket that was covering him and into the sleeping bag, with the blanket serving as a mattress. He kept looking around as if searching unsuccessfully for something.

"Oh," said Simon, "he probably wants a shirt. He always sleeps with a shirt or something."

"Well ..." said Gretchen slowly, "I suppose it couldn't hurt, so long as it is fairly loose."

Simon dug through one of the packs and found one of Yancey's shirts, a pair of pants, socks, and sneakers. He helped Yancey put on the shirt, and put the other items off to one side. This seemed to satisfy Yancey, who lay down and was asleep almost instantly.

Simon said that he'd take the first shift, but Gretchen refused to let him on the grounds that he'd been doing most of the driving for the better part of the day. To prove it she yawned mightily, and as much as he tried to resist

Simon was forced to echo it.

"Two hour shifts," declared Charlene firmly. "We're all of us too tired for longer ones."

She then grabbed Simon's hand and led him to the other bedroom, and each settled into one of the sleeping bags, using blankets as a mattress. Gretchen watched until the other two were finished their preparations, then smiled as she got up to turn off the cabin's lights, leaving only the fire for illumination. Within seconds the two were asleep, and Gretchen was alone with her troubled thoughts.

She and Charlene had been treated decently enough, considering that they were captives. Oh, sure, their guards had promised an interrogation, but nothing ever came of it, what with one thing or another. After seeing what Yancey had gone through, Gretchen shuddered to think of what could have happened and felt a cold, sick feeling in her stomach. Looking over at him, she could see him staring quietly into the fire. His eyes gradually closed, as if he was fighting to stay awake, but eventually he went to sleep. Then Gretchen was left alone with her thoughts, with a background symphony of soft snoring from the bedroom, and the soft grunts and mutterings from Yancey. The night passed slowly for her, but she had no problem staying awake, and didn't bother waking the others for their shifts.

The first glimmers of dawn found Gretchen still absorbed in her thoughts. During the night she had stirred only to add wood to the fire, which had proven to be adequate to the task of keeping the small cabin warm. The fire had been burning long enough that the stone chimney had grown quite warm, and this added its own share of radiant heat to the cabin. The fire was beginning to burn low, once again, so Gretchen added some wood to it. Glancing at the sunlight beginning to shine through the window, she decided to light a fire in the small stove, and put on some water for morning tea. The chair creaked softly as she got up. Picking up some tinder and larger pieces of wood that were near the fireplace, she walked over to the stove. As quietly as she could, she got the tinder and wood into the stove, checked that the damper was open, then started the fire. After a sluggish start, the chimney started drawing properly and the fire started going in earnest. Her noises, minimal as they had been, had woken up Simon, who quickly walked into the room.

"Dammit, Gretch," he said with a sigh, then he hissed out quietly, "we were supposed to take shifts."

She just smiled, and continued her search for a pot or something to boil water in. "Wasn't sleepy. 'Sides, better to have you two fully rested than all of us barely rested."

Simon couldn't argue with her logic, so he settled for gently pushing her away as he pulled out the battered kettle from out of the stash of supplies. "How did he sleep?"

"Well, enough. Though I .... "

Gretchen was interrupted by Yancey, who had suddenly sat upright and was looking wildly around and breathing hard. Seeing the other two standing there, he closed his eyes for a moment, breathed deeply several times, and calmed his breathing. He climbed out of his sleeping bag, put on his pants and shoes, looked at the fireplace and the almost-exhausted supply of wood, then without a word he took the log carrier and went outside. Gretchen looked worriedly at Simon, who simply said, "He'll be OK," as if he was trying to convince himself of it.

Yancey made a couple trips for wood, moving stiffly and somewhat slowly. By the time he was done his self-appointed task, the water was heating up and mugs had been placed on the small table. A mumbled complaint was heard from the direction of Charlene, who, to the amusement of Simon, turned out to be even worse of an early riser than he normally was. For breakfast, they decided to finish off the eggs and milk, and treated themselves to a couple of cookies each. Gretchen was not too impressed with their choice of camping foods, but that didn't stop her from enjoying the treats. For his part, Yancey nibbled on a bit of scrambled egg and drank his tea with small sips. He did not join in the conversation at all, but simply sat staring at the fire, lost in his own thoughts.

When Gretchen suggested that she should examine his wounds, he simply got up, took off his shirt and pants, then lay down on his sleeping bag. Gretchen bit her lip, but went about her task. There was little enough for her to do. None of the wounds looked inflamed or worse than before, so all that was required was putting antiseptic ointment on the wounds that required it and changing the dressings. Throughout all this, Yancey said not a word, simply staring straight ahead. When she was done, she stepped away and Yancey dressed himself carefully. Then he surprised them by putting on his jacket and walking out. The two women made to get up and go after him, but Simon said quietly, "Leave him alone. He's alright."

They looked at him with intense questioning stares, but he simply stared down into his cup of tea, his hands wrapped around it.

A silent minute passed, then Gretchen angrily said, "No, he bloody well is *not* all right. One of us has to go out to get him."

Charlene was startled, as she had rarely heard Gretchen swear, although she was in full agreement with her long-time friend and sometime-lover. Something was most definitely wrong with Yancey, and Simon's seeming indifference simply did not make sense.

"He's fine," Simon repeated in faraway voice. "He's been through this sort of thing before."

The two women could only stand and gape. Gretchen's face grew angry, and she opened her mouth, but was interrupted by a wave of Charlene's hand. Charlene took a chair across the table from Simon and said simply and quietly, "Simon."

When there was no response, she repeated with kind insistence, "Simon."

To their shock, Simon's eye's watered, and he angrily used his hand to scrub the tears away.

Gretchen was becoming fearful, for she had never seen Simon act this way before. She didn't know Yancey all that well, but Simon she had spent years working with and hanging out with as friends. She could see the emotional pain that he was in, and racked her brain trying to think of the reason. Charlene opened her mouth to say something, but Gretchen held up her hand to stop her, and interjected quietly, "This is about when you two were young. When you were growing up. Isn't it?"

Simon stood suddenly, and for a moment it looked like he was going to throw his cup into the wall. Then he drew a ragged breath, calmed himself, placed the cup on the table, and silently looked down at it. Then he strode to the middle of the room and stood there staring at the door, quivering with nervous tension. Closing his eyes, he once again used deep breaths to calm himself, and it didn't take very long for his breathing to return to normal. Opening his eyes and looking beyond the door with a faraway gaze he said in a dull voice, "You don't understand what it was like."

The two women sat quietly, afraid to intrude into this moment.

"Little Shithole. That's what everyone called the town, young and old. Had a real name once, but that's the only one we ever used. Dinky little nothing in the middle of nowhere. Once there was some mining and logging, but that petered out when we were kids. Buncha people left, but there was enough work for a small town. Sort of. Enough to pay for food and booze. Nasty sort of social stratification, too, based on if your parents had work. Mine had odd jobs, once in a while. Some dads got better and more frequent work. Yancey's dad had one of the few full-time jobs. In the off-times, a lot of parents drank. My dad did. Sometimes he'd hit me. Started with just the odd cuff on the head. Then more often. Then the slapping started. Went to school with bruises, but nobody asked questions. That's just the way it was. Being at the bottom of the social totem pole, the other kids just ignored me.

Except Yancey. He always sat with me, and made sure I was OK. Shared his lunch when I didn't have anything. Told me jokes to make me laugh. Then his dad lost his job, got no part time work at all, and that left Yancey and his family at the bottom of the social ladder. Failures that all the rest of the losers could look down on. Then his dad took to drinking. Hard and mean. Started hitting Yancey. Real bad. A lot. And no one said or did anything. Lots of kids showed up with bruises once in a while, but Yance sometimes couldn't even walk properly. But he didn't say anything, and no one asked. Just shrugged when I asked him about it. So I just made sure he got fed and wasn't alone."

Gretchen finally blurted out, "But no one did anything? What about you mothers?"

Simon turned to her and smiled sadly, "A lot of the kids never got hit, or at least not hit more than a couple of times. Some had it a bit worse, like me, but in my case it sorted itself out. My mom laid down the law one day, after Dad grabbed me and started slapping me and laughing. She grabbed me, sent me to my room, and threatened to kill him if he ever touched me or her again. He just laughed at her, so she grabbed a bottle, broke it across the table, and waved the jagged edges in his face. I remember how scared he looked, and was so glad of it. He never touched me again, but things were never good between my folks after that. And my Mum was always cooler towards me after that."

"And Yancey's parents?" Charlene asked quietly.

Simon's sad smile turned into frozen ice. "His dad got worse. Whenever something went missing, or he was looking for money, he'd grab Yancey and beat him to 'confess' where he'd hidden it. I remember one day that Yancey and I were talking about things - you know, how kids do. My dad had finally stopped hitting me and Yancey was happy for me. Said that he hoped that his dad would stop one day, too. Then he asked if my dad stopped hitting me because he and my mom had sex. I remember just looking at him and shaking my head. Apparently his mom tried to stop the beatings, but wasn't strong enough, so she resorted to bribing him with sex. In front of Yancey. His beatings got less frequent, but more violent. If the sex wasn't good enough, his dad would beat him anyways. So his mom ended up doing pretty much everything and anything that sick bastard could think of. All in front of Yancey, 'cuz that's what his father wanted."

Shaking his head, voice ragged with emotion, Simon continued, "Keep in mind, this was our childhood conversations. It was all just the way things were. We didn't know any better. Didn't know that it *could* be better. Just knew that it was wrong, and the only thing we could do was to endure it and hope it would end one day."

Pausing to wipe his eyes, he continued his narrative. "Anyways, sometimes Yancey's injuries would get so bad he could hardly walk. He'd go off on his own, treat the swellings by dangling the damaged limb in the cold water of one of the local creeks. Bathed any bruises and cuts, too. Lucky he didn't get an infection, I guess, but it seemed to help. Sometimes when he didn't show up for school, it was because he'd gone off to the 'healing waters' as he called them. I'd go looking for him after school, and make sure he was all right. Like now, he wouldn't say a word, wouldn't show anything. That's how he fought back against his father, you see, by not giving the sick bastard what he wanted."

Gretchen and Charlene could only stare at this recitation of horror. Each had heard of, even experienced, inflicted violence, but this was beyond their experience.

"Anyways, Yancey's father died after a few years of that. His mom had taken up drinking by this point, and just kept going with it. Made a cursory effort to feed and clothe Yancey, but it wasn't much. My mom made sure that he got some decent meals a couple times a week. We weren't very well off, but she couldn't let that go by, especially since he'd helped me through my own rough times. Things were actually not too bad after that. We ran wild through the woods, the pair of us. Bottom of the social ladder we were, but we took care of each other."

"Jesus Christ, Simon," Gretchen said as Simon grew silent. "Bloody hell. Didn't the teachers or police do anything?"

Simon just shook his head. "That's just the way things were in Little Shithole. Nothing could be done. Yancey just had the worst of it. Some of the teachers, though, tried to compensate by helping us scholastically. So we ended up with all the tutoring we could hope for. Then one year an old lady died and left her books and stuff to the school library. She was a real bibliophile, and there were hundreds and hundreds of books on all sorts of things - novels, history, science, the arts, and we devoured them all. Yance, especially, seemed to finally start coming into his own. Then there were the videotapes and DVDs - documentaries, various TV series, and the like. Keep in mind that we didn't have any Internet or even much in the way of TV or radio! All that kind of stuff didn't reach us until, oh, the summer before our last year of high school, so that treasure trove was our first big link to the outside world."

"What about Yancey's mother, Simon, what happened to her?" enquired Charlene.

Simon replied simply, "She died that last summer - the booze finally killed her. No loss. Only me and Yance attended her funeral. Yance was underage, of course, but close enough to his majority that no one there cared about that. He'd been taking care of himself for years, anyways - himself and his mom. The welfare money dried up then, but because our marks were so good our teachers helped us get summer jobs. Yancey was an assistant with a plumbing outfit, and I got on with the road crews for the Ministry of Transportation, and that was how we earned enough for college."

Gretchen knew that Yancey never went to college, but never learnt the reason, so she asked, "Why didn't Yancey go to college? It sounds like it was something you had both planned to do."

He snorted before replying, "Yep. That was the plan. Me for biz school, and him for science or engineering or something. He wasn't sure what, but we were both going to get the hell out of Little Shithole. Leave and never come back. But something came up ..."

Simon's voice trailed off for a moment and then he recovered, "Anyways, Yance decided to become a private detective. Bought the Busted Flush and went to a community college in Thunder Bay to get his license. Then off to Toronto to ply his trade for a year and a half, then he moved to Ottawa. The rest you know."

There was silence for a few moments and then Charlene cleared her throat.

"Uhm, so what you're saying is that Yancey's taking care of himself now the same way he did when he was young? Keeping everything bottled up and washing his wounds in the streams?"

Simon shook his head, "No, it's not like that. He'll talk when he's ready. He just needs to sort things out in his head first. Hell, if that'd been me, I'd have been catatonic by now, and no lie. Yancey's tough, but not in a stupid macho way. For all that we loathed Little Shithole, we both enjoyed the forests. It was always our refuge, you see, our safe place. For Yancey it's, well, 'sacred' is too strong a word for it, but very special. It heals his soul, if you will. It always has. So leave him be, for now."

The two women looked at each other and shook their heads, not fully understanding how Simon could just let his friend go off. Simon, for his part, was concerned for his friend but not overly worried. This was ugly stuff, to be sure, but nothing Yancey couldn't handle - with a bit of Simon's help, perhaps. The ladies just didn't understand, but they would. Of that he was certain.

Gretchen finally broke the awkward silence. "What I don't understand is why the police would sit back and do nothing about all that."

Simon just shook his head sadly. "Like a lot of small towns, Little Shithole used the OPP as the police force. When we were very young, the town was about three times the size it was when we left, thanks to logging and road crews and such. That made them eligible for a modest-sized detachment. When the town shrunk, somehow the detachment stayed nearly the same size. But think about it for a minute. Being posted to a dead-end place like that, or even just about any small town in northern Ontario, is going to be viewed as temporary for pretty much every police officer. Or used as a punishment posting. In either case, they just put in time doing the absolute minimum until they can get transferred to a larger town. The ones that stick around are mostly the ones you don't want. Every so often, though, you get a good one. Someone who gives a damn and tries to do their best. Doesn't happen often, but they are truly gold. There was one of those that got transferred there, back when we were, oh, ten or twelve. Constable Dundee, his name was - Donald Bates Dundee. Didn't take crap from anyone, not even his Sergeant, who was not one of the good ones by the way. Didn't blindly follow the book, but didn't stray too far from it. Everyone got a fair shake from him, and he seemed to truly love his work. Wonder what happened to him? Gotta be long gone by now. Doesn't matter, I guess."

Everyone was silent for a time after that. To break the awkward silence that had fallen, Gretchen began tidying up the remains of their breakfast. The others pitched in to help, and within a few minutes all the utensils had been washed, and the few scraps disposed of. There was still no sign of Yancey, and the women were getting concerned. Simon, however, insisted that they get set up to analyze their intelligence from the Tears facility, not to mention figure out the logistics of survival. Although unhappy about it, neither Charlene nor Gretchen could argue with the logic. So they began discussing how best to set up in the small space available to them. They had just started that discussion, when Simon slapped his head, and suggested that survival matters take precedence. Like checking the gas level in the Busted Flush, the cabin's electrical system and plumbing, those sorts of minor details. The two women agreed and everyone exchanged guilty looks. They were all slightly off their game right now, and that would have to be taken into consideration.

After a brief discussion, they agreed that the first order of business was to take a small tour of the area around the cabin to check things out. They could check out the Busted Flush along the way. There were enough coats and scarves for everyone, if one counted towels as scarves, and off they went outside. They first checked out the Flush, and saw that there was only a quarter tank of gas left. Moving on, they observed the solar panels at the top of the cabin, and made a note of where the wiring went to. Once back inside, they'd check out the battery system to see if there was the possibility of charging phones and laptops. The firewood situation looked pretty good, with several bush cords of aged wood neatly stacked. That would last them a good long time, but they decided that it might be worthwhile to move a cord or two to the porch by the door for easier access. Continuing their tour, they could see a good-sized stream meandering along the back, with dense bush to either side. There was no sign of Yancey, so after a quick debate they headed back to the cabin, each grabbing an armful of wood as they passed they wood pile.

This was a good place to hole up, they agreed. The cabin itself was not visible from the road, and any smoke was mostly hidden by the tall trees. If there was any wind whatsoever, any smoke would be well dissipated by the time it cleared the level of the tree tops. Several trips later, they decided that the porch now held enough wood for at least a couple of days. With those basics taken care of, they went back inside. Inspecting the solar battery system, they found USB outlets for charging small appliances. Not sufficient to charge the UPSs, but the Flush could do that, Simon declared. Grabbing all the phones and laptops, they plugged in as many as it looked like the system could handle. Judging by the charger's display, Simon decided that charging everything up would deplete the batteries to the point where they'd only have enough for a couple hours of the cabin lights. After a brief discussion they agreed that it was more important to charge everything up, at least for now. With this done, they set to work unpacking and arranging maps, notes, and other stuff they'd need when they started analysing data. As well, they made sure that all the flashlights and lanterns were at hand and ready to use.

Gretchen, by this point, was getting somewhat unsteady on her feet, so the others urged her to take a nap. She protested, but not too strongly, and within a few minutes was quietly snoring away in their primary bedroom. As she slept, Charlene and Simon discussed a number of things without getting into any great depth.

Charlene described her kidnapping and imprisonment, and Simon talked about what they had found in Herman's databases. This segued into a discussion of Herman, and how his last project had gotten started. There were many pauses and times of silence, but by this time it was all comfortable and companionable between them.

Simon was, at this point, pretty sure that Charlene was the one Gretchen referred to as 'The Source', and finally got up the nerve to ask if that was the case. Charlene actually blushed a bit, then admitted it to be true. Simon laughed softly, and told her about how some of her information had been used. This led to telling her about some of the things he had seen after the terrorist attack, and the effect on the business community. Charlene listened intently, and her journalistic training allowed her to gently steer the conversation.

The more she heard from this young man, the more impressed she became. Gretchen had always spoken highly of him, but this was her first chance to talk with him first hand. To her mind, this was one to watch. He was talented, tough, and genuinely cared about people and the state of the world. A rare combination in her experience.

Night was falling when Yancey finally returned. The table had been set for supper, and they had set a place for him. The haunted look on his face was almost gone, but he still spoke not a word. They were eating MREs, and Yancey nodded and gave a slight brief smile when they passed one to him. The dinner talk was fairly light, centring around when and how to go about getting more supplies.

After the eating was done, they cleared the table and moved to the centre of the floor where a map was spread out. In the light of the fireplace and the low cabin lights, they discussed possible strategies regarding when to go, how to pay, who should go, who might be looking for them, that sort of thing. Yancey appeared to be listening, although his attention often seemed to wander to the fire or the window. When pressed for an answer to some question he just gave a little smile and shrugged his shoulders. Clearly, he wasn't quite ready to focus on the problems at hand, and no-one forced the issue. There was no real urgency on the supplies issue, so they decided to let it ride until tomorrow or the day after.

They finally agreed to call it a night, and were talking about shifts amongst themselves. When they turned to ask Yancey a question, they discovered that he had crawled into his sleeping bag and had gone to sleep. They decided to leave him be for the time being, and resolved on three-hour shifts.

Gretchen was chosen to take the first shift, since she had slept last, and was admonished to wake Simon up this time. When the time came, she did indeed wake up Simon, who took his shift. He watched the others sleep, and cast more than one worried glance at Yancey, who appeared to be sleeping soundly.

At the appointed time he woke up Charlene who stumbled up to take her post. The past few days had taken a toll on her reserves of strength, and she was finding herself envying her young friends for their ability to bounce back so quickly. She sat staring at the fire and then woke up with a start with the sun shining in her face. The fire was not only burning better than when she had started her shift, but there was more wood at the ready than there was before.

Startled she looked around, but saw that Simon and Gretchen were still fast asleep. Glancing at Yancey's bedding, she saw that it was empty. The door quietly opened, and Yancey walked in with a bucket of fresh water and a handful of small branches. He looked at her with a vague smile, then without a word headed to the stove and began to quietly set a fire going in it. Once that was going, he put some water in the kettle to boil, and put the rest of the water into a pan, which also went on the stove. With the water set for boiling, Yancey began setting up the small table in preparation for breakfast. By the time the water had boiled, the tea pot was ready and Yancey set the tea to steeping, making more noise than was necessary.

Charlene wondered about this, as he had been so very quiet earlier, but then Simon sat up and made his usual morning sounds as he got out of bed. This caused enough disturbance to wake up Gretchen, who sat up and made her own variety of morning sounds. By the time those two had shuffled to the table, the tea was ready and poured into cups by Yancey. They each selected an MRE and began eating without saying much. Clearly, none of them was a morning person, and being out in the woods hadn't changed that.

With breakfast done, conversation started to pick up. Yancey, who still hadn't said a word to anyone, got up, put on his coat, and walked out the door. They all stopped talking for a moment, then Gretchen turned to Simon and glared at him.

"He's fine. Really," Simon insisted.

Charlene favoured him with an expression of moderate disbelief, which caused Simon to blush and look down into his tea, harumphing.

There was an unspoken agreement to postpone discussing this, and they began to discuss next steps. Simon suggested that they start looking at the original databases, plus the notes he and Yancey had made, so very long ago. It certainly felt like an eternity.

That would give everyone a common starting point, he felt. He got some push-back from the two women, who, not surprisingly, wanted to start with something of more immediate concern, like the 'Harvest of Souls' operation. Simon explained how he and Yancey had put together the scraps of information from the database to discern the Sword's transportation network, and how this led them to the Tears of Joy. The women looked at each other, shrugged, and then agreed that they didn't yet have enough background to be of much use. So, they set up to look at the original data, with the original notes spread around them in a semicircle. Simon started to explain the methodology, but Gretchen shushed him with a wave of her hand, declaring that she knew enough about his methods to figure it out, thank you very much. If they needed his advice, they'd ask for it. Simon just grinned. It felt good to be working with Gretchen again. While the ladies reviewed the original data, he spent the time taking a quick overview of the data that had been harvested from the computers at the Tears facility.

When they next checked the time, they discovered that it was nearly noon. Gretchen looked pointedly at Simon, who sighed resignedly and got up to go check on Yancey. In truth, he was beginning to agree with her - not that he'd ever admit that to her. So he heaved himself upright, put on his jacket and toque, and went outside. The day was bright, with only a few wisps of cloud visible. Simon took a deep appreciative breath, then shaded his eyes with his hand and looked around for his friend to no avail.

Whistling softly to himself as he thought about where he would go if he were Yancey, Simon quietly ambled along until he got to the stream. Pursing his lips and harrumphing, he decided to go upstream. It just seemed like a more fun place to be, with the water gurgling past him with the promise of mysteries to be explored just around the next bend.

Continuing his casual amble, he had to choose his footing carefully in several spots, but that was half the fun. Finally he reached a bend in the steam that curved around a pair of very large boulders. The path along the stream itself was blocked, so he glanced towards his left to see if there was a path around, and then felt something drop on his toque.

He quickly looked around, but saw nothing untoward. Then he looked up to see if a bird had shat on him, but again found nothing of consequence, so he took off his toque to look for signs of avian desecration. The toque was unblemished, so with a puzzled look he put it back on his head and continued picking his way around the boulder. Another slight impact on his head brought him to a halt. As before, he looked around and upwards, but once again could not discover the source of whatever it was that had hit him. A dim memory was beginning to vaguely form, when a rustling sound above him caused him to look sharply upwards again. And found himself staring at an onrushing blizzard of moss, twigs, and other debris avalanching towards him.

"AGGGHHH!"

His cry of dismay was answered by snorting, derisive laughter. Glancing upwards as he brushed debris from his hair and spat it out of his mouth, he saw Yancey's grinning face above him on top of the boulder. As a childhood memory of similar attacks by Yancey bubbled into his consciousness, he closed his eyes as if in pain, spat out the last of the debris, and said with enthusiasm, "Asshole."

To the heartfelt curse, Yancey could only start laughing again. Some things never got old.

"Just keep walking around the boulder. Where the two boulders meet makes a sort of ladder, loosely speaking. Are you sure you're in good enough shape for a wee climb?"

Muttering darkly under his breath, Simon walked around the boulder and saw where it was jammed up against another large boulder. Peering at the two, he could see some minor ledges and such that might be considered climbing aids, so he took a running leap to get started, and carefully scrambled up to the top without losing too much of his skin. When he got to the top, he found Yancey sitting quietly, eyes closed, with a small contented smile on his face.

Yancey calmly told his friend to sit and remain silent for a bit. With various mutterings, Simon did as requested, and his heavy breathing quickly evened out. They both sat there quietly, surrounded by the trees on each side of the stream. The gurgling of the stream provided a complex regular rhythm that was punctuated by irregular faint snatches of sound. Yancey smiled and pointed to them in turn. The leaping of fish, the faint rush of wings as birds flew by, the call of soaring hawks, the gentle padding of small animals coming to the stream to drink. The sun gently warmed both the rock and the silent watchers.

Simon sat enjoying the view, then without turning, reached over and poked Yancey in the shoulder with a stern forefinger.

"Are you ready to stop playing silly buggers?"

Yancey inhaled sharply, as if in pain, and clutched the attacked shoulder with a moan. Without looking over, Simon said with a sneer, "It's the other shoulder."

"Are you sure?"

"Yep. Saw it myself."

"Oh. Damn. Well in that case, yah, I guess I'm done."

There was silence for several seconds, then both of them started snorting with barely suppressed laughter as they kept staring out into the wilderness. It went on long enough that both had to wipe eyes and blow noses. The smile faded from Yancey's lips, but not his eyes as he softly said "I know that I was a mess. I got the shit kicked out of me, both physically and emotionally, and I just kind of shut down. Just like when we were kids, I guess."

He turned to Simon with a serious look on his face, "I

was at the end of my rope there, Simon, just before you came for me."

Another brief pause, then Yancey turned away and hung his head, "I've never been in a situation that I couldn't at least see a way out of. But not this time. And I was afraid that I could be broken. Could be made to turn on my friends."

He paused to look at the half-healed scars on his hands, then carefully touched his face, "I thought that I could handle anything. And the simple beatings I *could* handle. But then the real torture started. The bastard was an expert, Simon, an experienced pro. It was all so very clinical and detached, as if I were simply a vessel for the information they wanted. A container to be opened up, emptied, and tossed away."

He turned to look at Simon, his face devoid of emotion, "I thought I'd seen bad people before, Simon. Hard-cases. Evil, even. But this lot ... I thought I understood them, based on the data we've seen. But the data doesn't tell the whole story. Just like that extra guard that was there that we didn't know about, the Sword is a whole new level of evil that none of us have ever had to contemplate, much less deal with, before."

Simon looked evenly at his friend, fully aware of the heartfelt anguish he must be feeling. Yancey had always been the strong one, the one with the plan, the one with faith in his ability to deal with anything and make a better future.

"So I shut down, Simon. I just couldn't deal with the pain and shock and horror. I couldn't help you or the others any more, and that just made me too ashamed to face any of you."

"Yance ..." Simon began.

With a small self-deprecating smile and a waggling of

his hand, Yancey quieted his friend. "I know, I know, but I wasn't thinking too straight at that point. The shock, the stress … everything just felt like a big crushing weight. So I had to get my head straight. We're in the fight of our lives, and I needed to get my focus back. Fast."

His face cleared and one side of his mouth raised in an almost-smile. "Think of the mind as a muscle. What I've been through is like overstressing a muscle - it gets strained, sprained, and torn. Like a muscle, the mind needs to heal. And that is what I've done here. Gentle exercise for both mind and body. Long walks, hills and trees to climb for extra exercise, chopping wood, all good for the body."

Yancey gestured around, "Hey, how much more restful and easy on the eyes can any place get? Gentle for the mind. And for mental exercise? Well, tell me, how many different species of fish have you seen today? What size? How many hawk and osprey nests can you see on each side of the stream? How many different species of birds have you seen? Think of it as an exercise in situational awareness."

Simon just smiled calmly at him and shook his head.

Yancey chuckled, "Yah, it's a soothing setting, and that helps at one level. But seeing is not the same thing as observing. My experience as a PI has taught me that, and this place allows me to practise and hone that skill in an environment with a certain amount of distraction and background chatter. Like getting a damaged muscle back into shape. And to get the mental kinks out."

Yancey paused for a moment then continued softly, "I ran away from you all because I couldn't stand the thought of being around people. Couldn't handle the stress of having to be polite and act normal. Whatever that is. But this place has allowed me to heal, given me time to think, and the opportunity to interact with the world at my own pace."

Simon looked carefully at his friend, whom he'd known since childhood. Yancey not only sounded more like his old self, he really did look better. The physical wounds would take a while to heal, but his soul was no longer damaged.

"The ladies were worried."

"Sorry 'bout that."

"Wouldn't have bothered you out here, myself. Knew you were fine. But they made me come."

"Yah, well, maybe it *is* time for me to ease back into things."

"That would be nice, you coming back after your little vacation and all. There's work a-waitin'."

They both grunted their amusement at the exchange. Some things never got old.

They sat and enjoyed the warm sun for a few minutes more, then headed back to the cabin. Yancey still moved somewhat carefully and gingerly, but Simon could see that he was moving better than before. Then a thought occurred to him.

"Uhm, Yance, have you been bathing yourself in the stream like you used to?"

"Hell, no. All sorts of nasty bugs and parasites in these forest streams. I boiled water and let it cool down before I washed in it."

Simon smiled to himself as they walked back to the cabin. It was good to see that sometimes cherished childhood rituals could be tempered by adult sensibility - and yet still retain their magic.

CHAPTER FIFTEEN
Council Of War

The four friends had been at the cabin for nearly a week, and were beginning to settle into a comfortable rhythm. They made a good team, too. Gretchen and Simon had spent so many productive years working together that they quickly fell into their old patterns that had cracked many a thorny analytical problem. Charlene had years of experience as an investigative reporter, and was exceptional at analyzing the big picture and asking piercing questions. Yancey had his own set of analytical skills that were a good complement to Simon's, and his experience as a PI meshed nicely with Charlene's skill set.

Yancey wounds were healing well, and he was moving with only moderate stiffness. Even better, from the viewpoint of his friends, his mental state was much improved. If not the big sloppy smiles of old, at least the smiles were no longer thin and forced. And his sense of humour was beginning to return, although both women could have done without the return of the punning that both men revelled in. His keen mind rose to the challenge of analyzing their treasure trove of data, and he flung himself into that with something approaching his normal passion.

Of course, one of Yancey's first questions after he'd regained his equilibrium was about how well his improvised firebomb had worked.

Simon grinned, "Yance, it was a thing of beauty. Not the huge blast that we were hoping for, but good enough. A nice big bang, a bright fireball, some ancillary flames, but it didn't do any real damage. Which was good, 'cuz then the Tears people could wave it off to the cops as a silly prank that did no harm so no need to investigate it, thank you very much. On the down side, it didn't last very long, which is why the guards came back your way so quickly."

Yancey took a deep breath and sighed appreciatively. He was rather pleased that it had worked at all, if truth be told.

"Just like old times, eh, Simon?"

Simon raised his head as if gazing at old memories, and nodded happily.

Charlene and Gretchen looked at the two of them with something less than awe, and shook their heads disgustedly.

The two young men just laughed at their reaction, and everyone's mood was lightened considerably. Charlene was moved to smilingly enquire, "Had problems with authority, did we?"

"Oh, yeah," laughed Simon, "but it wasn't like we made a habit of it."

"Yep," added Yancey. "Just because you look helpless doesn't make you powerless, and you need to remind them of that."

Everyone turned to look at him, even Simon. Yancey got a faraway look in his eyes, and his face grew very still. Then he snorted with amusement and gave his head a slight shake. He looked up at the others, with a small, lopsided smile. "It is, after all, every captive's right to mess with the minds of his captors. When the Deacon started his initial questioning, I endured a bit of slapping around, and then when he asked me to confess I played the hysterical fool game a bit before quieting down, then told him that the code name of my contact was 'the muffin man'. Then I asked him "Do you know the muffin man?".".

Simon stifled a guffaw, as the two ladies looked on without understanding what either of them was talking about.

"How far along did you manage to string it?" Simon managed to get out between snorts of amusement.

Yancey replied, "As far as "he lives on Drury Lane". Then he caught on. I suppose my bursting out loud laughing may have given him a clue, too. Got cuffed across the face for it; then he stopped himself and took a break. When it all resumed, it was as if it never happened, and they were back to being cold, clinical professionals."

Simon gave two thumbs up, and the two young men were lost in a fit of laughter.

Gretchen and Charlene were aghast at this story. For one thing they were still concerned about the torture that Yancey had endured on their behalf.

"Dammit, Yancey! What the hell were you thinking, provoking them like that?" Gretchen finally blurted out in horror.

Yancey got his laughter under control, gave a couple of happy snorts, then shook his head, "No, it had to be done. Truly. To prove to them that just because someone is bound, that doesn't make them helpless. And it proved to me that I could get to them, that they had weaknesses that could be exploited. Humour is the best way to combat their kind, and the best morale-booster for a prisoner. Unfortunately, that only worked when they were trying to convert me and get me to voluntarily confess my sins. When they began trying to break me and rip out the information, well, that was a whole different thing."

The look on the faces of his friends made Yancey realize that perhaps they might have unresolved issues about what had gone on. So he gently but emphatically added, "Hey, it all turned out alright. Gretchen and Charlene got rescued, I got rescued, and we got some really good intel out of it. Yeah, I got torn up a bit during the op, but I *did* manage to walk away from it. My injuries are healing nicely. Right, Gretchen?

Gretchen sighed and allowed that his injuries really were healing with no apparent problems.

Yancey pressed home the point, "OK, and we've begun bringing everyone up to speed on what we know so far, and taking a first look at all the lovely new intel we acquired. Right, Charlene?"

Charlene just smiled and nodded her agreement. She could see how Yancey was making sure that the team was not being dragged down by negative thoughts, and her estimation of his abilities went up a notch.

Yancey paused and looked around at the group. "OK, gang, that just leaves one truly important question. Who's up for some tea before we quit for the night?"

The laughter that greeted this was more than the mild humour warranted, perhaps, but signalled a welcome clearing of the air.

The next morning they agreed that it was finally time to risk a trip to fetch more supplies. After some discussion it was decided that Simon and Gretchen should be the ones to go, on the assumption that a young couple would be less memorable. Their supply of cash was limited, so after some debate it was decided to stick to basic foodstuffs like rice, beans, flour, and tea. If there was any money left over, maybe get some bacon and eggs, or whatever was on sale. Looking at maps, they chose to go to one of the larger stores, as that would probably be the safest, as well as offering the possibility of items on sale. After a bit of debate, they decided to get a minimal amount of gas for the Busted Flush. Gas was expensive and they weren't using much of it. So Simon and Gretchen went out, leaving Yancey and Charlene to fret for a couple of hours. The stay-at-home pair passed the time discussing the sorts of stories that Charlene liked to cover at her newspaper. Both were pleased to find a kindred soul in the other that enjoyed hunting out hidden truths in a messy world.

Simon and Gretchen returned to find the other two yakking away like old friends, but the conversation quickly shifted to examination of the results of the successful expedition for supplies. They had been lucky enough to hit a day of good sales, and managed to stretch their money to cover enough food for two weeks, perhaps a bit longer if they were careful. Another welcome purchase was a large supply of various newspapers. All of them were voracious readers, and the rest of the day was spent catching up on the news of the world. The only mention of the attack on the Shattered Palace was a small piece in a couple of the papers that described a 'military training accident'. The two papers that mentioned it at all had it buried deep inside - the rest ignored the story completely. None of them were surprised at this, but both Yancey and Simon sat very quietly staring out the window for some time after reading that. The rest of that day passed quietly, as they read the papers and brought various items to each other's attention.

That evening, the conversation drifted into how the ladies had been 'acquired' by the Sword, and why.

"Well," began Charlene, "after Herman's murder, I

knew that I was going to be on someone's list of people to question or silence. They knew that I was involved with Herman, and were obviously going to be curious about what I might know about his research. I was his editor, after all. I'm afraid that Gretchen got caught up simply because she knew me. As for the actual 'acquisition', one night there was a knock on the door and when I opened it the gentlemen standing there flashed badges and insisted that I come with them for questioning. Once in the car, they drove for a bit and I just … fell asleep. Woke up in a cell at the Tears facility, where they allowed me time to clean myself up before escorting me to another room for questioning. The questioning itself was all done professionally, with no overt threats. More like a questioning by police, than anything. In fact, they worked very hard at giving the impression that they were from an official, but very secret, organization working on a case affecting national security. Fortunately, I knew little about the details within the databases, and nothing at all about where it had come from. Only Herman knew it all, and he was dead."

Gretchen took up the tale at this point. "My own 'acquisition' was pretty much identical, although I didn't find out that Charlene was there, too, for over a day after arriving. Aside from what they said during the questioning, I overheard some of the guards talking. As Charlene said, we got picked up to see what we knew about some sort of leaked information. They initially started talking about how Charlene and Herman had gotten hold of the information, but then become more concerned about stuff that came up during questioning. Apparently looking at my background they found mention of Simon, and their anomaly-detection algorithms saw that of all my acquaintances, he was the only one who had left town. They discovered that a car had been rented, and that the intended destination was Ottawa. They looked to see who Simon knew in Ottawa and came up with Yancey, a private investigator. Then you disappeared from view and that got someone scared, so they decided to take 'harsher measures', whatever that meant."

Yancey and Simon exchanged looks, then Yancey turned to the ladies and explained, "The 'harsher measures' was someone torching my apartment. That didn't make sense at the time, and even less now, as it sounds like they weren't sure about my level of involvement. Probably some lower-lever operative got nervous, what with the attack on the Shattered Palace about to take place."

Gretchen nodded, "Makes sense. A couple of days after that, there was a big panic over something, and they stopped questioning us. Even forgot to bring us a meal, a couple of times. Really strange. Up to that point they had been so professional and clinical - almost polite. Except for some of the staff - all male staff, by the way - kind of leering at us when they thought no one else was looking. Some of the guys looked real hard and moved like soldiers, with crisp efficient movements. Others looked like they had worked out, but didn't move like the soldier types. Then there were a couple that were something on the flabby side - those were the ones that leered. About a day after the panic started, all the soldier types disappeared. Day after that, the body-builder types were gone, too. Just the two creeps, and they kept referring to someone called 'the Deacon'. We never saw him, though."

Yancey started rapidly tapping the tips of his fingers together; something Simon had only seen him do when stressed. "Did they say anything about my office, or anyone else in the same building?"

Simon looked at him.

"I'm worried about Mama and his wife."

Simon sat upright as if punched. "Oh, shit, Yance, I forgot about them. Damn. Do you think anything happened?"

"I don't know, Simon. I have to assume that they went to the office, if only to look around. Mama knew that something was up, and he's no fool. I'm pretty sure he'll be safe."

Yancey sounded as if he were trying to convince himself.

"Mama?" queried Gretchen. Then realization hit her, "Oh. You mean that nice restaurant owner and his wife who had that place near your office?"

Her hand flew to her mouth, and she stared with horror at Charlene.

Charlene made 'calm down' motions with her hands before speaking, "No, no one mentioned your office to me, Yancey. Or anything about your friend. I agree with you that in all likelihood he is safe. At that point you were only a person of interest, and only a mild interest at that. That fire at your apartment doesn't sound like something a competent operative would do, and I can't believe they'd have too many dolts working ops in Ottawa, of all places. No, it sounds like you two probably got out just ahead of them, especially since they picked up your trail so quickly, then just as quickly lost it. How did you do that, just out of interest?"

Seeing that Yancey was still lost in worry about Mama, Simon told them about laying the false trail about going to Montreal to find Gretchen, then doubling back on the Quebec side. Charlene laughed and clapped her hands, "Great fieldwork, Yancey. You'd have made a fine investigative reporter."

Yancey, knowing high praise when he heard it, gave a

135

lopsided grin and tilted his head at her. Then his smile faded and his features softened as he asked Charlene about the man who had put together the databases that were at the heart of all this. Charlene's eyes misted as she told them about Herman, and how one tip had led to another. How they set up things so very carefully to protect themselves. Just not careful enough as things turned out.

Keeping his voice gentle, Yancey had to ask, "How, exactly, did Herman get his hands on all this? The stuff about the gaming of the elections was one thing, but all those details about Infinity Ascending and the Sword? Where did that come from?"

Charlene could only shake her head, and her eyes flashed as she thought of those databases and how Herman had died acquiring them. "Now that I've started to see the depth and breadth of the data, I'm beginning to wonder that myself."

Yancey sighed and then stated firmly, "Well, I think we'll have to put off that aspect for a while. We really don't have the time to worry about the source of the data right now. As far as we could tell, it was all accurate. Still, it is a mystery, and probably going to be important at some point."

The others all agreed with him, and on that note they decided to pack it in for the night.

After that, the analysis of the data absorbed all their energies with but few such breaks. Charlene and Gretchen had to be brought up to speed on what had been found within the original databases. Charlene focused on the background information on Infinity Ascending and the Shattered Palace, while Gretchen turned her efforts towards double-checking what the guys had deduced concerning the cadres of influence and control. They took frequent breaks to bring the other up to speed on one aspect or another and discuss the implications.

Yancey and Simon focused their efforts on the data downloaded off of the Tears of Joy network during the two rescues. That was raw intelligence of the first order, but much of it consisted of encrypted information. It turned out that most of the encryption, like everything else on their network, was standard stuff that was breakable by people with reasonable experience. Which Yancey had. This struck them as odd, and they all paused to discuss this, on the chance that it was planted. They agreed that it would be logical to use commercial off-the-shelf stuff, since it made things easier in terms of training and maintenance, just like any other large organization. In addition, it might have been good internal politics for them to use the products of their membership. That seemed to be a reasonable hypothesis, so they went back to their tasks.

Much of the data was decrypted with little difficulty, although some of it was impervious to their efforts, and Yancey and Simon poured over it. A lot of it was in the form of emails, and those proved particularly illuminating.

They found a dossier regarding Yancey that had been sent to the Deacon, along with the instructions to get information out of him by any means. The dossier was interesting on several counts. First, it showed that their records of him were modest - consisting only of official documentation including, to everyone's surprise, his tax records. He had been investigated only because of his links to Simon, who in turn was linked to Gretchen, who in turn was linked to Charlene. However, the fact that he was a private investigator had raised some red flags. The team sent to check his apartment made some sort of error that caused the fire, the exact cause of which was unknown, but the team was to be transferred to the Fist of Tolerance for debriefing and discipline.

There was a reference to the report of another team that had been sent to Yancey's office. Yancey quickly found the referenced report and scanned it. Apparently the team had identified themselves as police detectives to avoid undue notice. A rental car had been found parked outside the office ("Geez, Yance, we just missed them by minutes," said Simon, his eyes opening wide), which they had towed away for forensic analysis, which was still pending. There was one local witness, the owner of a nearby deli, who cooperated fully with the investigators. He told them how the two subjects had decided to go to Montreal in search of the female subject. This was in keeping both with the cover story planted to cover her disappearance, and verified by credit card purchases at a gas station just outside of Ottawa. Questioning of the gas station attendant indicated that the two subjects had claimed to be on their way to Montreal, as evidenced by their request for directions and purchase of the required map. A team would do a search of the detective's office presently, but strictly as a formality. No further action contemplated at this time. Agents in Montreal were alerted. Witnesses were all fully cooperative and were warned to not discuss this with anyone. No further action was required.

Yancey leaned back with an explosive sigh, his head hanging loosely. Mama was safe. That was one enormous weight off his chest. The others had all paused at this display of emotion from him, and expressed happiness when he told them what he had found. Simon knew that Mama's possible fate had weighed heavily on his friend.

With only brief breaks for food, they all laboured at their

assigned tasks. Sometimes Simon or Yancey would need to answer questions from the women, but for the most part the men worked at their tasks while the ladies worked through the initial research. Once they had done that, the women shifted their attentions to helping the men deal with the new information, with special emphasis on the Harvest of Souls operation. It was quickly discovered that the operation had been delayed for at least four weeks, due to operational security concerns. Half of the security forces were to be transferred back to their original postings to ensure operational security of those locations. On learning this, there was much fist pumping and smiling among the group. Whatever their battles had cost the four friends, it looked like the operations of the Sword were being interfered with.

In addition to this, a recent email sent to the Deacon at the Tears of Joy said that due to the loss of the two female guests, a special security team was being sent to his facility to evaluate personnel and to improve their security protocols. This brought a smile to them all, and a nastier one to Yancey's face.

Yancey told everyone to pass along any photos to him for analysis. This brought puzzled looks from his companions, and they wondered what sort of analysis he was considering - wasn't it enough to just look at them? He laughed and firmly disagreed with that notion. He went on to explain that, unless special measures were taken, photos taken with digital cameras had extra information within them that contained such things as the serial number of the camera, possibly the GPS location, and so forth. If the serial number was still there, then they could associate specific pictures with specific cameras used by Sword operatives. Anyone with decent security awareness would disable the associating of GPS coordinates with photos, but slip-ups can happen and they might get lucky. He had to admit that this was probably going to be useful more in the long run, but said that he'd run into one interesting picture from his own current analysis of the Sword data.

He flashed up a picture of a recent riot in Toronto, that showed protesters and police hitting at each other. The others shrugged. It had been a popular picture in the various media for several days, and was old news. Yancey grinned and told them that it had been attached to an email in the Tears database. The two women shrugged again, but Simon started looking thoughtful. They all became quite alert as Yancey revealed that the photo in the email had all that extra information he'd been talking about, embedded inside it. And that meant that it had come from the camera that had taken the picture.

"That doesn't prove too much, Yancey," interjected Charlene, "just that the Sword had access to the original file."

Yancey turned to her and said with a mischievous grin, "True enough. But there are other pictures in another email that came from the same camera. And those pictures were part of a report that examined the security setup at the Tears facility. That picture of the riot was taken by the Sword."

Charlene jerked back as if shot. "They leaked it," she exclaimed, then held up her hand to halt further discussion as she thought furiously. Her face grew angry, and she spat out, "No - not leaked. Fed. Fed into a willing media outlet. Or a photographer working in the media. Damn!"

She fell silent, fingers drumming on the tabletop as she digested this unpleasant piece of news. It wasn't surprising, she supposed, but dammit it just wasn't right.

Charlene was a journalist who truly believed in her heart of hearts that the profession was a calling, with an extraordinary responsibility to do the right things and to do them properly. This would not do, no, not at all.

"We can't use this as any sort of proof, you know," she finally said wearily.

Yancey replied cheerily, "Nope. But it does let us know who to watch more carefully. One more thread to trace. And it might be useful in the future, when used in conjunction with something else. Best of all, they don't know that we know."

Charlene snorted and waggled a finger at Yancey, "You are a devious man, Mr. Franklin. You'd have made a good reporter. OK, how do we keep track of all this?"

Yancey replied that he had set up a database to store the photos and associated emails, so just toss them over to him and he'd enter in the data. Gretchen spoke up and suggested that they might want to automate that by writing a script to dig through all their emails and update the database in bulk. Simon chimed in and suggested that if they centralized the storage of all the decrypted emails, they could make a script to put them on Yancey's database.

Charlene was following along with the discussion carefully without comment. However this last exchange forced her to ask, "Hey, aren't you centralizing everything anyway?"

Gretchen and Simon looked at each other guiltily.

"Well," said Gretchen.

"Uhm," added Simon.

"You forgot, didn't you?" said Charlene sternly, making it sound like an accusation rather than a question.

"Well," repeated Gretchen. "We all got so wrapped up in our own analysis and tasks …".

Charlene just smiled wryly. She'd seen this sort of thing happen before when there was a big story with time pressures. The others had also had experience with crunch-time situations, and they all looked guiltily at each other. Yancey broke the silence by getting up and heading to the stove.

"Tea break," he declared firmly. "Definitely time for a tea break."

"I like how you think, Mr. Franklin," said Charlene with a laugh as she struggled to her feet. Squatting on floors was something best left to the young, she thought with a sigh. After the brief respite, they gathered around the small table with their tea and cookies. After several minutes of comfortable and companionable silence, Yancey quietly spoke up.

"We're starting to make mistakes ... rookie mistakes. We've had the shit kicked out of us, we've fought harder and faster than we've ever had to, doing things that we never dreamt of doing, and now we've been thrown together to do or die. Literally."

The others looked at him coolly at first, and then slowly nodded in understanding and acceptance.

"Charlene, you've been our rock. You've been asking all the right questions, helping us to dive into the analysis. Simon and Gretchen, you are a well-oiled team, no doubt about that. But what we're missing is a strategy. No, no, listen to me, please. Charlene, you're see this in terms of stories and investigations, and the rest of us are experts in data analysis of various flavours and that's how we've been attacking this. But that isn't enough."

He looked at each in turn, his face calm but intent.

"We are fighting an organization that has been around for over a century. They have influence in the highest levels of power, they have shit-tonnes of money, and their reach is world-wide and multinational. Canada is being used as a battleground, as a prize to be sliced and diced. For my part, my focus is on saving *our* country. That's about as much as I can worry about right now. For me, that has to be our strategic goal. *Everything* else has to be focused on that, our tactics have to be shaped to that end. We are the ones best situated to begin the fight to save our country."

Yancey stopped, and cleared his throat, somewhat embarrassed by the display of his intense feelings. The others looked at each other, but no one knew how to respond.

Finally, seeing as no one else was going to speak, Simon cleared his throat and said, "Alright, Yance. You've got a point about our making mistakes. And probably even about our equilibrium being wobbled enough to affect our work. There's a shit-tonne of data left to analyze. Some of it, like the fancier encryption, is beyond us. So what do we do with the information? I take it that you've got something more in mind than a simple data dump onto the Internet, or Charlene publishing some stories."

Yancey smiled his big sloppy crooked smile, "Yep. Been giving it some thought. Best part is you aren't going to like it - no, not at all."

The women stared at him with eyes large and rounded. Simon just sighed, closed his eyes, and shook his head as if in pain - he could guess at what was coming.

"Our immediate goal has to be to stop this Harvest of Souls operation. We know that it's postponed, but it'll be happening soon. What it is, exactly, we don't know. Where it takes place and when, is also unknown. All we know is that it involves the transportation of children - and that can't be good, knowing the Sword. We need to figure out filters and scripts that'll dredge up stuff related to that, as quickly as possible. Then we have to publicize all this, but it has to be done carefully, structured in a way to cause the most damage. A big data dump is the worst possible way to do it. A careful, controlled approach will be necessary. I'm thinking a timed release of stories, Charlene."

Gretchen chimed in, "Why not just release the whole thing? Give the data to the authorities, as well as publicize it. Heck, we could even put the data up on one of the open source sites."

They all paused for a moment, then turned to Yancey as he cleared his throat. "Not going to work, not with this lot. These are very, very dangerous people who have a lot of powerful allies. Any evidence given to the authorities will be disappeared, or declared top secret, or given to a committee for unspecified study, and that'll be the last anyone will hear of it. I've personally seen this happen over the years - and for much lesser crimes. I'm sure Charlene has, too."

Charlene slowly nodded her agreement.

Yancey pressed on with his argument, "Look how well the attack on the Shattered Palace was covered up. Not so much as a peep from the newspapers - nothing that strayed from the official story. That means a detailed cover-up at the highest levels. Simply releasing this stuff will get the data disappeared, not to mention ourselves. And don't kid yourselves that we won't be made targets. No, I think the best way to deal with this is to be very careful about who we trust, slowly release bits and pieces to get people used to the idea that something is horrifically wrong from the top down, and keep the enemy so off balance that they won't have time to deal with us. We need to be careful about how we present all this because, let's face it, what we've uncovered sounds like something from a silly conspiracy novel - on the face of it anyways."

Charlene's eyes were unfocused as she balanced the types of stories this represented, with the best way to introduce an unsuspecting public to a series of revelations this large and far-reaching. "There's an election coming in fourteen months or so," she said slowly, "might want to keep that in mind, too."

"Yep, we need to take that into consideration so that the timing of our revelations has the maximum effect on the Sword, and the least risk to ourselves," answered Yancey brightly. "And that brings me to the subject of politics. This is going to be largely a political battle, fought in political terms. That's one of the core pillars of the Sword's assault on Canada, and the most vulnerable, I think. We need to put someone into the political side of things for the next election, who can represent determined opposition to the Sword and everything it represents."

Gretchen and Yancey immediately turned to look at Simon. Charlene looked startled for a moment and then joined the chorus of stares. Simon jerked his head back as if struck.

"Are you out of your frickin' minds?" he hissed intently.

Gretchen just laughed at him.

"Who is that is always getting involved in election campaigns, hmmm? On the local, provincial, *and* federal levels, I might add?" she said with wide-eyed innocence, fully enjoying Simon's discomfiture. "Who knows all the campaign insiders, hmmm?"

Simon was blushing furiously and beginning to splutter.

"Simon," said Gretchen in a quiet and serious voice, "it really does make sense. You know all sorts of party insiders in both the Liberal and NDP parties. What's more, they respect you, they really do. You wear your political heart on your sleeve and don't play or support stupid power games. You, my friend, have earned a lot of respect from your peers on The Street, too."

"Charlene," pleaded Simon, "what about you? You're known."

Charlene raised both hands and waved them as if waving away a problem, "Nope, nope, not me. I'm a reporter. I reveal things that people want left buried. They may respect me, but basically they're afraid of me and my kind."

"Think, Simon," said Yancey quietly but firmly. "This makes sense, and no kidding."

Simon's mouth opened and closed several times with a sound coming out. Then his eyes unfocused as he began to think - really think - about what his friends had been saying. Finally, he began to nod.

"Yeah, OK, I guess I do know the political side better than anyone. But there's a long time to the next election. Yes, it takes time to set up a campaign, but there's more to it than that."

The others looked at Simon with interest.

"Think about it. The vote-rigging is the most obvious part of the problem. But it's a big stick, not a subtle tool. The ConRefs won a majority, but not a tremendous one, in a hard-fought election. That means the rigging is being done selectively, for any number of reasons, I would think. Hmm, first and foremost would be to not make the election look rigged. A bit of a 'duh', I agree, but there are implications. How are the losers chosen?"

The others looked surprised at this new way of looking at the problem, but kept silent.

"The Sword is about control, right?" Simon asked the group, "So it pretty much stands to reason that they'd use the rigged voting tool to maintain control, not only of the country but of their own party. It would allow them to punish dissent, eliminate rivals, and reward obedience. So what if their majority is smaller than some might want - a majority is a majority. Which leads to the obvious task of checking with my contacts and getting their feel for the results of the last election."

"Uhm, Simon, that's been analyzed to death for the past couple of years," Gretchen pointed out.

"Yep," he replied with a grin "But not in light of this new information. It's not just a case of win or lose, but rather who got in and out that was unexpected, and why. Did certain polling districts go against type, or was it the entire riding? We don't tell them what we suspect, of course, but most of them just love to talk politics and process to anyone who expresses the least bit of interest."

"Or even no interest whatsoever," said Gretchen dryly, remembering election-time encounters with some of Simon's friends.

"Well, that would seem to be what we need to do," announced Yancey briskly. "Simon, you go to Ottawa for a few days to talk with your contacts there. Charlene, you go back to your old job and start writing stories. I guess we need to work out which stories to do first, but that's another discussion."

Both of them nodded slowly, their minds obviously elsewhere working on the implications of the strategy.

Gretchen looked at Yancey and asked, "What about me?"

Yancey sat for a moment, then opened his mouth to speak but was interrupted by Charlene, "She comes with me."

All eyes turned to her.

"She's got data analysis skills that I'll need, and is pretty good at the computer security thing. My people are good, but she's better at a lot of things."

Yancey nodded, "Good idea. I wasn't too keen on you heading back into the mouth of the lion's den on your own. Gretchen, what do you think?"

Gretchen snorted, "As if I'd let her go off on her own."

"And you, Yance, what about you?" enquired Simon.

"I cover your backs, doing the back and forth thing. I *am* an experienced private investigator, after all," he said with a grin. "I'll be the field investigator, poking into the shadows and being the eyes and ears for the rest of you."

"That's a good plan for our side of things," opined Gretchen, "but how can we stop the Sword's immediate plans? Our best efforts so far have only slowed them down. Everything we've talked about so far is longer-term stuff. To take down this Harvest of Souls thingie, we're going to need serious help. Like from the police. Why can't we go to the OPP with this?"

Simon and Yancey looked at each other, and then at Charlene. The older woman sighed and said gently, "And tell them what, love? The Sword has far too many informants and bought cops. By the time our evidence got examined and kicked around, they'd have heard about it and sanitized the situation. No, the boys are right. We need to figure out exactly what the Sword is planning before we can even hope to figure out how to stop whatever it is."

They all looked back and forth at each other and then at Yancey.

He gave a broad lopsided grin and said, "All right, we have a plan. Now let's dive into that data and save some kids."

Charlene held up her hand and asked quietly, "What more can we do with the data, Yancey? Haven't we gone about as far as we can?"

She was a bit taken aback when the others just chuckled.

148

Yancey shook his head and said with a smile, "Nope. We've just scratched the surface, taking a quick look at it all and grabbing at the obvious bits. Now comes the hard part where we really dig into it. Rather than looking at the contents of the emails, we can look at the headers. From there we can build up an idea of who is talking to who."

Charlene shook her head somewhat irritatedly, "Yes, yes. Reporters have been doing that sort of thing for years. Take the data and figure out the network and relationship patterns."

Simon decided to step into the discussion, "True enough, but if we add timestamps to that we can see how the communications might vary over time. Maybe correlate that with known events, and maybe figure out if certain personnel are associated with certain actions or events."

Still smiling gently Gretchen piped in, "It's like the networks you and I have been looking at with the original data, but fancier."

By this time Charlene's expression was becoming more thoughtful. She pointed a finger at Yancey and asked, "OK, now how does the content of the email figure into the analysis? Beyond the obvious, that is."

Yancey smiled broadly, "Now you're getting the hang of it. Yes indeedy, we can do lots of fun stuff with the content. First step is to build up a concordance, and see what subjects are most important to which person. Then we can run a sentiment analysis on it to get some idea of how they feel about that subject. Maybe get a feel for nationalities and education levels."

Charlene was nodding thoughtfully by this time. "So we can build up an idea of who is talking to whom and about what, figure out who the important players are by how well connected they are, and get some idea of timelines.

Hmm, are there any attachments to those emails?"

"Good thought," said Simon, "and, yes, there are. I'm assuming that you want those analyzed for their metadata as well as their content?"

"Oh yes. Many a story has been broken because of a document's metadata," Charlene answered, smiling happily at the memories. "But what about the encrypted data?"

Yancey jumped in at this point, "We'll keep trying, but for now I don't think we should worry too much about the ones we can't crack. For one thing, analysing what we've got will keep us going for a while. For another, the simple fact that someone is sending or receiving a message with non-standard encryption is pretty telling in and of itself. Oh, and we can take an even closer look at the email headers."

Charlene just looked at him with a puzzled look and shook her head slightly in puzzlement.

"Lots of good stuff can be gotten from the email headers, love," interjected Gretchen. "Sure there's the date and name of the sender and recipient, but also the route that the message took to get from sender to recipient. That gives hints as to the locations of each, but that can get obfuscated by using a VPN. Still, worth a look."

Yancey agreed, "Even if the physical location is obfuscated, it is still worth associating specific people with specific routings. Building up patterns is really important, even if what the different elements mean isn't apparent right away. Over time, details leak out and finding out the truth about one element can illuminate several more. Or help provide a sort of fingerprint that can be used to identify a specific player."

"Speaking of the players," said Charlene, "Gretchen and I came up with an idea that might tie into the email analysis. Gretchen, love, maybe you might want to explain about those group ownerships?"

"Oh, yes, I had almost forgotten about those," Gretchen said excitedly. "So, I was going through the analysis you guys did. Good stuff, guys - I appreciate the time pressure you were under, but some of the shortcuts you took bothered me. I took a different approach and it appears that different Sword cadres control different groups of companies, and the membership in those groups varies somewhat over time. Charlene?"

The older woman leaned back as she took over the explanation, "Once Gretchen explained that to me, the first thing that occurred to me is that sometimes transfers of control end up with bruised feelings. Unhappy people sometimes say things they shouldn't, to people they shouldn't. I was originally thinking along the lines of putting out some feelers once we get out of here, but maybe a better first step would be to check those emails of yours?"

Simon and Yancey looked wide-eyed at each other, then hung their heads sheepishly.

Charlene laughed happily, "You forgot about checking your email data against the old database, didn't you?"

For a change, Gretchen didn't harangue the guys because, in truth, she hadn't thought about that either. Not that she was going to tell them that. Instead, she changed the subject by asking the men about the estimated timeline for all this analysis.

Yancey looked thoughtful for a moment before replying, "We've done some initial first-looks, but there's too much to be analyzed by hand. The first-pass cleanup looks done, and we've made a stab as writing some initial scripts to do some of the things we've just talked about."

He paused as he turned towards Charlene, "It's all raw

data, and anything we do in terms of automated cleanup or analysis has to be thoroughly checked before we can trust any results. It's a big job, and really easy to get absorbed entirely by it, I'm afraid. But I'd say we could start to have something useful in a couple of days, maybe. That sound about right, Simon?"

Simon nodded thoughtfully, his gaze focused somewhere in the distance. "Yeah. Probably have the basic communication network relationships in a day, and the rest of the raw analysis done and put into databases a few days after that. Interpretation of it all is going to take a lot more time than that, of course. It's gonna be a huge help having four of us working on it, especially when we start integrating the new data with the old."

Charlene smiled softly at the sight of her three young friends gazing into the distance and nodding softly to themselves. She'd had many opportunities over the years to witness specialists wander off into their own minds, and was honest enough to admit that even reporters were prone to it at times. She let them be for a minute, then snapped her fingers several times to get their attention, then asked the group, "Are we going to get any more work done tonight?"

They all agreed that perhaps it was time for a cup of cocoa and then to bed. There was a lot of work to be done, but sometimes it was essential to take care of the human side.

CHAPTER SIXTEEN
Bleak Homecoming

Yancey slowed the Busted Flush and pulled over onto the wide gravel shoulder, then came to a stop. They were passing through Timiskaming en route to North Bay, and from there to Ottawa. After leaving the cabin they had filled up on gas and supplies, paying with a credit card, so they were well supplied for the trip.

"What's the problem, guys?" queried Gretchen.

"We've been driving for a while and I thought we could use a break. It's easier for Simon to read the teeny-weeny symbols on the map when we're stopped. His eyes aren't what they used to be."

At the sound of his name the aforementioned navigator raised his head, muttered a rebuke that promised dire consequences at some future date, and then said that there was a picnic site indicated just down the road. Glancing at the gas gauge, he added that it might be time to start thinking about where to gas up.

Gently pressing the accelerator and pulling back onto the road, Yancey then turned to Simon and said, "Hmm. Good thought. Let's talk it over when we get to the picnic area."

Simon sighed and nodded his agreement.

"There's the picnic area," said Yancey a few minutes later. He pulled off the road and drove into the area, then stopped the car and turned it off. The sudden silence spoke volumes as they looked around. There were three picnic tables arranged in a large semi-circle, none of them in very good repair. The tops were warped and peeling, and the seats were about the same. The fire pits looked as though they hadn't been emptied in a very long time. The waste containers were full, and there were empty bottles of beer and liquor scattered about. A short distance away was a collapsed swing set and crumbling wooden climbing steps. Yancey and Simon got out of the car and stood leaning against the roof as they looked around. The ladies quickly followed and stood off to one side, gaping.

"Holy crap. This looks like something from Little Shithole," observed Yancey.

"Yeah," agreed Simon, without sounding happy about the memory. "I thought other parts of the North kept their facilities in better shape, though."

A glance from Charlene caused Simon to quickly add, "No, truly, it really did look like this when we left. Maybe not so many empty bottles, though. And not much better when we were young. There was a similar sort of swing set when we were kids, but that didn't last for more than a few years. Guess the Mayor never did manage to get those government grants he was always talking about."

"Oh, he got them, alright," Yancey said with a sneer, "he got them year after year, but somehow only certain projects for certain people got the money. Damn little for community projects, unless someone's pockets got lined."

Gretchen opened her mouth to say something, but Yancey raised his hand to silence them all. His mood had changed from friendly banter to an intense focused alertness.

"Someone's coming. Stay close to the car, each next to a door, and make sure that it is ajar. Be ready to jump in if I give the word."

They could all hear the sound of tires on gravel, becoming louder as the unseen vehicle got closer. Within a few seconds the sounds were just beyond the brush that hid the road, and then a car suddenly pulled into the picnic area and came to a sudden stop. The paint scheme and roof lights showed it to be an OPP cruiser.

"Let me doing the talking, keep both your hands on the roof of the car, and don't move," breathed Yancey quietly to the others.

They could dimly see a figure behind the windshield, sitting there gazing intently at them. Then it opened the door, climbed out and donned a hat, then strode purposefully towards them. As the figure drew closer, they could see that it was a good-sized man wearing an OPP uniform, the eyes hidden behind sunglasses. The mouth was working, as if chewing on something.

"Good afternoon, folks," said the officer in a strong but neutral voice. "Might I ask what you're doing here?"

Yancey could merely stand and gape at the officer. No one said anything, and the officer was obviously beginning to become irritated and was opening his mouth to speak when Yancey interjected, "Corporal Dundee?"

"That is *Sergeant* Dundee, sir, and whom might you be?"

"Corp ... that is, Sergeant Dundee, sir, I'm Yancey Franklin. I knew you in Little Shithole. I grew up there."

Sergeant Dundee stood immobile except for his chewing, his face impassive. He removed the sunglasses and carefully studied each of them. Then his face lit up with a smile and he strode forward with his hand extended. "Young Mister Franklin, it has been a few years. You are looking well," he said shaking Yancey's hand warmly. Then he turned to Simon, "And Mister Thane. There is never the one without the other," as he shook Simon's hand equally warmly. Turning to the women he said with a twinkle in his eyes, "And a good day to you, ladies. I am Sergeant Donald Bates Dundee, in charge of the OPP detachment for these parts. You're travelling with a dubious pair here, so be sure to watch yourselves."

Charlene stepped forward with a laugh and extended her hand, "We have learnt that all too well, Sergeant Dundee. But they're more knights errant than scoundrels these days, so we keep them around. I'm Charlene, and my young friend is Gretchen."

Gretchen greeted the Sergeant with a lop-sided smile and a wave. He greeted each in turn, then stepped back to regard Yancey and Simon with a warm, if puzzled, smile.

"Of all the people that I never expected to see again, you two are about top of the list," he finally said. "I think we need to catch up on things."

The last was stated with a firmness that would allow for no disagreement, as he motioned towards one of the dilapidated tables. Simon grabbed their portable chairs from the car, and hauled them over, then started setting them up. Gretchen grabbed a large thermos of tea, a handful of plastic cups, and a bag of pastries. Charlene reached into the car and emerged with a ground sheet which she placed over the table to give a somewhat more hygienic eating surface. The Sergeant looked a bit startled at the flurry of activity, then stepped back and watched in amusement at the well-synchronized motions of the group. It was obvious that they were used to working as a team, and he nodded slightly to himself in approval. The refreshments were also welcome to him, as it had been a long morning patrol covering for one of his subordinates. Within a short period of time, they were all sitting comfortably, sipping on tea and munching on pastries in companionable silence.

Dundee looked questioningly at Charlene, then said, "Excuse me for staring, ma'am. But you look familiar, somehow."

He paused for a moment or two and then snapped his fingers, "You're that reporter. You did that article on the OPP a few months back. And others, now that I think of it. You're very good. Haven't seen too much from you lately, though."

Charlene smiled warmly at being recognized. "I'm more of an editor these days than a reporter. That piece about the OPP was just an excuse to get back out in the field for a change. Well, that and covering for one of my reporters who came down with a nasty flu."

Dundee returned her smile. He understood all too well that being in charge often interfered with the fun parts of a job.

"So, what brings you to this neck of the woods, with young Franklin and Thane, here? Working on a story?"

He accepted a cup of tea poured from a thermos, and held it in his hands while it cooled. He found the heat soothing on his hands. He found himself feeling the cold in them more keenly these days.

Charlene calmly answered, "Of a sort, yes. By the way, how did you come to know these two troublemakers?"

Dundee grunted a laugh, and Simon and Yancey bent their heads to hide embarrassed grins.

"Ma'am, these two troublemakers and me go back a good many years. Not bad kids, you understand, but sort of ... mischievous, I guess you'd call it."

Charlene responded with a laugh and nod. Gretchen

made no effort to hide a broad grin.

"So, gentlemen," Dundee said turning to the men, "what have you been up to? You never went back home, as far as I know. Not that there was ever much there for either of you, and certainly nothing or no one to go back for. And I see that you still have that damn car."

While waiting for a response he blew on his tea and took a careful sip. He was pleased to discover that it was actually reasonably good, and took another small sip.

"True enough, sir, but I'm working on a case," replied Yancey evenly. "I don't know if you've heard, but I got my private investigator's license and that's what I've been doing since I left. Simon, here, got his business degree and has been working on Bay Street. Well, that is until that tank attack blew everything to hell down there."

The Sergeant allowed as he had heard about the attack.

With a rapid exhalation that puffed out his cheeks for a moment, Yancey continued, "Well, Simon heard a few things about some business deals that didn't appear to be kosher, so he came to me. I started poking around, and there appeared to be some elements in common with an old case of mine. My first case in Toronto, actually, less than a year after I left home. It involved runaways from up North being promised a better life in the city, which ended up being in prostitution, and then some of them started disappearing."

"Runaways are a fact of life up here, Mister Franklin," Dundee replied softly. "Once they get to a big city, well, the streets are not a welcoming place."

The mood of the group was quite sombre by this point. The others had heard about this case while at the cabin.

"No sir, they are not," replied Yancey grimly. "But these kids were being groomed for the trip in their communities, and then funnelled to specific front groups in Toronto.

Mainly girls, but some boys, too. Someone in their communities spent some time playing with their heads, getting them primed and ready for specific groups in Toronto, which on the surface were hostels aimed at kids from the North. Once in Toronto the real head games started, and they were made ready for the job. But once in a while one of them would disappear, and any of their friends that started asking questions disappeared, too. The local cops didn't care. To them, one or two fewer hookers was no big deal. I looked into it, and the missing girls all had the same sort of background - all from small towns in northern Ontario, and all left while still in high school. Digging into the computer records indicated that they even had some teachers in common, even though they came from different towns. That got me intrigued, so I dug some more into those teachers. Turns out that they moved from school to school up North every few years. And within a year after their arrival, the number of runaways would increase, then decrease after they left. I went to the cops, but they still didn't give a damn. So I went after the so-called hostels, but the ones that I knew about closed up shop, seemingly overnight. At the same time, the Department of Education computer records of the schools got locked down tight, citing 'privacy concerns'. Dead kids and dead ends. And nobody seemed to give a damn. Then some of the cops started hinting that I shouldn't be poking around so much, or bad things could happen. So I stopped looking into it, took a few smaller cases to pay the bills, then left Toronto for Ottawa. Been there ever since."

Yancey paused for a moment before plunging on. "Then Simon mentioned to me about the strange activities of some companies, and a couple of the names matched some of the clues I found in that case. I remembered a few strange goings on up here just before I left, so I figured it might be worth checking things out. Gretchen used to work with Simon and needed a change of scenery, and Charlene is always on the lookout for stories and wanted some time away from the job. So here we are."

Dundee had listened carefully to this story, and his face made it plain that he was not too sure about it. Then he looked carefully at Yancey. "Oh, and you just happened to remember details from a years-old case of no consequence?"

Yancey lifted his chin, and looked at him with pain-filled eyes sunk deep into a stern face. "No one else cared, sir. *Somebody* has to care. *Somebody* has to hold those responsible to account. All those kids, for all those years. All those years and up to the present day, sir. There's more to it than just turning a few runaways into prostitutes. It has to be stopped."

"Good for you, lad," murmured Sergeant Dundee. "Do you by any chance remember the names of those hostels?"

"One was 'The Golden North', and the other 'Friends of Wandering North'," replied Yancey instantly.

Dundee took off his hat with one hand, and with the other scrubbed at his short, grey hair. He sighed deeply and looked off to the side, seeing things that only he could see. Unpleasant memories.

"I got transferred out of Little Shithole just after you two left. To a place a couple hundred klicks east of there, to help with a couple of small towns. Had quite a spate of runaways a few months after I got there. Nothing out of the ordinary, really, just kids getting unhappier and unhappier and then one day ... just gone. No clues about where they went, either, except for the last one. The boy hitched a ride on an eighteen-wheeler, and the driver reported it after hearing a report on the radio. The kid was long gone, of course, but a small pamphlet had dropped out of his pack during the ride. Picture of a big happy sun with outstretched arms, welcoming a figure with a backpack. Promised a warm cot, a warm meal, and advice if it was asked for. No questions asked, and no payment required. All funded by ex-northerners who wanted to give back. Called themselves 'Friends of the Northern Wanderer'."

The others could only sit and stare incredulously at him.

He sighed, then shook himself and continued, "I tried to follow it up, but got nowhere. The pamphlet was put into the evidence locker, but somehow went missing. Enquiries to the police in Toronto either went unanswered or came back claiming that no group of that name existed, that the address given was a fake, and that runaways were always to going to happen, so stop bothering them. I kept hammering away at it - there were too many kids and too many parents to ignore. The spate of runaways in the area stopped, so I was told to drop it and get back to real police work. Runaways were a fact of life, I was told. Well, I cut back on the enquiries but kept poking away at the police databases anyways, and wrote up some reports. Then when promotion time came around they gave me my sergeant's stripe and transferred me here. Ran it as one-man detachment for a couple of years. Kept my nose clean, then got a few constables assigned. Been here ever since, in charge of the small detachment. Still tracking runaways and odd disappearances, but nothing officially. Sort of a hobby, you might say."

Dundee then gave a probing look at Yancey, "From what you've been saying, though, there's a lot more to it."

It was not a question.

"Yessir." Yancey replied. He glanced quickly at each of the others, then inhaled sharply before continuing, "A lot more. We don't have all the details, but we know something about the people behind this. These are very bad people, Sergeant. Bad people with deep pockets and powerful friends."

Again, Dundee regarded each of them carefully before continuing. "And yet here you are - all of you - digging into things that powerful bad people don't want dug up."

Charlene chimed in, "Yes, Sergeant. And we will continue to keep digging. As horrible as this is, it is only the tip of the iceberg, I can assure you."

She glanced at Yancey, who nodded his encouragement to keep going.

Taking a deep breath, she plunged on, "Sergeant, we have reason to believe that this group is involved not only in recruiting children for prostitution, but also for other types as sexual services, possibly even for sale as slaves to foreign buyers. There seems to be an entire network setup for collection, transportation, and distribution. Big money and big names. And one good reporter has already been killed following this story. That's why I'm here 'incognito', as it were, and not alone."

Dundee shook his head and said an emphatic, "Shit," then rubbed at his face with both hands.

The group held their collective breath at this. They had put a lot of trust in this near-stranger, perhaps too much.

Lowering his hands, and raising his head to look at them, Dundee said in a firm voice, "There have been a lot of strange disappearances all over the North over the past few years. Too many to be explained away as runaways. On top of that, recently the number of orphans disappearing has increased sharply. The rumours talk about runaways being drawn into prostitution all over Canada, but that never made sense to me. Budget cutbacks over the past few years have all but gutted Social

Services, and even the OPP is getting stretched too thin up here. We can't handle anything but the most urgent cases these days. What's more, there have been some altogether strange things happening. Soldiers scurrying about, supposedly on manoeuvres. Too many police officers turning a blind eye to things that they shouldn't. Companies have always treated the North as if it is a pool of resources to be strip mined as desired, but lately it's gotten a lot harsher. Like you said, Mister Franklin, too many people have stopped caring."

He paused and looked thoughtful, as if weighing decisions of consequence. No one dared to say anything.

"Mister Franklin, Mister Thane, ladies - why are you doing this? What is it that you think you can do?" he said finally.

"Sir," said Simon quietly, "they aren't all-powerful or all-knowing, as much as they would like everyone to think so. By accident, we have each of us learnt too much to back away - even if we wanted to. As for fighting them, well, we've done that successfully before, believe it or not. We have to try. We have to hit them so hard, so publicly, that the authorities have to step in whether they want to or not."

The others each nodded, then Yancey took up the narrative, "Things are coming to a head, and soon. If we could get access to the records of disappearances that might help us to figure out where and when the next big collection is being made."

Dundee sat motionless for some time, studying each one in turn. Finally he nodded to himself as if he'd just come to a decision. Reaching inside his jacket, he fumbled with a hidden pocket for a moment and then pulled out a data stick. He held it out to Yancey, who stepped forward to take it. Dundee's eyes bored in Yancey's, and he kept hold of the stick as Yancey put his own hand on it.

"I haven't been able to do anything officially. Not after they reprimanded me. It might be nothing or it might be something. But like you said, someone needs to look into this and stop it. I haven't said a thing about it to anyone at my posting, but one of the constables recently made enquiries about how I might be coming along with it. Not wiseass cracks, but enquiries as if it were more than an old cop's obsession. So I put everything onto this data stick and erased it off my computer. This is all of it. All there is."

"Sir," said Yancey evenly, "I swear to you, on my honour, I will follow up on this and track down whoever is responsible."

The others had each sat upright, with equally intense looks on their faces.

Dundee let go of the data stick with a big sigh. He was in deep now, for better or for worse.

"There's one more thing you and your team have to know, Mr. Franklin …" Dundee said quietly, "there's an APB put out for you. All of you. Something about being material witnesses to some unspecified serious crime. Anyone seeing you is supposed to detain you, alert HQ, and wait for a special team to come and take over. Never seen anything like that before."

He paused and a faraway look came into his eyes. "Policing was all I ever wanted to do, and I've always been proud to do it. Proud of the OPP, too. Sure it has its problems, but it does a *lot* more good than harm. There are a lot of good officers, too. I've seen too much good being done to say anything against it. But …" he sighed and paused for a heartbeat before continuing, "but there's always been a small dark spot in our work here in the North. Not big, but something not right. In the past year or two that small dark spot seems to have grown. And lately there's been some strange things coming out of HQ. Like that APB on you."

Dundee turned to Yancey, "I always rather hoped that you'd join the Force, Mr. Franklin, but I also knew that probably wasn't in the cards."

He sighed and shook his head.

"You all had better get going. I can give a false sighting report. Say that you're heading west along the 560. That'll take the heat off you as you head to Ottawa, if that's still where you want to go. But that's the best I can do, I'm afraid."

He paused for a moment, then grunted and pulled out his wallet and pulled out some money. "Better not use any credit cards for a while. Here's some gas money. No, no, just take it. You're going to need it."

The group each thanked him profusely, and everyone shook his hand. Yancey handed the data stick to Gretchen, "Make copies of it as we go."

They all turned to get into the car. Yancey was the last, and he paused just before getting in, turned to Dundee and said firmly, "We'll get them, sir," then he got in the car, started the engine, and pulled carefully away.

Dundee stood and watched them leave, staring after them long after the Busted Flush was out of sight. What he hadn't told them was that he'd heard about Yancey's case in Toronto, although not in detail, from the local police who had made enquiries about the background of a new private investigator who kept sticking his nose into places it didn't belong. He'd passed along the little he had, just omitting a few of the more colourful youthful indiscretions, and that was the last he'd heard. He'd gotten a similar request from the Ottawa police a couple years later, but that was strictly a routine background check, and he had made sure to give them the same information. That was the last he'd seen or heard of young Mr. Franklin until today. The lad had good instincts, and a good soul that had risen above a rough childhood. It looked like the youngster had chosen the correct path, after all, and was still sticking his nose into secrets that others wanted kept hidden. The thought of that pleased him, and rather a lot.

He decided that he could afford to wait ten minutes before filing his report, and knew just how to word it to deflect attention from them. There was going to be hell to pay for this if it was ever discovered, he thought, and a lot more than he had let on. At least a reprimand, and maybe a demotion - or even the loss of his pension. But that didn't matter. He was a police officer, sworn to serve and protect. Nothing had ever before stopped him from fulfilling his oath, and nothing ever would.

CHAPTER SEVENTEEN
The Finance Minister's Press Conference

It was a medium-sized press room, with a raised area at the back for several sets of video equipment. This time, however, there was only a single video crew from the AJF News Service. The front of the room held the usual lectern, with rows of Canadian flags to either side. The backdrop was filled with graphic representations of red maple leaves. Near the bottom, but still visible by the video cameras, was the logo of the ruling Conservative Reformation Party. The room held more empty seats than filled ones. The media had been told in no uncertain terms that they should only send experienced financial reporters, given the nature of the event. There were no other details of what the announcement would be, so all the media, including the newspapers, went along with the request. They were learning that it was better and easier to go along with government requests than not. This was another part of the stratagem that had come from the government's deep-think teams.

The quiet buzz of whispers amongst the reporters ceased as three men strode into the room. Two of them were rather large, with the look of attack dogs, and they took positions at either end of the stage. The third man, older and thin to the point of emaciation, radiated a strength that caused all eyes to focus on him as he strode up to the lectern. He stood there, hands lightly grasping either side of the lectern, no notes visible anywhere. In truth, no notes were required. This was the Finance Minister, and he had a fearsome reputation for keen intelligence and lack of mercy for any who questioned him.

"You are all no doubt aware of the Prime Minister's recent amazing successes at obtaining new treaties with our economic allies. These treaties have led to ancillary, less formal, economic agreements that will be of immense benefit to Canada. Building on these agreements, and after fruitful discussions with international business leaders, this government has decided that it is important to help shepherd along the influx of new companies into this great nation of ours. We have taken as our model the examples of world class economic and corporate guidance to be found in the United States of America, in their states of Delaware and Nevada. To this end, Canada will be modifying its laws governing incorporation to rationalize them into a single, simplified set of regulations that will apply across the country. This will allow a company to be incorporated as a special federal corporation, with governance to be carefully regulated according to a new, comprehensive regulatory regime. This new regulatory regime will include a new Court of Commercial Appeals, which will deal exclusively with the new federal corporations. We have taken every measure to ensure that everyone's rights will be protected, while at the same time streamlining the process for these new federal corporations. This new corporate structure, combined with the improved regulatory environment, will encourage companies, new and existing, to set up shop in

Canada. You will be supplied with background material to assist you in preparing your stories. Now, are there any questions?"

The Finance Minister recognized the representative from AJF News, listened to the question, and gave a detailed response. The more cynical among the reporters thought that both the question and the answer sounded well-rehearsed.

While this was going on, several of the reporters positioned at the rear of the room began whispering amongst each other. It was quite obvious that only a couple of favoured reporters were going to be recognized, so the others kept themselves amused whilst listening with half their attention.

"Bloody wonderful ..." snorted one older reporter softly, "another hollowing out of the Canadian business scene."

A young reporter turned, and with something of a sneer replied, "How can you suggest that? This actually sounds like it might be useful - for a change. Anything to attract more companies to Canada is going to help." He followed this up with a disrespectful sniff.

Another reporter, also somewhat older, replied with a sneer of his own, "Kid, you might want to check your facts. Delaware, despite being the place where tonnes of companies are incorporated, including most of the Fortune 500, is home to no corporate headquarters. It's all done on paper, or rather computer files. Hell, there are special incorporation agencies that handle all that, and one tiny office can hold the incorporation records for tens or even hundreds of thousands of corporations."

The first reporter chimed in, "It's all done there because Delaware corporate law shields companies and their directors from scrutiny from governments, shareholders, and the general public. They have special commercial courts, too, but they exist solely to protect the corporate interests."

The second older reporter added, "Yep. And it's often used as front for getting corporate assets offshore to evade US taxes, or to launder dirty money. Everybody wins except the ordinary citizens."

The young reporter just gaped at the two older ones.

"Come to think of it," said the first reporter, "weren't there rumours floating around about possible changes to our banking regulations? Hmph, maybe they're trying to turn Canada into a sort of offshore tax haven? Now wouldn't that be something?"

Both of his colleagues looked incredulously at him, and then sat back in their seats with eyes narrowed as they thought furiously. The younger one alternatively looked at one, then the other. He didn't follow everything that was said, but it sounded like there might be a story in it, if he could just figure out what they were talking about.

About that time the press conference came to an end, and the Finance Minister strode off the stage with his bodyguards in tow. As the reporters filed out, the first reporter turned to the younger, "Say, kid, don't you work for Charlene Blaverston? She'll love to hear about this."

"Sort of," was the reply from his young colleague, "but hadn't you heard? Ms. Blaverston's gone on sabbatical. All broken up about the death of her friend, apparently. I had just joined her group when she left - never had a chance to meet her, actually. The new editor had fired the old financial guy, so he told me to cover this. Gave me his ID badge, too, so that I could get in. Luckily the photo was kinda blurry, and we both wear similar glasses."

The heads of the two older reporters jerked back. This was news to them. They each grabbed an elbow of the young reporter and guided him away.

"Hey, kid, you know it's traditional for the old financial reporters to welcome the new ones with a drink, right? Well, here, let us buy you one or two."

"But it's not even lunchtime," protested the youth.

"All part of the tradition, kid, all part of the tradition."

CHAPTER EIGHTEEN
Home Sweet Home

Yancey and Simon were driving through Ottawa, looking around with somewhat bemused glances. It all seemed so normal, so ordinary, so unchanged. Rather anticlimactic, if truth be told.

Each had tried and failed several times to speak, but words simply failed them. Gretchen and Charlene had flown back to Toronto earlier that day, and the car now seemed quite empty without them. After everything they had been through the past few weeks, it just seemed wrong, somehow, for things to be back to normal again. All their carefully discussed plans seemed so out of place here, with so many people laughing and going about their normal daily routines. The urge to simply accept this normality and put aside the previous events as a bad dream was very strong in both of them.

"Time to turn our phones back on, Yance?"

"Not yet ..." replied Yancey tersely, "we need to drive around a bit more. Get a feel for things."

Suddenly he grinned, "Damn, we've been out of the loop too long. Too long in the bush."

As tense as he was, Simon had to return the laugh, "Yep. Hope the ladies are handling being back in a big city better than we are. Probably are, come to think of it, city-bred folk that they are."

Despite the gradual loosening of their nerves, both kept a careful watch around them, alert for spying eyes. Although the splitting of their forces was really a necessity, no one was very happy about it. Taking a commercial flight to Toronto seemed like the best way for Charlene and Gretchen to go back home. Charlene was quite confident in her ability to stay off the radar, in terms of living arrangements, and to ensure their security overall. Given that, and the necessity for Simon to start checking out his contacts in Ottawa, they really had no choice but to split their forces. They really did need to plug back into the normal world at some point, and it might as well be now.

Yancey and Simon ended up driving around for a bit before settling down. Yancey knew of a couple of decent rooming houses that would probably be a safe place to stay at for a while, and they needed to go to one of them before too much longer. Then there was the question of arranging transportation for Simon. There was a slight possibility that Yancey might be able to pick up a car "off the books", but public transportation was still a viable option. A lot depended on how things stood with Yancey's various contacts. Then there was the question of when to start plugging back into the phone system and Internet. Charlene and Gretchen could plug in anonymously at the newspaper, but for the guys it was a dicier proposition. The initial plan was to keep any access to a minimum, and to keep in touch only a certain times, via digital dead drops. Charlene had called it 'Moscow Rules', but only Yancey had understood the Cold War reference.

After being passed by several police cruisers without

being pulled over, they began to breathe more easily. After discussing preferences, they decided to go to one of the boarding houses and establish a base of operations, however temporary it might be. Yancey had used both of the places in the past. The owners were unaware that he was a private investigator, and were willing to ask no questions so long as the rent was paid in cash. Their first choice was a large house with a garage that might have parking spaces available. Upon their arrival, the owner was happy to see him and was able to provide two modest rooms at a reasonable price. To Yancey's pleasant surprise, the garage was empty and available for a small extra fee. Upon getting the keys, Simon and Yancey hauled up a backpack each and put them into their rooms. There was little enough to go into the backpacks, but it was expected of them, Yancey explained. It was important in a field op to do whatever was normal for that time and place.

After parking the Busted Flush in the garage, Yancey decided that a walking tour of the area would be the best way to familiarize Simon with the lay of the land. At the very least, he wanted to point out a couple of places best avoided after dark, and a couple of dicey-looking areas that were actually quite safe. They walked around for an hour, finding the various bus routes, taxi stands, and places that a car might park without being obvious. The modest exercise and lateness of the hour had sharpened their appetites, so they stopped at a small restaurant that had changed ownership from the last time Yancey had been in the area. As they walked in, they were engulfed in a wall of delicious smells.

"Wow, Yance, that smells good. I'm starved."

Yancey's stomach growled in agreement as they sat down at one of the few tables. Hunger aside, everything really did smell good, and vaguely familiar. He sighed then reached for the menu to study it.

"Looks pretty good, Simon. Smells a lot like Mama's place, too. Hope the food's as good. Some of the dishes are the same, too. Maybe we should try those?"

A good-looking young woman came to take their order, then wandered off into the back after they'd made their selections. In a few minutes she returned with their food, and presented it to them with a smile before wandering to the back again.

They meant to eat slowly and savour the meal, they really did. Alas, the combination of good food and their recent culinary privations caused them to practically inhale it. About half way through the meal the feeding frenzy subsided, and they began to eat more sensibly. That is, swallowing one mouthful of food before starting the next. Eventually they slowed down to a more civilized pace, and allowed themselves time to breathe between mouthfuls. This allowed them to speak, and they used this new ability to make complimentary comments about the food.

Wiping his mouth with the napkin, Yancey leaned back and said with a satisfied exhalation, "That was good. Not as good as Mama's, but damn good."

"Gotta agree with you on that, Yance. The spices aren't quite the same, are they?"

"And what is wrong with my spices?" said the voice of the young woman who had served them, now sounding rather irritated.

The men spluttered and blushed as they looked up into her face. Except this time she was not smiling - no, not at all.

"Uhm, miss, uhm, that is …" Simon choked out.

"Sorry, ma'am, we meant no disrespect," Yancey

managed to get out before pausing for breath. "This food is very similar to what a friend of mine used to cook, and I've eaten at his restaurant all the time for many years."

"And just who is this 'friend' of yours?" said the young lady in a tone that was becoming increasingly cool.

Yancey looked over at Simon for support, but his friend seemed too paralysed to help. Typical Simon, thought Yancey - he'd break into a Sword stronghold without a care, but he'd quail before an angry woman.

With a small sigh Yancey replied, "We all called him 'Mama'. Even his wife."

"It be good to see that my name be remembered. Eben by folk who never call, no, and never write," a deep voice intoned sadly.

Both Yancey and Simon jerked their gaze from the young lady to a figure that had moved silently from the kitchen without their noticing.

"I can handle these two, Uncle," said the young lady in a prim voice that brooked no interference.

"Mama," breathed Yancey, who was somewhat overcome at the sight of his friend. Then he jumped to his feet and the two friends clasped hands and shook them vigorously. Both were mighty glad to see each other. Simon just leaned back in his chair and beamed. The world had just taken a major turn for the better, as far as he was concerned.

For his part, as soon as he got over the initial surge of joy, Mama looked carefully at his young friend. There were changes to be seen by those who knew and cared for him. New lines at the corner of the eyes. The sight of new, half-healed scars on Yancey's hands and face, and the way he stood and slightly favoured parts of his body worried him, for Mama had a pretty good idea of what those meant. None of that worry showed on his face, though, as

176

he greeted Yancey and then Simon. These were good boys, and he was very glad to see them again.

"Uncle, I hate to break up your party, but I really need to keep the front clear. Don't make me call Auntie. She told me to keep an eye on you while you're here helping me, and not to let you cause any trouble."

Mama laughed and herded his friends to the back, where the kitchen was. The young lady collected their plates and passed them to the men, stating firmly that they could at least do some work while they gossiped. The young men grinned in reply, and went to work washing dishes while catching up with Mama. Yancey began by apologizing for making him a target for investigators. Mama raised a large eyebrow at that, for he had been hoping that would be news he could spring on them. That 'askance look' was one that Yancey was all too familiar with, and he had to laugh out loud.

Still chuckling, Yancey told Mama, "Hey, I *am* a trained investigator. The report I saw mentioned that there'd been full cooperation and no follow-up would be required."

All humour left his face as he added, "These are very bad men, Mama. I'm glad that you took my advice to be completely open with them. I was worried about that."

Mama snorted as he replied, "T'were easy 'nuf to do, Yancey-boy. I know cops, and they weren't any sech thing, no matter what badge dey flash. So I ticken de patois an' be de dumb black mon, eager to please de white bosses. I know they type. Give dat type what dey expect, and life be easy."

The young men laughed at the thought of Mama playing dumb. He was many things, they knew, but dumb was most certainly not one of them. And they, too, knew the type of mental blindness that Mama referred to. Knew it, and always treated it with the contempt and mocking it deserved.

After that there was a companionable silence as dishes got washed and the kitchen got cleaned. The familiarity of the work combined with the reunion of old friends was calming for all, and Mama carefully noted how both of the young men now seemed much less tense. Less like soldiers returning from battle, and more like the boys he remembered. The new lines and intensity around the eyes, though, that stayed on both of them. There was also a new toughness to them, as if they had been tested - and tested hard - but come through with their souls intact. Mama didn't speak of this to them, but simply helped them feel welcome and back home. He knew that the boys would tell him what they could, when they could.

"Where you boys be stayin'?" Mama enquired.

Yancey told him, and Mama nodded his approval, then carefully said, "You both be welcome to stay with us, you know."

The young men shared a quick look and then shook their heads.

"Thank you, Mama," said Yancey with sincere thanks in his voice, "but we're still on a case. An incredibly dangerous one. I can't expose you to any more trouble than I already have. Just knowing me has put you - still puts you - in harm's way. No one knows we're back in town, but that's going to change soon. We can't see you anymore after this. It's just too dangerous for you."

Mama looked carefully and steadily at each of the young men in turn before he spoke in a low intense tone.

"You be good boys, and I t'ank you for your concerns. But I know a bit 'bout bein' in harm's way. The wife and me know how to take care. Tell me what you need. Me'be I c'n help, me'be not. You got a good place to stay. Do y'need a car? Dat Busted Flush stand out lik'a sore t'umb,

Yancey-boy."

Simon and Yancey could only stand there and blink. It took all of their control not to let their jaws drop. Nothing ever fazed Mama, but this was a side of him they'd never seen. Yancey took a deep breath to clear his mind as his thoughts raced. Mama had been a source of friendship and strength for many years, one that he'd depended on. This new battlefield was incredibly dangerous for everyone, combatants as well as the innocent. The silence stretched between them for a handful of heartbeats.

"Mama ..." began Yancey as Simon put a hand up to stop him. Yancey looked at his friend and gave his head the tiniest of shakes, and Simon stood back with a neutral expression.

Yancey looked at Mama intently before continuing, "This is really dangerous, Mama. Think drug cartel or terrorist dangerous, but worse. We need all the help we can get, and that's for sure, but ... but you're family, Mama. I can't let anything happen to you."

The tightness in his throat prevented Yancey from continuing. Mama gave him a gentle look and nodded his head, then he looked at Simon and saw a nod agreeing with everything Yancey had said.

"Boys," Mama said carefully, "I t'ank you for that. More than I kin say. But if this be as bad as you say, better I have some warnin' and knowledge. No? And I know how to cover m'tracks so they's clean and stays clean."

The two young men stared at each other for a moment, and Simon nodded. Yancey turned back, and getting a firm grip on his emotions thought furiously about what to tell Mama. He paused for a moment and stared intently at his friend before continuing.

"OK," he began with a slight sigh, "we *are* up against it, Mama. Simon and I helped stop another attack by the bastards that used the tank to attack Toronto. After that, we rescued Simon's friend Gretchen from another bunch of those bastards."

Yancey paused to control his emotions as he looked down at his hands and flexed them carefully. Mama saw this and said nothing. This only confirmed his suspicions. Finally Yancey looked up and continued.

"But we found out about some other operation they're planning. Not an attack, so far as we can tell, but transporting a cargo of some sort. We need to gather enough information to figure out what that is and how to stop it. We also need to figure out who they are and how to stop them at an organizational level. Gretchen's gone back to Toronto to work with a contact of hers on that end. Simon knows some people in Ottawa to talk to. We've survived so far by being invisible, off everyone's radar, but we can't do that anymore. So we've got to make ourselves impossible to find, yet still be out and about. I can do a lot to shield our activities on the Internet, and we can use burn phones to communicate, but we have to physically move around to see people. That's going to expose us, and we don't know who their agents are or where they are."

Mama nodded thoughtfully, "There be any way to identify dem?"

Simon nodded, took a notepad from his pocket, drew the lemniscate figure on it, then tore out the page and handed it to Mama.

"That's their symbol. They're awful coy about it being seen, but they do enjoy being sly about displaying it. Almost like a secret handshake."

Mama studied it carefully, then held it up to show to the young lady who had been quietly standing behind the young men.

"Seen this around, Camille girl?"

She studied it carefully, as both Simon and Yancey looked aghast at each other and then at Mama. Neither of them had realized that she had been listening.

"No. But I'll take a look around. Might be a person or two I can ask about it, maybe. Have to think about that. Come back tomorrow, about this time," she said in a clipped, neutral tone.

Simon gaped at her for a second then blurted out, "But this is dangerous. Mama, you can't let her in on this."

The young lady just looked at him disdainfully and said, "I know how this sort of thing is done. Now leave out the back door and come back tomorrow evening for supper."

Mama just chuckled at their confusion, then added his own encouragement, "Best be listenin' to her, boys. I'll be workin' on gettin' some new wheels for ya's both. Oh, and stay in your room 'till then. Work on your 'puters or the like. And your plannin'. Oh, and here be some food so you not be starvin'."

With that, Mama started filling up bags with various foodstuffs that would last two hungry lads until the next evening.

"Uncle!" declared a prim female voice, "How do you expect me to make this place profitable when you insist on giving away my food?"

Mama just chuckled and passed the food to the young men, and escorted them out the door.

As they walked back to their rooms, Simon and Yancey were both shaking their heads in wonderment.

"What was *that* all about, do you think?" asked Simon in a low voice of wonderment.

"Pfft ..." exhaled Yancey sharply, "damned if I know. I suppose I should be more worried about it than I am, though. But if Mama says something is so, then it is so, and no doubt about it. Though I don't recall him ever mentioning a niece. Cute, too."

Simon grunted his agreement with that last comment.

They walked along in silence and were almost back at the rooming house when Yancey turned to Simon and said with a big sloppy lop-sided grin, "You know, I do believe that I'm starting to feel better about this. I really am. Wonder how the ladies are making out?"

Simon just laughed as they walked into the boarding house, "Raising all sorts of hell, I have no doubt."

* * *

Yancey and Simon tried to make productive use of their time while waiting to regroup with Mama. They decided to stay in their rooms, the better to prevent being seen by hostile eyes. Weeks of hiding had made them a bit paranoid.

Yancey had arranged for access to the boarding house's Wi-Fi system. For one thing, it was the expected norm. For another it gave them some access to the Internet for the first time in weeks, albeit in a limited fashion. It was far from a secure or fast connection, so they decided to limit themselves to checking a couple of throw-away accounts that each of them had. As an afterthought, Yancey suggested updating their map applications. Both activities were normal and innocuous.

Simon let out an exasperated sigh, "Damn, I wish I could check my real email accounts. You sure we can't even send a message to Gretchen and Charlene from here?"

His query was met by a patient shaking of the head from Yancey. "Nope. Not even if this were a normal stakeout. Places like this get a discount from their service provider by disabling the encryption options and allowing deep packet analysis for marketing purposes. Encrypting our messages isn't an option, because it raises too many flags, and we don't want that right now. So we act boring and dumb, not calling any attention to ourselves."

"I understand that, but when can we get back to normal? Gotta do that sometime, Yance. We all talked about this. Staying off-line for this long raises others sorts of flags."

Yancey nodded in agreement. "True enough. But this isn't the place, that's for sure. Maybe at a coffee shop or book store. My security protocols can make that safe from anything except TEMPEST monitoring. Alas, it isn't unknown for those public places to have that sort of equipment, believe it or not. Not too common around here right now, but I had a couple cases that uncovered some of it. Their Wi-Fi was fully encrypted, and that was a big selling feature for the service. What the customers didn't realize was that the business had bypassed the encryption by monitoring the computer itself, not the communications. The law is kind of vague about the legality, but no police force will lay charges over it."

Simon's eyes went big. "What? I haven't heard a thing about that. Isn't that equipment bulky and expensive?"

Yancey answered with a snort, "It used to be - but technology marches on, my friend. The cases I was involved with had the sensing antennas embedded in the tabletops and fed the data to the recording computer. That's the easy part, actually. The hard part is teasing useful information out of the raw signals - the keyboard signals, the video signals, that sort of thing. There's actually several security firms that have done that sort of analysis for many of the most popular computers. The analysis software is only moderately expensive, and requires a pretty powerful computer to do the analysis in real-time, but it is all off-the-shelf stuff. A lot of the larger airports have it, actually, run by the various security services. Everyone can honestly claim not to be listening on the communications, or decrypting secret data. Which is kind of true, at least in the legal sense. The faint emanations from the device being monitored are not legally a signal, as such. Of course, there are rumours now that the laptop and tablet manufacturers want to incorporate anti-TEMPEST technology to guard against such monitoring but the various national security services won't let them. And on it goes."

Simon listened to this with a look of stunned incredulity. "How the hell do you keep up with all this? No, wait. How do you even manage to function with that level of required paranoia? Seriously."

Yancey answered with an easy laugh, "Long practise, my friend. That and whiskey."

This was greeted by a less-than-happy look.

"No, no, it's really not that difficult," Yancey insisted with a wave of his hand. "Keep your communications encrypted, that's the basic thing. Then just be careful about what you say and where. Basic situational awareness, really. As for the fancy monitoring stuff like TEMPEST, well, all of my devices are shielded. Their emissions can be attenuated with a thin conductive material - I paint the inside with conductive paint and use an off-the-shelf conductive skin around them. Not perfect, but will beat all but the more advanced sensors. I've experimented with putting small spoof-generators inside a laptop, but that tended to interfere with the operation of the device. So anything that requires real security I reserve for doing at my office. Which leads us to the next item on our to-do list." Yancey sighed and shook his head slightly.

His friend responded to the sigh with a laugh. "See, that's what I was talking about with that paranoia crack. You really don't want to trust a site that's been visited by Bad Guys, do you?"

Yancey snorted before replying, "Laugh all you want. Yeah, I can scan it six ways from Sunday, but a real pro will still be able to monitor it somehow. Like I told you and the others, it all depends on how paranoid the Sword operatives were. Based on the emails from the Tears facility, I should be in the clear. As should you. And the ladies, so long as they don't draw too much attention to themselves. But the fact that one of them got over-eager and torched my apartment makes me wonder if they took a similar overachiever approach to my office."

Simon grew serious at the reminder, and nodded.

Then Yancey grinned, "But that is for tomorrow. Tonight ... we feast!" With that he reached over to grab the food that Mama had packed, and quickly laid out a meal for them on the small desk.

That got a laugh out of Simon as they both fell upon the food with a will. As usual, filling up on excellent food boosted their spirits considerably. Both agreed that Camille seemed to be getting the hang of this cooking thing, though they agreed that it would probably be safer not to say that to her face.

Sprawling as best they could in the modest room, they sat in comfortable silence for a time. "It was sure great to see Mama again," opined Simon. Yancey nodded his agreement.

"Yeah. I will admit to having a load off my mind after talking with him." He paused for a moment and sighed, "But I can't help but feel that maybe I was too eager to drag him into this. Whaddya think, Simon?"

His friend thought a moment before replying. "Well, we

185

really could use some help, Yance. We've been freakin' shit lucky so far. That won't last, you know. Can't last."

Yancey nodded thoughtfully in reply, but didn't say anything.

Simon continued, "And, geez, he seems to actually have some experience with this sort of stuff, somehow. You ever hear about that?"

Shaking his head, Yancey quietly said, "No. Not a word of anything like that. I've known him since I got to Ottawa, years ago. Had a lot of heart-to-heart's with him, too. He's a good man, Simon, a truly good man. Can't say I'd ever want to be stupid enough to cross him, though, not after seeing him deal with those punks that tried to shake him down for a protection racket a few years back."

The memory of that brought a happy smile to both of them. Mama had easily swatted the punks away when they tried to attack him, so they had come back at night and firebombed the front of the deli. Yancey tracked them down and ensured that their precious cars became so much inert metal, and all their on-line accounts trashed. Simon had tracked down the banks they were using and caused some grief concerning those. Mama had no more problems after that. The police weren't too happy, but couldn't do anything officially. They became somewhat happier when the gang decided to move out of town, apparently deciding that Ottawa was not a nice place to live.

Yancey face suddenly twisted as if he'd just bitten on a very sour apple.

"What's up, Yance?"

"Gah. Thinking about being shaken down by punks reminded me of all the bills that are due or past due or soon to become due. Office rent and bandwidth charges and VPN accounts - oh, my."

Simon laughed, "Well at least you won't have to pay rent on your apartment any more. Wonder if you'll get your security deposit back?"

Yancey favoured him with an unhappy glare. "Oh thank you so very much for that. Oh, crap - that reminds me that I need to get in touch with the landlord." He paused for a moment then added with some heat, "Double crap - I need to talk to the cops about that, too. I can explain being out of town, I guess, but I won't be able to explain not contacting them about it. Can't leave it too long or they'll assume that it's regarding a case and then they'll want to know about that. GAH!" He buried his head in his hands.

Simon nodded in sympathy, his own face a study in unhappiness, "Yep. That reminds me about my own bills that are piling up. We'll both be alright for a while, but something needs to be done to get some money in."

Yancey nodded sadly. "You know, this saving the country thing is a lot of fun and all - but the pay sucks."

"Hey, Yance, do you think Mama needs someone to wash the dishes at his deli?"

Simon deftly dodged the pillow thrown at him.

CHAPTER NINETEEN
Return Of The Dragon

The security guard sat upright in his chair, resplendent in his new and freshly-pressed uniform. The security station itself had been there forever, and was as lavishly marbled and chromed as the rest of the entrance foyer. Old though it was, its size and location was like a breakwater, forcing visitors up to him before they were able to pass through the gates on either side. His chair was raised off the floor slightly, giving him a psychological and tactical advantage. Young and new to the job, he exuded an imposing hawk-eyed vigilance that would brook no impertinence or funny business from any visitors. He rather fancied himself akin to Heimdall, guarding the rainbow bridge into Asgard.

Thus it was when the doors flew open, he readied his steeliest gaze with which to turn upon the visitors. In marched two women, neither of whom he had ever seen. The older of the two opened her coat to reveal a corporate ID badge attached to the collar of her suit. The younger woman trailed behind with a slight smile on her face. As they arrived at the front curve of the security desk and prepared walk around, they halted as the newly-installed turnstile failed to let them pass. Turning to the guard, the older woman took off her ID badge and waved it at him. He motioned them to return to the front of his desk, it being beneath his dignity to move his chair to the side.

Taking the card from the frowning woman, he examined it then stated brusquely, "Sorry, ma'am, but this is an outdated identification. All regular employees were issued new identification last week. How did you get this?"

"Excuse me. I'm Charlene Blaverston, editor-in-chief of the investigative reporting desk. I've been away for a few weeks and didn't get the new ID."

The guard looked at her suspiciously, "Security was informed that all employees had been issued their identification cards. We would have been told if there were any outstanding. If you'll just stand over there without blocking the doorway, I'll arrange for someone to come down here and we'll sort this out, by the by. Oh, and could you both please have any and all personal identification ready for inspection. Thank you for your cooperation."

Mindless adherence to security protocols was his first mistake. His second was missing the storm clouds gathering on Charlene's face when the turnstile failed to open. His third, and final, mistake was being rude and dismissive to her. Gretchen tried very hard not to openly grin, and for the most part succeeded. She truly loved to see smug functionaries get eviscerated.

Charlene fixed him with a basilisk stare that would have caused anyone who knew her to run away.

"Young man," she began coolly and calmly, "I am Charlene Blaverston, editor-in-chief of the investigative reporting desk. I have held that job for a good many years, and have worked at this newspaper for longer than you have been alive. Is Frank Hayden your supervisor?"

At the guard's slow nod, Charlene continued, her voice

189

still calm and even, "Then call him, please. Right now. Tell him who is waiting at the front desk. Do it now, please."

The guard shook his head in negation, "Sorry, ma'am. Supervisor Hayden is in conference, and not available for some time. You can either wait by the door like I advised earlier, or come back later in the day. Perhaps you'd like to make an appointment."

Charlene looked at him for the space of several heartbeats, not blinking. Then she smiled, reached into her pocket, took out her phone, and dialled a number. The guard was beginning to feel as if he was somehow losing control of the situation, so he tried to tell her not to make phone calls inside the building, but Charlene just made shushing movements with her hands, turned sideways, and otherwise ignored him. Gretchen's hidden grin became somewhat less so.

"Hello? I'd like to speak to Frank Hayden, please. Oh, in a meeting is he? Is this Christine? Hi, Christine, this is Charlene Blaverston. Yes, thank you, I did have a nice bit of time off. Look, I'm having an issue at the security desk out front. It seems that new badges got issued, and the guard won't accept the old one. Yes, I agree totally. Oh, that would be lovely, thanks so much. No, no, please don't let anyone else know I'm here, yet. I was *so* hoping to make it a surprise in the newsroom. Why, thank you, dear. Yes, I'll be sure to drop by to say 'hi' before the end of the day. Bye."

With that, Charlene terminated the call, returned the phone to her pocket, and turned to face the guard with a serene, yet somewhat predatory smile on her face. The guard's aplomb was beginning to slip away, but he kept his face composed as he returned Charlene's stare. The tableau remained unchanged for several minutes. Then the sound of feet running quickly down the stairwell behind him grew louder and louder, and several seconds later the stairwell door was flung open and feet were heard running on the marble floor towards the guard station. The guard jerked his head to the side as a figure ran to the locked turnstile and halted, leaning over it to talk to him.

"Supervisor Hayden!" blurted the guard, "I …"

"Oh, shut up and buzz her in," said the middle-aged man in clipped tones. He turned to Charlene and said in a much warmer tone of voice, "Ms. Blaverston, I am so happy to see you back! You left so suddenly, and no one knew how to get in touch with you. I *do* apologize for this mix-up. There is no excuse for your old badge being rejected without checking with the Security Office immediately." This last was directed towards the guard, who hastily unfroze and pushed the appropriate controls that unlocked the turnstile with a loud *buzz*.

Both of the ladies moved through the turnstile and Charlene extended both of her hands towards Hayden and warmly clasped his hands.

"Oh, Frank, it is so good to be back among friends. Don't worry about this nonsense. These things happen. Oh, could we get a visitor badge for my friend?" she said turning and nodding at Gretchen, who gave a slight wave to him.

Hayden removed a spare badge from his pocket and handed it to Gretchen, who attached it to the lapel of her jacket.

"Just give my office the particulars at your convenience, Ms. Blaverston. You know I don't like to bend the rules, but in your case, well …"

Charlene shook her head firmly, "No, Frank, I appreciate that but let's not get into the habit. Gretchen, dear, please pass the guard your driver's license. We'll pick it up on the way out."

Gretchen handed the young guard her license, tilting her head in a brief, sympathetic nod. To his credit he gave a small, weak smile in return, then bent his head to enter the information into the security system.

"Where are you off to?" queried Hayden.

"The newsroom. No one knows that I'm coming, as I was rather hoping for it to be a surprise. Would you care to join us on the trip up? I'd love to chat and catch up," said Charlene with a warm smile.

Hayden led them to the elevators, pressed a button, and chatted happily with Charlene as they waited for an elevator to come. He was careful to make sure that Gretchen felt included in what was essentially a private conversation, and both ladies were impressed by his gentlemanly manners. During the wait, and the long trip up, Hayden gave her a short summary of the new security measures installed as a result of the terrorist attack not so long ago. Charlene nodded and made approving noises, then asked about who had taken over in her sudden absence. Hayden carefully studied the elevator's display for a moment before answering in a soft voice, "Jud Philson."

"Oh, Christ," Charlene couldn't help but blurt out.

They were almost at their destination, so Charlene asked quickly, "How bad?"

As the doors opened, Hayden said quickly and quietly, "Watch your back."

Charlene flashed a grin at him, then turned to Gretchen and gave a quick waggle of her thick eyebrows. Gretchen and Hayden exchanged glances, and he tempered his with a soft, knowing smile. He would have liked to stay to watch this, but he really did have other business to attend to. Not least of which was scheduling a session with that young security guard on security protocols and the value of using professional judgement.

The two ladies stepped off the elevator and into the office. With a brief glance around, Charlene led the way down the aisle, looking straight ahead. Gretchen, for her part, was happily looking around. She had never been inside a newsroom before, and was determined to see as much of it as she could before the fireworks started. Despite all their discussions and planning, this was very much an unknowable event. It all depended on whether Charlene had been declared MIA or cut loose. So far, it looked like the former.

What struck Gretchen about the newsroom was the continuous melange of sounds. Not quite a roar, but certainly not silent. Their passage was continuing along unnoticed, then Gretchen felt, rather than saw, a silence ripple out around them as they walked. A ripple of silence followed by a change in the sounds. The muted roar of the melange gave way to a ripple of whispered conversations. They approached a walled office at the end of the room, the only private area in the entire department. The door opened up with a bang, and a young-ish man stormed out to investigate why he wasn't hearing the sounds of proper work. He came to a halt while still mostly in the doorway.

"Hello, Jud," said Charlene, calmly standing before him, "good of you to keep things moving while I was away. But now I'm back. Why don't we step into *my* office and you can bring me up to speed on what I've missed."

She stepped forward, giving Philson no choice but to step back or step aside. He chose to step aside to let both ladies into the office, and then he closed the door. Although startled, he quickly regained his composure, and went to sit down behind the desk, leaving the ladies standing bemused. With a brief puzzled look at Gretchen who had assumed a carefully neutral expression, he looked at Charlene, leaned forward, put his folded hands on the desk and spoke in a pleasant-sounding voice, "Well. This is a nice surprise. No one expected you back. So soon, that is. What can I do to help you today?"

Charlene looked around briefly, snagged one of the visitor chairs and motioned Gretchen to take one herself. The visitor chairs were new, replacing the ones which she had carefully chosen to be both comfortable and welcoming, with rather hard, uncomfortable ones. She snorted softly at the sort of mentality that indicated.

"As I said, Jud, I'm back. I want you to bring me up to speed so that I can resume my duties."

Philson looked at her carefully before replying with his most engaging smile, "Well now, Charlene, I'm sure that we can arrange something for you. Why don't we find you a desk in the bullpen outside so you can ease your way back into things? No need to rush into anything. Take it easy for a few days, take it slow. Better for everyone that way, don't you think?"

The last was said as a statement, not a question.

Charlene favoured him with a polite smile, of the sort one might use on a child who was having difficulties in understanding. She let the silence drag on for five seconds, then ten. When she finally spoke, it was in quiet voice with a neutral tone, "Jud, I am the managing editor-in-chief of the news department, and I am back to resume my duties."

"Charlene, you have to understand - you left suddenly and have been away for some time. Without telling anyone where you were or when you were coming back. We've covered for you ... *I've* covered for you. We're really busy, and now isn't the time to start upsetting things. What I think ..."

"Jud, am I or am I not the managing editor-in-chief of this department?"

This was delivered in the same quiet voice, but the tone was no longer neutral. In fact, it was rather chilly.

Philson sighed like a man pushed to the edge of his patience after trying to deal with a difficult subordinate, "Now see here, Charlene ..."

"Jud. Am I or am I not?"

The voice was almost as quiet, but the tone was like the crack of a whip as Charlene stared mercilessly at Philson. He started to unfold his hands and lean back, then changed his mind and re-folded them, sitting not quite forward enough to be comfortable. The tip of his tongue flicked out briefly to nervously lick his lips. This was not going according to plan. Dammit, the old bat had no right to do this to him. No right at all. He sat back suddenly, and his hands tightly gripped the side of his chair. Then he relaxed them and drummed his fingers briefly before gripping the arms again, as calmly as he could manage.

"Well, I suppose strictly speaking that's true, Charlene. I mean, there's been nothing official, as such. I mean, you should have told Them Upstairs before coming here."

Charlene smiled frostily at him as she purred, "You mean I shouldn't have offered you the respect and courtesy of coming here first?"

Philson began to sweat. Dammit dammit dammit. It just wasn't fair. He was just starting to get this place whipped into decent shape after she had ruined it - let it chase irrelevant stories, let it alienate advertisers and all sorts of powerful people. He was just starting to prove to Them Upstairs what modern news coverage really meant, and how profitable it could be. He opened his mouth to speak.

"Get out of my chair, Jud," said Charlene sweetly.

Philson could only gape at her, frozen with his mouth open.

"Get out of my chair, *now.*"

Although the volume of the voice was at a normal speaking level, the tone of command was so strong that Philson found himself jerking unthinkingly to his feet. He came around the desk, alternating apologies with complaints about the treatment she was giving him after all that he had done for her. Charlene simply stood, pointed him to the chair she had vacated, then walked around the desk and sat in the chair. *Her* chair, despite the desecration of it by someone unworthy of being called an editor. She rotated slowly side to side, glancing outside the window at the frozen tableau of reporters gazing towards them. She snorted, shook a finger at them, and they all scurried back to work. Many of them were smiling. The normal auditory madness returned at full volume within seconds. Charlene gave a brief, happy sigh. She was home.

Then she turned to Philson, who stood in an upright sulking pose in front of her.

"We really are very busy, Charlene. Lots of stories on the go."

She favoured him with a kindly smile, "We always are, Jud, that's what we do. Now, why don't you take a few minutes to give me an overview, then we'll call a meeting of the senior reporters to see where everyone is with those stories of yours. Hmmm?"

Philson nodded, then jerked his head at Gretchen, and asked, "What about her. What's she doing here?"

"Jud, say "hello" to Gretchen."

Jud just glanced at her, gave a dismissive snort, then shook his head. That's all the department needed - another favourite friend parachuted in to do busywork.

"So what, exactly, are her duties supposed to be?"

Gretchen gave him a brief, closed mouth smile and waggled her fingers at him in greeting. This guy was really beginning to annoy her.

Charlene shook her head slightly, "You'll find out soon enough. In the meantime, just carry on with the overview."

After a somewhat stiff start, the overview went better than expected. Unexpectedly, despite his reputation, Philson was actually quite well organized and had a good handle on the current lot of stories. There were more minor stories than she would have liked to see, and too few investigative ones. Particularly lacking were the hard-hitting investigative ones that their office was known for. In fact, in her absence none at all had been started, and some of the ones she had authorized were cancelled. Those would bear asking more questions about later. It was inevitable for some investigations to end up in the waste basket for any number of valid reasons, but something didn't seem quite right. Philson finally wound up his summaries, and everyone sat back in silence. For Gretchen, this was all fascinating stuff, but she could tell that Charlene wasn't happy about something.

Charlene asked Philson how soon a meeting of the senior reporters could be convened. He said with some pride that it could take place right away, as he made sure they were all at their desks working for most of the day. Charlene told him to gather them all up into her office and he hurriedly went about his assigned task, closing the door behind him. Charlene closed her eyes and let out her breath in an exasperated rush. Gretchen cocked an eyebrow at her, but said nothing.

Charlene grinned wryly, "In some ways things aren't so bad. But in others ..." she let her voice trail off.

In answer to Gretchen's quizzical look she added, "He's been changing the editorial direction of the stories. Too careful not to not dig too deeply, playing it too safe. That's not how we do investigative journalism. Not here, thank you very much."

People started filing in and arranging themselves around the big table. It might not be a round table, Charlene thought to herself as she got up from behind the desk, but she'd set them up against any roomful of knights. They were better. They were *journalists*.

Motioning to Gretchen to stay where she was, she went to her usual chair at the table. Philson only needed a brief glare before he moved. The ensuing discussion gave Charlene better clarity about what was going on with the current lot of stories. Finally, as the discussion wound down, one of the older reporters pointed towards Gretchen and asked what her role in all this was.

"Ladies and gentlemen, may I introduce to you Gretchen Sinclair."

Gretchen nodded respectfully to the group and several of them nodded back - but not all.

"She's going to help us with a variety of things. Her primary task will be to help with the info-security for our department, focusing on any devices taken out of this building or left at home. She'll help to set everything up with the latest security software and, equally importantly, help with ensuring that our communications remain as secure as possible. This isn't in any way meant as a slight against Frank Hayden and his team, but Ms. Sinclair has more experience with these matters. As investigative journalists we have an obligation to ensure the safety of our sources, as well as ourselves. Yes, Jud?"

Philson leaned forward with a condescending smile on his face, "I'm sure you mean well, Charlene, but there are corporate computer security programs that are applied company-wide. There is, in fact, a real cost savings to be realized by standardization. And while you were gone, I set up ... or rather, contracted to be set up ... special software to ensure the safety and integrity of all our communications and data. It's all government approved software, too. In fact, by using their qualified vendors, we saved a bundle."

A number heads nodded in agreement with Philson. Charlene could only look at him with a stunned look on her face. No one saw Gretchen go white as she put her hand over her mouth in horror.

"Let me get this straight, Jud ..." began Charlene in a hollow voice, "you installed government-supplied security software on all of our devices? On the phones and laptops as well? And let an outside contractor do the work instead of our own people?"

Philson nodded happily. It had been a major managerial coup for him, and had made Accounting very happy.

"Did you at least have our own people check their work?" asked Charlene hopefully.

"Of course not," was the terse reply. "There was no point. It was all fully guaranteed by the government, and came with an on-site warranty service. No need for us to waste manpower on it at all. They even came here to work on our desktop machines."

"Gretchen ..."

Without a word, Gretchen got up and went to the computer at the desk. She pulled a memory stick from her purse and plugged it in, then clattered away at the keyboard for a bit.

"Scanning. This may take a few ... oh shit. This is not good."

All eyes turned towards her, dubiously. This had all the

earmarks of some foolish demonstration. Philson openly sneered.

"Charlene, does Mr. Hayden have computer people on his staff?"

Charlene looked at her quizzically and replied in the affirmative.

"Tell him to send them up here. Right now. Bring their kits. Now, now, now."

Philson started spluttering, but Charlene picked up the phone on the table, dialled a number and snapped, "This is Blaverston. Computer security breach in progress. Newsroom. My office. Right now," then put the phone down.

All eyes were swivelling between Charlene and Gretchen. Less than a minute passed before a pounding of feet was heard, and seconds later a team led by Hayden burst into the room. Charlene pointed at Gretchen, who stood up and waved them over. Hayden indicated for one of his team to check it out. The young man sat down in the chair staring at the screen while Gretchen explained what was going on, in a low intense voice. He calmly sat there, then as Gretchen began pointing out what was happening, his eyes went wide and his head jerked up.

"Sir ... she's right. Something ... several somethings that shouldn't be here are active on this computer. At least one of them is sending information somewhere. Do we disconnect, shut down, or attempt a trace-back?"

Hayden and Charlene had been watching this without speaking. Hayden opened his mouth, but Gretchen spoke up first, "Shut down. I recommend an immediate normal shut down of all the computers to halt the downloading. A normal shutdown won't look suspicious. We can try a trace-back later."

Hayden looked at his tech specialist, who nodded his

agreement. The rest of the team added their own agreement, and Hayden simply told them to go to it. The team worked quickly, getting every computer in the newsroom shut down.

"Where do we go from here, Frank?" asked Charlene.

"Hmm, suggestions, people?" Hayden queried of his team.

One of them spoke up quickly, "Take all the laptops to the basement. No Wi-Fi there."

The rest of the team quickly accepted this idea, so Hayden asked, "What about the desktops? Move 'em or analyze in-place?"

Another team member spoke up, "Take this one to the basement first. Once we find out what we're dealing with, we can decide how to proceed."

Hayden nodded and told his team to get started. As all the laptops in the newsroom were being collected, Hayden turned to the group around the table and told them to use their cell phones only if they absolutely had to, and even then only for voice calls. He then went off to help his team carry the compromised equipment to the basement. As he went he nodded to Charlene and said that he'd be in touch. As he closed the office door, he gave Gretchen a wink. She returned a wan smile.

Charlene opened the door, leaned out and yelled, "Stop lollygagging around you lot. We still have work to do. It's Old School time, boys and girls. Get to it."

Throughout all this, Philson had sat back in his chair, a stunned look on his face. After the office door closed, people sat back down around the table chattering back and forth, occasionally glancing at Gretchen, who had sat down in one of the uncomfortable visitor chairs. She wasn't quite sure what to do with herself, but she projected an image of calmness despite her inner turmoil.

"It was the latest and greatest in computer security."

All eyes turned towards Philson, who had lifted up his face and was speaking in a pleading voice, begging them to understand.

"They came and gave a presentation and talked to Them Upstairs and everything was supposed to be perfectly safe."

Charlene asked quietly, "They? Do you have names?"

Philson nodded unhappily, looking like he was about to burst into tears, "I've got some brochures and stuff. Demos and powerpoints are on a data key they gave me. In my desk. Ah, goddamn it, Charlene, I was just trying to get things right. They came and made it sound so perfect and … and … oh, *fuck*."

"Jud," Charlene said softly and calmly, "you got scammed. It happens. Now, what I want you to do is to go to one of the unused desks in the bullpen and write down everything you can remember. Treat this like an investigation. Hell, there's probably a good story in this. You want in on this, Jud?"

Philson looked up at Charlene, wiping at his eyes. The angry, hungry look on his face was all Charlene needed to see. With a thankful nod he exited the office, closing the door softly behind him. Charlene turned to the others, looking at each in turn. They still all looked somewhat stunned by the sudden turn of events, but Charlene's mention of a story had gotten their attention. She could see the hunger of a predator in their eyes. Damn, she loved this job.

"You all heard that? There's a story here, even if it means we endure some ribbing. And don't doubt that we will. But, and this is a big but, what if we aren't the only ones? Who else has fallen for this scam? Is this some criminal gang or is the government? There are lots of

202

questions here, people, but first we have to warn the other media outlets. Gretchen, can you put together some information about what people should be looking for?"

Gretchen nodded, looked around the top of the desk, then grabbed a pad of paper and began writing.

"As soon as she's done, I want you all to start calling up your contacts at the other media. Start with the newspapers, then radio stations, and so on. Tell them we'll fax over instructions on what to look for. Yes, fax. Every newsroom worth its salt has one, and now it's gonna get used for something other than spam. After you've done that, we'll start the investigation. Make photocopies of Jud's notes once he's done, then we'll meet back here to discuss them. Oh, one more thing. He gets a byline."

This was greeted by sneers, jeers, and groans, but Charlene was adamant, and she looked intently at each and every one of them in turn.

"Hey! That's enough. Yes, he screwed up. We all have. But he's one of us now, despite his MBA and management roots. Everyone who works on a story gets a byline, you know that. And, who knows, we may even be able to make a real reporter out of him."

The groans that greeted her this time were of a more collegiate nature. Young Jud had shown some talent, however misplaced, and in all honesty this latest idiocy had sounded good to all of them at the time. So they were willing to cut him some slack and chalk up his being something of an asshole as due to his exposure to management.

Damn, thought Charlene to herself, she really did love this job.

All the reporters trooped out of her office, after being admonished to finish the stories they were currently working on, or pass them on to the junior reporters. They still had a newspaper to put out, after all.

Charlene closed her eyes, sighed and shook her head smiling. Then she turned to look at Gretchen, who was sitting quietly at the desk.

"Are things always this chaotic?" asked Gretchen with something of a plaintive note to her voice.

"Sometimes they're worse," Charlene assured her without a trace of humour in her voice, "much worse. But this went a lot better than we expected, all in all, didn't it?"

Gretchen laughed so hard that she had to wipe the tears from her eyes.

"At least they won't be thinking of me as some useless drone that you foisted on them."

"No, they won't, will they? That'll help, a lot, when you start helping out with the advanced data journalism stuff. There are some bright minds here - I wouldn't have it any other way, of course. But what you and Simon and Yancey do is at a whole new level. I learnt an awful lot these past couple of weeks."

"Thanks, love. You know, I'm really looking forward to this. I really am. But I hope I didn't step on Security's toes with all that. Security people can be awfully touchy about outsiders putting their grubby hands on their systems."

Charlene assured her that wouldn't be a problem. She'd seen Hayden winking at Gretchen, and that meant he was satisfied.

Gretchen was happy to hear that, but couldn't help admitting that she missed Simon and Yancey.

"Yes, I know what you mean. It's nice to be back at work, but I do miss them."

"And their silly sense of humour."

"Always made me laugh."

"Of course, then there were the burp and fart jokes."

"And the puns."

"Suddenly I'm not missing them so much."

"Hell, no."

They looked at each other and laughed. Some things never got old.

"Well, my girl," said Charlene breaking the nostalgic moment, "we need to get you down to HR and get you officially on payroll. The company's gotten enough free work out of you."

CHAPTER TWENTY
Deliberations Of The Council

It was a modest room. Not so much stark, as unburdened by extraneous distractions. The table was round, and was large enough to seat twelve people comfortably, with a computer at each position. There was a carafe of water and a glass of plain design for each participant. The chairs were comfortable without being overly soft. The lighting was sufficient to the task of reading many documents for a long period. It was, in short, designed for real work without inflicting the distraction of discomfort.

The door opened and in walked the twelve participants of the meeting. Each of them wore simple, loose clothing, all in shades of light grey. There were no distinguishing marks of office upon any of them. They each moved to their assigned chairs without undue haste or noise. There was no wasted motion, but it was obvious that they did not consider smiles and nods to be wasted, for they greeted each other warmly without speaking. When all were seated and had greeted each other, one of their number raised a hand.

"I am the First Ascendant, and I speak for Infinity Ascending."

This announcement was greeted with a polite bow from each of the others.

"The Twelfth will now lead us in our prayer for Divine guidance."

The appointed man, for they were all men, bowed his head and intoned a simple, eloquent, and heartfelt prayer. At the end, everyone joined in the "amen".

The one called the First raised his hand again for their attention, for such was their way.

"Brothers, this meeting is to discuss a variety of issues of importance. Before we begin, is there any old business that needs to be discussed?"

There was a low murmuring between several members, but most shook their heads in negation. The First nodded to the dissenters, giving them the floor. One of them rose, bowed to all present, then spoke quietly.

"My pardon, brothers. There is old business, but it can wait. The matters before us are more pressing. We request, though, that the next meeting of the Ninth Level be allotted at least an hour's extra time to discuss these matters."

The First replied with a nod, "That is a reasonable request, and I thank you for your understanding. Now, is there any other old business?"

This time there was no indication of need, so the First carried on with the agenda.

"Brothers, we have a very full agenda for this meeting. I pray that you focus all of your attentions and powers of thought upon it. We have reached a critical juncture along The Path. The general velocity of travel has increased faster than expected. Although many projections have been borne out, there are a number of troublesome indicators and worrying trends. If I may, I would like to discuss the outliers before we discuss our successes. May I continue?"

All of those seated nodded their acceptance.

The First began his discussion with the status of the major competitive powers in the current situation. He refused to call it 'the game' or refer to the others as 'players' as so many of the Sword, and a few of his own council, did. He prefixed his discussion with an overview of the failed attempts of the Council to reach out to, and the Sword's attempts at exerting control over, these competitors. These major powers had all, for various reasons, developed a strong societal need to have colonies of some sort. Unfortunately the current state of the world precluded the creation of overt colonies, and the Council's efforts had been directed to heading off the crisis points that these needs would engender. The Sword had, over the years, come up with a standard ploy of creating or supporting nationalistic groups. These groups, by their very nature, became more focused over time and therefore more brittle and vulnerable to properly-applied control techniques. It was an often-successful technique used to good effect for the neutralization or control of many organizations, as well as nations. However, it often produced mixed results. At best.

The Sixth Ascendant was called upon to give a summary report on the current status of China. The main concern here was that the many years of stagflation had resulted in increasing internal unrest. In an effort to get more value for their investments, the Party had decided to massively increase investments in various offshore tax havens, expecting that this would be more beneficial in the long term. The unfortunate side effect of this was to drain off the funds required for domestic programs, causing further civil unrest. Part of this was caused by the increasing failures of the power-generation infrastructure.

China had invested heavily in 'green' technologies, such as solar and wind power, in an effort to wean itself off coal. In fact, they had produced much of that equipment for the rest of the world, as well. Unfortunately, the pressure to produce quickly and cheaply had resulted in systems that failed much sooner than expected, putting unforeseen pressures on other power-generation methods. Of course, this premature failure was soon going to become important in the rest of the world as well. Study groups, led by Ascendant Five, had projected that there would be a large and important opportunity to allow for a resurgence of nuclear power. This played in nicely not only with many of their client companies, but also with their overall philosophy of central control.

Another major cause of civil unrest was the large, and growing, gender imbalance. For many years, the availability of tests to determine the sex of a foetus, and the cultural propensity for male children, had led to an ever-growing excess of male children being born. The official numbers showed only a modest imbalance, but the truth was far worse than the outside world was allowed to know. The Party's response to this was to put as many of the excess males as possible into the armed forces, hidden in off-the-books Special Forces. This appeared to be working, but exactly how this might play out over time was unknown.

An even larger growing source of unrest was the problem posed by the so-called "ghost children". These were extra children born despite the official government policy of one child per family, and as such were not eligible for official recognition. Rich families could afford to buy official status for their extra children, but for most parents this was simply not an option, and this inequality created dangerous social tensions. The number of these ghost children with no place in society and no hope for their future was a small percentage of the total population, but their numbers still totalled in the millions overall.

Of more immediate priority was China's long-standing and insistent demand to be treated as a world power, despite their economic stagnation. This had been partially mollified by allowing them to establish bases in the Canadian province of British Columbia. These bases were informal, but de facto, colonies answerable only to the Chinese government. The most troubling aspect of these colonies was the almost total absence of women. This had caused problems with the local population, and was bound to cause problems that the local government could not ignore. After some debate the council decided that further study would be required before a course of action could be determined, although all concurred that the matter was of some urgency.

The concerns caused by Russia were outlined by Apostle Eight. Post-Putin Russia had become much less bellicose, but increasingly isolationist. It was on friendly terms only with former Soviet bloc allies, and even those links were becoming more tenuous each year. The current leadership was composed of what used to be referred to as 'oligarchs', who had clawed their way to power after the dissolution of the former Soviet empire. They seemed to be content to take care of their own internal issues, with little contact outside of that. They had created, if not an Iron Curtain, then at least one that was increasingly opaque. They were currently rebuffing all of the Order's attempts to reach out to them, although they had expressed an interest in gaining access to areas in northern Canada. After deliberation, the council decided to put this under active consideration.

Apostle Ten rose to summarize the problems posed by

India. It desperately wanted to be seen as an important player on the world scene, but its severe population pressures were causing problems for them. Like China, they also had a gender imbalance, but fortunately their own birth control strategies had not created a similar caste of 'ghost children'. Their solution for the excess males was also to hide the problem within their armed forces. Speaking of which, for some reason they continued their drive to build and maintain a large, complex, and expensive navy. Not to mention their ongoing research into and expansion of their nuclear weapons capability. They also insisted on attempting a large number of scientific 'spectaculars', although they had managed to maintain a modest presence in space at a reasonable cost. They were becoming increasingly demanding of recognition, and it was hard to know how mollify them. One suggestion had been to give them an economic foothold in eastern Canada, similar to what was granted to the Chinese on the west coast. After considering the issue, the council decided to set aside the issue for further study, but acknowledged that the matter was of increasing urgency.

After the summaries were completed, the First thanked each of the presenters and looked carefully, but confidently, around the table before continuing.

"It is important to remember that these territorial concessions are being made to channel these current and predicted social instabilities into peaceful and controllable ways along The Path. There are other potential flash points, of course, but these are the major negative inflection points seen by our analysts and their projections."

One of the Ascendants signalled his desire to speak. The First nodded at him and bade him to share his thoughts.

The Ascendant rose and bowed to his compatriots before speaking. "I have no insights to offer at this time, but would like to add a piece of information that may be too recent to have reached everyone's attention. It had been known to us for some time that several nations were working together on a secretive project inside North Korea. Recent intelligence reports indicate that this group includes China, India, as well as several powerful factions from the Middle East. Interestingly, Russia seems to be definitely excluded from this group. The details of the research being done inside North Korea is sketchy, but indications are that it is of a biological nature, possibly involving medical treatments of some sort. The research facilities are well-funded and appear to be of the highest quality. How this might be connected with what has been discussed so far, I cannot say."

With this, he bowed to the First and sat down. The First thanked his colleague for the valuable information, then paused and suggested a brief break. The next part was going to be difficult and fractious, and he wanted everyone to be fresh. After everyone had completed their refreshments and resettled into their positions, he continued.

"I am bringing up a potential, and I must stress that word, issue with our current operations," he said in calm, measured tones. "The Sword has always been our most important tool. They have performed heroically over the decades, since their creation shortly after our order began. They have been our eyes, our ears, and our hands when establishing our influence in the world. But I must stress that this council has historically had its own separate avenues, albeit on a much more limited scale. There has been a worrying tendency, accelerated in the past decade, of dependence on the Sword to the detriment of these independent tools available to us. Given how events are accelerating faster than our projections indicated, I urge this council to once again reinstate these independent tools."

Of all the items discussed, this last one generated the most heated discussion. The overwhelming consensus was that the accelerated pace of developments mandated that the Council place more faith in, and operational decisions into the hands of, the Sword. The First bowed his head signalling his acceptance of the will of the Council. But in his heart, he was very worried that the tail had begun to wag the dog. And this tail, unfortunately, was well aware of that.

CHAPTER TWENTY-ONE
Silent Snow

The surroundings were austere to the point of bleakness, but quite functional. Many of the computers were set up on the floor, and of necessity their users joined them. Bundles of wires for power and communications forced people to take care in where they walked, lest they trip. Many of the original lights in the room were still not functioning, so there were temporary auxiliary lights in widespread use. The people in the room seemed to be either focused on their computer screens or scurrying around. The scene appeared to be one of barely controlled chaos.

However, it soon became evident that what the cavernous room lacked in furniture and comfort, it more than made up for in design and efficiency. The perimeter of the chaos was carefully feeding information to a central command and control area, and this group was better equipped than the others. There were tables for the computers, white boards to display written information, and chairs for most of the people populating this group. There was a definite level of noise, but it was clipped and professional, as was the appearance of the residents therein.

On one of the largest displays was a map of Ontario. There were a number of symbols on the map, and several of them appeared to be in motion. Notations relating to them were being written by hand on white boards to either side of the display. Several people were staring intently at map, pausing only occasionally to refer to tablet computers held in their hands. Runners from the chaos at the periphery made a steady stream to and fro as they rushed up to whisper information, pass some pages of written information, or to draw attention to something on a computer screen.

One man at a desk in the centre picked up a phone and barked orders for combat teams to make ready to leave on short notice. He had just put down the phone when a runner came up, stood at attention, then presented a sheet of paper.

"Sir, the targets of special interest have been located in Ottawa. Shall I dispatch a team to follow and monitor?"

The man at the desk nodded in reply, then returned to staring at his screen and scanning the written reports. Matters appeared to be coming to a head.

CHAPTER TWENTY-TWO
Letter To Gretchen

Hey, Gretchen :

Lots of interesting things happening here, so probably time to give you an update on what we're doing.

Oh yeah - don't forget that this is a one-time-read email. But you knew that, didn't you? Wouldn't make any mistakes, would you? Not like that one time a few years back. Tee hee.

Anyways.

We're settled in, now. Got a place to stay and everything. Nothing fancy, but clean, as the saying goes. The locals have accepted us as one their own, as it were. But more on that later.

The important thing is that we're using Yancey's office as a base of operations, and he's squared being away with the local cops, after the fire in his apartment. That last task was a bit tense, let me tell you. As we discussed up at the cabin, it is a tad sketchy to just kinda saunter back into town after your apartment building has been torched and just act like nothing ever happened. As usual, Yancey handled it with aplomb. Yah, he fretted about it for a couple days, but one day we were out walking about and he spotted a police detective that he knew on the other side of the street. Told me to fade into the background, and then he dashed across the street and walked up to the guy. Whoa, the look the detective gave him would peel paint. Really pissed at Yancey, and no fooling. Who, I must say, just stood there with that big sloppy grin of his and spun the yarn we'd worked out about being out of town, came back to find apartment torched, went to ground to check things out, yadda, yadda. Well, the guy was still pissed, jabbing his finger into Yancey's chest as he talked, then eventually calmed down a bit. Damn near gave me a heart attack, it did. But the dude calmed down enough to stomp off and leave Yancey standing there grinning like a fool, waving goodbye. Then Yancey waltzed across the street, motioned me to walk ahead of him, and then when we turned a corner he let out a quiet laugh and did a fist pump. Turns out that detective was one of the honest ones who didn't hate Yancey's guts (are you surprised at how rare that is?) and was more upset about what Yancey might have gotten himself into than anything else. Turns out that although Yancey's apartment was totalled, there was only minor water and smoke damage to the rest of the building. It also helped that this sort of thing had happened a few years ago, and a leak from the cops turned out to be the problem, so Yancey had earned a bit of leeway from that. So we're square with the local cops, at least for the moment. Oh, and we're not bothering to go back to the apartment - ain't nothing there to salvage. Yancey said he'd cancel his lease by phone or email - doesn't want to face the landlord, I guess.

That went so well that Yancey decided to head out to his office and check things out. Yah, I know we all talked about how chancey that was, but Yancey said he got a good vibe off of the detective. So that, and the emails on the Tears server, convinced him that now was as good a time as any to check his office. We went back to the Flush and picked up some gear that Yancey wanted, then headed out. Oh, forgot to mention that we got some new wheels - dirt bikes. So cool. And less conspicuous than that damn land yacht. Anyways, off we went, and got there without any problems. Did a quick look around, and saw nothing funky, so we parked the bikes and went inside.

Yancey had one of his magic doohickies out, but couldn't detect any listening devices. So we made coffee (Remember that time you came up to visit him with me? Well, he's gotten even better at it. It was really nice to have good coffee again.), and poked around without talking about anything in particular except how awful it was to come back after a camping trip and find that his apartment had been torched. Still nothing untoward detected. Yancey is really good at that dissembling thing ... he babbled away like some teenage girl (your allusion, dear friend, not mine!), all the while waving his magic thingie around. Without skipping a beat he went to a cupboard, brought out what looked like a metal detector and a weird gun-shaped thing with a display screen on it, and spent the next hour waving both of them over every square inch of his office. We actually found one small listening device, too, attached under one of his workbenches. Damn! Then he took another magic box, and waved it around the office. This one had a strange-coloured strobe light that flashed every so often.

Once that was done Yancey finally explained what was going on. It was all to check for listening devices, of course. Turns out that some are always active, some are mostly silent and only sometimes active, and some are video-only. The first scan was for the ones that were on, and that showed zip. The metal detector thing was actually an EMP generator (that's electromagnetic pulse to plebes like us) and the gun thingie was an IR camera. The EMP generator heats up any electronic device, and the IR camera detects anything that gets warm. So simple and elegant, once one thinks about it. Anyways that's how we found the one passive device. The flash thing was used to detect any video cameras by way of the bounce-back reflection from any optics. Now that is cool.

Anyways, at that point Yancey declared the office to be safe. Not guaranteed safe, of course, but enough that he'd feel safe working there again. Good enough for me!

We poked around a bit, and it looks like the Sword operatives missed the original data key of Herman's and the copies we made that we had left behind in a hidey hole. Not only that, but it looks like they fell for the fake data line that he'd installed, and the fake servers. The line had a pretty obvious tap put into it, and the servers had their hard drives taken, but that is it! Now, Yancey allowed as a truly brilliant operator could have spoofed it all, but given what we know we decided that the Sword had done only the obvious minimum. That means the hidden servers and real T1 line are trustworthy. So very good to have proper Internet access once again. Oh, and Yancey had some cash stashed in the hidey hole, so we still haven't had to use our credit or debit cards, which is one less worry.

By that point we were feeling hungry, so we popped on down to Mama's for some food. It was bliss, Gretchen, pure bliss. Although I *was* surprised that Yancey didn't pig out like he usually does. Seems determined to keep off the weight he's lost. Gotta agree with him there, and I kinda like having lost some weight myself, but don't tell him that. And Mama asked after you, by the way.

After satisfying our inner selves we went back to work,

and Yancey had another trick up his sleeve. Turns out that he had a couple of mechanically-driven cameras hidden in his office that used old-fashioned film. Nothing electronic, all plastic, nothing that would show up on any modern scanner! The film was from a client of his, who produces it for various science experiments. It's actually a photosensitive polymer that's insensitive to light until activated with UV, which gets done after it is put into the camera. Very impressive. Anyways, it apparently gets triggered when the fake servers or T1 line get hacked - sort of like a dead man switch. Takes a picture every second or so, for about a minute. He developed the film, and it revealed some pictures of the ones who broke in. Not high-def, but good enough to see faces. We've scanned those, and I'll send you a copy in a separate email. We didn't recognize 'em, but that is no surprise.

All that, and guess what excited Yancey the most? He found his dulcimers to be still intact. Remember those from the time you were up here? He had just made the things, and was teaching himself how to play. Well, anyways, he was thrilled to find 'em both - the one you play on your lap, and the one played like a guitar but with fewer strings. Mountain dulcimer and strummer, Yancey calls them.

By that point it was getting late, so we called it a day. Grabbed some takeout from Mama's, and headed home, feeling pretty darned pleased with ourselves. We ate the food (oh, Gretchen, it was soooo good) then Yancey started strumming on the laptop dulcimer. Then he shoved the strummer thing into my hands, and showed me a few basic chords. Then we started doing a few simple songs. Then we started singing along as we strummed - old folk tunes, then some old country and western songs. Then Yancey started wailing away on some classic Twisted Sister and George Thorogood songs. I kept up the best I could, and we both sang away. Perhaps a bit too loudly, 'cuz the neighbours started banging on the walls. Guess they aren't lovers of the classics. So we called it a night. Anyways, since then, everyone has assumed that we're failed musicians. Works out well, except that the landlady now wants our rent in advance every few days. Apparently she used to date a musician.

I'd like to leave on a happy note, but there is one strange thing you need to be aware of. We have noticed, on the odd occasion, people lurking about that don't quite fit in. Not often, but they somehow kind of move along when we do. They're easy enough to get loose of, and Yancey insists that we do so any time we go out. Not sure if they are actually following us, or if it is just happenstance. Keep your eyes open, Gretchen.

Have made some progress on establishing a network to gather intelligence on the Sword. Will update you on this later, when Yancey decides that it is safe to do so. Analysis of the data is proceeding. Will let you know if we find anything.

Anyways, that's all for now.

Toodles.

S.

CHAPTER TWENTY-THREE
The Dragon's Lair

Gretchen finished reading the much-anticipated email from Simon, and leaned back into her chair with a contented sigh. It was good to hear that the boys were not only safe and sound, but making good progress. The thought of some of their small adventures forced a giggle out of her. This caused Charlene to raise her head from her own work and look quizzically at her young friend.

"Anything you'd like to share, dear?"

Gretchen was still smiling, and passed over the tablet she had been reading with another chuckle. "The boys are fine, and seem to be up to their usual antics."

Charlene gave a small snort of amusement as she took the tablet and began reading. In truth, she'd been a bit worried about them. They were good boys, but she still felt a bit protective about them. Such thoughts were brushed aside as she quickly read through the message. "Oh, dear," was her only comment, as she covered her mouth with her hand. "Perhaps it *is* for the best that they are on their own, for the time being. They seem to have established a good cover story, and made their peace with the local law enforcement over the torching of Yancey's apartment. I'm not entirely comfortable with their establishing an intelligence-gathering network. But, Gretchen, what's with that rather out-of-character ending to the message?"

Gretchen gave a small laugh, "That's how I know it is really from Simon. We set up a series of simple code phrases back when we had a job at the same firm. We dealt with enough sensitive stuff that we had to take care that our emails actually came from each other. He got the idea from Yancey, actually, and decided that it would be a good thing to set up before things got too sensitive. As things turned out, he was right. We actually did get a few spoofed emails trying to have one of us send some information files, or to feed us false information. Not too often, and not recently, but we kept up the habit of it. The word "toodles" indicates that all is well. If he'd used "ta ta", that would have meant that he wasn't sure about something, and that I shouldn't take any action until he got back to me. The phrase "Anyways, that's all for now" indicates that the information he just sent is valid. If he'd used the phrase "Talk to you later", that would mean that the information was compromised somehow - maybe he thought it was bad but was passing it on, or he was sending some misinformation on the chance that it was being intercepted. Now, if he'd said "Talk to you later, love", that would mean that all hell was breaking loose and that I should get the hell out of Dodge. We never had cause to use that one, but set it up just in case."

Charlene had listened to this explanation with a thoughtful expression. She sometimes forgot that Gretchen and Simon had dealt with high-security issues in the past. And, of course, Yancey's PI work had honed his skills in such things, too. She gave a small, soft sigh as she chided herself for thinking of Simon and Yancey as 'boys'. Those 'boys' had swum in some dark waters, and those dark waters held sharks. She shook her head slightly as she noticed Charlene looking at her with a puzzled look on her face.

The older woman grunted softly in amusement and simply said, "I'm so used to working with investigative reporters that I sometimes forget that you civilians can have investigative skills, too."

She grew more serious as she continued, " It sounds like Yancey and Simon are well on their way to re-establishing themselves, and building up their own investigative resources. They're quite correct in not sending us the details, too - 'need to know' has got to be our mantra, I'm afraid."

Gretchen grew thoughtful as her friend talked, then replied, "Even so, I think that they are on to something with their looking at the socio-economic angles. We can help them there, I think. They're going to have their hands full getting re-established and doing data analysis and setting up that new intelligence network of theirs, and with just the two of them to do all that. We've got more resources here than they have, so how about we turn our attentions to any new economic and political trends? We could send them summaries and such as required. Might even be a good story in it, you know."

Charlene had to smile at that last comment. Her young friend and lover was showing the instincts of a good investigative reporter. "A good idea. We'll grab the economics reporter and have a brainstorming session. You've got recent experience on The Street, so you'll have some good insight into that. I'll give you his name, and you set it up, OK?"

Gretchen replied with a wolfish grin. It was time to dig up some good dirt and get the country ready for the big revelations to come.

* * *

Charlene walked into her office to find Gretchen seated at the big table with a young lad who looked like he was just out of J-school.

"Excuse me, Gretchen, but isn't this the time for the meeting with the economics reporter?"

Gretchen just grinned mischievously, "Charlene, meet your economics reporter, Sherman Seyonson. Sherman, say hello to Charlene."

Sherman rose quickly, but with a distinct lack of grace. He stumbled forward holding out his hand to shake. Charlene shook it with a puzzled expression, and motioned for everyone to sit down.

"Hello, Sherman, I'm very pleased to meet you. But I was expecting to meet with Paul. Paul Younman, that is."

Sherman began a stumbling explanation, but was quickly waved to silence by Gretchen.

"Charlene, it seems that Mr. Younman was let go shortly after the start of your ... sabbatical. Sherman, here, was hired as his replacement. It turns out that he's been to the latest economic news conference, and picked up some interesting background information while he was there. Sherman? Just tell Charlene what you've been telling me."

Sherman turned a deep crimson, and tried but failed to make coherent sounds. Charlene sighed to herself but didn't let it show. Typical new J-school grad reaction to meeting an editor, she realized. Worse, actually, since as far as he was concerned this was a new editor. Poor kid.

"Sherman? Stop." Her voice was soft, but firm. "Pause. Take a deep breath, then let it out slowly. Trust me, this is a bit of a shock for both of us, OK? Good. So you're our new economics reporter?"

Sherman seemed to have gotten control of himself. He managed a brief nod and a smile, then started over. "Yes, Ms. Blaverston. I was hired I guess a couple days after you left. Mr. Younman got into a big shouting match with Mr. Philson. He was the one who hired me, you know. Mr. Philson, I mean."

Charlene nodded, just to keep the narrative going.

"Well, I don't know what it was about, but it ended with a lot of yelling between the two. Mr. Younman stormed out, and Mr. Philson said that the old fa..., I mean, Mr. Younman, was gone and I was taking his place. The Finance Minister's press conference was the next morning, so Mr. Philson said to take Mr. Younman's press credentials and cover it. So I did - fortunately the security people cared more about checking that I was really from this newpaper than who I was. The conference itself was really interesting, even if everyone else here thought it was pretty lame stuff."

Charlene allowed herself a small friendly smile, and nodded understanding.

Encouraged, Sherman continued. "But what was really interesting were the comments some of the other reporters were making. Like there was some really weird background stuff that no one else would talk about. Anyways, after the press conference was over, they took me out for drinks. Said it was a tradition for the new guys."

Sherman actually blushed a bit at the memory of the one-too-many drinks, and Charlene actually laughed at his expression. "Yeah, Sherman, it is. As much to find out what you know, as anything else. But mostly friendly fun."

She was rewarded with an excited bobbing of his head.

"Yes, ma'am. It was that, all right. They really wanted to know about you and your sudden departure, but I didn't know anything. So they started talking about the press conference, and some of the background stuff they mentioned. Sounded pretty far out there, to tell the truth. So when I got back I wrote it all down, and did a bit of digging. Uhm … well, I did the digging the next day, actually."

Both Gretchen and Charlene had to chuckle at the expression on his face.

"Don't worry about it, kid," Charlene said in a friendly tone. "Don't do that too often, but it sounds like you got more out of them than they got out of you. Well done."

Sherman perked up at the praise, and nodded his thanks before continuing. "Ma'am, I think there might be a story in this. It really does smell. At best, the economic benefits for Canada are pretty minimal. I did some work on comparative international investments when I was in university, and this is way out of the norm for these sorts of thing."

Gretchen nodded, and added, "Sherman and I were just talking about that when you walked in, Charlene. This recent announcement is just one of a series. As Sherman suggests, it all sounds a bit 'off'. He thinks it might be worthwhile looking at the background of some of the others. He's got some interesting data to look at, too."

The three of them discussed Sherman's findings and suspicions for a few minutes, until Charlene thought that she finally had a handle on it. There was a pause, and she looked thoughtful for a moment, then nodded. "OK, Sherman. I'll admit that you surprise me, but it looks like you've got good instincts. Start with this latest announcement - that's got a real back story that we can run soon. Maybe by the end of the week. Look, you've done good work and have some good material here. I'd like you to work with another reporter to write it up - say, Betty. You know her, right?"

A tinge of unhappiness showed, but Sherman nodded.

Charlene noticed and said brightly, "You'll share the byline, don't worry. This is an important story, and I see this as part of a series. You've got the technical skills and instincts. Here's a chance to hone your reporting skills, and Betty's a good person to learn those from. One of the best, actually. OK, so pass on a copy of all your data and whatever you find to Gretchen and myself. Now off with you. You've got a story to dig up."

Sherman had brightened up considerably by this point, and fairly bounced out of the room. Charlene sighed. Betty was not going to be happy at having to play 'training sergeant'. Her prediction was borne out as she saw Sherman talking excitedly to her, and Betty favoured Charlene with a glare before returning her attention to an oblivious Sherman.

"She going to be OK with this?" Gretchen asked.

"Oh, yeah. It's a good story, and it'll take the two of them to pull it off properly. She'll thank me later."

Charlene turned and focused her attention on her young friend. "This is something the boys have to be told about, to make sure they're aware of these things. There's been a lot of economic announcements lately. Big ones, coming seemingly out of nowhere. Everyone seems to think that it's all a bunch of the same old hot air, but with what we now know, I'm worried about what it might be leading up to."

Gretchen nodded slowly, "Yep. I know some folks from The Street that I can talk to. Got some lunch dates lined up this week, and this'll be one more thing to query about. The one thing that sticks out for me from what Sherman was saying is the long-term planning that this all implies. There's got to be traces of that around. And we need to find out what other plans of that sort are around."

Her older friend simply nodded, and looked as if her focus was partially elsewhere. Then her attention snapped back to Gretchen. "I may have been wrong earlier. It's probably a damn good move for the boys to set up an intelligence-gathering network. The more eyes and ears we get on this stuff, the better. Things seem to be moving quickly, and I'm beginning to get the sinking feeling that time is against us."

CHAPTER TWENTY-FOUR
Silent Witness

Although only back in town for a few days, Yancey and Simon had already established a pleasant routine. Up early, then a walk to Camille's restaurant for a hearty breakfast to start the day. She was beginning to smile a bit more as she got to know them. However she still charged them full price for their meals, and made them help with the washing up afterwards. Neither complained, as Camille quickly proved to be a good conversationalist, possessing a keen mind and a studied view of society. The lads were careful not to reveal too much to her, but because Mama trusted her implicitly, they allowed themselves to discuss some aspects of what they knew if only in general terms.

After breakfast, they would go to Yancey's office. Now that they were reasonably sure that no more monitoring devices were in place, they were beginning to get back to analyzing their data. Simon had been worried that the Sword would get suspicious if their bugs stopped working, but Yancey just laughed. "Nah. Those were all standard, off-the-shelf things. They checked me out, so they know that I know about stuff like that. Hell, there was anti-snoop gear out in plain sight! No, they put that stuff in just out of habit, just in case I got sloppy. They'd probably be more suspicious if I missed them, come to that. I thought about keeping them intact and feeding false data to them, but that gets too complicated. We like simple. Fewer ways to screw up."

Once assured that the office and data links were safe to use, Yancey did a check of his off-site backups. Happily, only two of those showed any signs of tampering, and both of those were old ones that Yancey used for secondary backups of his cases. The new ones he used for primary backups and the ones that he'd set up for communications between the four friends were untouched.

"You sure about that, Yance? We're trusting those things with our lives, you know."

Yancey just gave a big sloppy grin, "Well, if they had been compromised, we'd be dead or worse already. So don't worry."

"Not helping, Yance. Not helping at all."

"OK, OK, worry wart. They've got similar protections as the fancy encrypted read-once-only technique we set up for the emails. In theory it might be possible to decrypt it - not likely but theoretically possible. But that can't be done without leaving a trace ... sort of like a smudge on a piece of paper. No electronic smudging means we're safe."

"Well, if you say so," mused Simon grudgingly. "I thought I was up on that stuff, but you do seem to have a knack for the truly devious stuff, my friend."

"That *is* my job," replied Yancey with wide, innocent eyes. Then he grew serious. "Well, it was, anyways. Now we've got something rather more serious to work on."

Their current analysis consisted of attempting to integrate Sergeant Dundee's data into what they already knew. It helped to flesh out the patterns they'd already detected of illicit transportation of goods. Which, as they now knew, was all too often human cargo. The new data showed transport through Dryden, which implicated the Tears of Joy facility even more strongly. They were currently trying to discern patterns of movement over time, in an effort to guess what any future efforts might be. It was all very confusing, and they struggled to understand what it might mean.

However involved they got in the data analysis, Mama made sure to keep them well supplied with nourishment. He and his wife, Alvita, would drop by several times a day with food, coffee, and tea. Sometimes they'd drop off the supplies and quickly leave the young men to their work. Other times, when they sensed that a brick wall had been hit, or an argument was getting heated, they would stay and chat.

Their third day of analysis found them working well into the night. Alvita came by with their supper to find the two men nodding vaguely as they stared at a whiteboard that was covered with notes. After laying it out on a spare table, and gathering the remains of the lunch, she went and stood quietly by the young men. They looked up, a bit startled, as it wasn't her usual habit to stay when things were quiet.

When she was sure that she had gotten their complete attention she said in her calm, mild voice, "Have you boys been givn' more t'ought to how we can be helpin'? I know dat Mama and Camille have spoken to you about dis."

Yancey and Simon just gaped at her. Then they looked at each other, then back at Alvita. She just smiled and a said, "Best be eatin' the food while it be hot. Sit."

The command to sit was given in a tone that brooked no disobedience, so the two men quickly sat down, frozen at attention. At a mild glare from her they unfroze and began eating. Their hunger quickly overcame their confusion, and they focused on eating the truly delicious food. While they ate, Alvita sat with her hands folded in her lap, happy to see the young men focus on something other than work. They worked far too intently for far too long, in her opinion.

When the feeding frenzy abated somewhat, Yancey looked up somewhat guiltily. "The food is very good, Alvita, thank you."

Simon added his own, rather more muffled thanks, as his mouth was full.

Alvita just smiled calmly, "T'ank you, boys. Now, back to my orig'nal question. What t'oughts you be havin' on that?"

Yancey paused in his eating, took a large slurp of coffee, and wiped his moth with a napkin. Then he sat back and regarded the older woman. Simon quietly followed suit, content to follow Yancey's lead on this.

"Alvita …." Yancey began.

"No, Yancey. You be needin' our help. We have experiences in dese t'ings, Mama and me. And young Camille, too. We don't know the details, 'cuz you tryin' to shield us, an' bless you bot' for dat. But we don' need 'em. We lived t'rough dis afore. Back home. Da Old Home." Her eyes seemed to focus on things only she could see, then she shook her head as if to dispel the images. "Did we never tell you how we meet - Mama an' me?"

Yancey just shook his head. This was a whole new side of Alvita and Mama for him.

Alvita smiled happily, "We meet in Canada. Live all our lives down in da Islands, often in da same big town, but only meet here after we escape."

She saw the stunned expression on their faces, and explained. "Yah, escape is what I say. You know 'bout how's they's set up as offshore tax havens?"

The two men just nodded.

"Well, what you don' know is how it be to be livin' dere. Not for the Rich Ones - oh no - for de real folks."

Alvita looked intently at the men, "It not like de books or movies. Everythin' be set up for the Rich Ones. Everyone else expected to serve. Some servers better off, but only for a few closest to da Rich Ones. Started out years ago as just one more type of job. Now it be da only job. For you. For you chil'ren. All so polite, all so peaceful. But no hope for betterment, not for most. Any complainers get dealt with, real harsh. Obey and serve, and life be sweet."

Her eyes began to blaze, "Be sweet if all you be wantin' is to serve. In all ways dat da Rich Ones be wantin', wit'out complaint." She paused to catch her breath, and to collect her thoughts. She inhaled sharply, and shook her head before exhaling equally sharply, then continuing.

"It be one t'ing to be poor but have opportunity to make y'self better. It be another t'ing to be poor and have no hope. So some of us fight back against de Big Evil. No, not wit' violence. We try legal ways - police, media, organize workers, all dat. We believed in da power of goodness. But it be too late for dat. De Big Evil have claws in all t'ings. All de media, all de police, all de lawmakers. An' most folk? Well, for some it be good life. For most, it just be de way t'ings be, and canna change de way of t'ings. So those who fight da Big Evil need be leave, if able. Some not able. Some too broken to start over. Some dead."

Her voice faded into a whisper, as eyes focused on things seen a long time ago. Then she took a deep breath and continued speaking, but her gaze was still on images of long ago. "My sister ... Camille's mudda ... it were too late for her. She talked of formin' a union to help make life a bit better. Her body be found all broken up, but police say it were accident. So I take Camille and I run to Canada. I lie and say she my own daughter so we stay toget'er and make a life. So I work hard, put Camille into school. Then I meet Mama. We be two sorry fools from a land of sun, and we meet in a land of snow." She laughed softly at the irony.

Yancey and Simon remained very still and silent as they attempted to absorb Alvita's story. They had both heard some stories of life in a tax haven, of course, but this was beyond anything they'd ever heard of or imagined.

Alvita focused her eyes on Yancey and Simon once again. "Boys, dat be many year ago. T'ings be worse now. We both keep in touch with some of da old foolish ones down dere, dem dat stay for one t'ing or 'nother. Some we send money to, and some we help to leave and make new lives here. But da Big Evil be here, now, and flexin' its claws. So - I ask again. What can we be doin' to help?"

Yancey looked at her, not knowing what to say. Then he shook his head, "No. You've done enough. I need to keep you safe. You and Mama and Camille. I'm sorry that I told Mama and Camille anything about this. It's my fight, now. Mine and Simon's."

Simon simply nodded his agreement.

Alvita's eyes flashed and her soft voice became harsher than Yancey had ever experienced. "You listen to me good, Yancey Franklin. You be a good boy, and a good friend to Mama and me. But there be times you be needin' a good smack upside you head. You be a smart boy and known' many t'ings. You and young Simon, here, both. But *we* know da Big Evil, and its ways. *We* have lived wit' it, watched it, and fought it. Those be t'ings that you not be knowin' 'bout. When da Big Evil get da dirty money inside, evert'ing change. Laws be passed to help only dem and they kind. Life turn shiny bright on de outside, but hard and dirty on de inside."

Then her eyes and voice softened, and she took Yancey's hands in hers. "But you have had some knowin' of dey claws, do you not? No, don' be lookin' away, Yancey Franklin. Both Mama and me kin see the damage dey brutes be doin' to ya, but Mama wanted us not to be sayin' anyt'in. Just know that we be here for ya if you be needin' us, and watchin' ya back. And yours as well, young Simon."

Yancey's hands gripped the older woman's hands tightly, and she returned the grip. Then all three of them began clearing their throats, and Alvita released Yancey's hands.

"I'd best be gettin' dese dishes back to be washed," and with that she quickly gathered everything up and quietly left.

Yancey and Simon could only look at each other in shock.

Finally, Simon broke the silence. "Holy shit, Yance. Did you ever know any of that?"

Yancey just shook his head, not trusting himself to speak. Finally, he wiped his eyes, blew his nose, and stated simply "We're not going to get anything more done here. Let's just call it a night."

Simon agreed wholeheartedly, and so they shut everything down, set the alarms, and went back to the rooming house.

* * *

The next morning, they got up and walked to Camille's for breakfast. Simon hadn't slept at all well after the revelations of the previous night, and still felt unsettled. It gradually dawned on him that Yancey didn't look unsettled at all. In fact he looked as if he were engrossed in thinking about a problem.

They got to the restaurant and placed their usual order. Yancey was unusually quiet, and simply sat sipping on his coffee, responding to Simon's attempts to make conversation with noncommittal grunts. Simon recognized the symptoms - his friend was worrying at a problem and working through a solution. It was nice to see Yancey back to normal, Simon thought, but he could at least pretend to be civil to Camille. She was cooking their food, after all.

While waiting for their food to arrive, Simon passed the time by glancing through the local paper. It was one of those ultra-local small tabloid papers, with no real news in it. But it was interesting enough, and helped to pass the time. From time to time he would mention some piece of trivia, like a lost dog being found, announcing it in bright happy tones. This was a game he'd played before - the trick was to see how long it took to get Yancey's attention. Sometimes it took the most outrageous embellishment of a story to do so, and Simon always enjoyed the challenge. Still, there were rules to the game, and Simon carefully adhered to them. The embellishments must be carefully calibrated, so as to properly gauge the depth of Yancey's descent into the realms of thought. Besides, it was more fun that way.

"Oh, look, Yancey, that lost dog I mentioned was actually one of a litter. It seems that they were all born with two tails."

Grunt.

"Hmm, well now, this is interesting, the reason the search party was out looking for the dog at all is that the girl's mother is the leading light in some community organization or other. Just goes to show, ya, doesn't it?"

Grunt. Slurp.

"Yah, looks like her organization is in charge of some special weekly event. Waitaminute, oh, it's a musical of some sort. Maybe we should go, do you think?"

Grunt.

"Hey, the next show is this evening. Might do us some good, ya know. Getting out and about, and all. Whaddya think?"

Grunt.

"Well, you might have a point. I mean, who wants to see a show about dogs? The advert talks about girls showing off their puppies. Sounds dull."

No grunt this time, so Simon risked a peek from behind his paper. He saw Yancey staring balefully at him over the lip of his cup. The eyes were not quite focused, Simon thought, so he decided to up the ante a bit.

"The second act of the show doesn't sound much better. Says the girls will be offering to spank monkeys. Whatever that means."

Simon was rewarded with a strangled incoherent growl, and he leaned back just enough to evade Yancey's hand as it tried to snatch the paper.

"Oh, sorry, Yancey. Did you say something? Dear me, I was so engrossed reading these fascinating stories in the local paper."

Fortunately, Camille chose that moment to bring in the food, and put the plates in front of each of the young men. Yancey sat back down with a snort and a shaking of his head.

"Don't pick on Yancey, Simon," Camille admonished. "He's not had his breakfast yet."

"Yeah," sniffed Yancey sulkily, "what she said."

"And you," said Camille sharply, pointing a finger at Yancey, "stop sulking, and eat your food. And because you two are being such brats, you can stay and wash dishes after you're done."

Yancey laughed, "You were going to make us stay and wash up anyways."

Camille's only reply was to shake her head sadly as she walked back into the kitchen.

Still chuckling, Yancey dove into his food with gusto and Simon followed suit. Neither spoke for several minutes, the better to give the delicious food the attention it deserved. Then, when the last bit of egg was mopped up with the last bit of toast, they leaned back into their chairs and sipped contentedly on their coffee.

"So ..." said Simon softly, "looks like you've thought of a plan, then."

Yancey nodded. "The beginnings of one, perhaps. Been thinking about what Alvita said last night."

Simon's mood grew sombre, but before he could say anything, Camille's voice called for them to bring their dishes and lazy selves to the kitchen for the washing up. "Duty calls," was all Yancey said with a smile, and both of them hurried to obey the summons.

While the men were cleaning the breakfast dishes, Camille leaned against the doorway.

"Been asking around about that lemon eight thing you mentioned the other day."

"Lemniscate," Yancey corrected.

"What I said," she retorted. "Anyways, it has been seen around. Not much, but some. Always in the company of hard-looking rich men."

"Rich men?" asked Simon.

"Must be rich. They acted like they own the Earth and all within, is what I was told. And what did Auntie talk to you about last night? Seems to have set you both into a blue funk."

Simon and Yancey exchanged glances. Finally Simon broke the silence, "She told us about how she and you and Mama left the Old Home. And why."

Camille's gaze looked far away for a moment, then she inhaled sharply and shook her head. "Yes. I thought that might be it. Back to fightin' the Big Evil, is it?"

By the end of her reply, her voice had a distinct sharp edge to it that the men hadn't heard before. Neither quite knew what to say.

Then Yancey said softly, "I tried to tell her to stay out of it this time, that it wasn't her fight any more. Not hers, not Mama's, and not yours."

Camille's back straightened, and her face became a study in ice.

Yancey appeared not to notice as he continued speaking softly but urgently, "But she's right. It's not my place to tell anyone not to fight. But, Camille ..." he looked up at her intently, ignoring her anger.

"Camille, what I *do* have is experience in probing into dark places and uncovering secrets others want to keep hidden. Simon and I have fought this Big Evil and though we haven't always been successful at it ... we're still alive, still causing grief for them, and we'll continue to cause them as much grief as possible. Yes, we can use your help. But all I ask is that you hold off on any more enquiries until I talk to Mama and Alvita again. Today, I promise. I've got some ideas that I need to run by them. I won't freeze you out, or try to smother you with protection. You have my word of honour on that."

Camille stood like a study in granite for a handful of heartbeats, then nodded briskly. "You'd best be off, then. Got lots of work ahead of you, I be thinkin'".

The two men left quickly, walking back to the rooming house to pick up the Busted Flush. The forecast promised sleet later in the day, so use of the motorbikes was contraindicated. As they walked, Simon said softly, "This is an ugly business and going to get uglier, Yancey. Hope you've got a good plan."

Yancey answered with a grunt, "So do I, Simon, so do I."

* * *

After getting to the office, Yancey outlined his plan to Simon to get his initial reactions. As expected, neither of them was too happy about it, but the necessity of it was clear. Then Yancey suggested that it was time to bring in Mama and Alvita, and Simon agreed. Yancey walked over to the diner and simply told them that he'd been thinking and needed to talk with them when they had some time. Mama and Alvita simply looked at each other, then nodded and suggested that now was as good a time as any, and should they bring along a few things to eat? Yancey laughingly allowed as that might be a good idea, and ended up carrying one of two large containers of food and coffee back to his office.

"Hey," said Simon upon seeing the delegation enter the office, "expecting an army to show up? That is a *lot* of food."

"Can't do no good thinkin' onna empty stomach," Mama intoned solemnly. Alvita simply smiled and patted Simon's cheek. After locking the front doors, and setting up a small buffet on a spare table, they all sat down and heaped their plates with the food. After nibbling on some of the savoury dishes and one of Alvita's perfect pastries, Simon and Yancey shared a look and a nod, then Yancey

241

began talking.

"Mama, Alvita, I've been thinking a lot about you've both been telling me. Been whipsawing back and forth on what to do, who to trust, how to protect everyone, that sort of thing. I've not been at the top of my game, lately, and I'm sorry for that." He held up a hand to forestall the comments he saw on their lips. "No, it's true. But that has to end now. We've got no more time for that sort of thing. The important thing is I've got a plan of sorts, and Simon thinks it isn't totally bat shit crazy."

Simon rocked his right hand back and forth a few times, but smiled as he did it.

Yancey took a deep breath and carried on. "OK, this is what needs to be done. Mama, Alvita, you are both absolutely correct - we need your experience and your contacts, both. We need to set up our own intelligence network, to figure out how the 'Big Evil', as you call it, is organized and what they are planning to do. We need eyes and ears out there. But - and this is the vitally important thing - we need these people to be watchers only. Silent witnesses to what goes on. Any action, and I mean *any* action, has to be done in conjunction with the appropriate authorities."

The two older people looked at each other, then shook their heads. "Ain't gonna work, Yancey-boy," rumbled Mama. "No, it will not," Alvita agreed sternly. "Dey own and control all de levers of power".

Yancey just shook his head. "No, it really does have to be this way. Every underground group in history that has allowed itself to use violence has turned feral - without exception. Violence breeds paranoia and extremism, and that creates an understandable backlash from the rest of the citizens. We can't neutralize a poison with another poison. We don't want to create yet another version of the

Big Evil. And from what we can tell, they don't control everything or everyone. They influence or control a lot of the ones at the top, but that's about it. There are still a lot of good people out there - trust me on that."

Mama bowed his head and shook it, hearing Yancey's words but not quite believing them. Alvita just sighed and closed her eyes. Simon and Yancey exchanged glances, and then Yancey walked up to the two elders, knelt before them, and placed one of his hands over each of theirs.

"It has to be this way. It may be the same Big Evil, but the place and time are different. Please, trust me on this. We need watchers, not agents. We can't set this up like a revolutionary network, either. That always ends badly, no matter how righteous the original cause is."

Mama and Alvita looked at Yancey, then Simon, then exchanged a long look between themselves. Finally, Alvita spoke softly, "We understan' what you be sayin', Yancey. But there be ways to set these t'ings up. De standard cell form be proven by time."

"No, Alvita, no cells. Nothing formal. I understand that you will want to protect your contacts. Fine. I don't need to know who they are. But let them know who I am. You two can be their primary contact, but they need an alternate contact, just in case. I can give them safe ways to send emails and send data to you or me. That's the sort of thing I know how to do."

Mama allowed as that was true, and Alvita grudgingly agreed. "OK, Yancey, if that be de way you wan' it to be. I know you have deep knowledge of sech t'ings. Fine. So, what is it that you need of us and our friends?"

Yancey stood up and began pacing back and forth, as was his wont. "Information. Simon and I have got some information about them, some of which is going to appear in the newspapers in the near future. But we need more, as much as we can get. Look, you say the Big Evil bought its influence with its money. Can you get details of that?"

Simon chimed in, "If money is involved, the banks are involved. The banking system down there is centred around hiding information. Any details you can get about accounts, business information, and the like would be great."

"Oh, you mean like de shell companies and trust funds?" asked Mama.

"Exactly," Simon said as he leaned forward with excitement. "There were some leaks about that sort of thing some years ago, and that raised a lot of interest for a while, but was just a one-time thing and got buried. Money is the key here, I think. Where it comes from, who is controlling it, that sort of thing."

Mama spoke up, "We know some folk in da Old Home wit' access to dat sort of information, m'be."

Yancey nodded and added, "That helps us figure out who the players are. But we also need local information. Mama, remember I told you about the big operation involving children?"

Mama nodded.

"That's our immediate problem. We know that something is going to happen, but not where or when. The only thing we know is that it involves the transportation of children. So anything we can find out about that would be really useful."

Mama and Alvita nodded at this, and Alvita added, "That be all fine and good, boys, but how else do we be fightin'? You spoke, Yancey, of stayin' wit' da system. Dat mean politics, no?"

Simon spoke to this, "Good point, Alvita. Yeah, and I'm going to be working on that angle. I've done some work on political campaigns in the past, and have some contacts that I want to see here in town. Haven't had the time, yet."

Mama looked thoughtful. "Best be makin' the time, Simon-boy. We be spread t'in for sure, but need to cover all de bases right quick as we can. It take time, and lots of personal talkin', to build up dat sort of t'ing."

Simon looked at Yancey, "He's got a point, Yance. We've been busy getting re-established here. That and analysing the data we do have. But he's right about the face-time."

Yancey nodded, thinking quickly. Personal relationships were definitely not his strong point, as he had always depended on Simon for that sort of thing. "You've got a point, there. OK, Simon, start talking to your political people tomorrow. Mama, Alvita, how soon can you be putting the word out to your contacts to keep their eyes open and report back to us?"

Alvita just shook her head sadly, "Camille be startin' that already, I be fearin'. I go talk to her first t'ing, and let her know 'bout all dis. We got some contacts of our own, too. Folk from de Old Home livin' here have been feelin' jittery for a while, now. Too many old bad memories comin' back to life in dis New Home."

Mama reached over to hold his wife's hand, and she smiled back at him and added, "She a good girl. Like our own flesh, she is. But she got a lot of her mudda in her."

The group spent some time discussing how best to set things up to communicate. Yancey promised to set up a series of safe data drops and email sites on the Internet, and to set up some data keys with the necessary programs. All anyone had to do was to insert the data key, and boot up. The keys held a special security operating system and had all the necessary encryption programs. He explained that journalists had been forced to develop these sorts of techniques, and it could be set up and used by anyone with minimal training. Mama and Alvita nodded, then mentioned the necessity of using burn phones as not all of their contacts had access to or the training to use computers. The initial planning session continued for several hours.

The Silent Witness Network had begun.

CHAPTER TWENTY-FIVE
Contemplations Moving Forward

Mama and Camille sat at a table in her restaurant sipping on coffee, taking advantage of a lull between customers. Camille sat leaning forward staring bemusedly into her coffee, as Mama looked on with a tolerant smile.

"I must say, Uncle, that your two young friends are not what I expected."

"No?"

"Really, they seemed quite frivolous when they first came in here." She paused to glare are her uncle, and said in mock seriousness, "You know very well that you have a weakness for helping wandering souls."

Mama gave a deep-throated chuckle, "And what be changin' yer mind, girl?"

Camille snorted softly, "Well, I've had a chance to watch them at work, for a bit. Thought at first that it was a brighter and lesser pairing, sort of Holmes and Watson. But that is most certainly not the case, is it?"

"Nah, nah, they be a true team," was the bemused answer.

"That be true, uncle", Camille answered, her carefully nurtured Canadianized speech beginning to slip. "They be having different strengths, but have no trouble letting the other take the lead when necessary. But squabble! Yoi, it be like like a pair of brothers going at it if one dares to slip off what the other perceives as the correct path." Her eyes rolled at the memory of watching this. "A most interestin' pair of young men, these friends of yours are."

Mama smiled as he replied, "They's good boys, Camille. They grew up together. I know Yancey pretty well, and have a had a chance to talk with young Simon some, over the years. Good boys. A girl could do worse. A lot worse." His grin grew more than a little mischievous as the last was said.

Camille coloured slightly as she grimaced, shook her head, and waved her hands dismissively. "No, Uncle, I've no time for such things right now. The business takes all of my time." She paused for a moment and grew more serious. "And now you want to get back into the old ways. Change the world. Fight de Big Evil."

She shook her head as if to chase away unwanted memories. "Uncle, you and Auntie have raised me like I was your own daughter, and I couldn't feel more loved." She paused and looked wistful, and said softly, "But there be times I miss my mudda so much."

Mama smiled gently and placed his large hand over her much smaller one, and said softly, "We all miss her, Camille. She were good people. But she understood da need to stand up for da right thing. No cost too high, sometime."

"But why us, Uncle?" Camille did not wail or beg, for she was stronger than that, but there was a tone in her voice that demanded answers. "Why us again? We done da fightn', for all the good it did us. We all be losin' so terrible much, and now t'ings finally be goin' good. M'be if we just be waitin' it out, t'ings work out OK."

Mama looked at her sadly, knowing full well the truth of

what she said, and how upset she must be if the patois was coming back into her speech.

"Not goin' ta get better, girl, unless they's stopped. Da Evil has it claws in dis country and is startin' ta squeeze. *Hard*. Just like back home. But this time, there not bein' a safe haven left for fleein' to. Ain't none left but dis place. Canada took us in, treated us good, and gave us a fair shake to make our own way. Gave us opportunities we'd never have back home. Tain't perfect here, not by long shot, but dis place gave us a new life, a decent life. And now dey's needin' our help. Time to pay back what we owe."

They sat there and finished their coffee in companionable silence, each fully aware of the difficulties in the looming battle, and what the stakes were. But they were Canadians, and knew that their country was worth fighting for.

CHAPTER TWENTY-SIX
The Game's Afoot

The days passed by all too quickly, with not enough hours in the day to get everything done.

While Yancey focused on data analysis and setting up the Silent Witness network, Simon spent the bulk of his day touching base with his political contacts. On top of this, Gretchen kept up a steady stream of stories that she thought the guys should be aware of.

The news on the political front was interesting, to say the least. The ruling Conservative Reformation party seemed to be cranking up the economic announcements in the long lead-up to the election due in fourteen months. The Liberal and NDP parties spent more time attacking each other than they did the government, and the new Liberal Democratic Party was making a surprisingly good showing. It had been created just before the last general election by MPs and party supporters of both the Liberal and NDP parties, outraged and repulsed by the seeming institutional stupidity in their parties. Although new, it had garnered only a few seats less than either of the parent parties. Its fresh progressive dynamic clearly resonated with the voters, and it seemed to be attracting the best and brightest of the progressive-leaning supporters. The party leaders of the Liberals and NDP pooh-poohed the LDP as a one-shot wonder, of little consequence, and contented themselves with taking shots at each other.

"Y'know, Yance, the LDP could have a real shot in the next general election," mused Simon one evening, as the two sat sipping tea. This ritual had been established during their time at 'the cabin in the woods', as they always referred to it, and had kept it up.

"How so?"

"Well, they did amazingly well in the last election, even though they had been organized for only a few months. We've got a year and a bit to the next one, and that gives them time to really come together properly. Funny thing is, it started out as a silly protest thing - sort of like the old Rhinoceros Party. Remember them? Well anyways, it isn't a joke any more. With the Libs and NDP engaged in mutual assured destruction, the LDP is really the only opposition party doing its job. And doing it well, by all accounts. They've got a lot of experienced MP's, so the new ones have been able to get up to speed in record time. They're light on detailed policies, but what they've got is pretty impressive considering they're starting from scratch."

Simon paused to take a large slurp from his tea, and refused Yancey's offer of a pastry. Despite Alvita's temptations, both of them were managing to keep to their resolution to stay trim. Well, more or less.

Yancey grinned as he put the box of pastries off to one side. He let the silence grow for a few seconds then gently teased, "Ah, but there's more. I can tell. I am a detective, ya know. Can't hide anything from me. I see all and know ..."

"Oh, just shut up, will you?" snapped Simon with mock anger, "I was getting to that part. Hell, can't a man pause for a sip of tea without being harangued?"

Yancey's eyes flew open, and his right hand slapped up against his chest, "Moi? *Moi?* Would *I* harangue *you?* I'm … I'm … shocked. Shocked and hurt. Truly. Deeply."

He punctuated the depth of his shock by quivering his mouth and making soft, sobbing sounds. The effect was effectively ruined, shortly thereafter, by his soft snorts of laughter.

This got Simon chuckling, and it took nearly a minute for the two of them to regain control of themselves. The laughter finally died down, and Simon's face grew more serious, "They even made some hints about me joining them. Not very subtle ones."

Yancey smiled, "Well, the plan was for you to get into the political side. Although, in truth, I just kinda assumed it would be with one of the traditional parties."

"Yah, me too," was the bemused reply, "but I didn't realize how truly screwed up they were. I mean *really, really* screwed up, from the top down. No one can understand it, either. It's like there is always something happening to get them riled up over some old wound or imagined slight."

"Almost as if someone was helping it along?" mused Yancey.

"That was my thought," replied Simon quietly. "Although that could easily be explained by normal political back room nonsense helped along by ConRef people gently throwing sand in the gears of their opponents. Dunno. It's like you always say, Yance, never attribute to malice that which is more properly attributed to stupidity."

Yancey snorted his agreement. To his mind, stupidity and politics seemed to be such natural bedfellows. "OK, so the LibDems are the voice of sanity, it sounds like.

What sort of role were they hinting at?"

Simon's voice was thoughtful as he replied, "That's interesting, actually. Many of them recalled my work in the back rooms, and were hoping to lure me into that side of things. Especially on the analytics side - lots of fun stuff there to work on. But here's the really interesting bit. Some of them even suggested running as a candidate in Toronto. What's more, it was the more senior MPs making that suggestion. The ConRefs have Toronto sewed up, but some people think the support is brittle, especially in the financial districts. They said many of the same things that Gretchen said up at the cabin, mentioning my work there and the good impression I made on a lot of folks. Kinda embarrassing, to tell you the truth."

Yancey stayed silent. His friend was far too modest for his own good, and never thought of his gentle and kind nature as being anything special. But Yancey was very much aware of Simon's keen intellect and strength of character, and was gratified that others finally seemed to be taking proper appreciation of that.

"You interested?"

"Hmm, not sure. Always kinda figured I'd do the political thing from the inside. Maybe as an assistant to an MP, or party insider. I guess if they're serious about running candidates, they need to start picking them now. It'll take time to build up the organization in ridings they don't already represent, and that's a lot of ridings. Hmm, ya know ..." Simon's voice grew quiet as his eyes unfocused as thoughts roiled in his mind.

Yancey just grinned softly, and took a quiet sip of his tea. Running for office was probably the best strategic move, actually. Gave them more options - good options. But he said nothing, and waited for his friend to finish his thinking.

After a couple of minutes in silence, Simon inhaled sharply and once again focused on his surroundings. "I need to talk to some people back in Toronto before I decide. But ... yeah, it makes sense to run. For one thing, it'll be a great platform to discuss issues, and maybe lay more groundwork for exposing the Sword's operations. We've not got any firm plans on how to do that. Hmm, timing will be important ... yah, this could work out nicely."

Then he noticed Yancey sitting there quietly, with a gentle smile on his face.

"But you'd already figured this out, didn't you, oh master planner," he said accusingly.

"Some of it, sure," was the quiet reply, "but you're the master of the political angles, not me. Simon, it really does make sense from both a tactical and strategic point of view. Running for office would be a helluva commitment, though. And a helluva risk, being so public and exposed. You up for it? Really?"

In response, Simon raised his mug of tea and made a salute of it, "Illegitimi non carborundum," he intoned solemnly.

Equally solemnly, Yancey raised his mug and repeated the toast. They clinked mugs, then drained the cold contents with a shudder.

"Blah. Well, that was disgusting," belched Yancey with a shudder. "Want a refill?"

"Only if we wash it down with one of Alvita's pastries," was the reply.

Yancey raised an eyebrow at the request for a pastry.

"Hey," Simon retorted, "some things are worth celebrating the right way."

With a laugh, Yancey agreed and passed over the box of

pastries after selecting one for himself.

* * *

A couple of days later Simon returned to Yancey's office in the afternoon to find his friend standing in front of a whiteboard, his hands wrapped around his head with fingers interlaced. This was, as Simon well knew, an indication of deep thought. Or an ice cream headache. Very serious stuff, in any case. The only real surprise was to find Camille sitting at a table, a small smile on her face as she observed Yancey at work. Simon nodded a greeting to Camille, then held a finger to his lips to encourage her to keep silent. With a turn of her head, she simply nodded a greeting at him, making no other sound or movement.

"Greetings, Simon," Yancey intoned as his left hand lifted off his head and pointed unerringly at his friend. "I deduce that you have already eaten."

Camille frowned at this, then turned and sniffed, "He's right. I can smell the food on you. And a cigar or something, too." She sniffed deeply several times, and her frown deepened. "Curry." Sniff. "Basil." Sniff. "I know that spice mixture ... you ate at that Thai restaurant, just off of Bronson, didn't you?"

The last was said quite accusingly, with not a trace of humour. Camille took her cooking seriously, and expected customer loyalty from these two.

"Uhm ..." began Simon.

"And you had a meeting with the party chairman of the Liberal Democratic Party," Yancey intoned without turning around.

"Well, uhm ..."

"Further, I can deduce that you came back here in a cab from the Standard Cab Company. And the driver was a

255

swarthy man wearing a tattered, blue cloth worker's cap of the sort usually seen in the southern part of Germany."

By this time both Simon and Camille were gaping at him. Then Simon sighed disgustedly, sat down heavily, and said to Camille, "Just ignore him. He just likes to show off his observational skills." Then he turned to Yancey and said, "It gets really old, and I'm not playing that game anymore." He paused and then said somewhat contritely to Camille, "Yeah, we went there but I didn't have any choice about it. No, really."

Camille just sniffed, and refused to look at him. So she turned back to Yancey, "Alright, oh mighty detective. I can see how you figured out how he'd eaten ... that was pretty obvious. But how did you know who he's seen?"

Yancey lowered his arms and turned around to face them. His face held a large lopsided smile. "You observe, but you do not truly see. You have all the clues, but ..."

"That will be quite enough, Yancey Franklin," snapped Camille primly, "you will tell me, or I will see to it that Auntie never gives you ... either of you ... another pastry."

Simon just rolled his eyes and sighed, "Why am I included in that? I warned you not to indulge him."

For his part, Yancey just laughed and walked over to the table and sat down. He stared at Camille, waggled his eyebrows and said in a poor imitation of Groucho Marx, "Fill my cup with coffee and my hand with a pastry, and I will tell all. I wouldn't do this for anyone else, but you have the eyes of an angel and my soul burns to cater to your every whim." As he said this, his eyes grew large and soulful like those of a puppy.

Camille glared at him with a basilisk stare, then sighed and filled his cup from the carafe she had brought, and passed over the box of pastries. "This had better be good.

Or else," she warned. "And you weren't supposed to be eating so many of these, anyways."

Yancey paused to take a bite of pastry and a sip of coffee, and closed his eyes while heaving a happy sigh. It had been a long time since breakfast, and thinking was hard work. It burned a lot of calories, or so he kept telling himself and anyone who would listen.

A low growl from Camille caused Yancey to hurriedly swallow and explain. "OK, OK. The cigar smell is pretty distinctive, as you said. Simon came home yesterday with the same smell. When I complained about it he said that he'd been in a room with a cigar smoker who just happened to be the aforementioned party chairman."

Camille nodded, "Alright, fair enough. But what was that nonsense about the cab. Simon, is that accurate?"

Simon froze in mid-grab towards the box of pastries, "Uhm ... well, yeah. Can't figure out how he knew that one, though." He completed his grab of a pastry, then sat down to take a bite and chew thoughtfully while glaring at Yancey.

"My friends," Yancey said in mock-friendly tones and opening his arms wide, "the answer is before you. Open your eyes and gaze upon the true wonder of my ..."

"Spill the beans or face a dulcimer up the whazoo when we get back to our rooms," interrupted Simon. Camille nodded her emphatic agreement.

"Spoilsports," chortled Yancey. Then he turned and pointed at the large computer screen that was off to the side of whiteboard he'd been studying. "The security camera I've got pointed out front caught Simon as he pulled up. The feed from it shows up in the window at the bottom left of the screen."

Simon and Camille looked at each other in disbelief, then at the screen, then at each other again, then simultaneously shook their heads.

"You've been putting up with this for how long?" enquired Camille incredulously.

"Ever since we were kids," Simon assured her, his face a study in long-suffering patience.

Yancey just laughed softly and happily ate the rest of the pastry and sipped on the coffee. When he figured the other two had gotten it out of their systems, he looked at Simon and asked, "So, how did it go?"

Simon paused to pour himself a cup of coffee before answering. "It's like we figured. They want me to run in one of the downtown Toronto ridings, where I live and work. I had fired off an email to Gretchen about it yesterday, and had her to do a quick check of the LibDem organization. Got her answer just before the meeting. It all looks on the up and up, Yance. Both she and Cha...I mean, her contacts … approve. Very much so, in fact."

Camille pretended not to notice the slip. She was not offended in the least at the secrecy, and in fact quite approved of it. She knew about Gretchen, of course, and how highly both of the young men thought of her. She leaned forward and enquired intently, "So, have you decided?"

Simon gazed deeply into his coffee before answering. "Yeah, probably I'll run. I need to talk to some people back in Toronto about this, and see how firm my support is there. The party chairman was fine with that. In fact he seemed pleased at how carefully I was going about this - and who the people were I'd be talking to. Of course, they've got no organization down there right now, but he knows a few people who might help if they like the candidate. It's a big risk, you see, for any business that goes against the ConRef's. The … well, loathing might be too strong a word, but dislike pretty strongly seems to fit

... and at levels higher up the corporate food chain than I had suspected. But with the government controlling more and more of the economy these days, and doling out the best contracts to their friends, well ..."

"That's how it begins, Simon. The Big Evil gettin' its claws in deep," Camille said sadly.

They all fell silent, lost in their own thoughts for a time. Then Simon shook his head, looked at Yancey and said accusingly, "And you, my friend, were doing your best to divert us just prior to this little recitation of mine. No, no, don't deny it. Just spill it."

It was Yancey's turn to gaze into his coffee, but only for a few seconds. Then he raised his head and looked at his two friends carefully.

"Simon, I think I've figured out who's behind the Sword. Camille nudged me towards it."

Simon jerked upright. Camille just looked confused.

"Look," explained Yancey, "I was getting nowhere with figuring out the Harvest operation, so I started thinking about the bigger picture. It's not enough to stop this or that operation ... it may be necessary, but we need to understand the overall scheme that all these different aspects and operations fit into. I've become convinced I'm missing something, something important. Camille came in not too long ago, and we were talking about what happened at Old Home. How things changed over the years. Just before she arrived, I was going over some of the stuff that Gretchen sent, the stuff about the recent government economic announcements and some of the background she'd dug up. That's when it struck me."

He had their complete attention now.

"The types of operations, the types of economic controls, the mindset required. Simon, it looks as if the City of London is behind this."

His pronouncement was greeted with silence. The silence grew, and was finally broken as Simon said quietly but with no trace of humour, "Yance, buddy, you've lost it. No, seriously. You need to take some time off from this, and step back."

Yancey sprang to his feet and began pacing. His right hand waved as if to dismiss Simon's objections.

"No, hear me out, please. Yes, this sounds like some paranoid delusion. I'm well aware of that. But the facts fit, all too well, Simon. Look, let me bring up ..." Yancey's voice held a pleading tone.

"Yancey, no. Just no. Stop it," Simon's voice was harsh.

Camille could only gape at the two of them. She had never seen them like this, nor had she heard Uncle mention this sort of behaviour. The two just glared at each other for a moment, and she felt that she had to intervene. "Could you please explain to me how a city in England could be causing this?"

"Camille, it is nothing ..." Simon began.

"Stop," she commanded, and Simon shut his mouth with a snap. "Let him be speakin'." Her voice took on a tinge of the patois that only showed itself when she was upset. The two of them glared at each other.

"That's OK, Camille," said Yancey softly. "He's not entirely wrong, you know. It really does sound crazy because it's an old conspiracy theory."

The other two turned to look at him with puzzled looks.

Yancey sighed.

"Look, Camille, as Simon can tell you, I've enjoyed reading about crazy conspiracy theories my whole life. They not only take on a life of their own, but sometimes they can get inside a person's head and mess them up. Sort of like an ear worm that makes the mind run around in circles like a dog chasing its tail until it gets lost inside itself. That's what Simon's worried has happened to me."

Simon made a terse nod, although his angry demeanour softened somewhat.

"In fact, Simon's caught me getting wound up about things more than once. I can get a bit ... obsessive at times."

Simon's nod this time was friendlier, with the hint of a smile.

"But not this time, Simon. Upon my honour, I might be on to something. That's why I need you to check out my logic on this. I agree that is sounds like idiotic conspiracy nonsense. But, just hear me out. Please."

Simon looked intently at his oldest and dearest friend. Yancey was the most brilliant person he'd ever met, but his flights of logic sometimes took him to places that Simon was afraid his friend wouldn't be able to return from. And yet, Yancey had always managed to keep a grip on reality. And, if truth be told, those strange flights of logic often led to real solutions. Simon sighed deeply, then nodded. "Fine. But I'm going to need a fresh cup of coffee for this. And I can't promise to leave the pastries untouched."

Yancey smiled his thanks. "Coffee does sound good."

Camille surprised them by pouring the coffee and setting pastries in front of them, without saying a word. She was keenly aware that this disagreement was born of love and worry, not anger. She didn't understand why they had disagreed, but was eager to find out.

They sat in silence for a minute, sipping on their coffee, but ignoring the pastries. Then Yancey slowly got up and began pacing back and forth. Simon smiled slightly ... this was typical Yancey in explanation-mode.

"First of all, Camille," began Yancey, "London is actually two cities. There's London, proper - that's what everyone thinks about when they talk about London. Then there's the City of London. That's part of the downtown area, about a mile square, that houses the major economic activity of the country. Most people, even those living in Britain, aren't aware of the fact that the City of London is its own little empire, quite separate and distinct from the rest of the country. It has legal powers and a degree of independence not allowed any other city or town within Britain. For example, corporations are allowed to vote in its elections, and those votes outnumber those of the permanent residents by over three to one. There's all sorts of reasons given, but it all boils down to one thing. Money. It's been a centre of wealth for centuries, millennia even."

Camille just looked at him unbelieving. She glanced at Simon, who just nodded. He'd heard all this before.

"Truly, Camille. The City of London existed before any written records in Britain. But it existed, and exerted so much power, that when the Normans conquered England in 1066, they reportedly left the City alone. In fact, they seem to have curried favour with the bankers there. Over the centuries, the rest of the city grew up around it, but the core - the City of London - remained its special independence. Any time over the centuries when kings or parliaments threatened to reduce it to the status of a regular city, somehow that never came about. Money was doled out, sometimes silently and sometimes obviously, but doled out it was, and in great quantity. From the mists of time up to the present day."

Camille just shook her head, "What does this all have to do with the Big Evil?"

"Europe has always had spots that catered to the rich and powerful. Places to safely stash money, no matter how it was obtained, and keep it safe. Places like

Switzerland and others. But the City of London was special. It sat apart from Britain, yet increasingly integrated into the web of commerce. In fact, there are those who say it pulled the levers of power for Britain's colonial empire. Then came the two World Wars. Horrible wars that shook the fabric of Europe and fractured the old empires, while allowing new ones to arise. Financially exhausted after the two wars and with no empire to loot for money, Britain became all but bankrupt, living on dreams of past imperial glories. Except for the City of London, which retained quite a lot of economic clout and figured out ways to expand it. Britain had retained its various island protectorates throughout the world, and the City figured out ways to use those as havens for the rich to stash money so that it couldn't be traced or found or taxed. A lot of the initial funds came from organized crime, kleptomaniac despots, and various spy agencies during the Cold War. But the City didn't care, so long as the cash flowed in and it could rake of a piece of the action."

Camille nodded, "I have heard tell of those past days. Wild times, from the sounds of it. But not so bad for most."

"True enough, Camille. Not so bad. Then the multinational corporations got into the act, wanting to avoid taxes. That led to even more innovative banking schemes set up by the City. More wealth flowing around, and over time it became done by electronic transfer, not physical money. The next big thing was setting up special laws for corporations, with lax reporting standards, and government protections. That led to a lot of companies incorporating in these far away locations, so that the head office located there gets all the profits, and pays little or no taxes. Lots of schemes to hide and obfuscate and hide behind the shield of government protections. But that meant arranging for compliant governments, and compliant civil services, and more and more control over how those countries were run. Sound familiar, Camille? "

"De Big Evil," she whispered. "Dat be why it be everywhere." Her patois was thick by this time as the implications of what she was hearing began to sink in.

"Yes," said Yancey softly, "because it was a web of control that spread over the world. It has become so large that even declared enemies of Britain routinely use the City to do their banking with impunity. The amount of money being sucked up into the City's control is staggering. Much of Africa's wealth gets sucked out of it and put into the City's banks before it can get taxed, and that's a big reason behind that continent's economic problems."

"But there are other places that do this sort of thing, Yancey," Simon interjected.

"Yep, but none on the same scale. Some of them, like Cyprus and Iceland, suffered financial meltdowns and the depositors lost billions. That just made the City's banks look better and better. More growth, and more control over the global economic levers."

"OK, fine, but how does that involve the Sword?" Simon asked, "You've just described an economic cancer, and one that's been known for a long time. But there are international agreements in place, or being negotiated, that will force more and more transparency on those tax havens."

"Exactly, Simon. Keep that last point in mind - it's really important. But to address your first point. We know that the Sword has been around for just over a century, right?"

Both Simon and Camille nodded.

"And the ones who started it were of the economic and

political elites in Britain, right?"

Again, both nodded.

"The City of London has been around for many centuries. It has survived by grabbing control of everything it could get its grubby paws on, and keeping control, until it controlled Britain and its empire. I'm not saying that it started Infinity Ascending. In fact, I rather doubt that it did. But once Infinity Ascending formed the Sword to be its covert action arm, it became a Player. And stayed a Player, exerting more and more control over the decades, while staying out of sight. How did it do that? How did it exert that much control while staying hidden? And why the sudden increase in Sword militancy in Canada?"

Simon and Camille just stared at him.

"And now, think about your second point, Simon. The City is used to thinking in the long term - generations, in fact. Yes, transparency is slowly being forced on the City's economic empire. They saw this coming and so they needed a new place to stash the money, and to weave a web of mirrors and walls around it. Think about the latest economic announcements. Not just the handouts and sellouts to the foreign multinationals. Not just the economic chaos caused by the tank attack on Bay Street. No, I'm talking about the fundamental re-jiggering of our laws and corporate governance. The last big announcement talked about making our corporate governance something more along the lines of the state of Delaware, of all places. They're creating a new secrecy state for their activities, but this time it's got more resources and size and clout than any number of small islands."

Simon groaned, and Camille just stared at him.

"Argh, I've been so busy with this political stuff that the

implications of that didn't hit me. Until now. Shitshitshithshi ..." he wound down as he noticed Camille glaring at him.

"Uhm, sorry for the language, Camille, but ... this is bad. Delaware is sort of the American answer to the City, in some ways. Their state laws are set up to allow very low taxation of any corporation headquartered there. And that headquarters can be a post office box ... in fact, that's all it is for tens of thousands of corporations, including most of the largest ones in the US. Worse, it has a special legal system set up for corporations, and it is so heavily biased in favour of business as to be flat-out anti-consumer."

"But that gives us an insight into their next step, Simon," Yancey stated quietly. "That's just the first step. Next is rejiggering the banking system, removing transparency regulations, that sort of thing."

"Wait, what about all those new international agreements you talked about?" asked Camille.

Yancey said sadly, "I've started checking on those. Turns out that Canada hasn't signed any of them, or at least any of the ones I've been able to check so far."

"Oh, shit-on-a-stick," whispered Simon. "It's really happening. That would allow the City to give up the other places while setting up a new system here that would put the old one to shame." He turned quickly to Camille, "Sorry about the language."

Camille shook her head, "Not a problem - I was going to say worse."

The group fell silent, each lost in their own thoughts for a moment. Then Camille spoke up, and said in a soft voice, "Are you two OK?"

That got their attention, and they looked at her with puzzled expressions.

"You were so angry with him, Simon. And Yancey, you seemed so cold to him for a bit. Is everything OK between you?"

The two men looked at each other, then back at her.

Finally Yancey spoke, "Well, yeah. Why wouldn't everything be OK?" He turned to look at Simon and shrugged.

Simon was a bit lost in his own thoughts and said in a somewhat distracted voice, "Yeah, yeah. What he said."

Camille was beginning to glare at the two of them by this time. This was not at all what she had expected.

Yancey smiled, "We've talked about the City of London thing before. Years back, when Simon was in university, I convinced him to write a paper about it. Not about the conspiracy side, mind you, just the fact that it was a powerful autonomous entity within Britain."

Simon simply snorted softy on hearing this, but remained for the most part lost in thought.

"And he's still a bit sore about it, perhaps," Yancey said with a smile. "His prof gave him a failing grade, saying he'd never heard such nonsense in his life. So I supplied Simon with all sorts of hard data, some of it proudly proclaimed by the City itself. Simon had to go to the Dean over it, but the prof was forced to give him a passing grade. Great fun, all in all. At least I thought so. Simon's memory of it may differ."

Simon's mind was obviously still not quite in the here-and-now, but he managed to mumble, "Idiot prof. Left at the end of term. Real twit." Then he lapsed back into a thoughtful silence. The other two simply looked upon him quietly.

Then Simon looked up with a start, "I gotta get to Toronto as quickly as possible. We need to see if there are any whispers of this on The Street. There's gotta be people who have figured this out." He glanced at Yancey who had an amused smile on his face. "Sorry, Yance. You're good, but there are people who are true savants about this sort of stuff."

Yancey laughed, "No offence taken." Then he grew thoughtful, "But you've got a helluva good point there. There *are* people who are geniuses in this sort of stuff. It does beg the question as to why this isn't already out there."

"Fear."

The two men turned to look at Camille.

"They see da Big Evil and its claws. They see da comin' storm, and stay silent. Can't say as I blame 'em, neither." Camille's patois was back.

Simon glanced at the time. The time had flown by, and it was now early evening.

"I'll call the airlines and see if I can get a flight out this evening. Yancey, email Gretchen to tell her that I hope to be coming down this evening and will need a place to stay. Flight info to follow. Oh, and tell her to keep her ears open for any news about banking regulations. May as well get started looking into that stuff."

Yancey nodded and went to a computer to do as he was instructed.

Simon turned to Camille, "You best go tell Mama and Alvita about what we've been discussing. We really need to start identifying some of the people associated with the Sword. Or the City, or whoever it is we're fighting now. If anyone in the Silent Witness has access to any banking records in Old Home or the City of London, that'd be a big help. Anything to do with tax haven stuff. Corporate or individual."

Yancey looked up from his task to interject, "But all those layers of obfuscation will make identification impossible, won't it?"

Simon replied quickly, "Yep. But it might give us some patterns of behaviour. Sort of like fingerprints. At some point we can start matching names to the fingerprints, and that could be a really useful." His smile was predatory, "And with an election coming up, it could prove to be *very* useful."

Yancey and Camille gave answering predatory grins, then went off on their assigned tasks. Simon picked up a phone and dialled a friend who worked at the airport. The online booking systems were all well and good, but sometimes it took a human contact to get the job done fast.

* * *

The next afternoon found Yancey pacing in his office, alternating between sheets of paper and the screens of the several computers he was using. After Simon had left for the airport and Camille returned to her home, Yancey was left alone to do what he did best - sift through massive amounts of data, extract useful threads of information, and build up an idea of what was going on. This was what he had been doing for years, and all that experience and expertise was being used to attack the problems facing them.

A knocking at the front door forced his attention back to the here-and-now. A glance at the security camera feed showed that it was Camille, and she was carrying a small package. Uttering a small exasperated sigh, he got up and let her in. That done, he turned without a word and went back to his ruminations. Camille just smiled. Simon and Uncle had warned about this sort of thing, and she wasn't surprised or offended.

A quick glance at the empty but unwashed coffee pot,

showed that it was unlikely that Yancey had had any rest since the previous evening. She did a quick cleanup, set the coffee pot to soak itself clean, and went into the work area. Yancey was back to pacing and glaring at the material he was studying, so Camille quietly placed the coffee and food she'd prepared onto one of the spare tables. Not pastries this time - proper breakfast food, hot and savoury. She used her hands to fan the aromas over to where Yancey was. It took a bit, but finally his head jerked upwards with a snap.

"Oh, food. Great. Need that. Thanks." And with that he strode over and for a couple of minutes focused entirely on eating and sipping coffee. Then he let out a contented sigh, leaned back in his chair, and sat with his eyes closed and savoured the smell of the coffee.

"Camille, thank you. From the bottom of my famished heart, I thank you. You are truly an angel of mercy. And one who makes the very best coffee. I used to think Mama's was the best, but yours is even better. Feel free to tell him I said that, by the way. He agrees."

Camille gave an amused snort. Yancey's eyes were still closed as he focused on the aroma of the coffee. "What?" she asked innocently, "No offer of marriage? Uncle and Auntie always tell me about how you offer to marry them for *their* food."

This got Yancey to actually open one eye to study her for a moment, then it closed again. His face assumed a mien of total serenity. "I've known them longer. I'm not the kind of boy to rush into anything, you know."

This got a rare, full-throated laugh out of Camille. "Oh, so true," she said with amusement, "Careful and slow consideration of all things, that's you. A true master of moderation."

Yancey responded with a hurt, "Harumph."

"So what are you working on so hard that you ignore rest and food? Simon warned me to keep an eye on you," enquired Camille.

That her remark had hit its mark was evidenced by the way Yancey suddenly sat upright with a guilty look on his face.

"No, no. I had a bit of snooze. Really. Well, a nap, actually. Well …"

Camille laughed again, "Never mind. What's with all these papers and markings you got here? And those bouncing blobs on those screens?"

Nothing distracted Yancey like an excuse to talk about whatever he was working on. He stood up and walked over to one of the computers. Camille followed, her features bemused.

"OK, so after Simon and you left, I started thinking about what we'd been working on earlier - how to detect patterns of movement. Then that got me thinking about their various operations, and that got me thinking about this Harvest of Souls thing. Remember that?"

Camille simply nodded.

"Well, I've got a bunch of dates and times from some of the data Simon and I collected from the Tears facility. The other set of historical records that we got from … I mean, recently acquired … gave me some more dates and times. So I crunched it all and set it up like a schedule. See on that screen over there?" He pointed to one of the other computers.

Again, Camille nodded. It was just a list of dates and places as far as she could see. "So what did you do with that? Throw it into a spreadsheet?"

Yancey grunted in amusement, "Nope. The sort of analysis that I do on stuff like this isn't something spreadsheets can do, or at least not easily. I like to use R with a bit of Python and Ruby. Gives me better control for data manipulation and visualization. Like merging data sets and matching them to geographic data."

Yancey continued excitedly, "Like I did with that mess of data there. The interesting thing about all that is that all those places and times can be mapped into something resembling a transportation grid. Like on that other screen over there."

Camille looked at the indicated screen and saw a coloured web of lines. "Alright, then, a grid. Does it relate to anything?"

She heard Yancey clatter at the keyboard briefly, then a map of Ontario appeared superimposed on the calculated grid. It lined up perfectly with existing roads and cities.

"You're right, Yancey. But I'm not sure how that helps us."

Yancey just smiled. "My first thought, exactly. Not much there that we don't already know. But notice how it got plotted, with the most travelled routes showing up as thicker lines. All very nice, of course, but one of the things you learn when analyzing data is to look at the outliers. If you look carefully, there's a few places that only get visited occasionally. So I set it up a different way. I decided to see how things varied over time. That's what those bounding coloured blobs are that you mentioned when you first arrived. It shows different shipments, sorted by time, as they get tracked."

Camille stared at the screen with greater interest. "Can you superimpose the map on this one?"

Yancey smiled, "Yep. I turned that off to better concentrate on the movements. Try watching for a bit as I speed it up. Don't focus on one spot, but rather try to take it all in at once to spot overall patterns."

As she had been instructed, Camille stared at the screen

at the coloured blobs moved at a moderate pace. It took about a minute before ending and then repeating.

"Speed it up," she commanded.

This time it took about thirty seconds to loop.

"Faster."

The loop now took ten seconds. She was staring very intently at the screen, now.

"Twice as fast. And just loop continuously."

The loop now took five seconds to complete before repeating. The blobs flashed by so fast as to be lines, with the occasional flash to indicate a rarer route.

"There." Camille pointed excitedly at one of the intermittent flashes. "That one's special. The other flashes look almost random, but this one is regular. Like a heartbeat. Not quite that regular, but more so than anything else. Where is that place?"

Without a word, Yancey superimposed the map over the still-pulsing blobs. The 'heartbeat flash' that Camille had noticed was just outside of Dryden.

"The Tears of Joy," Yancey said softly. "We know it's used to house Sword people for a stop-over while travelling, hold prisoners, to forcibly extract information from prisoners, and who knows what else. Now it appears that it is used for something on a fairly regular basis - and has for some time."

"But what, Yancey? Why the regular shipments?" Camille shuddered as she remembered what those 'shipments' might entail.

"A number of those would be Sword personnel just passing through, I would think," replied Yancey slowly. "But I can't help but think there's something more. We know that kids have been moved out of northern Ontario for many years, and funnelled into big cities as prostitutes and drug mules. Some of those trips correlate with groups of disappearances. Taking those groups out still leaves a lot of trips there. Simon and I have taken an estimate of the staffing levels the Sword seems to have in Ontario, based on the information we have, and used the Sword emails to guesstimate the number of passing-through staff. That still leaves a significant number of trips there, but the pattern is different. Here, watch."

Yancey clattered at the keyboard for a few seconds, and the screen now showed only the trips to the Tears facility.

"OK, here's what we were looking at originally, isolating only trips to Tears. Five-second loop."

Camille saw the same fairly regular pattern as before, but more clearly now that the extraneous trips had been removed. She nodded and glanced at Yancey. He pressed a couple of keys, then said, "OK, removing the known groups of disappearances and estimated Sword passing-through."

The pulsing of the light became less frequent and regular, but still had a puzzling rhythm.

"And that's what I was trying to figure out, Camille. Some reason for those regular trips when everything else is accounted for. Something else is going on there."

Camille was staring intently at the screen, then queried, "Any way to correlate those with, say, any other criminal activity?"

Yancey smiled, "Good point. But without access to the police database, I can't do stuff like that. I've got a list of those dates, but nothing there stands out. It's just that every so often, there is a burst of one to three trips to the facility. Then a slight delay of a few days, then the same number of trips away from it, always to southern Ontario. The data isn't more precise than that."

"Maybe some unaccounted for trips by their staff? You did say that it was just an estimate."

"Thought of that," was the thoughtful reply, "but this seems to be a different pattern of behaviour than any of the other trips. I fear we've pushed our current data to its limits."

The two stood there contemplating the screens, but were startled by a banging on the front door. Yancey took a quick look at the camera feed. "It's Mama. And he looks excited about something. I'd better let him in."

Within seconds, Mama was inside and the look on his face was not one that boded glad tidings. "Yancey-boy, I just hear word from some friends in Toronto. There be somethin' bad goin' on. Childrens be kidnapped."

"What?" exclaimed both Yancey and Camille at the same time.

Camille quickly added, "Uncle, sit you down here. You breathin' too hard."

Mama waved her away. "No time for that, Camille. Glad to see you here. Yancey," he turned towards the young man. He paused briefly to catch his breath before continuing, "I know some folks from Old Home that be workin' for Rich Ones. Dey tell me that de kids be kidnapped. Not just one fam'ly, but hear tell of at least five. All nearly de same time. They get to talkin' after work, and dat's how it come out that so many be happenin'. No police involvement. De parents keep t'ings on de down low, as Rich Ones like to do."

Yancey stared intently at his friend, "Names? Details?"

Mama held out a piece of paper, "All de details be here, Yancey-boy. Names of children and when taken. Even have license plates of some of de cars that take them."

Yancey had been looking at the information on the paper, but his head jerked up at this. "How is that possible, Mama? Where did you friends get this sort of information?"

Mama just shook his head sadly, "Yancey-boy, we folk from de Old Home be everywhere. Lots of dirty jobs need doin' that go beggin' for people to do 'em. So the ones like us get those. When we work for Rich Ones, dey no see us. We de invis'ble ones. Gard'ners and maids, mostly. But some work security. And dey see t'ings. Have access to the security cameras. Dat's how dey know the kids gone. Dat's how dey get license plates." Mama paused for a moment before continuing, "And Yancey, some say dey see your lemon eight sign inside de cars when doors open."

Camille turned to Yancey, "Dey be taken to de Tears place for sure, Yancey."

Thinking furiously for a moment, Yancey said softly, "Don't know that for sure, Camille. Might be. But the one thing for damn sure is that this is too big for us to stop on our own."

"But how we save de chil'ren?" Camille pleaded.

Yancey looked away, towards the computer screen and its rhythmic flashing. Then he looked back at them with a grim smile. "I think I know someone at the OPP who can help us. But a phone call won't do it. Gotta do this in person, I think. Gonna take a few hours to drive there, so let's take a few minutes and get started on this properly. Mama, I need as much information as you can get me."

Mama nodded and turned to Camille, "You be known' some folks that be workin' for de Rich Ones. Call 'em. Ask if dey see somethin'."

Camille nodded, and when Yancey pointed to the phone, she trotted over and began calling.

"Yancey-boy, I be goin' back to de deli. Alvita be out, but I call her back. She know some folk, too. We make calls from dere, usin' de burn phones you get us." And with that Mama turned and strode out.

Yancey took a deep breath, then let it out slowly. The first thing to do was to email Gretchen and Simon with this information and to let them know what was going on. Maybe Charlene could do something with it. Whatever happened, there was going to be a story in it for her. There was equipment to collect and pack into the Busted Flush. Then it was off on a trip to see Sergeant Dundee and discuss with him what the police could do to help rescue those kids.

It was time to take direct action against the Sword.

CHAPTER TWENTY-SEVEN
The End of Tears

The long solitary drive had given Yancey plenty of time to think, and his thoughts hadn't been altogether pleasant. It had taken longer than Yancey had wanted to finally get on the road, but it was time well-spent. Mama had obtained a more complete list of the known kidnap victims and their families. As had been initially noted, they were all children of the rich and powerful. No ransoms had been demanded, so Yancy was pretty sure that this was an attempt to force the cooperation of their parents. An even more chill-inducing thought was that perhaps the Fist of Tolerance planned to 'convert' the children more firmly into their creed. In any event, Yancey knew that he and his friends had to somehow shut down the operation as quickly as possible.

Once he had the complete list of victims, he had emailed Gretchen and Charlene to let them know what was going on. After a quick flurry of emails, it had been decided that they would hold off on any enquiries until they heard from Yancey. He told them of his plan to contact Sergeant Dundee, and Charlene had approved of it, as he seemed to be the only police contact they could trust. Nobody wanted to risk the lives of the kidnapped children with any rash action, and everyone was aware of the Sword's ruthlessness.

Yancey even had a chance to exchange a couple of emails with Simon. The latter had spent a weary night struggling with flight delays and bad weather at Toronto that had forced all flights to circle until conditions cleared. He had just landed, hours later than expected, as Yancey was about to leave. Because they had discussed secure communications before Simon had left, Yancey left it to him to give those details to the ladies. Given the pervasive monitoring of phone calls by businesses and governments, they had long since decided to use only encrypted emails for most communications. Voice calls were to be reserved for emergencies only. Once re-established in his office, Yancey had set up yet another layer of secure mail drops and burn phones, and Simon would let the ladies know about those.

Those things were, unfortunately, the only things that he could influence or control. His biggest concern was about the reception that Sgt. Dundee would give him. Yancey was pretty sure that Dundee would either be able to help him or would point him to someone who could. Dundee's comments about not entirely trusting his own staff, combined with the fear that the call might be monitored, had convinced Yancey that a face-to-face meeting was the only viable option. A lot depended on how Dundee reacted. Yancey was betting his life, and the lives of the children, on his faith in the old police officer.

Finally arriving at his destination, Yancey was in a position to safely telephone Sgt. Dundee. He stopped outside of a restaurant, went inside and used the pay phone to call the police detachment. He asked for Dundee and was put on hold for several minutes. Finally, the phone was picked up and Dundee's reassuring voice was heard enquiring who it was that was calling.

"Hello, Sergeant, this is Yancey. I need to meet with you to discuss that old case we talked about a while ago. Do you have time to meet with me?"

The only sound Yancey could hear was the background hiss of the telephone line. Finally Dundee spoke, "Wasn't expecting to hear back from you so soon, son. You sure this is important?"

Yancey could tell that the sergeant was being careful of what he said. It was probably best that both play that game, he thought. "Yes, sir. I think you're going to want to hear about this. At your convenience, of course."

"Well," came the measured reply, "I have a break coming up, so could spare a few minutes. You in town?"

"Yes, sir."

Another brief pause.

"OK, meet me at the deli on Main Street. I'll be there in a few."

"I'll be there, sir."

With that, both of them hung up.

Yancey looked around and spotted a young waitress lounging behind the counter reading a newspaper. "Uhm, excuse me. I'm supposed to meet a friend at the deli on Main Street. Could you please tell where that is?"

She gave him a tired glance, then looked carefully around as if to see if anyone could overhear them. She leaned forward, and Yancey did the same. She said in a low voice, "Between you and me, that's a better choice than this place. See the street there? OK, go to your right and it'll be the second street. Hang a right again, and the deli is on the right-hand side of the street, a couple dozen metres down. Should be lots of parking at this time of day."

As he left, she gave a small wave and watched as he

walked out the door, making sure he saw her watching with appreciation.Yancey got into his car, feeling the young woman's eyes following him. Buckling up, he gave a small wave to her as he pulled away and drove down the street. He was mildly disconcerted by her attentions but felt rather pleased by it, if truth be told. Then he remembered why he was here, and quickly settled down to the business at hand.

Her directions proved to be accurate, and he found the deli with no problems. He parked the car, went inside, and quickly scanned it without seeing Dundee. So he strolled up and sat at one of the small booths. An older gentleman wandered over and with a slight European accent asked with a smile, "Good morning, young man. Or is it afternoon yet? Anyways, what can I get you?"

Yancey returned the smile with a large one of his own. "Actually I'll start with a cup of coffee. I'm meeting a friend here, so we'll order when he gets here. But that coffee of yours smells wonderful. What type of beans do you use?"

The gentleman, who turned out to be the owner, brought Yancey a cup of coffee and the two of them spent several minutes happily discussing coffee beans, roasting methods, and the best way to brew the perfect cup of coffee. Soon, Sgt. Dundee showed up, spotted Yancey, and ambled over. "I'll take the usual coffee and strudel, Frank, thanks. Oh, and bring a piece for my friend, too."

"Sure thing, Sergeant ..." replied Frank, with a big smile, "coming right up."

The two men simply nodded at each other and sat silently while Frank brought their order. After ensuring that everything was OK, he excused himself and went back into the kitchen explaining that he had some prep work to do.

"I'm told that this is the best place to eat," said Yancey with a smile.

Dundee just looked at Yancey with a neutral expression as he sipped his own coffee. The silence lasted for several more seconds before he finally spoke softly, "Why did you come back? The APB on you got cancelled, but you should have stayed away nonetheless. It's not safe for you to be here. Not for either of us."

Instead of replying, Yancey flicked his eyes towards the kitchen doorway where Frank had gone. Dundee grunted, "Frank's OK. Don't worry about him."

Yancey reached inside his jacket and pulled out a thin binder and held it across the table toward the sergeant. Dundee hesitated slightly before taking it, but then sighed and opened it up. "What am I looking at?"

"I found out where the next shipment of kids is being taken to, and when."

Dundee's head snapped upright, and his eyes blazed intensely as they bored into Yancey's. "You sure about this?" came the crisp query, all signs of mildness gone, as Dundee snapped into full-bore professional police officer mode.

"Yes, sir. I've got names of the victims, license numbers of some of the transport vehicles, the destination, and the delivery times. The only thing I'm lacking is a way to stop it."

"What's the source of this information?"

Yancey paused before answering. This could get tricky. "Confidential sources, sir."

Dundee's eyes bored into Yancey's. "Confidential sources, eh? You realize I need to confirm at least part of this before I can act, or convince the Force to act?"

"Yes, sir. Take a look at the list of names. Those are at least some of the kids being transported. And the list of license plate numbers can be verified as legitimate."

Dundee skimmed the sheets and began drumming his fingers on the tabletop, his face betraying deep concentration. This continued for a few moments as he thought about the problem. The drumming suddenly stopped, and his eyes focused on Yancey. "OK, let's head to my car. I can use the terminal there to check to see if any of these kids has been reported missing. I don't recall hearing about any recently, but it doesn't hurt to check the latest reports."

With that he got up and marched out of the deli, with Yancey following close behind. They got outside and strode a few metres down the street to where Dundee's squad car was parked. He unlocked it, motioned Yancey to get into the passenger side of the front seat, and walked around and got into the driver side. He started up the engine and began to type furiously at the terminal. He paused, read what was displayed, tapped a few more keys to scroll down the displayed information, then logged off and sat back with a heavy sigh.

"None of those names are on any reports of missing kids. Sorry, lad, but I need more than your word on this."

Yancey thought furiously for a moment before speaking, "Look, those are names of top-end families. Movers and shakers. People of influence. I don't think this is a simple kidnapping scheme - it seems more like the twisting of arms and not-so-veiled threats. They've probably been told not to contact the police. I might be able to do something about that, and have them put pressure on the police. Is there any way you can do anything about tracing those vehicles?"

Dundee thought for a moment, then shook his head. "Just verifying the existence of those vehicles won't prove much. Hmm, but maybe if we could see where they are right now..." His voice trailed off for a moment. "Look, I think that I might be able to do something, but official channels will take time. Let's go inside and see Frank. We gotta pay our tab, anyways."

With that, Dundee was out of the car, and obviously expected Yancey to follow. Puzzled though he was, Yancey got out of the car, and watched as Dundee carefully locked it then went back inside the deli. Once inside, he went back to the counter and yelled out for Frank. In a few seconds Frank came out, and cheerfully exclaimed, "Oh, you're back. Thought you'd skipped out on your tab, again."

The expression on Dundee's face chased away Frank's smile. "What's wrong?" Frank quietly asked.

"Frank, I think we may have a mass kidnapping and transport of kids going down, and it seems to be happening right now. It's going to take too damn long to go through official channels. My young friend here says he can help on contacting the parents and get pressure going from that end. But we need to track those vehicles. Do you know anyone who can help?"

Frank looked intently at Dundee, his pleasant expression replaced with something colder, more professional. "Might. Is this the real thing?"

"If my young friend here says it's real, then it's real."

Yancey kept his face under control, but he was immensely honoured by the trust being put in him. Frank's eyes scanned the young man as if probing into his soul. Then he nodded his head in a sign of agreement, and held out his hand. Dundee extracted the appropriate page from the file and handed it to him. Without another word, Frank turned and went back into his kitchen.

Dundee smiled. He was an old hand at these sorts of things, and knew that they couldn't be rushed. "Finish your coffee and eat your strudel while we wait for Frank. Keep your strength up. If your information can be verified, then we're going to be in for a long day."

Frank came back shortly with a thoughtful look on his face. "I called up some old friends of mine, and they did a search of traffic camera data. Turns out that all those vehicles were spotted at various points around the province. One group each starting from the Ottawa, Toronto, and Waterloo areas. The interesting thing is that they all seem to be heading north, and converging. Looks to be around the Dryden area."

Yancey nodded, grateful that their data analysis matched what was happening. "That would make sense. The Bad Guys have a facility there. It's been there a good number of years, masquerading as an executive retreat. I've got a file on it, with pictures and sketches of the layout."

The two older men gazed at him intently. "And why would you have that sort of information, young man?" enquired Frank in a firm, commanding voice. Dundee gazed at Yancey just as intently, but didn't say anything.

Yancey took a deep breath - he had to be careful here not to reveal too much. "I had reason to check it out, recently. Remember when we last met, Sergeant?"

Dundee nodded carefully.

"I told you that I was following up some leads on some unpleasant business. That place was one of the leads, but there was nothing really definite, so I simply did a quick check and filed the information away."

Dundee continued to stare are Yancey, and Yancey realized that the police officer was certain that there was more to it. Fortunately, he decided not to pursue the matter. For the moment, at least.

Finally Dundee broke the silence, "OK, so we've got

some decent intel. There's an OPP detachment there. Do we bring them in on this now?" The last was directed at Frank.

Frank looked thoughtful, then shook his head. "For a drop-off depot of that size dealing in kidnapped kids they have to have the local force either neutral or on their side. Best to leave them out of the loop until the last minute. But you both are missing one important point. We have no evidence of a crime." He pointed at the file that Dundee was holding, "We've got anonymous sources *claiming* kidnapped kids are being transported. Yes, we've got several groups of vehicles converging on Dryden - but that's not a crime. That's not enough for any sort of official action. We need hard evidence of some sort of crime in progress that we can tie those vehicles in with, or at least reasonable cause. Sorry, gentlemen, but that's just the way it is."

Dundee turned to Yancey and said, "Now would be a good time to get the parents - those Important People you talked about - to apply some pressure."

Yancey nodded, "Anyone special they should be calling?"

Dundee smiled a happy smile, reached into his pocket and pulled out a business card, "Yes, indeed. Here's the regional commander's name and number. He's got the authority to get things rolling. A real stickler for protocol, is old Georgie. Won't move his ass unless there's a fire under it. So make your call, young Mr. Franklin, and light that fire. Then I'll give him a call and give him a heads up. Lay the groundwork, as it were. Let him know that we're ready to go whenever he gives the word."

Yancey took the card with a lopsided grin and reached for his cell phone. This was a time for voice, not email. He dialled a prearranged number, and when a familiar feminine voice answered, he quickly said, "It's me. There's been no missing person reports filed. We need to light a fire under the police regional commander before anything can happen. Here's his name and number." Yancey read off the information from the card. Then he added, "Keep this line available for one more hour, just in case, and then dispose of it and start using the next one. I'll do the same." Then he hung up. It was up to Gretchen and Charlene, now.

He turned to Dundee and stated, "That'll get the ball rolling. I just hope it all happens quickly enough."

The two older gentlemen smiled grimly and Dundee said gently, "We can do some planning while we wait. There's no regulation that says we can't plan."

Frank added, "Why don't you get that file on the facility in question, young man, and we can go over the sorts of logistics we'll need. We'll need a sufficient force to take it, of course, then we'll need to transport those kids ... oh, and provide on-site medical teams. Go get the file, then, and I'll put up the 'closed' sign. Sergeant, why don't you make that phone call to Georgie? Then we'll get down to business. Anyone want more coffee?"

* * *

Gretchen made sure to terminate the call on the cell phone, then put it back into her pocket. Charlene was in the bullpen talking with a reporter, but Gretchen's wave caught her attention and she walked back to the enclosed office that she now shared with Gretchen.

"What's up?"

"That was Yancey. As we suspected, there's no official record of anyone missing, and the police won't move until the parents file a report and apply pressure."

Charlene sighed. "Well, we rather figured that this might be the case. Can't blame the parents for keeping it off the record, nor the police for not acting until they can confirm that something is wrong. At least I know a few parents on that list, and I'm pretty sure I can persuade them to file a report."

"Yancey gave me the name and phone number of the regional OPP commander. That'll save some time. But will it be enough?" She handed Charlene a slip of paper with the information on it.

"Oh, never underestimate these sorts of people, love," said Charlene grimly, "They hate any breath of scandal, but they hate being ordered about like ordinary people even more. If we give them a chance to get their children back, and to get back at the ones that took them, they'll take it. Once I convince the first few, they'll convince the others. It may take a few hours, but it'll get done. The trick will be to keep it all quiet, so I'll make sure that the Important People impress upon the OPP commander the necessity of maintaining operational security. And the cost to him if he fails to maintain it."

Charlene paused for a moment and her eyes glazed over as if looking at something only she could see. Then she gave her head a small shake, "Gretchen, these are phone calls only I can make. While I'm doing that, could you please help Tom and Phyllis with their stories? They're stuck on some of the data analysis aspects."

Gretchen grinned, made a sketchy salute, and left to assist her new colleagues.

Charlene grabbed a cup of coffee, made herself comfortable at her desk, and reached for her phone.

* * *

Nearly two hours had passed, and Yancey was beginning to get anxious. The two older men just smiled gently at him and told him not to worry, that these things take time.

"Besides," added Frank, "it'll take time for Georgie to clean his underwear after he starts getting those phone calls. Then he'll dither for a bit, trying to decide what is best for his career."

Dundee grunted his agreement, as he examined the photos and sketches of the Tears of Joy facility, as well as maps of the surrounding area.

"But when will we hear something?" Yancey persisted.

"Well," drawled Dundee, "once those fires get lit under his ass, Georgie will give me a call first, to confirm that I told him what I told him a couple of hours ago. Then after a few minutes of dithering he'll decide that it was really his idea all along, and that he's in charge. Then he'll delegate responsibility to someone else, myself in this case, so that if anything goes wrong he won't get the blame. So, assuming that the fires are lit, and are of sufficient heat, then I would expect a phone call pretty soon, now. In fact, why don't you and I head back to the station and start packing up for the trip? Frank, how about some supplies to take on the road? It'll take us a few hours to get there."

Frank nodded, "Sure. Drop by here on your way out, and I'll have it all ready for you. Now off you go."

With that, Dundee and Yancey went out to their individual vehicles. Dundee made sure that Yancey knew where the station was, and told him to park at the rear with the rest of the Force's vehicles, then meet him at the rear door. It was getting dark by this time, but Yancey found his way to the station without difficulty and parked as directed. He got out and stood outside the rear door, looking up at the CCTV camera that was there. In less than a minute, the door opened and Dundee motioned for him to enter. "We can wait in my office for a few minutes, then we'll start getting ready for the trip. Don't say anything to the constables about what's going on, or where. The less they know, the better, I think. At least for the moment." The thought of keeping his team in the dark clearly bothered him, but he knew that secrecy was vital if the rescue effort was to succeed.

They walked through the small squad room, to the stares of several officers. Without pausing as they marched through, Dundee told one of the officers to call the two who were off-duty and have them report in within the hour. Reaching his office, he opened the door, motioned Yancey to precede him inside, then followed Yancey in and closed the door. Without a word, he went over to the coffee maker, drew two cups, handed one to Yancey, then sat down with a satisfied sigh in his own chair. He waved at Yancey to sit, and take a load off for a few minutes.

"OK, Mr. Franklin, now we wait for the phone call from Georgie at Headquarters. Don't expect that it'll take too much longer." He blew on his coffee and took an appreciative sip. Yancey smiled and followed suit.

There was a knock on the office door, and a constable opened it up. He kept one hand on the door knob while he stood in the doorway. He gave Yancey a brief, puzzled look, then focused his attention on Dundee. "Hey, Sarge. What's going on? Fred and Charley aren't going to be happy about being called in. And their wives are going to be truly pissed at them and you over it, this being something of a special anniversary for both of them."

Dundee motioned the constable in, "Close the door, Samuel."

After the puzzled officer walked inside and closed the door, Dundee continued, "Look, I can't go into details right now for security reasons, but I'm pretty sure that I'll need everyone. Don't know all the details myself. Waiting for a phone call from Division, and that should come any time, now. Make sure that the patrol cars are all gassed up. Oh, and gas up this gentleman's Crown Vic while you're at it."

He turned to Yancey, "Give him your keys."

Yancey hesitated a moment, then passed his keys over.

"Oh, Samuel ..." began Dundee, "treat this one as if he were one of us, OK? Just gas up the car, nothing else. Oh, and pull a portable flasher, Force car markings, and a few tactical portable radios and data terminals from stores plus a few mag-mount antennas for them, and put them into the back seat of his car, please. Oh, and a few vests, too. May as well use his car to haul the bulky stuff."

Samuel looked a bit startled, but nodded. "Understood, Sarge. I'll get right on that, then bring back his keys." With a nod at Yancey, he left the office and closed the door behind him.

Yancey said nothing, but raised his eyebrows in surprise as he looked at Dundee.

Dundee simply returned a bemused look, "You know the layout of that place better than anyone, so you may as well come along. I won't be able to spare more than three people from my small station, and they'll be filling up one squad car. So that leaves you as my driver. 'Sides, I would dearly love to ride in an old Crown Vic one last time."

He paused to blow on his coffee and take a hearty slurp. He sighed happily, then looked at Yancey again, "Didn't think it'd be wise for anyone to know exactly who you are. That's why I'm not saying anything solid to the lads; just letting them draw their own conclusions. Won't be the first time we've had a visitor-who-cannot-be-named coming through here."

They sat in companionable silence for a few minutes, sipping their coffee. The quiet was broken by the ringing of the phone on Dundee's desk. He let it ring twice as he put down his cup, picked up the receiver, and identified himself. From the small grin on Dundee's face Yancey deduced that this was the Regional Commander, Georgie.

As expected, Dundee gave a brief summary of what he had told his commander several hours ago, then paused as the voice on the other end got rather more animated.

"Yessir, I understand the pressure you must be under, Sir," Dundee said soothingly. "Of course I'd be happy to take on-site responsibility for the operation. That won't be a problem. But what sort of support can I expect? I've only got limited resources here, and given the distance to Dryden, I have to leave at least two constables here. That gives me only three that I could take with me, in only one or two squad vehicles."

The voice on the other end of the phone burbled on for a bit, with only the occasional encouraging noise from Dundee.

"Sir, if I might suggest something here. How about if I pick up a few constables along the way? That way, we can build up a proper-sized team without depleting anyone's resources or raising too many red flags."

The voice babbled on for a minute.

"Yessir, I am fully aware of the need for operational security. But if we simply tell the others to join up with us, without revealing the final destination until the last minute, that should work out well."

Again, the voice babbled on for a time.

"Yessir, an excellent suggestion, Sir. Having you arrive by helicopter and provide air support would be a great help, Sir. Might I also suggest that you arrange for one of the large ambulance buses, as well? We know of at least seven kidnap victims, and there may be more. Yessir, thank you, Sir. I'll be on the road within fifteen minutes, Sir. I'll keep in touch with you via the encrypted tactical sets, Sir. Thank you, Sir. Until we meet at the site, Sir."

With that, Dundee gently hung up the phone, shook his head, rolled his eyes, and sighed softly. Then he looked at Yancey, "Well, we're on. Let's gather the troops, weapon up, and move out."

With that he got up and moved quickly out of his office into the squad room.

"OK, listen up everybody. We've got a secure take-down operation in progress. It's a bit of a commute from here, and we'll be picking up extra support along the way. I want to take as many as three people with me, but only if Fred and Charley are going to be getting here soon. Any ETA for them?"

Samuel piped up, "Fred's on his way here, but Charley's going to be at least another half hour."

Dundee thought for a moment, then said, "Fine. We'll leave the two of them behind to handle business here, and hopefully nothing major will happen. I want you three to come with me. You'll all ride in one squad car, and I'll ride with our friend here." Dundee nodded towards Yancey, then continued, "That'll leave two cars for Fred and Charley to use."

"As I said, I'm expecting to pick up extra officers and cars along the way. We'll be getting helicopter support at the target site. Because of operational security, I can't tell you the destination just yet. We may or may not be able to count on local support when we arrive."

He paused to let them digest that bit of news. They all looked thoughtful, but not surprised. This was not an unheard of in serious cases, nor was bringing in outside forces to handle something that local enforcement was too small to deal with properly.

"How long will we be gone, sir? Can you tell us that much?" one of the officers queried.

"A fair question, Smith. Hmm, at least a full day, I should think. Could possibly extend to two, maybe. Better take a minute to call your families and let them know. Anyone not able to go for two days? It's a stretch, I know, but I promise you that it is worth it."

He looked at his constables questioningly, but not without sympathy. A policeman's lot was never an easy one, especially not in a Northern posting. The three constables each sighed heavily, and one scrubbed at his head vigorously as he considered what to tell his long-suffering spouse.

"You did say that time was of the essence, didn't you Sarge?" the head-scratcher enquired.

"That I did, Chuck, that I did."

"Well, then," sighed the young man, "I guess there's only time to tell the missus about it and then hang up real quick. Shame about that."

That got a chuckle from all of the men, and general agreement that it sounded like the best way to handle the problem.

"OK, gents, take five to call home and to gather your personal kits. Then load up the squad car with your personal gear, tactical comm sets, and weapons. Anything bulky for the group we can throw into our friend's Crown Vic."

The others laughed, and one of them joked, "This is all just an excuse to ride in a Crown Vic again, isn't it, Sarge?"

Dundee's face grew serious, but his eyes twinkled, "I am

hurt to core that you'd think that of me, Constable."

Then his face broke into a grin as he added, "Now off with you. We leave in fifteen. Oh, and I've arranged for Frank to supply trip grub. My treat."

This was greeted with cheers as the men sat down at desks and picked up phones to call their wives.

Dundee turned to Yancey and tossed him a set of keys, "Here's the keys to squad car Five. Pop over to the deli and pick up the food, would you? We can divvy it up when you get back."

Yancey grinned as he caught the keys, "Don't think that this means you get to drive *my* car for the trip."

Dundee just growled and made shooing motions with his hands. Yancey laughed and left to pick up the requested supplies.

When he got to Jack's deli, he was a bit surprised to find several boxes of supplies ready for him. Jack pointed out which box held the coffee and associated condiments, and which held the edibles. He even helped Yancey carry them out to the car.

"Good hunting, young man," he said. Yancey thought that he detected a note of wistfulness in Jack's voice. But time was too short for lallygagging, so he got in the car, and with a wave to Jack he motored back to the station, parking at the rear.

As he pulled up, he could see Sergeant Dundee with the members of his detachment. It looked like Yancey had arrived just at the end of the briefing.

"Those are the tac frequencies we'll be using during our trip. Any questions?" asked Dundee.

All those present murmured to the negative.

"OK. I see our trip grub has arrived. Let's divvy that up and be on our way."

The appreciative officers descended upon Yancey, and

the boxes of food were quickly apportioned as necessary. Dundee tossed the keys to the Busted Flush towards Yancey and stated in clipped tones, "OK, lad, it's time to go. We'll lead the way, and the other car will follow."

With a contented sigh Yancey got behind the wheel of the Busted Flush, buckled up, and started the engine. Dundee got into the passenger side, and was surprised to see the five-point seat belt arrangement. Yancey grinned, "Can't ever be too careful in my line of work."

Dundee gave a brief snort of amusement, and buckled himself in, then turned to Yancey and gave a brief nod. The Busted Flush pulled out onto the road, followed by the police cruiser. The operation had begun.

* * *

The Busted Flush thrummed happily as it motored along the highway on the way to Dryden and the Tears of Joy facility. Yancey and Sergeant Dundee had barely spoken since they had left the police station. Dundee had a portable data terminal on his lap, and was typing furiously into it. He had mounted a portable tactical radio on the dash of the Flush, attaching it to the mounting holes left over from the car's previous incarnation as a police cruiser, and had the squelch turned down low enough that only a faint hiss was heard from it.

After about twenty minutes of this, Dundee sat up with a satisfied sigh, and stretched mightily. "OK, Mr. Franklin, you can stop matching the speed limit, now, and do whatever you think is safe for this old car. We'll be picking up another cruiser full of officers every couple of hundred kilometres, so by the time we hit Dryden we'll have ourselves a nice task force. Ambulance and helicopter support will be there by the time we arrive."

Yancey glanced at Dundee out of the corner of his eye. "I sure hope that those kids are actually there, after all this."

"Getting cold feet, Mr. Franklin? Don't worry, they'll be there. Traffic cameras in Thunder Bay spotted one of the target vehicles. And the license plate numbers you supplied match the DMV records. No, I have no doubt that your information is good."

He gave Yancey a quizzical look that became rather more probing than Yancey was comfortable with. "There's more to this than you're telling me, isn't there? You know damn well the kids are there and who has them. Anything you'd like to share?"

Yancey stared straight ahead without answering. He paused for a moment to gather his thoughts before replying with a sigh, "Sergeant ... yeah, there's more. But nothing that I can tell you right now. I ..."

"Never mind, son, never mind," Dundee said with a slight smile, "but anything you can tell me would be nice."

Yancey thought furiously before speaking, "Well, a lot of what I've got is speculative, to be honest. But I think that our target site has been operating for a while, though perhaps under different names. I'm pretty sure it was operating at the time all those runaways started disappearing. And there are indications that there are other facilities like it all over the country, but I don't have any hard information on those, or even locations."

Dundee sighed and nodded, "That's about par for the course. But at least we can shut down these sons of bitches. We'll get the others, too, never fear. If official channels don't work, then I think that Frank will be willing to help us out with his unofficial sources."

Yancey took this in then asked, "Sir, about Frank. He's more than just some civilian deli owner, isn't he?"

Dundee snorted in amusement, "Noticed that glaringly obvious little thing, did you?"

Yancey blushed slightly and replied, "Aside from his having contacts within the OPP that could track those vehicles, it was the look in his eyes when I picked up the food. A hungry, predatory look. Definitely wanted to come along."

Dundee actually laughed on that. "Yep, that's about right. Well, he used to be a Senior Staff Sergeant with the Force, and a damned fine one, too. Retired some years ago."

He paused and looked thoughtful before he continued, "The Force was everything to him. All he knew or wanted, actually, and he gave it his all for many years. But mandatory retirement comes to us all, and he needed to do something, so he settled up here and opened the deli. I have to admit, it is kind of nice having him around to bounce things off of, and the constables appreciate it as well. He knows all sorts of people in the Force, and is always happy to help out, in unofficial ways. I don't like to use his contacts too often, though. Not a good habit to get into. But it makes him feel useful again, and he's still got damn good instincts. Once a cop, always a cop, I guess."

Dundee got a faraway look in his eyes, and his voice took on a faraway quality, "The deli gives him a chance to be part of the community, in a way that he could never experience as a police officer. At least it gives him something to do. Heh - I'll probably end up buying it from him one of these days, myself."

Yancey looked sharply at Dundee, "Surely not for a few years, sir?"

Dundee snorted and replied with a smile, "Sure, sure. But it doesn't hurt to have a backup plan. But enough of that. We have a long trip ahead of us, and we don't need to spend all of it fretting about the upcoming take-down. Tell me about life as a private investigator. We don't get many of them up here."

Yancey laughed, and happily described his training and a few of more humorous and interesting cases he'd been involved in. That led to reminiscing from Dundee about some of his own early adventures, including his time in Little Shithole riding herd on a certain pair of young hellions. It was a pleasant way to while away the hours of a long trip.

The only sour note came when Dundee queried Yancey about his preferred choice of weapons during the raid. Yancey took a deep breath and let it out slowly before answering, "Don't think I want one, Sergeant."

Dundee looked hard at his young friend. He was well aware that Yancey was no stranger to violence in his youth, and that his time as a private investigator had required him to, at times, see the uglier side of life. The stories that Yancey had been telling him made that clear, no matter how humorous a spin was put on them. He also knew from Yancey's records that the young man had received firearms training during his private investigator course. So he fumed at Yancey and tried to impress upon him the seriousness and danger of the upcoming raid.

For his own part, Yancey was adamant about not using a gun. He'd seen too much violence and the effects of guns at the Shattered Palace. Not to mention that desperate struggle with the Sword soldier and the killing that was required to survive. No, he simply could not face holding a gun - not if it might be required of him to use it. He realized that this was a serious problem that would have to be addressed at some point, but not now.

"Mr. Franklin, you need to be able to defend yourself

and the officers around you. You don't have the training to go inside the building with the assault teams, so you'll be left outside. You must be armed."

Yancey glanced briefly at Dundee before returning his attention to the road ahead as he answered, "I won't carry a gun. Won't use it. I've … seen what guns can do."

Dundee sighed to himself. Something was wrong with his young friend, and he had a pretty good idea what it was. He'd heard that tone of voice, and seen that look in the eyes, before. Now was not a good time to find this out - but better here that at the site, he supposed.

"Mr. Franklin …" he began.

"I might have something just as good," blurted out Yancey quickly, "I've got a combat tomahawk like the army special forces use - it's got both a blade and a spike. I've even had some training on how to use it, too. You're absolutely correct that I need something. I've got a combat knife as well. With both of those, that will be good enough"

Dundee knew that this was not a battle that he was going to win, not if the problem was what he thought it might be. "All right, Mr. Franklin, I suppose that will suffice."

They proceeded in silence for some time before either one of them spoke. After that, they were both careful to keep the conversation light.

* * *

"Pull over just up ahead at that picnic site," Dundee commanded.

Yancey pulled over as directed, and left plenty of room for the other vehicles to pull up behind them. There were now five squad cars, each with two or three OPP officers, following the Busted Flush. They were stopped just outside Dryden, and Dundee wanted to brief everyone on what was going down.

"Alright everyone, listen up. From here on in, I want radio silence except on Tac-4. All communications will use the assigned call-signs, exclusively. No exceptions. No screwups."

Dundee paused to look at around at the assembled officers. There was a palpable tension emanating from the group.

"Our target is a commercial facility just outside of Dryden. I'll be passing out copies of maps of the area, plus photos and sketches of the facility in a moment. We strongly suspect that a number of children - at least seven and possibly more - have been kidnapped and taken to this facility. We have reason to believe that this facility has been involved with the disappearance of runaways in northern Ontario for many years."

The previously silent group broken out in excited murmurs.

"OK, OK, quiet down. It's time to shut these bastards down, and save some kids. We've tracked a half-dozen vehicles, supposedly limousines, converging on this location from across the province. Our intelligence indicates a normal complement of up to a half-dozen people stationed there, so that means at least a dozen hostiles on site, possibly more. They will be armed, and have shown a propensity for making witnesses disappear. So we've got to hit them fast and hard, and keep them off-balance. Above all, we need to make sure those kids aren't harmed."

One officer spoke up, "Sir, what about the local detachment? Will they be involved?"

Dundee shook his head, "No, it's been decided to leave them out of it until after the take-down is completed."

The group nodded. This was not unheard of for large-scale take-downs of this nature in small towns.

"OK, here's the handouts. Pass them around. We'll be coming in from two directions, silent until the last moment ..."

Yancey stood back and watched as Dundee briefed the other officers on the details of the rescue operation. All of the officers looked professional and in control, with only the expected level of tension. They certainly looked like they could get the job done. As for himself, Yancey was less sure. This was something totally outside of his experience, but he let none of his reservations show.

Dundee and the other officers were busily discussing tactics, and assigning tasks to specific groups of officers. Once again, Yancey's exact role in all this was glossed over, with the strong hint that he was not officially there. The officers all gave knowing smiles, and favoured Yancey with courteous nods. He nodded solemnly in return. This was not something that he was used tol.

Another unsettling thing was seeing OPP signage and license plates on the Busted Flush. Dundee had insisted on adding the magnetic-based logos to the Flush, as well as affixing OPP license plates over Yancey's existing ones. It would simply make things easier, he explained patiently, and Yancey had to agree. It really did make sense to eliminate any possible confusion between the Good Guys and the Bad Guys. To that end, he'd even convinced Yancey to wear a bulletproof vest with OPP markings on it.

Dundee had carefully asked Yancey once again if he wanted a handgun or a shotgun. As expected Yancey quietly refused but Dundee made him promise, on his honour, to wear the tomahawk and knife.

Dundee asked the group, "Any questions?" and

302

Yancey's attention snapped back to the here-and-now.

"What about air support?" enquired one officer.

"Good point. It should be here any time. As soon as we get confirmation, we'll synchronize our attack to its arrival. Ambulance service has been arranged for, and we can contact the fire department if necessary. Any other questions?"

There were none, so Dundee told them to gear up and stand by, and then walked over to Yancey.

"You OK, Mr. Franklin? Not your usual kettle of fish, is it?"

Yancey gave a tight grin, "No problems, Sir. We'd better gear up ourselves, I guess. Anyone need radios or vests from our supply in the Flush?"

Dundee nodded, and the two of them walked over to the Busted Flush. He made sure that Yancey took a vest - then gave a hard look until Yancey sighed and dug out the combat tomahawk and knife. As he was attaching them to his belt, Dundee took a quick walk around to ensure that everyone was geared up properly. A quick radio check showed that a couple of the radios had low batteries, so those were quickly replaced with spares from the supplies carried by the Busted Flush. With that done, everyone stood around quietly checking out their weapons.

Yancey heard a beep from within the Flush, and saw that an incoming message was waiting on the tactical computer. He called over to Dundee, and the sergeant hurried over. After a few seconds of typing and staring at the screen, he stood up and took a deep breath, then called out in a loud voice, "This is it, gentlemen. The helicopter will be here in about ten minutes. It'll take us that long to get into position, so saddle up and follow my lead in."

Everyone got into their respective vehicles. Before getting into the Busted Flush, Dundee slapped the portable flasher unit on the roof. That done, he got in and told Yancey to roll out.

* * *

"It's like deja vu all over again," thought Yancey as he raced down the road towards the Tears of Joy building. Half of the rescue team was coming from the north, and half from the south. Radio communication ensured that they would arrive within seconds of each other. Yancey could see the lights of the helicopter in his rear view mirror. This time one of the OPP squad cars was taking the lead, with the Busted Flush in the rear of the group.

They got to the front gate, and the lead cruiser plowed into it at high speed and smashed through. Yancey normally preferred more subtle approaches, but had to admit that it was effective. With the front gate down, all the OPP vehicles roared down the driveway towards the building itself. They could see several limousines parked along the side of the building, and shadowy outlines of others at the rear.

The OPP cruisers roared up and came to a halt - some at the front door, some at the side door, and a couple at the rear to provide backup. The police officers quickly piled out and ran towards the doors, as the helicopter activated its high-intensity spotlight and circled around. Yancey and Dundee hung back. Dundee to coordinate, and Yancey so as not to get in the way of the professionals.

Dundee lifted up a megaphone and identified themselves as police and that anyone inside should cooperate as the building was entered.

The police officers at each door swung their battering rams, and after several swings the doors burst open. Yancey winced at the crudeness of the entry, but had to admit that it was both effective and satisfying.

Police officers swarmed into the building, and Yancey could hear shouting as the officers announced themselves and demanded the cooperation of everyone inside. Suddenly several shots rang out, then the *boom* of police shotguns, then silence. More shouts were heard, and the tactical radios announced that the hostiles had been neutralized without police casualties. The shouts turned triumphant, and the radio announced that the children had been located. Another voice on the radio said that the ambulances were on their way, and that the children should remain in place until those had arrived.

Dundee announced that he needed to go inside to check on the captives, then he trotted off.

Yancey felt that the whole thing was rather anticlimactic, if truth be told. Which was a good thing, he sternly told himself. He took out his cell phone and snapped a few pictures of the outside of the building with the police cars. Then he walked over to investigate the limousines. He took a few pictures of the outside, then carefully opened the door of one of them. He inhaled sharply as he got a look at the inside. Although the outside looked like a standard limousine, the inside was set up for prisoner transportation with full-body confinement straps on the seats. He quickly took a series of pictures, then closed the door. He went to another limo, and found the same sort of interior setup. He made sure to take pictures of all the limos that were in the light, as he didn't want to use the flash.

Shaking his head, he put his phone back into his pocket. He could hear the sirens of the ambulances coming down the road. Suddenly, he heard shouting, followed by a shot. With a crash, the side door flung open and someone staggered out. Yancey stood very still, trying to decide what to do. The unknown combatant extended an arm, and fired a pistol into the open doorway. Yancey could now plainly see that the shooter was not wearing a police vest, and so had to be one of the Sword. He quickly reached behind his back, and with a snap of his wrist freed his tomahawk from the quick-draw holster. The Sword soldier was backing away from, while still facing, the doorway, and hadn't noticed Yancey.

Shouts came from the inside, and the soldier turned to run away. By this point, he was only a couple of metres away from Yancey as the lights illuminated his face.

It was the Deacon.

"You!" shouted the Deacon, "You have betrayed your God!"

The Deacon swung his right arm around to bring the gun to bear on Yancey, but Yancey had leaped forward to close the gap. His left hand grabbed the Deacon's right wrist to force the gun away, then Yancey twisted his body and the two of them fell to the ground, the momentum of the fall causing them to roll.

"I offered you salvation!" screamed the Deacon, as he strove to bring the gun to bear on Yancey.

The two of them were still rolling, one over the other, on the ground. Their struggles caused the rolling to cease and they found themselves suddenly sitting upright facing each other. Yancey's left hand was holding onto the wrist of the Deacon's gun hand, but Deacon reached over with his free hand in an effort to reclaim the gun. Yancey responded by jerking his left hand upward to keep the Deacon off balance, then swinging the tomahawk with his right hand. At the last moment he twisted the tomahawk so that the spike end faced downward. The point slammed into the Deacon's groin, ripping through the testicles, before burying itself into the ground.

The Deacon gasped as if shot, and Yancey ripped the pistol from his grip.

Several police officers poured out of the door, shouting, "Don't move. Don't move," at the pair.

The Deacon looked at Yancey with shock and pain. Yancey smiled a cold, hard smile and said in a low, intense voice, "Canada. Is. Protected. Never forget that."

Yancey was reward with a look of pure hatred. A hatred that was tinged - more than a little - with fear. Yancey simply continued to smile.

The police officers continued to shout their instructions as they ran towards the duo, but Yancey didn't really hear them. He simply held out his arms, holding the pistol by the barrel in his left hand. A uniformed officer took hold of Yancey's arm and helped him to stand upright. As Yancey continued to smilingly stare at the Deacon, another police officer took the pistol from him.

"That's hardcore, man. Really hardcore," the officer murmured approvingly to Yancey, as he observed how the Deacon had been neutralized.

Yancey just turned around and walked to the Busted Flush.

The convoy of ambulances had arrived by this time, as well as a bus. Medical personnel rushed inside and the children were being escorted out one at a time, with blankets wrapped around their shoulders, and gently herded into the waiting bus. The helicopter continued to circle, shining its high intensity light back and forth.

Yancey took a deep, even breath, but it came out as a ragged exhalation that formed a dense plume in the cool air. He kept his back to the Deacon as the latter was handcuffed, extricated, and then put onto a gurney and into an ambulance. Somehow Yancey didn't feel all that exhilarated about what had just happened. Maybe payback wasn't all that it was cracked up to be, he thought to himself as he rested his head on the cool roof of the Busted Flush.

* * *

The scene at the Silent Snow facility continued to be one of barely-contained chaos, but to this was added an extra layer of urgency. One of the men at a monitoring station got up and trotted over to the desk of the unit's commander, and handed over a printed communication.

"Sir, it appears that there is a large OPP operation in Dryden that involves the rescue of a number of kidnapped children from a facility there, the Tears of Joy. There are some indications that one of our targets of special interest may be involved. It appears that he was recently linked in some manner with that facility, and is now involved with the OPP operation."

The commander carefully examined the report, thought for a few seconds, then came to a decision. "We need to bring the target subject in, if at all possible. It'll take at least two hours for a team to get there, even by helicopter. It looks like the OPP Regional Commander is on the scene. Contact him through normal channels, and have the target detained pending our arrival. Dispatch a field team to pick him up. Go."

With that, the operative trotted over to another work station and began making the arrangements as ordered.

* * *

Dundee came out of the building with a grin on his face. It was a small, tight grin, but a happy one. He walked up to Yancey, to find the younger man leaning with his back against the Busted Flush, with his head back and eyes closed.

"We've accounted for all the kids on your list, and a half-dozen more besides. They're all in various stages of shock and some are damn near catatonic, I'm afraid. Their physical injuries don't look too bad, but some got slapped about pretty good. Mostly they're just scared out of their wits."

"They'll need counselling," said Yancey without opening his eyes. "The facility specializes in breaking people and instilling obedience. Even a light touch of that will be hard on the kids." Yancey's head dropped, although his eyes remained closed, "I wish we could have gotten here sooner. Before the processing had begun."

Dundee stared intently at Yancey, wondering exactly how the younger man had gained that information - and at what personal cost. But all he said was, "We got here as quickly as we could, and before the kids had much done to them other than a good scare. They'll be alright. But what about you? I hear you had a bit of scuffle with one of them as he tried to flee the scene. Good job on that collar, by the way."

He was interrupted by the squawking of his tactical radio. Dundee answered with a curt reply, then listened as he was told to get to one of the encrypted terminals for an urgent message. He grunted an acknowledgement, patted Yancey gently on the shoulder, and walked around the Busted Flush and got into the passenger seat to access the terminal unit. He spent a couple minutes alternately typing and peering intently at the screen. With a final flurry of typing, he got out of the car and stood up with a sigh. He paused for a moment to take a deep breath as he stared up at the circling helicopter. Then he walked around the car, looked carefully around to make sure that no one could overhear, then leaned towards Yancey, who by this time had opened his eyes to look around.

"I'm supposed to take you into custody, and detain you until some federal security types show up for you in a couple of hours."

Yancey's gaze suddenly focused intently on the Sergeant. He mouth went dry, and he couldn't think of anything to say.

Dundee just smiled sadly and shook his head. "Wish I could comply with the orders, but it seems as if you just kinda drove away before I could find you. Real shame about that. And with those Force markings and Force license plates, well, your car is going to pass for a Force vehicle, probably one of the unmarked cruisers. Aren't any records associating you with those particular plates, either. Damn shame about that. Don't rightly know how that happened."

Yancey's eyes grew wide as the import of Dundee's words sunk in.

"Sir ..." he began.

"Better get going, Mr. Franklin."

Yancey was insistent. "Sergeant, no, I can't let you do this ..."

Dundee interrupted him with a glare, "Shut up, Yancey. Just this once, *please*, listen to me. Just this once."

The two men stared at each other for a handful of heartbeats, then Yancey sighed, lowered his head, and gave a brief nod.

"Thank you, Mr. Franklin. You've done the Force ... you've done *me* ... a great service today. Those kids are alive and well because of you. We've shut down a terrible evil that has been plaguing the North for many years, because you came to me. This operation is obviously run by an organization with deep pockets and powerful friends. We'll get as many of them as we can, but that's going to take time. Time, it would seem, that you don't have. So go. I take it that you know how to disappear?"

Yancey just grinned and nodded.

"OK, then. Be off with you. Don't worry about the gear or Force identification, just go."

A lump came to Yancey's throat. This old career police officer was trusting him with an awful lot.

"I'll try to get all the gear back to you, sir. It may take a bit of work, but I'll see that it's returned."

Dundee waved his hand dismissively, as if the matter was of no importance.

Yancey shrugged out of his OPP vest, then got into his car, tossing the vest into the back seat. Dundee motioned for him to roll down the window, and Yancey complied.

"It was a real pleasure working with you on a case, Mr. Franklin. I always knew that you would have made an exceptional police officer. Thank you for proving me right."

The two shook hands solemnly, then Dundee stepped back. Yancey carefully backed up, got turned around, turned on the roof flasher and drove down the driveway and onto the road. He made a left turn, and headed north. After driving a kilometre or so, he turned off the roof light and continued on into the night.

He drove for nearly an hour, then pulled over at the crest of a hill. He got out, and examined the pictures that he had taken with his cell phone. They looked something that Charlene could use, so he quickly composed an email to her briefly describing the scene at the Tears facility and the number of kids found. Without sending the email, he quickly composed several other emails, one for each picture. Those he also put into the transmission queue without sending. Then he went to the trunk, opened it up, and extracted a long directional antenna, which he attached to his phone. Balancing it on the roof of the car, he carefully swung it towards the cell towers that he knew were south and east of Dryden. Within a few seconds he had locked onto one of them and had established a good connection. He then had the phone transmit all the emails in its queue, and that was accomplished in under a minute.

Smiling to himself, he disconnected the antenna, and set the phone to airplane mode, disabling all of its radio components. Then he re-stowed the antenna in the trunk, shut the lid, and got back into the car. He sat for a moment, then got out and removed the OPP identification from the sides of the car and tossed them into the back seat. He decided to leave the antennas and the license plates for the time being. His final task was to turn off the automated script that he'd left running to penetrate the facility's Wi-Fi network. He hadn't mentioned that small detail to Sergeant Dundee, and Yancey was still convinced that had been the correct decision. Or, more correctly, the least bad. There would be lots of time later to see what, if anything, had been collected. It had been a long shot, but one worth trying, especially given how long he'd been able to stay on-site. Enough time to grab a lot of those larger files that he'd seen the last time.

Getting back into the car, and checking the cell phone for messages, he discovered two. One was from Simon that consisted only of the words "kick ass". That evoked an amused grunt from Yancey. The second message was from Gretchen that simply said "stay safe". Yancey gave a small snort at that, but it brought a happy smile to his face. He sat for a moment, thinking about his friends. Then he shook his head to dispel the temporary lethargy, and removed the battery from the phone. He'd smash the phone, and dispose of it somewhere along the way home, probably in one of the innumerable small lakes that dotted the landscape. He had plenty of others to replace it.

He smiled to himself as he pulled back onto the road and drove, the Busted Flush thrumming happily. For now, it was time to head back to Ottawa. It was going to be a long trip back home, but Yancey didn't mind. Everything had turned out so well. He'd made a solid contact at the OPP with Sergeant Dundee, some innocent kids had been saved from the Sword, and the Sword had been dealt a major blow to their operations in the province. With any luck the police could uncover other the similar facilities in the other provinces and shut them down, too. Charlene had promised a series of articles to keep the heat on the police to keep digging at this. It was a good start to their plans to begin exposing the Sword and its activities. The Silent Witness Network was up and running, and had proven itself. They had a possible handle on who was pulling the strings behind the Sword. Things were starting to look up.

Probably best to take the back roads, he thought. Maybe even take a couple days to do the trip, stopping off somewhere along the way for a bit. Yeah, that would be nice. Find an unused campsite, or abandoned logging camp, and just sit and enjoy the fresh air and the woods. Maybe someplace with a nice stream, too.

CHAPTER TWENTY-EIGHT
Aftermath

Dundee walked out of the Tranquil Roads Executive Spiritual Retreat building, grateful to be taking a bit of break. It had been a long day - immensely successful and satisfying, but tiring. Helluva name for such an awful place, he thought to himself. A foul business, no matter how the name tried to disguise it.

It had been over two hours since Yancey had left the site and Dundee found himself worrying a little about the young man. Then he snorted at the foolishness of his thoughts. Young Mr. Franklin had proved that he was perfectly capable of taking care of himself, even when poking his nose into dark places that powerful forces wanted kept hidden. There was more to this than the young man was telling, of that Dundee was sure. But he couldn't help but feel that the youngster was keeping secrets in an effort to protect him. That thought produced another amused snort. His thoughts were interrupted by a squawk from his tactical radio.

He lifted the microphone up and acknowledged the call. To his surprise, the voice of the District Commissioner began blaring forth. Dundee glanced skyward to see his superior's helicopter still circling around, as it had for the duration of the operation. The voice was somewhat distorted, as the radio's audio processing software attempted to compensate for background noise of the helicopter, but the irritation in the Commissioner's voice was plain to hear.

"Dundee, the security team from Ottawa will be landing in a few minutes. Make sure the prisoner they wanted is ready for them."

This was going to get interesting, thought the Sergeant.

"Sorry, Sir, but he's not here."

"WHAT DO YOU MEAN HE IS NOT HERE?"

"Well, sir, he left just before you sent your orders. Said he'd be right back after checking on something. There was no reason to detain him, so I let him go."

"WHY WAS I NOT INFORMED OF THIS?"

"I just figured he'd be right back, and then I got called away for more urgent matters. We *are* very busy down here, as you know, Sir."

The sound of the helicopter became louder, and it appeared to be coming down for a landing on the lawn. Within a minute it had touched down, and a figure hopped out and came running over to where Dundee was standing. A few seconds later Dundee was staring at the Commissioner, whose face was livid with rage.

"Dundee, you idiot. Don't you realize how badly this will reflect on the Force? On *me*? These are federal *security* people, and they are flying in from *Ottawa*, for Christ's sake. What am I going to tell them?"

Sergeant Dundee quietly asked, "Sir, did it ever occur to you to ask why they wanted that person? He's the one that lead us here in time to save all these children. Children, I could point out, of some very important people. Just think of what would have happened if he hadn't stepped forward when he did."

The Commissioner's face grew even more livid, and his self-control slipped even more. "You don't understand anything, Dundee, you never did. Promotions are coming up and this will not look good on me, not at all. These are federal security people. Your failure will reflect badly on me, very badly indeed."

Dundee shook his head sadly, "You used to be a good cop, Georgie. What happened to you?"

The Commissioner's face went from florid to grey in the space of a few heartbeats. His mouth worked, but nothing came out for a few seconds, then his words finally came out in a hiss, "You're through, Dundee. I'll see you charged with disreputable conduct, conduct unbecoming, and whatever else I can come up with. You'll be lucky to get a reduced pension, if you get any pension at all." His rant wound down, and he gulped for air.

Dundee just shrugged and laughed, "Not important, Georgie. The kids are safe. An organized crime ring has had their asses handed to them. Nothing else matters. Especially nothing you say or do."

The Commissioner stood there gaping and making incoherent sounds. After a few seconds of that, he spun on his heel and stomped off back to the helicopter in a huff, like a child having a tantrum. Dundee just shook his head, his smile fading to a much sadder version, and then he sighed. Georgie really did used to be a good officer once upon a time, he thought to himself. The Force was a tough career, and no one came out of it without a few scars. But some just plain gave up on caring, and too many of those sort rose to command rank for Dundee's liking. Then he heard someone calling his name, and he turned around to see an officer waving him over. Dundee's smile became happy once again. There was work, good work, left to be done. It was good to be a cop, but maybe Frank could use a partner at his deli.

* * *

Charlene was in her newsroom office, standing in front of the table where the rest of her reporters were seated. Her face had a happy, predatory grin on it. All of the reporters knew that look, and they were intensely alert.

"Ladies and gentlemen, we have an exclusive story. The OPP just launched a raid on a facility near Dryden, and rescued a bunch of kidnapped children."

Everyone leaned forward, listening intently. They'd heard about some sort of an OPP operation, but no details had been released.

"We've got a report from an on-site witness. With pictures. And the names of some of the victims."

She passed out printouts of the pictures that Yancey had taken with his cell phone. There were enough copies for everyone, and each of them hungrily took a quick look.

"Those cars that look like limos on the outside but were prisoner transports on the inside? The kids were transported in those. The other shots show some exterior shots of the facility - it's supposed to be some sort of executive retreat. Very exclusive, very hush-hush. There's only a couple shots that show police officers, but we'll want to make sure that their faces are blacked out when we publish. Treat this like a high-end organized crime bust."

"Anything official from the OPP?" asked one reporter.

The organized crime reporter answered that, "Nothing much on the wire. Just an announcement of some sort of ongoing criminal investigation near Dryden. No details whatsoever. How did you get this, Charlene?"

Charlene just smiled innocently, "That's why I'm the

editor, youngster."

Then her face grew serious. "This has more implications than this one site, I'm sure. This is a supposedly top-end executive retreat that's been there for years. This is no small-scale one-off thing. It's large and it's organized. From what I've been able to gather, the police just lucked out in finding it."

She began pointing at individuals around the table and firing off assignments.

"Fred, you're the organized crime specialist. I want you on lead for this. Dig into it from that angle. Who's running this? How big is it? Is this province-wide or even nation-wide? That sort of thing."

"Jake, I want you to talk to the police in Dryden. Find out how this happened under their noses. Hammer 'em, hard."

"Phyllis, talk to OPP headquarters about what they know about this, and how it has gone on so long without being noticed. Again, hammer 'em hard over this."

"I know some of the parents, and I'll talk to them to see if they want to go on-record. My preliminary take on this is that this is a massive extortion racket of some sort, but who the hell knows what else was going on. Everybody else, keep up with the regular stories and features. If you hear anything useful, pass it on to Fred or myself. If anyone runs into anything database related or has problems extracting data from reports, see Gretchen. Questions?"

One reporter piped up, "Does anyone else know about the pictures?"

Charlene's smile turned predatory once again, "Nope. And I'd like to keep it that way until the next edition hits the street, if at all possible. Oh, and those pictures stay exclusive to us. We're not sharing."

Everyone around the table made happy sounds at the thought of that, with smiles matching that of the cat that had just gotten hold of a very juicy canary.

"AJF News isn't going to like this, Charlene," piped up one of the reporters, to the general sound of snickering.

"And they're going to like it less when we publish details that they don't have and can't get," was the happy reply. Not-so-muted cheers greeted that pronouncement.

"We've got a big job ahead of us. Lots of big, juicy stories to tell. Lots of nasty things lurking in the shadows that we can drag out into the sunlight. This is going to be fun, boys and girls. Now off to work, the lot of you."

* * *

The unmarked helicopter fluttered noisily through the sky, flying away from Dryden. Its inhabitants sat motionless, well aware that the empty seat was a mark of the failure of their mission. The co-pilot turned in his seat, pointed to one of the passengers, and tapped his headset as he held up two fingers.

The indicated passenger adjusted his receiver to the indicated channel and identified himself. He paused for a moment, then began speaking.

"Sir, we are on the way back to base. The target had been on the site, but the OPP had not detained him as requested, and his location is unknown at this time."

He listened to the other before replying, "The facility appears to have been sanitized. All paper records appear to have been thoroughly incinerated, and all electronic devices melted using thermite or something similar. Nothing left for a digital forensic analysis. Nothing to provide useful intelligence of anything beyond this single facility. Several prisoners were taken into OPP custody."

Another pause as he listened. "The police presence at the site consisted of both uniformed and plain clothed officers, all wearing police vests. No one recalled seeing any civilians. Is it possible that the subject is an undercover police officer? That might explain why he was allowed to leave without being challenged."

There was a brief pause before he spoke one last time, "Understood, sir. Returning to base. Out."

* * *

"This is Melanie Goldsmith of AJF News."

"In a breaking development, the Ontario Provincial Police announced a daring raid on a facility near Dryden, Ontario, suspected of being used for criminal purposes. Details remain sketchy. The OPP has cited the need to maintain a high degree of secrecy while they complete their investigations, so that all of those involved can be identified and apprehended. We at AJF News fully support this, and decry the attempts by some media outlets to bypass these necessary precautions in a feeble attempt to boost their sagging ratings."

* * *

Thomas Thansworth the Third sat staring in horror at the TV screen watching the breaking news from AJF. He was quite sure what those criminal activities were, that the announcer was talking about. Just as he was quite sure that in some way his own family was involved.

The evidence was quite clear, if currently a bit sketchy. Using the hidden books as a starting point, he had been able to slowly discover bits and pieces of information. The need for secrecy, and the lack of privacy, made gathering information a slow and tedious process. Even so, he had learned enough in his researches to know that these were not the sort of people that one wanted to make angry. These were enemies to his country and, whatever else Thansworth had been or done, he believed in the Republic and all that it stood for.

A real problem was that even with the limited amount of research he'd been able to do, there was too much information to keep track of in his head, so making notes was a necessity. Moreover, those notes had to be on paper to avoid leaving a digital trail. However, he was forced to keep those notes to a minimum because of the requirement to keep them hidden between research sessions. The need to keep his research, and the incriminating notes, hidden from everyone else was becoming harder.

He'd discovered that his private room was being searched on a regular basis, sometimes several times a week. That was his own fault, and he once again cursed his carelessness. To keep his wits sharp he'd stopped drinking. That, unfortunately, drew unwanted attention from his family who began to see him as something other than a harmless wastrel. To regain that coveted status he was forced to take up drinking again, but he was careful to limit the amount that he actually ingested, and surreptitiously disposed of as much as he dared. That caused most of the watching eyes to turn their attention elsewhere. Most, but not all. That's when the searches of his room started. To throw the unseen watchers off the scent he had taken to hiding small amounts of various mood-enhancing drugs. This had resulted in the searches becoming less frequent, but once in a while there would be a flurry of them. There were, at least for the moment, no monitoring devices in his room - he'd "borrowed" some equipment from the security detail to make sure of that.

Thansworth was well aware that he'd be able to deceive and misdirect for only so long before being caught, and he knew full well what the consequences would be. He was - he had been - a soldier long enough to be able to face the prospect of his own death with only modest apprehension so long as it meant striking a blow at the enemy. He also relished the opportunity to make up for his disgraceful performance at his last command, the Shattered Palace. He had to do something to regain his honour, and more importantly, somehow make up for the deaths of the soldiers under his command. He had to make things right.

There was a powerful enemy intent on subverting the country that he held dear -and his own family was fully enmeshed in that plot. He had access to information and documents detailing that plot and its participants. The problem was that he'd only get one chance to grab a large amount of it and run - his computer skills simply weren't good enough to hide his tracks very well. But run where? Who could he tell?

Thansworth hung his head and scrubbed at it with his hands. Everything in his life had turned out so very wrong, and much of that was his own fault. He'd spent so much effort focusing on his career, encouraged by his uncle, that his friends - real friends made at the Academy - had become lost to him. Over the years, some simply stopped reaching out to him as he became more distant. Some had given vent to their feelings when he had run roughshod over their careers in pursuit of his own. So many bridged burnt and so much to atone for.

With a deep sigh he raised his head and gave it a slight shake. None of that mattered. The past was over and done with, and he had no future worth caring about. The only thing that mattered was defending the Republic from a terrible enemy. There had to be someone he could pass this information on to, someone who could use it. His eyes narrowed in thought. There were no obvious candidates, but perhaps there was a way to discover one.

It was vital that a recipient be recruited before he did anything else. He'd only get one shot at doing a data dump, and then he'd have to somehow transfer it all to his contact. The strategy was decided, and all that remained were tactics. Feint and thrust - this was the sort of thing that he understood and was good at. It was time for a disgraced patriot to put those skills to the defence of his country one last time.

CHAPTER TWENTY-NINE
Judgement Of The Council

"Amen."

Everyone present solemnly intoned a response to the heartfelt prayer for divine guidance.

The council of Infinity Ascending was meeting to discuss recent events.

Apostle One quietly called the meeting to order and opened with his summary.

"Nothing must interfere with the upcoming elections in USA and Europe. Once those are secured, work can truly begin on consolidation and bringing reticent countries and groups onto The Path. It is through God's will that we will accomplish this. At long last, all will stand with us in our fight against The Darkness."

There were murmurs of assent from all present. This was the fulfilment of a dream long in the coming, and the thought of bearing witness to it was most heartening.

Apostle Eight begged leave to comment, which was granted with a nod from Apostle One. Apostle Eight rose and made a humble bow to his fellows before continuing. "Brothers, The First has in the past pointed out that there are regions of fragility - China, Russia, and India in particular. Based on our most recent projections, these could cause problems, especially given the methods the Sword used to stabilize them. I realize that the Sword's own projections show no problems, but I must confess to some disquiet at the discrepancies between the two sets of analysis."

With a nod to his fellows, Apostle Eight sat down.

Apostle Ten requested leave to speak, and he rose with a bow to his fellows. "There is also the matter of the recent failed operations in Canada. These may be small threads, to be sure, but even small threads can cause a larger unravelling. I would advise that some thought be given to this, so that our travels along The Path remain unhindered."

The Council deliberated in their quiet fashion, and decided that operations in Canada should be minimized, for the time being. There would be time to focus on the elections and other matters in that country after securing the governments of the others.

"Let the Sword hear and obey the Word of God."

CHAPTER THIRTY
Judgement Of The Sword

The Apostles of the Sword met in their usual stark surroundings.

The First Apostle leaned forward, his eyes bright. "Brothers, the Time is nearly upon us. Success is within our grasp. Once the upcoming elections are secured, we will control the major powers. Work can then begin to transform this planet into a true bastion against The Darkness. It is *our* efforts, *our* sacrifices, that have brought us to this point along The Path. It will be through *us* that God's will shall be done."

There was no unseemly demonstration of emotion at this exhortation, but all the others sat a little straighter in their chairs, and their eyes shone a little brighter.

"The primary item on our agenda is to discuss the details of each of the upcoming phases of our operations. But before that, let us deal with lesser matters. Apostle Eleven will give us a summary of operations in Canada. After that, we will clear up any other old business, then move forward with the important issues. Apostle Eleven, if you would enlighten us?

The man addressed by the First Apostle, took a moment to look around the table at each of his brothers in turn, then made a quick,deep nod of his head as a salute to the group. The obeisance completed, he began his report.

"Brothers, some of you may have heard about the recent police raid on the Tears of Joy facility in Ontario. It put an end to that facility's operations, including the current one that involved the processing of the children of people in positions of power. This is unfortunate, as that phase of the operation was incomplete, but sufficient of the elite have been brought under our control to serve our purpose, and the rest can be brought to heel with the threat of similar actions. This breach requires us to close down and sanitize others of its kind throughout the country. This is of no great loss, as all have long since served their purpose and were no longer of even secondary importance. Their loss is of no real consequence to our plans. Of some operational concern, however, is the loss of trained personnel. Of possibly greater concern, however, is that operatives of a new security agency were observed at the raid, although they appeared to have played a minimal role. We have no details about them at this time, but enquiries are ongoing. Of more pressing concern is that the Deacon of the Fist of Tolerance was injured and captured during the raid, and is being held by the police. On positive note, our allies in the City of London have been successful in their continuing operations to increase their control of Canadian economic activity. These are the only items of consequence occurring in Canada at the present time. I await your guidance."

There was a pause of a few seconds as the members of the group digested this information. The pause was broken by the First Apostle, who spoke with a cold smile.

"It is true that there have been unforeseen difficulties in that one country. A source of resistance appears to have arisen, and in the fullness of time it will be dealt with as we have dealt with all others. For now, the Council of Ascendants wishes us to minimize all operations there that do not directly pertain to the upcoming elections. This we shall do, but only for active operations. Continue to monitor this new security group, and any others who may pose a threat. As for the Deacon, we need to debrief him. We know the results of his failure, but not the details that led up to it. He has shown himself to be weak and unfit for his position. He needs to be extracted and debriefed, or debriefed in situ. We need to confirm that the facility was sanitized before it was taken. In any event, both he and any surviving members of his team will be eliminated for being incompetent and unworthy of our Order. But enough of that. Will this have any impact on the main Harvest of Souls operation?"

Apostle Eleven nodded to show acceptance of the guidance he had received before replying, "No - that is going ahead, but is a little behind schedule. There was some trouble arranging suitable transport, but that has been resolved. The failed attack on the Shattered Palace caused the loss of many of our troops, and it has taken time to reallocate resources from other parts of the country. The Harvest will proceed, and should prove to be a good source of profits in coming years once it has been established."

The First Apostle nodded to show his acceptance of this information before he spoke, "The slight delay is acceptable. This the first operation of its kind in Canada, and complications are to be expected. Canada is now sufficiently under the control of the Sword - it is time to exploit and harvest the bounty within. Now, is there any old business to be discussed?"

All present agreed that there was no old business that needed to be discussed at this time.

"Very well. But before we proceed with new business, let me emphasize one thing. Although unimportant to our plans, these recent setbacks have not only embarrassed our Order, but will be taken as a sign of weakness by our adversaries. The Council of Ascendants does not properly grasp these matters of vital tactical importance. It is therefore up to us to deal with such matters in order to preserve God's Path. Canada *shall* be prepared to be the sacrifice that pacifies our reluctant allies and rewards our friends."

"In God's name, and to His eternal glory, it shall be so. Now let us discuss matters of greater importance."

About The Author

Brian retired from the software development rat race to take up the carefree life of an author. He lives with his wife and two cats in Ontario, Canada.

For the latest news about this and forthcoming books, the occasional commentary on life, or to leave a comment (we love feedback), check out Brian's blog at

www.damnfoolpress.com/BrianGreiner

Books by Brian Greiner

The Ascending Darkness

#1 Darkness Creeps Forth
#2 Darkness Comes Reaping

www.ingramcontent.com/pod-product-compliance
Lightning Source LLC
Chambersburg PA
CBHW071052250626
47159CB00002B/457